JOSEPH PINTAURO, a former priest, is an award-winning playwright and poet. He is also the author of *A State of Grace*.

Cold Hands

by
Joseph Pintauro

A PLUME BOOK

NEW AMERICAN LIBRARY

NEW YORK AND SCARBOROUGH, ONTARIO

Publisher's Note

This novel is a work of fiction. Names, characters, places, and incidents either are the product of the author's imagination or are used fictiously, and any resemblance to actual persons, living or dead, events, or locales is entirely coincidental.

NAL BOOKS ARE AVAILABLE AT QUANTITY DISCOUNTS WHEN USED TO PROMOTE PRODUCTS OR SERVICES. FOR INFORMATION PLEASE WRITE TO PREMIUM MARKETING DIVISION, NEW AMERICAN LIBRARY, 1633 BROADWAY, NEW YORK, NEW YORK 10019.

 PLUME TRADEMARK REG. U.S. PAT. OFF. AND FOREIGN COUNTRIES REGISTERED TRADEMARK—MARCA REGISTRADA HECHO EN FORGE VILLAGE, MASS., U.S.A.

SIGNET, SIGNET CLASSIC, MENTOR, ONYX, PLUME, MERIDIAN and NAL BOOKS are published *in the United States* by New American Library, 1633 Broadway, New York, New York 10019, *in Canada* by The New American Library of Canada Limited, 81 Mack Avenue, Scarborough, Ontario M1L 1M8

First Plume Printing, September, 1986

1 2 3 4 5 6 7 8 9

PRINTED IN THE UNITED STATES OF AMERICA

for Corita

We live in the mind.

—WALLACE STEVENS

PART I

CHAPTER I

WHAT road was I on? Was it Daniel's Path or Town Line Road? How could I be lost in my own neighborhood? It must be a new road the real estate people had made. But no, there were last winter's potholes all over, and asphalt crumbs. No one used the damned road.

My pickup took sharp curves, over and over, up bumps and down, through the woods. I decided not to backtrack again—that's how I had gotten into this mess in the first place. But it seemed the road would go on forever. No crossroads. I was starting to panic. It wasn't just that I had taken a wrong turn somewhere. I didn't know *where* I was in the world.

It was happening again. That morning at the marina I was on the phone maybe five minutes when suddenly I didn't know who the hell I was talking to, if they called me or I called them. I had had to hang up and sit down; I was dizzy.

I remember a warm breeze came in through the window as I sat in the marina office staring out over Three Mile Harbor. Rounding the black buoy was my charter boat, coming back with a catch. I had to pull myself together to go out to meet her.

Three dentists from Virginia had chartered *The Escape*. They had caught a mako and tried to cut the poor fish up. Dried blood was all over the boat. I got to hosing it. When they left, I could hear my phone ringing in the office, but this time I wouldn't answer it. I just kept busy scrubbing the darkness out of the deck vinyl till it gleamed.

The dentists had cut out the jaws, then thrown the head into the water. I gaffed the mako head and angrily threw it in the back of my pickup, intending to take it to the dump, and . . .

"That's where I am, goddamnit, on some road trying to find that dump!" The mako head was still in the back. "I must have decided to take the north road to the dump," I was saying to myself, "the back way. I must be on one of those winding north woods roads, deep into scrub oak territory over near Barcelona Point, where it's desolate. No crossroads. No goddamn road signs." I did recall that I had started out to find the dump. I hung on to that.

I stopped the truck, turned off the engine, and sat there in the pickup, amid crumbling asphalt. Red-winged blackbirds cawed at my truck, then flew off toward an empty barn. I had stopped before an abandoned farm. An old rusty Esso gas pump stood near the garages. In back was a barn with a green asphalt roof that was about to cave in. Something was wrong with the trees there—some were bare, like it was winter, and others were still very green. Thanksgiving was a few days away and a frost was long overdue. Summer was begging to be put to death, like a crazed old woman wandering through our meadows. I could smell hay; the wind carried its sweetness across the sun-warmed field, though the field was now in deep shade. There had never been such a hot November in the Hamptons.

The old-timers shrugged and called it Indian summer. Farmers were happy: it brought them an extra crop of lettuce. They were still harvesting their potatoes in the warm ocean mists. Cabbage and cauliflower were growing like it was July, though the dark came early at five. Clocks had to be pushed back. Fuel-oil trucks were working overtime making deliveries in the twilight. But uncannily, frost was nowhere in sight.

People were weary of the heat. It was like living through two summers in a row. We had never seen it so hot so close to Thanksgiving. Television reported the equator was shifting and that the glaciers were receding. Some said the jet stream was changing; others thought up things like a collapse in the ocean floor, bringing the Gulf Stream up alongside Long Island.

For a while the Indian summer got everyone into a festive spirit, but by mid-November we had started to worry. Sudden frost had been known to kill birds. And robins were still everywhere. Snowy egrets, orioles, even wild canaries stayed behind in the hot weather. Poor birds thought the place was turning into paradise. Oaks were smart; they had let go of their leaves at the normal time. But the maples hung on, still green, soft and full of life. Timothy reseeded itself, and Russian olive trees set forth new springtime buds. Tulip and daffodil bulbs broke ground, thinking it was April. Crocus blooms were seen.

I was worried about all the trees and bulbs and how they would suffer when the frost hit. I was angry because we were running up electric bills for air conditioning, and I worried about myself because I kept forgetting things . . . like today, trying to find the dump, sitting in my truck in the middle of a deserted road, trying to remember who on God's earth I was.

There was mail on the pickup seat. *Rose Smith. Jim Smith. Box 201-A, Bridgehampton, Long Island.* My wife and children were nearby; I tried to hang on to that thought. If the Jim Smith on the envelope was me, what was I doing sitting lost on that winding road? I was sweating. The red-winged blackbirds were coming back.

"Working too hard," I told myself. I never dreamed it could all slip, like oily ball bearings from your fingers. Too hard. "Have got to take care of myself. Look at that weather vane shaped like a whale . . ."

What the hell started this? Something long before the mako head. But it makes me sick to my stomach to try to focus on it. No choice but to lean back in my driver's seat, drop my hands to my sides, and listen to the echo of ocean far away.

I was in the deep shadow of a wall of giant spruces. I looked to their tips, as though a sound would materialize there. A high gull was catching orange from the setting sun. A faint, faraway engine introduced itself, then the soft hiss of a highway, trucks. The old farm on my right had to connect to a working road, even if it was a dirt road. I gambled with the idea of continuing on, in hopes there would be a crossroad to that highway. The panic began to subside. My legs were loosening.

What had happened to me? It wasn't a loss of memory. It was more a feeling of *remembering,* as if my past had disentombed itself and was chasing after me, like a high-speed bulldozer. I had been in flight on that crumbling road.

I turned the key and let the truck roll along at fifteen miles per hour, hoping for the crossroad. I wasn't going to panic this time.

Indian summer may not have tricked the oaks, but it befuddled the roses. As I slowly rolled in my pickup, bumping over the asphalt crumbs, I could see roses trailing the broken fences, cultivated varieties now gone wild, climbing the cedars like poison ivy, turning into ground cover, spreading into the meadows, blooming yellow and pink, sweet things, giving us all that color long after they should. Other years, as early as September the frost would have killed the roses, sent their sap deep underground to hide at the roots, safe from the white death, the snow and ice.

The road was straightening out. About two hundred yards ahead I could make out a road sign. I pressed the accelerator to the floor. I flew. Then I braked, skidding on pebbles up to the road sign. The road doesn't cross; it's a plain left called Deerfoot Path.

I turned onto it and floored the accelerator. My engine screamed a straight run for two miles. At last I could see the tops of speeding trucks on the highway.

I merged into the highway, west, toward Bridgehampton. When

I saw a telephone, I pulled over, kept the engine running and jumped into one of the phone booths.

"Jimmy, that phone don't work." A voice startled me. An old woman pulling a shopping cart was coming toward the booth. "The other booth works." I slipped into the other booth. Her gnarled face came closer. "Whatsamatta? You okay, honey? You look pale."

"Who are you?" I asked.

She tapped her foot and put one hand on her waist, smiled and bowed her head, looking over her glasses at me. "Now I'm gettin' too old for you to be playin' your tricks on me, Jim Smith." She made a face of agony as she pulled her dress away from her body. "Purgatory, this weather." I kept an eye on her as I dialed numbers that came to me automatically. The old woman stepped blindly off the curb. She turned and bowed her head in order to look over her glasses again. "You tell that Rosie of yours to get you some iron pills before you fade away on us." She was wearing a maroon and gray dress printed with feathers, with a thin matching belt that hung in the dress loops.

A truck flew by her so close that it washed her with dust. She dropped her shoulders and flattened her hand to her chest. "Did you see that? I remember when this was a dirt road, and it took us two days to go to New York City. You know how quick these trucks make it from Montauk? *Two hours*. And they'd kill us to get there. Thank God, the summer folks are gone. I couldn't cross here till after Labor Day. Had to shop in the delicatessen; that cost me extra. But it's hot as summer. God's behind it. And the poor birds. I been shooin' the robins with my broom, the lazy things. 'Get south,' I tell 'em." She laughed.

She finished brushing the dust from her dress and turned. Have a happy Thanksgiving," she said with a sad little wave. She crossed the highway, dragging her frail, almost empty, shopping cart behind her.

"Hello? Rosie?"

"Jim! Where the hell are you? The kids are hungry."

"Rosie, I'm having a hard time here."

"Hard time doin' what? Where are you?"

"I . . . I'm across from the Country Kitchen."

"Yeah . . . so . . ."

"Tryin' to figure out . . . my way . . ."

"What do you mean? You all right, Jim?"

"I'm all right, a little dizzy. Which way? Which way do I go from here?"

"Talk into the phone. I can't hear you. Jim? We're waiting for you. I got lamb. Should I let the kids eat?"

"Huh?"

"Can't you hear me?"

I was looking east at something familiar—the Methodist Church. My mouth was drifting away from the receiver.

"Jim? What's your number there? Jim?"

My head buzzed as if electricity was passing through it. Voices were inside my head. Dark images, crowding.

I hung up. I jumped into the truck and turned the key. The engine had been running, so the ignition shrieked. I made a U-turn toward the church. I knew the street alongside it went to the ocean. Hull Street. So I followed it. Each crossroad came when I expected it. That was a relief. But images continued—a whole procession of people coming into my mind across a long bridge out of the past.

I steered the truck between the dunes up to the tide mark; the tide was fully out. The ocean was not calm, but white lines of foam moved inland in orderly flanks. I turned off the engine and listened to the wind. I let my forehead touch the steering wheel and I closed my eyes. The full moon in the southeast, the gently rumbling ocean, the sun softly going under, comforted me. In the dunes the Rugosa roses were reblooming even though the bushes bore an abundance of fat red fruit. The sky was changing before my eyes, growing darker, deep rose.

Willie Warren's pickup truck bumped up the dune abruptly alongside me. Willie, the son of the big landscaper in town, was about fifty, a loner, a well-known surfcaster who hung around the dunes a lot, fishing in his bathing suit all summer. Even in winter he would be seen feeding the swans in the salt-water lakes. You couldn't talk to him more than a minute and he'd be gone—a true loner.

"How you doin', Jimmy?" he called to me. "Birds are workin'." He pointed east with his binoculars.

"Why don'cha get down there?" I yelled, trying to smile.

Willie rolled his eyes in boredom. "My freezer's full. Wouldn't care if the fish left yesterday. Ain't gonna be no bait left in that ocean anyway if they stay a week longer. We need snow or a northeaster to scare 'em south. Goddamn summer people didn't have weather this good last July, right, Jimmy? Wanna go for a swim?" He laughed.

"Why don't you?" I laughed back.

"Air may be hot"—he chuckled—"but she's a mite too cool for swimmin'. Ocean you can't swim in's like a woman you can't touch. Ain't worth a damn." Willie laughed loudly, backing up his truck. "Enjoy yer turkey." You couldn't talk to him more than a minute.

Fans of black and purple bloomed out of the horizon. It was hunting season. Ducks were hiding out on the ocean to escape the guns. Sharks get some of them. I could see a faint glimmer of dead sand eels at the shoreline. Suicides. Spit themselves up to escape hungry packs of blues.

Millions of fish still feeding long past their migration dates. Stripers and weaks should have gone south long ago. It was hotter in Long Island than the Carolinas.

Like Willie, I come to the ocean a lot. I keep my poles and lures in the pickup in case I catch the gulls working over the water. I keep a shotgun too, cradled against my rear window, but I'm no hunter. When I catch a fish, I tag him for those oceanographic guys in Montauk, especially the stripers, then I let him go free. My sport is riding my pickup at dusk along the lip of the ocean, boosted high on fat beach tires, like I'm flying. I'll stop at the Sagaponack dunes to watch the stars come out over the Atlantic.

If I ever use my shotgun, it'll be on myself. Sounds terrible maybe, but my shotgun gives me strange comfort knowing I can kill myself in a few seconds. Shotgun cradled behind my head is my reminder that I have the last word with my ghosts. Shotgun makes the moon rising and the sea breeze easier to enjoy. Just like those sand eels. If them little things have their pride, then so does a man. I'll use the shotgun on myself if they ever back me to a wall. Swear on Christ!

As Willie's truck disappeared in my rearview mirror, I threw mine into reverse, backed up and headed north. Good old Willie brought me back. I could make sense now out of familiar sounds of trucks on the highway, moving west toward Southampton. I remembered the woman's name, the one who talked to me near the phone booth. She was Dorcas Corwin, who used to be proprietor of the Bridgehampton Florist. Her shopwindow used to have a dark green awning in the old days, and Dorcas had window boxes full of Thunbergia vines out front, cascading nasturtiums and big kegs of lemon geraniums. She used to water them every morning with a metal watering can. In the winter she made prom corsages of pink roses and silver ribbons, and for weddings, bouquets of white orchids and ferns. The shop wasn't there since she retired. What's there now? Oh yes, it's a liquor store.

It all was coming back, slowly, as I drove.

My wife's name is Rosie Foster Smith. Her father is Morton Foster, Chief of Police of Bridgehampton. She was a nurse when I met her. Now she's the mother of my two daughters, Erica and Karen. I live with them on Garden Street, two blocks east of the Methodist Church, off the highway, toward the ocean.

My lungs pulled in deep satisfying breaths for the first time in hours. I stopped the truck next to a potato field, grabbed the shovel from behind the seat, went in back and pulled the heavy mako head toward me. I walked deep into the torn-up field and buried the head. I jumped back to my truck and headed home.

I passed the movie house and I knew it opened at five but that no one goes. I saw the ticket lady reading a book and the manager standing in the yellow marquee light. I remembered everything now, even what happened before that mako head; and as I concentrated on that, an acid taste came to my mouth.

As I pulled into my driveway, Erica and Karen were waiting at the window. They jumped on me when I walked in the front door.

"Don't," I said, "my hands are dirty." I pushed them off.

"What happened?" Rosie was standing there with two cups of chocolate pudding. "I couldn't make any sense out of what you were saying on that phone."

"Nothing."

"I expected you to call back." Rosie stretched a kiss to me. "You all right?"

"My hands are dirty. I just threw a mako head in a field."

"Well, wash them. The girls ate. They're having dessert with us."

The lamb on the table had green pears around it and maraschino cherries. Rosie loved to fuss.

I kept my head down as I ate. I wanted to talk, to create a cloud of talk, but I couldn't make a word. To reassure them I was all right, I kept eating, but it didn't work. My stomach was full of struggling birds and my legs were beginning to feel like marble. My daughters' somber eyes were making things worse. The girls ate their chocolate pudding, trying all the while to keep their eyes off me.

"What're you lookin' at?" I asked. "Huh? Do I look funny?"

My younger daughter, Erica, resembled her mother: short and brown-eyed, with straight hair. Karen took after me. She was quite tall for her age, with blue eyes. Karen didn't move when I spoke. Her head rested on her hand, her dark wavy hair nearly touching the table. She tightened her thin lips on her spoon, looking at Rosie without answering me. Erica pretended not to have heard me. She inherited her mother's prudence.

"You finished your chocolate pudding?" Rosie asked. They took the hint and slid away from the table. "May I . . ." Rosie suggested.

"May I be excused," they said in unison.

"Go fill the bird feeders," Rosie said in return.

"We did," Erica said resentfully.

"Then just . . . go then." They went inside, their milk glasses still full. Rosie had a very worried look. "Jim, do you know you're extremely pale?"

I leaned back in my chair. The fork still in my hand. I rested it on my thigh to hide my shaking. The shaking was coming from inside, somewhere deep. I had no idea what was feeding it.

"I have a feeling . . ."

"Huh? I can't hear." Rosie leaned toward me.

". . . that all the years . . ."

"Jim? Should I call a doctor?"

My hands were shaking. The fork banged my dish as I tried to put it down.

". . . all the years will crash . . ."

Rosie's eyes opened wide. She pushed her chair away. It all happened in seconds. My legs, my shoulders shook. I stood up, my chair fell back behind me. Either I grabbed the tablecloth or somehow it had caught onto me, because I was dragging it, pushing right through Rosie, toward the living room. She screamed amid the noise of dishes crashing. Such a force of adrenaline was running through my arms that I picked up the floor lamp like it was a twig, and out of my lungs there came a roar, a sound I would never believe I could make—the cry of a wounded animal. I broke the lamp in half and threw it. The bulb exploded. Karen was struggling to get out the back door. I grabbed the fireplace poker and smashed everything on the mantel. I couldn't stop. Little Erica—out of the corner of my eye I could see her crouching against the wall. I could hear her whimpers over the noise. I picked up the plaid chair and threw it into the picture window. It landed on the holly outside. Glass clattered to the oak floor and onto the rug. I couldn't stop throwing things. It was as if, methodically, I was set on clearing the room, every stick of furniture.

Then I caught Rosie's face. She was holding the phone to her head, seemingly crushed against the banister. She was asking for her father. She must have called the station house. She hung up the phone and didn't move. I fell onto the couch, out of breath. I closed my eyes, wishing I could die, trying to understand what I had done, trying to find words in my mind to describe what I had done. I had no words, not one word.

I pretended I was passed out when the Chief walked into the house. He was a big man. I could hear the full sounds of gabardine swishing under his leather belts and holsters and the thud of his high shoes coming into the living room.

"Jesus H. Christ in the morning!" the Chief said. "Get the girls into the police car. You get your things, Rosie."

"Pa, should I call an ambulance for him?"

"Listen to what I'm tellin' ya, get outta this house."

"I don't understand."

"Karen, Erica, go into my car."

"Wait," Rosie screamed. "What the hell are you doing, Pa? Something's *wrong* with him."

"He's a sickie."

"Jesus, Pa, don't confuse me more."

"Rosie, you are a very stupid girl. I warned you about this man long ago."

"I'm calling an ambulance." Rosie's voice changed.

"He don't need no goddamn ambulance, I'm tellin' you."

"How do you know? He might've hit his head at the marina."

"He needs help but not the kind you're thinking of. I'm tellin' ya he didn't hit his head, Rosie. What'd he say to you?"

"How do you know he didn't hit his head?" Rosie demanded.

"I know. Now what did he tell you?"

"What do you *know*, Pa?"

"He try to lay a hand on you?"

"No. He was just pale at dinner. We were eating, and all of a sudden he started breaking things. Pa, go in there and check him for me. Please, Pa."

"Check him? How do you want me to check him?"

"Look at his eyes."

"Jesus . . ."

I heard several thuds of the Chief's feet coming toward me. I kept my eyes closed. I flinched when he unexpectedly lifted my feet onto the couch. I could hear his breathing; he was short-winded. Suddenly two thick fingers pressed on my eyelids, opening them. My eyes automatically met his. I couldn't prevent the reflex. There was a brief cognition.

"Nothin' to worry about," he said, standing. My daughters were crying. Rosie was telling them to stay in the house.

"Go into the dining room," the Chief ordered. "You girls get into my car."

"No," Rosie ordered. "Stay right here. It's all right."

"Goddamn you, Rosie, do what I'm tellin' ya."

"You come in here making things worse. He's my husband. I have to look after him."

"Rosie. I know what's eatin' this man."

"What? What's eatin' him?"

"It's nothin' an ambulance'll fix, so you might just as well leave him where he chose to lie. Goddamnit, Rosie, he's awake right now listening to us."

"What's *wrong* with him?"

"You gonna get yourself into the dining room or outside so I can talk to you?"

"Pa, you're scarin' me. Tell me what's wrong."

Then the Chief spoke, his voice weaker, uncertain: "He got himself arrested yesterday."

"Arrested? How?"

"He knows. He hears. He got himself arrested up in Hampton Bays, up in Boylan's territory last night."

"Arrested for what?"

"Why don't you pack up the girls and come to my place?"

"Are you crazy, goddamnit, Pa? Tell me what happened."

"It's not supposed to be any of my business?"

"What?"

"That's *right*. Goddamnit."

"What are you trying to do to me?"

"This man is very sick, honey, and I warned you."

"Jim was here last night. He was *here*."

"He was not here, Rosie. He was arrested at nine-fifteen last night up in Hampton Bays. Did you take the kids to the movies?"

"Yes."

"Well then, was he here when you got home?"

"He said he was ridin'."

"He was ridin' all right. What time did he come home?" Rosie didn't answer. "What time, honey?"

"After eleven."

"Damned right! I was never smooth like your momma—"

"Please, Pa."

"I smelled him. Never trusted the man from the first."

"I'm callin' a doctor. You can go, Pa."

"You are a stubborn bitch," the Chief said. "Right now he hears every goddamn word we're sayin'. Do you know that? There ain't nothin' wrong that a doctor can cure, unless it's a mind doctor. You made your bed, but you don't have to lie in it. I'll be watchin' this place all night. I'll have two cars watchin'."

I could hear leaves outside, strangely, the sound coming through the big space where the picture window was broken, and poor Rosie, following her father to his car. I could hear them arguing.

"Don't leave without tellin' me, Pa."

"Let your husband tell you himself. I warned you not to marry him."

"Pa."

"Didn't I tell you not to have kids with him? Let go a' me, Rosie."

"Pa, please. You're scarin' me. I'm scared. Tell me what he did."

"Rosie, I love ya, and I'd die for them two girls in there, but I ain't got the tongue to tell ya. If he threw a goddamn brick in a store window, or stole, why, Christ, I'd be laughin'. But he's a weirdo, your man. You go in there and find out for yourself what I been tellin' you for ten years. Maybe he'll tell ya what he did. I swear on your mother, if he don't, you'll be told, that I swear to Christ on. You'll be told, Rosie. So go inside, call your doctor. Do whatever the hell you got to, but I'm watching the house anyway. You keep the lights on and the shades up, you hear?"

I waited for the Chief's car to move out of the driveway, then I pulled myself up and looked at the mess around me. Karen and Erica watched me from the top of the stairs.

I'll never forget Rosie's grave face as she came toward me. "Hon." Her voice was squeezed. "Honey?"

"Don't ask me nothin'," I said, holding up my hand.

"Just . . . should I call anyone?"

"No."

"A doctor?"

"No."

"You all right? You're scarin' me, Jim."

"Don't be scared, Rosie."

"I don't understand what's going on. I don't know what to *do*."

"Nothin'. Nothin', Rosie. Let me think."

"Did you hear my father?"

"I heard him."

"You were arrested? It is true, what he said? Jim?"

"Lemme go down the cellar and think, Rosie."

"Just tell me *that*." She was looking at me as if I were a complete stranger, anger showing on her face now.

"I don't know what you mean." I stood up and started for the cellar door.

"I mean, were you arrested last night?"

"Yes. But I don't want to talk about it."

"What for?"

"Huh?"

"What were you arrested for?"

"Rosie, gimme a chance, gimme a break and I'll tell you everything. But now I've got to think 'cause I'm scared too. Things keep blanking out on me. Lemme go down the tool room and think for tonight. Gimme a few days to straighten it out in my own mind before I tell you. Gimme time, 'cause I'm very scared."

As I passed her, her eyes filled and her lips pressed tight together. She was more worried than I had ever seen her. I couldn't talk anymore. There was no flow to my words. They were like bricks in my mouth that I would have had to spit out one at a time. I only wanted to go down to hide, and rest.

If the house had been burning, I still would have pulled the cellar doorknob toward me, flipped the light switch and grabbed the banister to go down. I had to think, had to be closed alone in my tool room, the door locked. I stepped down the first few cellar stairs and looked back. Poor Rosie had gone upstairs. Our bathroom light went on. Then the door closed.

Wind was starting up outside. I loved the cellar on a windy night. The steps were a little mobile. I was going to have to shore them up. The old man who owned the house before us had them put in thirty years ago, just old two-by-eights thrown together with nails. Poor Rosie.

I pulled the door of the tool room closed and locked it behind me. The light bulb had burned out. I felt my way to the workbench in the dark.

In one last hope that I was dreaming, I stuck my hands into my pockets. If the small paper the cop slipped into my pocket wasn't there, I would have rejoiced. It would have meant that the arrest was a dream. Why not? A coincidence as grotesque as the one that had taken place could only happen internally, in one's mind, in a dream.

But my left hand found the paper. I pulled it out of my pocket, and dropped it on the workbench. I lit a match. I unfolded the paper. The cop's name appeared in the red glow: *Tato Manfredi*, and a telephone number, a Huntington exchange. That meant he traveled forty miles to the station house in Hampton Bays to go to work each day. Tato. It was his face that flashed before me when I swung the poker. Tato's face . . .

My mind flew across a bridge of years to 1949. I remembered the first time I saw Tato's sad, vivid face. I blew out the match and I was lost in the dark.

An oil burner pumped nearby, my house's monstrous heart. Pipes and ducts gurgled like intestines.

I hear the monster breathing, but I can't find his eyes. He is the truth. He is the man I really am. I am afraid to know him. So my mind hugs the cellar walls as it moves, careful not to bump the shelves where my memories are preserved, in glass jars that must be opened before they explode. . . .

PART II

CHAPTER II

MY father nicknamed my mother the "Flamingo," but her real name was Jeanette. She was tall and had dark eye sockets. I remember she was bone thin. Her feet were too large. Big hands with prominent veins hung down from long arms. My father nicknamed all his women; the names always fit. I have to force myself to call her Jeanette or I will see her as a tall, sad bird. She was fourteen when I was born; I was the only child of another child. She was a Southern girl, an orphan from a Baptist orphanage in Texas. Her hair was blond and she wore thick glasses. When last I saw her she was twenty and I was six.

I remember our apartment was small but high up, overlooking the Hudson River. It had wall sconces with bare bulbs and pull chains and crooked moldings. The walls were pimpled and painted high-gloss cream color. My mother's room had a blond wood bed and dresser.

My father was a Manfredi. They called him Buzzy. On one of his visits, Buzzy unbolted the large terrace door, letting in the breeze from the river twenty-two stories below. I remember him always in suspenders and dress shoes, as if he were ready at any moment to put on his jacket and start tap dancing out the door. The black hair of his arms crept like flames from under his starched cuffs. His shoes were shiny and noisy on the hardwood floors.

My father's hair was brown and straight, like mine. He often had to push it back from his forehead. He looked at himself in the mirror a lot. His eyes were crystal-like and turquoise color. His voice was brittle, as if he were unconscious of the beauty of his eyes.

The apartment always fell back to its dark state when he left. Then Jeanette's impatience with me became her only mood. Her hair started falling out of place. She went back to biting her nails, pacing the floor, tapping fingers, taking pills, sleeping, smoking. Ashtrays filled with cigarette butts. That's when she turned into the Flamingo I feared, yet she was all I had. She would hurt me, then beg for forgiveness. I had to anticipate her changes. But in the times she was Jeanette, holding me to her, I rested in her love. Those periods were infrequent, but when she was Jeanette, treating me like a child, it was beautiful beyond words.

"Santa Claus is up there."

"Where?"

"Up there." Jeanette pressed her finger on the glass, pointing to a window across the way that reflected the orange sun.

"In that room Santa's working with his little helpers, old men a hundred years old, making toys for good boys."

"One hundred years old?"

"Yeah, and no bigger than you. What would you like for Christmas dinner?"

"Pancakes," I answered.

On Christmas eve we ate the pancakes and then she left the

apartment. I lifted the kitchen shade, letting it flap all the way to the top in hopes that Santa and his one-hundred-year-old helpers would see that I was a good boy in every way. The night had turned the windows into mirrors. I could only see myself climbing a bench to the sink to wash the dishes. I hadn't finished when she rushed in, insisting that I get to bed immediately. I caught a glimpse of our little pine tree waiting in the corridor.

The next morning was extremely cold. The tree was on the terrace, faintly visible through steamed-up windows. But I could smell its fragrance in the house. I felt its needles under my bare feet. For one brief moment, she let me onto the terrace with my bathrobe wrapped tightly around me and the cuffs of my slippers turned up over my flannel pajamas. There were no packages.

"Take the stocking." The tree was not decorated. The wind was hard.

"Hurry, Cello. It's cold." It was not a real stocking, but one made of red flannel, trimmed with white. It had round bumps inside.

"Take it," she screamed into the wind.

The wind was loud coming up the sides of the building. It stung my nostrils. I looked for toys, but there were none. She pulled me inside, slamming the terrace door and bolting it.

Inside the stocking were tangerines, nuts, and two dimes. I threw the tangerines at the wall and scattered the dimes on the floor. The Flamingo slapped me.

"No. You are a *bad* boy. He knew you'd pull this. He can see the future, and that's why there's no toys." I could see she was afraid. Her glasses magnified the fear in her eyes. She kept fixing her glasses. She was sweating. Then suddenly she stopped dead, as if she were paralyzed. She pulled me near her, crying, caressing. "Honey, first of all there ain't no Santa Claus. That light don't come from inside that room across the way. That light is only the sun reflecting from there." She pointed behind her. "I was scared to ride the subway to Macy's for your toys. Scared I'd get lost and no one would know you were alone here."

My father phoned from Florida New Year's Day. Jeanette screamed into the telephone, "How can I send him to school?

Who'll pick him up? I'm scared to go out. I won't sign anything and you can't force me, you hear?" She glared down at me through her glasses, tears flooding her eyes so I could hardly recognize them. Still, her face was stone; only her mouth trembled. "All right . . . *when* . . . when you comin'? I'll sign. I said yes, didn't I? When you comin'? You're not lyin' again? Tuesday? Six o'clock? Tuesday, you promise? They'll find your kid here and me gone if you don't show up. I swear that."

During the next few days we emptied all the drawers and closets. We packed all her things in boxes. Father's things went into two suitcases. The small blue suitcase was for me. She packed it with care, folding underwear, seersucker pajamas, tops and bottoms, and shorts and shirts, and a sweater. Then she went to the kitchen and came back with an orange. She tucked the orange into my suitcase and snapped it shut. Then she put tags on all her boxes. The next day a man and woman from the Salvation Army came and took the boxes away.

"Cello . . . help me."

I awoke to her voice weakly calling me. I ran through all the rooms, but she was nowhere. Her voice seemed to come from the bedroom, but she wasn't in there. Then I went into the bathroom. She was there, in the tub. Her face white as porcelain.

"Cello, Mama's going away," she said.

I began to cry. She lifted her hand to touch my face. Her wrists were bleeding. I wanted her to smile and say she was fooling. I didn't want to see her wrists again. I went into the living room, turned the bench over, and sat inside. I played sailboat. For a while she sang. Then she called me, but I pretended not to hear. I waved to the maid cleaning venetian blinds in the apartment across the street. I made a ramp with books and rolled napkin rings onto the floor. I raced the napkin rings against each other. When I heard my father's key in the door, I ran into the closet.

"Jeaneaaaaatte!" I heard him making animal sounds when he found her, then screams. He screamed for help, for the police, for anyone.

I sat in the dark among umbrellas and shoes a long time listening to many feet walking on the other side of the door, heavy foot-steps, quick and light footsteps and voices—women's and men's—and my father's screams. It became quiet after a long while. I reached for the knob to open the door and peek out when it flew open to blinding light. My father was transfigured in whiteness. He wore a dark suit and a black tie.

"Come out," he said calmly, though his hands were trembling.

A woman stood behind him in a tightly fitted dress, a neighbor. She tried to bend to me, but her dress wouldn't let her. "Come, baby. Come." She took me by the hand and walked me to the elevator. We went down to her apartment. Her name was Mrs. Sadowski, and her feet puffed out of her high heels like balloons. Her apartment was painted many shades of peach and pink, and the living-room furniture was all white. Her toy poodle was white. He barked at me from a chair for an hour. I fell asleep on Mrs. Sadowski's couch.

When I woke up, my father was wiping my saliva from the white brocade with a handkerchief. I clutched his lapels tightly as he carried me back to our apartment. His large hands held my head to his lips, his mouth making tender noises. Suddenly I loved him. He was a giant. I wanted to stay in his arms forever, flying high above life, high up over the bleeding wrists and the barking dogs. When we returned to the apartment, Mother was gone.

The sun was red and everywhere when I walked with my father to the funeral parlor a few days later. There were no leaves on the sycamores and the sun glowed raw upon the orange brick apart-ment houses.

"You'll see your mother," he said, "I promise. But she is sleep-ing, and we can't wake her up. Don't you try to wake her up, you understand?"

At the funeral parlor, everyone was able to see Jeanette except me. I kept tugging at my father to bring me to her. I couldn't understand what was going on. Why all the people? Would she be in a bed sleeping? In a chair? Was she sitting somewhere up front? She might have been floating like a huge goldfish in a glass tank. I held my tears, afraid that if I didn't my father might change his mind.

Suddenly he was leading me through the crowd. My father's large hands lifted me high into the odor of flowers over her casket. The room grew silent. Jeanette was below me in a blue dress that I had never seen. Her hands seemed to have frozen in an attempt to clasp each other. Light blue rosary beads encircled them. Her face was a birthday cake, pink icing. Her mouth was closed against its will.

"Where are her glasses?" I asked.

"She don't need her glasses," Father answered. "She's asleep."

She was not asleep. Something worse than sleep had happened to her. Something terrible. His arms began to tremble. When he lowered me to the floor, I saw that my mother's casket was on a wagon on wheels. A tan cat sat under the coffin, looking at me.

The room began to get noisy. My father disappeared for a moment. I was in terror till I saw him in the crowd. I ran to him; I clung to his trousers till he lifted me. I would not let him return me to the floor. I encumbered him as he tried to shake hands with people. Several of them were trying to amuse me and cajole me out of his arms, but I held his lapels with fists.

"Let me go, goddamn you," he whispered, "let me go." I wouldn't. I clung fast to his lapels till they began to rip. Finally, he sat down with me.

I was feeling pain under my right leg as if a small animal was biting me. It was my father pinching me to force me off his lap. I squirmed and cried to myself and finally, like my salvation, his sister arrived, Fantasia.

"Your *zia* is here. Up. Get up." His eyes quickened with delight. He sprang up, leaving me dwarfed among wavy black skirts and long-trousered legs. I didn't realize that *zia* was the Italian word for aunt. I never knew I had an aunt.

I couldn't see Zia Fantasia, but I was aware of the increased activity as word of her presence flashed through the funeral parlor. The palms swayed in currents of people moving about. The room bustled with whispers, nervousness, smiles—and then silence as she entered.

Zia was taller than any man or woman in the room, and she was dressed in a luminescent frock of tan and a hat from which fell a

36

tent of veiling heavily banded with silk. Her shoes were silk and as tan as her stockings. The sleeves of her loose open coat and its hem were weighted with golden fur which, when she moved, spiraled in huge circles around her. From out of the fur of her sleeve peeked a thick bracelet of dazzling diamonds. Her Italian was musical, so perfect that no one risked speaking to her. In the paralyzed silence, her laugh, coming from inside her tent, rang a warning that she owned the hush that accompanied her. She came directly toward me.

"What is his name?" she asked with authority. She spoke in English.

"Cello," my father answered, smiling proudly down at me.

There was a mushrooming of fur and silk as she knelt before me. Her hand emerged from beneath her veiling, each long fingernail painted dark red. Perfume escaped as she lifted the veil. Her lips were bright red, her eyes minty crystals of green. She kissed me. She took my hands in both of hers. "Do you miss your mommy?"

"Yes." I felt the tears without knowing I was crying. I trusted her. She lifted me inside the tent of her veil. She stood with me in her arms, rocking me, walking. She spoke as if she knew me always. I watched her brilliant red lips speaking to me. I felt her breath.

"I want my mother," I said.

"I know, my lovely little man."

"When is she going to wake up?"

"No one knows." Tears filled her eyes.

"I'm afraid," I whispered.

"I know. I can't help you now. I have to return to Argentina, where I live, but I will come back for you. Do you understand what I'm trying to say to you? Don't worry."

"Yes," I answered, not really understanding how far away Argentina was, but believing her.

Father hired Mrs. McCarthy to teach me reading. She came each morning, wearing black pointed shoes and a black hat with a black curly feather in it. She never took off the hat. She spoke to me, but I hardly listened. She put tags on everything and I was supposed to identify them. Sometimes she tricked me by tagging wrong. *Chair. Table. Dish. Window.*

I waited for Jeanette to come back to the apartment. I watched the door so that she wouldn't slip in without my seeing her. If I missed the door for a while during the day, or while I had slept, I searched every room afterward to see if Jeanette had returned.

"Don't follow me from room to room, *please*, Cello," Mrs. Mc-Carthy said, stamping her foot. She was afraid of me; I heard her tell that to father. "There is definitely something wrong with that boy. He eats like a bird and sleeps with his eyes open."

I was afraid to sleep. Every time I closed my eyes I saw Jeanette in her casket. Closing my eyes was like opening them, really, on her face. During the day I could recall her as she was, but if it grew dark and I closed my eyes, I saw her in death.

Wakefulness had become my true sleep. Sleep was torment. I had it all backwards.

My mother unknowingly had given the whole world power over me. There was no parent to claim the feelings of my child's heart, and that was a dangerous thing.

The first person to claim that power was another child, my cousin Tato. The first time I met him was on a warm, sunny June morning. My father, his blond girlfriend named Pumpkin and I stood next to our suitcases at the door of our apartment. The long corridor had a damp smell, glossy green floors and walls. The light poured blindly from the large windows at both ends.

"Wave goodbye," my father said, jangling his keys. I waved to my sailboat bench, to the wooden floors shining in the blue light of bare windows. I waved to the window where I ate snow from the sill on winter days before Jeanette woke up, goodbye to the windows that caught the red sun every night. Goodbye cream-colored walls, cream-colored doors, shiny cream-colored molding around her door. Suddenly I realized I was being tricked.

Wave goodbye? If we left the apartment, how would my mother find us? I made a dash for her door. It had a skeleton key. I would turn it and lock myself in before they could catch me. But I never reached it. My father grabbed me. Suddenly I was fed up with him.

"No," I screamed. I would have killed him if I could. My arms were juiced up with power. I pounded his face and scratched. He put me down on the corridor floor and calmly locked both locks of the dark green steel door, as I kicked and pulled at his jacket.

"Now, now." Pumpkin gently tugged at me.

"No." I kicked and pulled. He put his keys in his pockets calmly, then turned. Suddenly I felt such a blow in my face that my neck ached and my ears rang. I heard screams from the floor below, but they were my own screams echoing in the stairwell.

"Don't you dare, you hear me?"—he slapped with each word— "dare . . . hit me . . . ever . . . ever . . . again . . . you hear?"

"Stop!" Pumpkin screamed. I was on the floor. He pushed her against the wall. I heard her skull knock.

"Mind your fuckin' business, you."

I couldn't swallow. My ear felt twice its size and was on fire.

As the limousine sped down the highway along the river, my father held his finger to my face threatening another slap, forcing me to suck back every sob, every drop of tear like a vacuum. I squinted my eyes tight and tried. I grunted. My grunts didn't annoy him. I had a terrible case of hiccups too. Pumpkin ignored the sounds coming out of me and, in a Tinker Bell voice, pointed out things I couldn't have cared less to see.

"Yek. Yek" was all I could answer. We rode over a bridge. It was the first bridge I ever remembered crossing. My face felt like rubber.

"Where?" The word blew from Pumpkin's lips above and behind me.

"What are you trying to say?" my father asked her with annoyance.

"Where are we taking him?" she whispered.

"To my brother Marco's," he said looking out the window. His eyes danced as we flew by the El pillars. Then he smiled broadly.

"What are you smiling at?" Pumpkin asked.

"My lunatic brother. Wait till you see his wife and kid. He married a fat Puerto Rican who owns a Puerto Rican wedding store." He burst into laughter.

"A wedding store?"

"Yeah. You know. She rents wedding outfits to Puerto Ricans."

"Don't make me laugh when we get there, you bastard. Don't you dare," Pumpkin screamed.

"This is Fay's Bridal Shop," Father said when the car stopped. Pumpkin stomped the floor of the limo, laughing.

In the windows of the shop there were four mannequins dressed in green sweetheart hats and green strapless gowns.

A fat woman in a green dress printed with large pink flowers came running from the shop. It was Aunt Silva, Tato's mother. Her hair was bright orange. She tried to speak Italian.

"Please speak English," Father said.

"Don't be such a hog," someone said as he pulled Aunt Silva away from the car. It was Uncle Marco.

Uncle Marco ceremoniously took my father's hand. He had a gray, homely face. His neck was very wrinkled. Long strands of hair wrapped around his pink dome like pen-and-ink lines. He smiled in a way that would not show his teeth. Then he reached back and pulled a boy to the door of our car. "This is your cousin. Shake hands with your cousin." The boy didn't move. His eyes were brown. "Shake his hand," Uncle Marco insisted.

"No." Tato smiled.

"This is your cousin Tato," my father said.

He was only a little taller than I. His hair was black as coal, short, falling just up to his eyes. His skull was large, his eyes almost angelic, but there was shrewdness in his black arched eyebrows and a liquid facility in his face that enabled him to produce a whole range of expressions.

Uncle Marco's annnoyance only amused Tato. My cousin finally smiled and held out his hand. It was damp with sweat. He had been running. His face was old, like a man's; you had to stare at it a long time to get used to it.

"Take Cello up to the roof," Aunt Silva ordered.

"You take him up," Tato said. Uncle Marco swung. Tato ducked.

"C'mon." Tato laughed.

He put his arm around me. The adults marched into the store while we took the stairway alongside the windows where the mannequins stood pointing into space. We climbed four flights, then Tato turned to me. "Did your mother die?" he whispered naughtily.

"Yes," I answered.

Tato threw his body against a black iron door. It swung out into the sunlight. He laughed as he turned and beckoned me into his world. "C'mon, Cello. Don't be scared."

The roof was an island floating in the sky. On the island grew those New York City weeds, the leafy ailanthus and silk trees. As the island floated, clouds moved in a train behind the trees. It was dizzying. Vegetable plants grew out of olive oil cans with dark velvety petunias—blue and yellow—their seed packets indicating their beds. In the middle of the roof there was a pigeon coop with angels painted all over it, angels of every variety, with golden wings and funny faces. Some were fat; they were painted vertically over horizontal planks. Long iron pipes, like flagpoles, supported whirligigs clacking in the wind, a man sawing wood, a goose flapping, a sailing ship and a black man tap dancing. An awning shaded wine barrels in the back of the coop opposite a grape arbor under which were benches and a table. Sunflower plants were everywhere, marked by packets, and though they were not in bloom, they were growing near wooden sunflowers which were.

I noticed his rocking chair before I noticed the old man. He came out of the pigeon coop walking with two canes and stopped short when he saw us. Tato had his arm around my shoulder, urging me toward the man. Except for the canes, the old man could have been the true Santa Claus. His head was a mountain peak, and his eyes were blue glass marbles, very pale blue, almost transparent, that glistened like cut glass.

"Are you Santa Claus?" The question took all my courage.

"He's the landlord, Mr. Possilippo."

I didn't let on that I didn't understand what Tato was trying to tell me, but I got the impression that a landlord was no less important than a Santa Claus. The old man laughed and turned away. He couldn't speak English very well, but he understood everything. He rested his two canes on the rocker and felt his way along the coop to a hose, turned it on and sprayed the tomatoes.

Tato knew exactly what to do. He opened the pigeon coop, went inside and shooed out all the birds. They flew into the sky. Then Tato filled pails with feed from a sack. I walked toward the coop and peeked in.

"Go in and see the angels." He meant the wooden room where the pigeons slept out of the weather. I walked over the strong odor of pigeon shit, toward the doorway of the inner room. When I got there, I looked cautiously inside. The odor was making me dizzy, but there were angels inside, very tall angels, fourteen of them, painted on the walls of the coop, which was really only boards. Sunlight leaked through the boards, seeming to come from within the angels' bodies. The angels were huddled in a ring out of necessity, their wings of gold and silver awkwardly squashed against one another, their vestments all different in design and color. Each angel wore a different expression—boredom, sorrow, joy—some looking up, some looking down and some staring right at the doorway as if I startled them.

The old man gently pulled me aside and passed into the room with his hose, watering down everything, making rainbows where the spray passed through the narrow bands of sun. He splashed the angels over and over without thinking twice, yelled to Tato to turn off the water, then dropped the hose. He shooed me out, then he and Tato took bamboo poles and began to wave the birds back down with loud whistles. Everything frightened me but made me want to laugh at the same time. I sat in the old man's rocker and watched. I wanted to run away, and I wanted at the same time to take a bamboo pole and reach it up till I could touch the birds in the sky. The birds zoomed in circles, like comets. When they came closer, they resembled oversized flapping stars. I clung to the wooden rocker, which was worn smooth as bone. After the birds were back in the coop the old man lifted me to his lap and took out a cigar. It was short and bent like a twig. He lit the cigar, then held the match for me to blow. He waited, eyeing me, holding out the match. I watched it burn nearer his fingers. He didn't budge. Then, to save his fingers, I blew.

"Good," he said as if he were amazed at my expertise. "Tomorrow we gonna paint da sky."

"Bullshit," Tato said through laughter.

"Sa not bullsheet. See over dere? It's peelin', da sky." The sky in the west was dark, except for a long horizontal tear over the horizon. A rare green color showed through and peach veils of foggy light spilled out of it onto the world.

"His mother died," Tato said.

"Shut up," the old man commanded. He dropped me down, lifting up his canes. He walked slowly toward the host of angels and the coop. "C'mere." He was calling me. The coop was busy with pigeons eating and drinking when I walked in. He hung his cane on a nail, then slowly bent to lift a pure white bird into my hands. I had to enfold its wings I was so afraid. I felt its energy burning through its silky body, its little heart beating wildly.

"Who you want?" the old man bluntly asked Tato.

"Midnight," Tato said.

"Take Midnight," the old man said with finality. The old man picked up his two canes and went out. Tato cautiously followed a blue-black bird around the pen with open hands. He enfolded it and lifted it. His face was ecstatic. He looked at me appreciatively.

"Mine? This is my bird?" I asked.

"He gave it to you." Tato smiled. "And he gave me Midnight. That one's a baby you got there. He never flew yet. What are you going to name yours?" Tato asked.

I thought of Jeanette at the west window over the Hudson, placing crumbs for the sparrows. I remembered their tiny footprints in the snow. Snow shooting into the dry hot rooms of our apartment through slightly lifted windows. Snow from the outside world that came gently to the earth. I named my pigeon Snow.

I almost didn't care when my father and Pumpkin stood up from the small round table of anisette and cookies and coffee to leave. My father left a pile of money on the table. Uncle Marco could not keep his eyes off it. My father kissed me with cigarette breath and a rough scratch of his beard.

"You're going to stay here, with Uncle Marco." Aunt Silva was holding the blue vinyl suitcase my mother had packed. Pumpkin bent to me. I felt sorry for her, as if she were just another child of his, an older sister who could not escape him. She did not kiss me. She seemed sullen and tired now.

As the limo drove off with Father and Pumpkin, Aunt Silva and Uncle Marco began to run, elbowing each other as they squeezed through the doorway. Their four hands landed on the pile of money, but Aunt Silva's hands hit first. She rolled two bills and handed them to Uncle Marco, putting the rest in her brassiere.

"What, are you crazy?" he said. She doled out two more. "You think I'm afraid to go into your brassiere? C'mere." She hit his hand with a spoon. He laughed and she laughed. Uncle Marco grabbed the neck of her dress and her brassiere and, closing his eyes against the barrage of spoon whacks, he pulled until her two huge tits popped out like giant jellyfish. The money fell to the floor. She put her foot on the roll and wouldn't budge until Uncle Marco left the house.

Outside he called Tato. "Go find Pimples and Sharkey and set up a game. I don't mean no cheap game." He slipped Tato a dollar for himself.

"You can't go with him. He has to go too far," Aunt Silva called after me. I sat near her a long time, watching her clean up. Then I asked, "Can I go to the roof?" I waited for an answer, but she just went on cleaning. I stood up eventually and slowly walked up the stairs.

In the middle of the third set of stairs I made the mistake of looking down. I was afraid to go any higher. I just stood still, waiting, realizing what father had done to me. I wanted Jeanette. I had forgotten about her in the excitement. I wanted to cry, but I was afraid to.

The old man appeared on the landing with his two canes. "Come up." He smiled. It was easier with him waiting for me. On the roof the sky was dark red. It was chilly. The old man sat down in his rocking chair. His hands, like large soft clamps around my ribs, lifted me to his lips. His clothes smelled of cigars. His old sweater was scratchy to my face, but beneath it his body was warm as a radiator. We drifted back, far back, then far forward, back and forth. He hummed a song as we rocked. I felt the vibrations of his humming on my face and in my chest. My lungs hummed the old man's song along with him.

I let go, my tight fists surrendering, a little at a time, to sleep.

Tato was a kind of mother of his own world. He was known in the streets as an arbitrator. Gangs of older boys respected him and exchanged favors with him. He mothered Mr. Possilippo on the roof and literally made the old man's world possible—shopping for necessities, carrying twenty-five-pound feed bags up the four flights, dragging up fertilizers, delivering pigeons and picking up new ones. The old man paid him movie money once in a while, and Tato had to accept or the old man would become embarrassed and even angry. The small payments kept the hierarchy of the rooftop fixed and unchangeable.

I thought that life on the roof had no end. I thought the old man was born old. I thought the summer was a permanent condition that we were trapped in blissfully, with no need ever to leave.

Those summer nights on the roof Tato and I slept on an old mattress under Mr. Possilippo's old green vegetable-store awning. I could hear the old man snoring nearby and the sound of trucks in the street, muffled car horns mixed with soft arguments in Spanish, and laughter. But the sounds, like the stray lights from below, had no connection to our place of peace and darkness. We slept like gods, unseen, far above the world of man. I often thought of the Flamingo at night. But then she was just a puppet of my mind; the dark blue night with its millions of stars was more real. Sometimes I imagined I heard the angels whispering to each other inside the coop.

I learned to run in an old pair of Tato's black sneakers. Soon I could make it with packages up the four flights in a flash. I tried anything they let me do, even whistling the birds down at feeding time with the bamboo pole. But like the old man, I was afraid of the streets. I only observed them from the roof. I had a lookout post in the northeast corner where I could sometimes see Tato coming back from deliveries.

Uncle Marco seemed intent upon deposing Tato and was his only enemy. Uncle Marco hadn't had a job in years. In spite of everything, whenever he asked to borrow money, Tato emptied his tin box of change without a word.

Each morning Aunt Silva held court in her shop. Her large body was enthroned behind her sewing machine as she gently threw orders to Tato, who made her wishes incarnate—running errands, making change for customers, boxing, brushing lint, ironing, reaching, stooping—responding with solutions. Mother and son were a wonder to watch. But this cooperation didn't extend to the rest of their lives.

Out of the shop, Aunt Silva's orders were not so gentle, and sometimes there were terrible fights. One afternoon we were going to the movies. Aunt Silva called us from the window of her apartment over the shop, red dye dripping down her forehead, a white plastic cape under her chin; "Taaatoooo."

"What?" Tato yelled. She disappeared. "Fuck." He kicked the air. "I'll bet she wants a Pineapple Duce." That was a soda drink. We climbed the stairs slowly. "How can she drink that shit? It's always in the back of the soda case and the bottle caps are always rusty." When we entered the room Albert, the local hairdresser, was rolling her hair.

"Ouch. No, it's okay, Albert. You son of a bitch, where were you? C'mere." She fished in her change purse.

"Go get you a Pineapple Duce, right?" She didn't hear Tato.

"Go get me a Pineapple Duce." She rolled out a dollar bill. "Albert, you want somethin'?"

"Large Coke in a container with ice, please." She waved the bill at Tato.

"You hear?"

"Why the fuck didn't you tell me from the window?" He grabbed the money.

"Go to the store and shut your filthy mouth."

"Get your own Duce and Coke." Tato threw the money on the floor and turned.

"Hey, get him." Aunt Silva jumped up, knocking over Albert's tray.

"Jesus Christ, Fay, you knocked over the whole goddamn thing."
Aunt Silva caught Tato by the hair. I ran into the hallway.

"I ain't your fuckin' slave," he snarled into her face.

"Who said you ain't? Huh?" She slapped him. "Huh? Who said?" Aunt Silva's lips were tight and her fists white as she banged Tato's head to the wall with a thud that made the windows rattle. Suddenly she doubled up in a scream. "He kicked me. The little bastard. Grab him, Albert. Right in the cunt he kicked me."

Albert, who was more than twice Tato's height, grabbed Tato by the wrist. Tato dragged him toward the hallway.

"Hold him." Aunt Silva went for the broom. Albert wore a smile as he pinned Tato's arms behind his back. Aunt Silva pushed the broom bristles into Tato's face. Tato screamed. Tato's ten dollars drifted to the floor. Aunt Silva noticed it immediately and grabbed it.

"Where'd you get this?" She could hardly breathe. And while Albert held Tato, Aunt Silva slapped him in the head in rhythm to her own words: ". . . little . . . little son of a bitch . . . Where'd you get this?"

Tato slipped down beneath her blows out of Albert's grasp. Tato grabbed the broom from her and struck Albert in the head with the handle, then swung.

"No," she screamed. He landed such a resounding crack on Aunt Silva's backside that the blood rushed to her face. Tato grabbed a nail file from the floor. He held it like a knife. Tears flooded his eyes, but he blinked them away as he spoke. "If you ever . . . touch me again . . . I'll wait till you're asleep . . . and I'll stab you to death . . . you hear? I'll kill you. I ain't your slave. Give me my ten dollars."

On our way back from the movies, Aunt Silva saw us coming across the street. She ran out of the shop holding a handkerchief in her fist. Tato froze in his tracks.

She was crying. "Please, listen to me." She tried to put her arms around Tato. "You're gonna feel so bad, my baby."

He pushed her away. "Whatsamatter?"

"Mr. Possilippo died." Aunt Silva said it as if she were pulling his life-support plug.

He was found in his rocking chair with his head on his own shoulder covered with the blanket that Tato had put on him.

The old man had one son, Tabs. Tabs decided the wake should be in the apartment, one floor above the Fay's Bridal Shop sign. The funeral was to be on the same day as one of Aunt Silva's weddings, a big one for which the girls wore the rented sweetheart hats shaped into sea-green hearts and their dresses were trimmed with green roses. The wedding party showed up during the wake to have photographs taken at the shop. There was a christening in the second-floor apartment. Spanish music played and the guests ate food out of paper dishes on the stairs. My skin tightened whenever we passed the old man's doorway. I wouldn't let Tato out of my sight.

The morning of the funeral Uncle Marco took all the wine from the roof and ransacked the place. Tato and I ran alongside the black funeral car in which Tabs and his wife sat. We went to the funeral mass.

I was amazed at the huge church, its gigantic windows shooting down ribbons of colored light, and the music, and how everyone didn't bother each other there, but sat quietly and peacefully. I loved best the lady in blue standing on a snake with a moon under her feet, because she had a white bird, just like Snow, shining over her head.

That night, after it was all over, we were falling asleep on the roof and Tato began to cry. He hid his face in my side. I was afraid of his crying; I turned softly, pushing him away with my legs. I couldn't help it. Tato's sobs died quickly, as if they were in a bottle submerged in the sea.

Tuesday morning Tabs' wife Ruth, in a black dress, said, "May I?" and stepped softly through the black door onto the roof. Her hair was blond and short, her veins showed thick and blue through the skin of her hands. Her fingers were long. She had the hands of an old woman, but her face was young. A silk scarf of pale gray hung loosely around her neck. Her eyes were blue and twinkled child-like out of veined and darkened sockets. Her tiny voice and manner in some passive way made a demand for the most careful, gentle treatment. I liked Ruth. She commented accurately upon the loveliness of things, the size of our cabbage. She didn't laugh at our lettuce growing in tubs with tomatoes, basil and parsley. She understood.

She pulled her feet together, peered into her camera and clicked. She shot the pigeon coop from a distance, then asked us to get some of the pigeons to come out. Tato and I opened the chicken-wire door and dropped some feed, but they wouldn't emerge, so we went inside. I picked up Snow gently, and Tato picked up Midnight. We carried them carefully into the sun. The woman smiled and stepped forward.

"Get closer. No, to each other. And smile. Wonderful." Snap. Snap.

She kept saying, "Why didn't Tabs tell me about this place?" Tabs appeared at the black door. "Darling." She went to him.

"Where the hell you been?" He was in a bad mood.

"Oh, darling, what's wrong?"

"Crazy old man." Tabs was dressed neatly in a dark blue suit with a silky light blue tie and black shiny shoes. His slick dark hair went straight back. He had his father's eyes, but a very large nose diminished their brilliance. His eyes darted to the pigeon coop. "Jesus Christ." He said, "Jesus Christ," every time he touched something. Then he wiped his fingers with a clean white handkerchief. "Crazy old man." He walked toward the coop as if he might at any moment fall into quicksand, placing each shoe carefully.

He peered at the birds. "Can you eat these goddamn things?"

"They're *pets*." Ruthie laughed. "Let me get a picture of you."

"You, wait downstairs," he commanded. She blushed and stepped out of his way. "No more water up here." He unscrewed the hose.

"The birds need water, the vegetables—" Tato protested.

"Fuck the birds and fuck the vegetables." Tabs didn't understand the latch of the chicken-wire door, so he broke it open. "Let them go live in Central Park."

"They'll only come back."

Tabs eyed the open feed sack. He emptied it into the garbage pail. Dust flew up all over him. "They'll wise up when the food is gone. Fuckin' crazy old man." He went into the coop. "Out," he commanded the birds. The birds hit the fencing. They wanted to get out but he was swinging too wildly.

"Tabs?" She was worried about him. Tabs was breathing heavy and sweating, totally abandoning his blue suit to the dirt from the hose as he rolled it.

"Do you realize this roof can cave in from all this dirt and water, Ruthie? You walk around with your camera like some fairy. That crazy old man didn't even have insurance. You want to get sued from all these monkeys when the place crashes down? Huh, fucking fairy princess?" Something hit his shoulder. It was white. He slapped it. Pigeon shit.

There was very little rain that August. Soot covered the roof, the overgrown lettuce, the tattered leaves of the grape arbor. The rest of the vegetables were clean. We wore ourselves out carrying water up the stairs to save them. Tabs gave Uncle Marco everything on the roof in exchange for cleaning it up. We worked for Uncle Marco, emptying tubs and dropping the dirt from the roof into the first-floor yard behind Aunt Silva's shop.

Our main concern was the pigeons. Tato was ready to do anything to save them. Our hope was that, after Tabs saw that all the dirt was gone from the roof and nothing was left but the birds, he would allow them to stay.

Uncle Marco walked around smoking the old man's cigars with arms full of produce. "You like paella?" Uncle Marco asked me one night at dinner.

"Yes." I nodded my head insincerely. We ate neatly, leaving the chicken bones on the red and white checked oilcloth. Tato kept his eyes down. Uncle Marco was drunk.

"Where'd you get that wristwatch?" Aunt Silva asked. The watch band was too big; it hung from Uncle Marco's wrist.

"I won it." He laughed, showing the dark red hole of his mouth.

"Liar. You traded it for the old man's wine press."

"Fat ass." His hand reached under her dress.

She jumped and slapped him. "Get your filthy breath off my table."

He put his chin down on the oilcloth next to his wine. "Hey, Tato, you like paella, huh? Hey, porto?" He picked up one of Tato's chicken bones. "Small bones this chicken. Jesus, looks almost like a pigeon." Tato's head sprang up. His eyes sparkled like a hawk's. They darted to the large bowl.

Aunt Silva came forward. "Don't believe him. They're Rock Cornish hens."

Uncle Marco smiled at Tato and shook his head. "Who gave you the Rock Cornish hens, Silva?" Uncle Marco asked.

"He gave them to me, but do you think this coward would go to the trouble to kill those pigeons and clean them? They're Rock Cornish hens, Tato."

Tato pushed his chair away and darted for the stairs. I followed him. When I pushed open the black door to the roof I saw Tato, his hands dangling at his sides, his face pale, walking in circles. His eyes were thrown back as if he were in a trance. He cried, dry sobs. Suddenly he was throwing up. The sight of the vomit made him scream. He walked to the left and turned to the right and stopped. "A place to go, a place . . ." He stopped and screamed one loud scream into the sky. I looked into the coop. Then I understood. There were only six birds left.

Snow was there. Midnight was gone. Aunt Silva appeared at the black door in her apron, the dish towel still in her hands. Tato fell into her arms. She saw the empty coop.

"That mother fucker. We gotta get rid of him," Aunt Silva said.

Uncle Marco had tied their feet with string, stuffed them into a burlap bag and brought them to the chicken market, where he made a deal.

Mr. Possilippo had a carrying case, a box with a handle, for transporting the birds. It had sides of screening. After that day I put Snow in it and kept him with me at all times.

Tato never got over it. His eyes looked terrible, he had a cold and earache, but even worse, his spirit was killed. He hardly ate, talked very little, even to me. And though the August nights were getting cold, he slept on the roof. Aunt Silva literally forced me to sleep on the couch. Each night she threw a blue chenille bedspread over me. She probably thought that without me on the roof, Tato would come down to sleep in the apartment. But he didn't. Uncle Marco had struck a fatal blow.

"Can you keep a secret?" Tato asked one day.

"Yes."

"I'm going to kill him."

Aunt Silva kept money under a lace doily on her chifforobe. On top of the doily was the wooden base of a bell jar that contained St. Rita and some dry roses and a brown gardenia corsage tied with a silver ribbon. Aunt Silva kept her money there because Uncle Marco was too superstitious to steal under the gaze of that stern woman in black who looked out from her bell jar. St. Rita held the cross of Jesus Christ with Jesus nailed on it before anyone who approached her.

The plan was that Tato was going to pretend to be falling down the flight of stairs to force Aunt Silva into the hallway, while I was to open the door to her bedroom, pull her chair to the chifforobe, stand on it, then take no more than three singles, bring the chair back to its place and slip out and close the door.

"What are you hangin' around for?" Aunt Silva asked as we put the plan in motion. I didn't answer her. She often accepted silence from me without a fuss. "Where's that other one?" Meaning Tato. I wanted to speak, to act natural, but I couldn't. I was so scared I almost wanted to confess. Suddenly, there were Tato's screams and the awful sound of the hollow wooden staircase resounding like a kettle drum. Aunt Silva fled. I sat there stunned. The whole thing seemed so real I almost ran out myself. But as Tato prescribed, I found myself pushing open the bedroom door. I could smell the peach satin spread that covered the bed, her Evening in Paris toilet water, the odor of rose sachet coming from the chifforobe drawers. The Marie Antoinette doll sat up on the bed in a pool of bouffant dress and smiled at me as I pulled the chair across the floor to the chifforobe. The space was narrow and the chair caught the peach satin spread. Marie Antoinette keeled over as if she had fainted. I left the chair and reached over trying to set her up straight, but she kept falling over. I wisely left her to her faint. I got up on the chair—no sound from the hallway or anywhere, just the whir of the electric clock in the room—with St. Rita peering through the bell jar, up to her waist in dry roses, trying to see through the dusty glass of her bell house, pretending she was a statue, pretending she could not move.

The money was in a flat roll. Fives, tens. I heard the organ music at Mr. Possilippo's funeral in my head for a moment. Then silence, just the chair scraping on its way back to the corner, then the whir of the clock. I pulled a five and suddenly all of the bills flipped out of the coil. I had to scoop them up from the floor. I put two fives in my mouth then wrapped the rest of the bills back up into a roll. On tiptoe I stuffed it under the doily. The satin bedspread shrieked as I pulled Marie Antoinette up by the arms. She managed to stay up and watch me disappearing behind the closing door.

I had taken too much money. Tato accepted it all anyway. "Wait on the roof," he said and slipped out the hallway into the sunlight.

From the roof I spotted him at the west corner, where some boys twice his size pitched coins against the liquor-store wall. Tato talked to one of them, then gave him money. The boy bounced on his long black-sneakered feet into the liquor store and came out with a brown bag. Tato took it and walked so close to the building wall that I couldn't see him.

It was a gallon of red wine. We scraped the label off with our spit and knife.

"What are we doing?" I kept asking.

"Go see if the coast is clear on the stairs."

I looked. Nothing but the steep hollow well of stairs and quiet. "Clear."

Tato went to the old man's cabinet, which was open because Uncle Marco had broken the combination lock. He got on his knees and searched among some cartons on the bottom shelf. He returned with a small box, like a cocoa box, except instead of a cow the trademark depicted a rat. The top came off easily. Inside was bright blue powder. Tato patiently shook the blue powder into a garden trough and poured it carefully into the gallon of wine. When the wine threatened to spill over Tato returned the screw cap.

"There's enough poison in this wine to kill everybody in Brooklyn." Tato held the gallon as if it were a huge bomb. He was sweating. His breath was short. His nose runny. "He's gonna find this and think it's the old man's homemade. He's gonna drink it and die."

We were having one of those chilly August nights. Aunt Silva felt Tato's forehead and said he was hot, so she made his bed and threw the blue chenille spread over the couch for me to wrap myself into. Later, when she was asleep, I went into Tato's room and slept with him. When I slept alone I was revisited with those visions of my mother.

In the middle of the night the door creaked. It woke me suddenly, but I pretended to be asleep. Out of the corner of my eye a massive shadow of someone eclipsed the kitchen light. He closed the door behind him. I could hear his breathing, the slow rustling sound of his movements toward the bed. I shook Tato but he didn't stir. I shook him again; he pushed me away. The rustling sounds of clothing and someone in them, moving. Then the mattress depressing. The form was sitting on the bed right next to me. I heard the chain of the light switch, then suddenly there was a quick, white flash of light in which I saw the pale face of Uncle Marco and the black hole of his open mouth. He had a glass of wine in his hand.

"The bulb blew," he said.

Tato sat up in the darkness. "What?"

"I wanna talk to you, and the bulb blew out." Tato turned on the little lamp behind him and rubbed his eyes. Uncle Marco dropped a dollar on the bed. He was drunk.

"I wanna tell you about the man who ate his dog. Did you hear about the man who ate his dog?" he said to me. I didn't look at him.

"This really happened in Italy," he slurred. "This man ate his dog. Everybody got disgusted. So the mayor of the town, in order to make this man feel bad for what he did, the mayor came to his house with a basket of food. In other words, saying, You're so poor you have to eat your dog? So now here's charity, a basket of food for you, you bastard. He just clams up and takes the basket. So years later, it turns out that the mayor's dog dies. So while the mayor is shovelin' the dirt on his dog's grave, the guy shows up and says, 'What happened?' 'My dog died,' the mayor said. 'Did you love the dog?' the guy says. 'Sure,' the mayor says. 'So you throw your dog that you love in a hole and put dirt on top of him?' 'Sure,' the mayor says. 'He's dead.' So then you know what the guy said? He said, 'When my dog died, I ate him, so he wouldn't have to go into the ground. He went into me instead.' " Uncle Marco poked Tato. "And with him, guess what he had? He had the basket of food that the mayor gave him, all rotted after all those years. 'Here,' he said, 'you can shove it up your ass while you're at it.' "

Uncle Marco waited. "That's the story." Tato said nothing. Uncle Marco said, "Look, I'm sorry about the pigeons. It was a joke. You wanna punch me? Punch me." Uncle Marco waited, then stood up. "Well, I ain't taking the dollar back, so tear it up if you like." Tato stared at him but said nothing.

"What are those droopy eyes of yours saying, porto?" Tato said nothing. Uncle Marco realized he would get nowhere. Tato could never forgive him; his eyes said so. Tato calmly tore up the dollar in front of Uncle Marco, and Uncle Marco left.

The next morning Uncle Marco was dead. His death wasn't as frightening as Tato's mood, the quiet in the house and shop, the endless rain on the day of the funeral.

Father arrived for Uncle Marco's funeral. When he came back from the burial, I did everything to avoid him. It seemed to puzzle him. "Talk to me," he demanded.

"Where's Pumpkin?" I asked simply.

"Forget about her. Soon I'm taking you away from here. Don't worry. You hear?"

"I don't want to go away."

"Well, you can't stay here. Do you want to *stay* here?"

"Yes," I answered.

"No. You can't stay."

Tato's eyes darted to mine. My father left that night.

The next morning, Tato, Aunt Silva and I were alone in the kitchen. Tato sat on the blue kitchen chair staring into space. He looked exhausted in the fluorescent light. Aunt Silva leaned over and put the coffee pot away.

"Are you satisfied now?" said Tato, tears filling his shining brown eyes. His lips quivered.

"Don't start that in front of me. I'm dried up, all dried up," she said.

Tato didn't move from the blue chair. Tears rolled down his face.

Aunt Silva sat down with her back to us, her elbow on the table. She pressed her two fingers to the side of her head. "Go away. Go play," she mumbled.

"It's raining," said Tato.

"Go in the hall. Go somewhere."

He slipped off the chair slowly. I followed him to the roof. The black tar was wet and reflected the low gray sky. The rain was too late. There were no vegetables, no trees, just a few plants in cans, and they were too haggard to benefit from the rain. Tato seemed to be looking for anything of the old man's to touch. He brought some coffee cans that had filled with rainwater into the coop for Snow and the five other birds.

Tato opened the old man's cupboard and looked down at the gallon with the rat poison in it. I could see Tato's face reflected in it, distorted in the foreground. He squatted and unscrewed the cap. I was afraid it might spill and touch my shoes. I didn't want to breathe its aroma. I hoped he'd put it back out of sight, but he kept staring down at it. I went to the black door, pretending to check on the stairs, but really I just wanted to get farther away from the gallon, as if it were a bomb that might go off. Then I realized that something was happening to Tato. A red flush had come over his face. His eyes shot to me.

"Cello!" His stare drifted. He blinked.

"What's the matter?"

"Don't you see?"

"Where?"

"The wine."

"What about the wine?"

56

"It's full. He never touched it." Tato jumped up and ran past me down the stairs. I followed him, leaving the open gallon under the gray sky.

Aunt Silva was in the shop. "Of course he died of a heart attack," she was saying as I walked in. She was a little alarmed by Tato's rapid questions.

"Where'd he get the wine he was drinking that night when he died?"

"Under the sink in the kitchen. He hid the old man's wine there. Don't say nothing to Tabs," she warned Tato, " 'cause he stole the wine from the old man's apartment."

"When did he go into the old man's apartment?" Tato asked.

"After we found the old man dead."

"Where'd he get the key?"

"Off the old man."

Tato's eyes shifted to me. It was so good to see he was returning from that faraway place. "Probably got the old man's money, too," he said, smiling.

Aunt Silva had us swear that we would never tell that Uncle Marco took the old man's keys and went into his apartment. We swore.

"C'mere," Tato whispered to me.

"Where?"

Tato pulled me into his room and closed the door. Then he pushed me into the clothes of the closet and got inside with me. He closed the door. We were standing amid Uncle Marco's boots and overcoats, the dusty smell of leather and wool.

"Where are you?" His cold hands cupped my face and turned it. His lips touched my ear. "We didn't kill him," he whispered. He clung to me, his lips pressed to my ear, repeating over and over, "We didn't kill him."

In the dark of the closet his words shone like stars in my mind. He cried into my neck. I stood stiff as a pole for a long time, feeling his tears on my skin.

Tato slept like a stone all night, breathing long and deep. The next day he called the old man's bird supplier, and they came by with a large carrying case. We said goodbye to them each by name

—Mickey, Serafina, Angelo, Ralph and Terrubimbo. Snow was the only one left of all Mr. Possilippo's birds.

"Who is this?" Aunt Silva wrinkled her brow, held one ear and spoke into the phone in her best Spanish. "*Sí. Sí. Claro.*" She waved her hand in a circle for us to come to the phone. She gave the phone to Tato.

"Yeah? Yeah?" He listened. "Yes." He smiled. "He's okay. He's got his own pigeon. Yeah."

I could hear a woman's voice in the receiver. Tato gave me the phone.

"Do you really have a pigeon?" she asked.

"Yes."

"Do you know who this is?"

"Zia Fantasia." I remembered not only her voice but the perfume I associated with it.

"Shall we go to my house that sits in the middle of the sea? Shall I come tomorrow for you and Tato and your pigeon? What is his name?"

"Snow."

"Is it white?"

"Yes."

"Shall we all go?"

"Can Tato come with us?"

"But of course. He must come."

"All right," I said weakly. Aunt Silva seemed to approve. I gave the phone back to Tato. He listened, smiling. Slowly the old craftiness was coming back into his eyes. They shone with both incredulity and delight as they came to mine.

"Tangerine? Like the kind you eat?" He cupped the phone and made an announcement: "She's bringing her girlfriend with her. By the name of Tangerine."

CHAPTER III

THE year was 1950 but the limousine was not a Cadillac. It was a vintage Packard with red cloisonné hexagonals on the hubcaps and a hood ornament of a woman on the radiator cap. The chauffeur, whose name was Henry, was hired for two days along with the car. He smoked Lucky Strikes. His little head was lost in a black cap.

When I reached the open door of the limousine, it was like entering a party. The first thing I saw was Tangerine's pocketbook. It had bamboo hoops for handles, big black orchids printed on white linen. It was lying at her feet, which were tucked into white pumps with blond wooden platform soles. Her breasts were bullets under a red elastic tube. She wore a large beauty mark on her bare shoulder and a choker of colored balls around her neck. Her skirt was white, with hundreds of pleats which cascaded to the seat of the car when she moved her legs. A white felt military hat had white netting which was pulled tightly over her face. Her earrings were small glass fruits—bananas, oranges and pears. The white veil was the feature that most beguiled me, because her mouth was large and always in motion, and her big teeth seemed yellow in contrast to it. The white netting was soiled by her glazed cherry red lipstick and her mascara. Her long eyelashes kept getting trapped in it, but Tangerine's laughter was proof that she liked the way she looked. She was laughing at my sneakers, which were too big for me.

"Who's the lady up front?" Tato asked, pointing to the figure-head.

"The *putana* of the wind." Tangerine sent her laughter over my head toward Tato.

Zia Fantasia lifted me up from the street into the car and sat me between them, putting her arm around me. Her perfume was the same she was wearing the day of my mother's wake, and her green eyes were so striking that her green earrings and the large green jewel in her ring couldn't compare. She wore a black suit with padded shoulders, black suede shoes and an ivory silk blouse. A black net covered with giant black sequins hung in back of her head, holding her chestnut hair. Her lips were shiny dark red. The suit had black glass buttons, but my eye was caught by her brooch of many colored jewels depicting a man playing conga drums and a lady dancing.

Tangerine's long fingernails made loud screeches when she scratched her stockings. The noisy stockings shrieked whenever she uncrossed her legs.

"The woman up front is the goddess of speed," Zia said to Tato, brushing his hair aside. "Are we ready, Henry?"

Henry was putting the pigeon carrier on the seat with Snow in it. "Right away, madam," Henry called back.

"I know what a *putana* is," Tato announced to Tangerine.

"You do?" Tangerine said with a laugh. "I think this one is old enough for anything, eh, Fantasia?"

Zia was mildly annoyed. "This is Tato and Cello. This is my friend Elena," she said.

The woman in the white veil slapped Zia gently. "My name is Tangerine."

"That is her nickname." Zia smiled with embarrassment.

"How old?" Tangerine tickled me.

"Six," I said.

"Too young," she huffed. "How old are you?" She poked Tato.

"Too young." He grinned.

"Oh, yeah?" Tangerine laughed. She said something in Spanish to Zia.

"I understand Spanish," Tato answered.

"He's ten. Aren't you?" Zia said, holding his head and kissing him.

He looked at Zia with surprise, mesmerized by her. "Yeah, I'm ten," Tato said shyly.

Henry was in his seat. He started the engine and in a few moments we were looking back at the tenements of Brooklyn from high above. Our car was a soft gray room of quiet that floated over New York City like a rocket ship.

We were all asleep hours later when Henry said, "Misses. Misses." The big Packard sat on a platform of cracked asphalt near a wall of tall sea grass swaying in the wind. We got out of the car near the breathing sounds of a sleeping giant. It terrified me until I realized it was not breathing but the rustling of the tall sea grass (or phragmites, as Zia called them). We walked along the wall of the huge whispers of the giant's sleep until we came to open sand and water, a peninsula that stretched like a finger into the bay. There were houses behind us toward the mainland, but before us there was nothing, only the peninsula of sand and a house that appeared to be a ship sitting on the water. The four of us slowly made our way toward it. It was the first time my feet felt sand. Zia held me by one hand and carried Snow in his case in the other. Henry breathed around the cigarette in his mouth and carried a suitcase in each hand.

The beach and sky had totally ignored the formality of the

61

house. Sand gathered in drifts against the front doors and along the porch which ran around the whole house. A pond, which had been unnoticeable from the phragmites, now sparkled east of the house. The doorway was trimmed in mint, purple, lavender and ruby glass. Zia opened the doors into a radiant foyer. Before us stood two monstrously large bronze statues of American buffaloes. I refused to pass between them. Their angry wild eyes were level with mine. Zia lifted me and knocked them with her knuckles. They made a hollow sound. She ordered me to do the same. Still, when she put me back down, they warned me with their eyes. The house opened before us: red carpets up the stairs, sun pouring down from up there and a hall light that was lit in spite of the sun. The light was shaped into a green flower of glass, painted with white veins, like an inverted tulip.

Two large rooms stretched on either side of us. The dining room with a black marble fireplace and a huge black marble clock, a golden woman reclining over it. The walls were paneled, but above the paneling they were painted, continuing the scenery that was visible through the windows. A large modern table with rings for legs stood near a floor lamp with a lead-glass shade which depicted orange trumpet flowers. The modern chairs were upholstered in black fabric appliquéd with palm leaves.

In both rooms the ceilings were entirely of glass, of sky appearing through dogwood blossoms, white clouds, seagulls and robins on the wing. A large heron flew with open wings on the living-room ceiling. The walls were shelves filled with marvelous artifacts, books and framed photographs.

Tangerine was opening shutters. The new light revealed a large red couch against French doors, which Zia began unbolting. Tato helped Tangerine let down large dark green awnings all around the porch. The wind and the blueness of the bay entered the house, sparkling, as sheer curtains lifted into the rooms, riding on air. I spun a globe of the world which moved on wheels, and I climbed up to shelves of mineral specimens, stuffed animals in bell jars, birds, butterflies, bone and scrimshaw, Indian vases, shells, dried eggs and model boats. Paintings of wild animals were on every wall. The closer I moved to the couch, the more I saw of the sea. And sailboats, real sailboats.

Upstairs there was a room for each of us, a pure white sunny room with walls of wainscoting material. From the windows we could see nothing but water—green-blue, moving northwest gently under prisms of light in the distance. I felt I was on a ship. Our rooms were nothing but windows, a bed and a closet. Tato and I had no clothes to put into our closets.

That night, going to bed was like lying down in a white box in space with windows to let in the stars. It was so dark that the stars came right to the horizon. I listened to the water and the wind in the dark. It was the first time I had slept in a room alone since my mother was alive. I waited for the terrible visions of Jeanette to appear in the darkness, but they didn't come. Tato was close. I could see him in his bed across the hall. The moon shone on his face. He was looking right into its light, making shadows with his fingers. My bed was large and the sheets crisp and slippery. I felt the air flowing around my head. While the green-tulip hall light guarded us, I drifted sleeping into the long dark night.

Next morning Zia Fantasia appeared, clasping her hands, in the hallway between our rooms. "Our car is here. Quickly! We're going to buy bathing suits. Hurry."

The four of us started out by buying plants in the Southampton Village Tropical Greenhouse. They loaded Henry down with palms, orchids, clivias, orange trees and philodendrons. A parrot in a huge wire cage sat in the middle of the greenhouse. Tangerine adored him. Zia arranged to rent the bird. They bought more things than I could possibly remember.

In one store Zia rubbed my arm with various perfumes. "Which do you like?" she asked. I pointed to the one with a bird on top of the bottle. The bird reminded me of Snow. She bought it immediately. I was happy, so dizzily happy. Tato kept reaching for my hand for his own security; even he was dazzled. They bought slips and panties, boxes upon boxes of lingerie, sandals and straw fans, incense, straw chairs, candles, lime water, seaweed in bags for baths, cans of teas, tins of wafers, charlotte russes and foods of every kind.

"What do you want? Anything?" Zia kept asking us. I couldn't answer her. I was so overwhelmed I couldn't tell the difference between seeing and having. In one shop I peeked into a small old Victrola. The proprietor wound it up for me and put the huge silver head down on an old record:

> *"Tangerine, you are all they claim,*
> *with your eyes of night and lips as bright as flame."*

Of course Zia bought it! A cabinet full of records came with the Victrola. But the most wonderful things we bought that day were water wings—a pair for each of us—that inflated into giant swans.

We had to stuff ourselves back into the car with all the boxes and bags containing straw hats, paper umbrellas, cold creams and suntan oils, pajamas, chenille bathrobes, kimonos embroidered with dragons, peignoirs, seersucker sunsuits, silk stockings of different colors, matching garter belts, four pairs of rubber beach shoes, many pairs of bathing suits, slippers, hand mirrors, nail files, combs and green hair slime for wave-setting, nail polish, dozens of lipsticks, compacts of powder and rouge, lettuce in cellophane, caviar, sausages, sodas, milk, eggs, many cans of crab meat, cases of mineral water, champagne, gin and whiskey, fresh mint, tomatoes, lemons, ice cream, an ice bucket, begonias, palms and geraniums—and a rented parrot named Fenimore, which Tangerine called Finamore. Zia tried to use Tato's full name, Guglielmo, but he wouldn't answer to it.

"Come, squeeze on my lap," Zia said to Tato as the car surged northward and onto the bay road toward Jessup Neck, where the house was. Tato refused to sit on her lap. "You are like your grandfather, thick-headed." She knocked his head. Zia looked away, then put her finger to her lips indicating silence.

That afternoon after all our things were in their places, we put on our bathing suits, and Tato and I took a walk near the water.

Zia accompanied us in her new cotton dress, which she wore comfortably and simply. She was a different woman in that dress; she looked like a peasant mother.

"What do you think happened to your mother?" she asked.

"She died."

"You are right. She died." She pressed me to her as we walked toward the large smoky clouds over the beach. A yellow and orange shell caught her eye. She bent to pick it up. "How beautiful." She let it go into my hand.

There were others on the beach. Tato and I tried to touch every one. We brought the best to her. She made a pouch of her dress and carried them home.

After dinner, while Zia was taking a nap upstairs, I found myself alone, and I panicked. Chairs, drapes, lamps, seemed to be alive. I was afraid they would turn on me. I would have joined Zia upstairs, but as I approached the two giant bison near the stairs, I changed my mind. I heard laughter and followed it out to the porch. I saw smoke rising from under the porch. I made my way down the stairs.

"Cello," I heard Tato whisper. Tato stuck his head between the steps. "Here, under the porch." He had a cigarette in his mouth. I joined Tato and Tangerine in the cool, sandy bed under the porch.

"Where's your aunt?" Tangerine asked.

"Upstairs, sleeping."

"Good," Tangerine said. She lit another cigarette, imprinting it with dark red lipstick, and put it into my mouth. "Hold it with these fingers," she said. Tato was giggling mischievously as she selected the proper fingers on my hand and stuck the cigarette between them. I took a deep drag, pulling in my stomach. Tangerine's face showed her amazement at my ability. I blew the smoke out of the side of my mouth. "You *bandidos!*" she exclaimed.

We smoked for her and laughed, but I only pretended to laugh, even when Tangerine tickled my legs with her long fingernails. I was so happy to have found Tangerine and Tato I didn't care whether we had fun or not.

In the evening Tato and Tangerine played checkers with the chess set. The horizon just after sunset had turned deep red and black. Huge smears of sky dwarfed the beach. But overhead was still luminescent blue, and the bay reflected it. Holding a cork ball with nine treacherous hooks hanging from it, I waited for Zia. It was a fishing pole that Zia had taken from the racks, rigged with a painted lure that looked like a toy fish. I had to rest the tip of the pole on the porch railing because I was not strong enough to keep it up. Zia appeared with a beach chair and flashlight and a folded sheet. We didn't take the high route to the cliffs but walked along the sand. The cool mists from the breakers were invigorating. Stars were forming overhead, but there was no moon. When we reached the rocks beneath the high cliff, a rush of warm dryness out of the south hit our faces. Zia spread the sheet in its drift and set it on the sand near the chair. The sun was down, but the world held onto its light like a sponge.

Several times Zia cast the lure clumsily, then reeled it in. Then with a sound louder than the wind, she cast far into the twilight.

"Good," she said. She stuck the rod firmly through the arm and seat of the chair and sat down.

"Where did you learn to fish?" I asked.

"Your grandfather."

"Did you ever catch a big one?"

"Not even a little one." She laughed. "Grandfather caught great ones." She scanned the water. "What will we do if we do catch a fish?"

"Eat him," I said.

"Poor thing." She smiled. I followed her eyes to the vast bay. It was the first time I realized there was an economy of life in the sea. I felt sorry for the fish we were going to catch.

"I don't even know how to take a fish off the hook," Zia said. She stood up suddenly. "Should we let our fish go free so he may grow and have babies?" she asked.

"Yes," I shouted.

"You saved him"—Zia pointed to me—"and he doesn't even know it."

She reeled in the lure and secured it to the pole. My teeth

were chattering. Zia flapped the sheet in the wind, lifted me to her and wrapped the sheet around us. My knees curled under her breasts. I could smell her warmth and fragrance. My head fell upon her shoulder. My face was warmed by her neck and my own breath. Her fingers tucked my hair behind my ears.

"Oh, my God, look at that moon!"

"Moon? Where?" I lifted my head.

There was an orange moon. Its presence was sudden and monstrous.

"How could anything so large come near without a sound?" Zia asked.

"Can we get moon burn?" I asked.

"No"—she laughed—"the moon is cool." She paused and then said, "That moon is how I love you."

"Huh?"

"Very, very big and very golden."

My head fell back upon her shoulder. "I love you like a white bird." I yawned.

"A white bird? How is that?"

". . . . like a white bird."

In my sleep I heard the white sheet snapping and I felt it fluttering around me. I opened my eyes for a moment and saw stars rocking in the black heavens, Zia's face in the foreground of the whole universe, looking down at me. She was carrying me back to the house.

"Whenever you see the moon full like this one, talk to it and I will hear you."

"Talk to the *moon?*" I grinned.

"Yes," she said, "and I will too. And we shall always be together that way."

Someone was reading in the rosy light of the silk lampshade as Zia carried me into the dark hallway. I could barely make out the green-tulip light, upside down, shining. A step at a time brought it closer to my eyes. I zoomed under it as Zia turned into my room. She put me down, standing me against the wall. Half asleep, I heard her turning the bedcovers down. Suddenly I was flying; again, she had lifted me. My feet touched the cool bedsheets. I was standing on the bed as her hands undressed me quickly. She pulled my ankles, letting me fall, centering me on the white field. I wanted her to think I was asleep, but I couldn't hide my smile. I smelled the warmth of her face bringing a kiss. Then she pulled the covers to my chin and left me alone, closing the door partway.

The wind followed her. It leaped up the side of the house to my window and across my face, full of the odor of the sea. I thought of my fish swimming off safely in the dark waters toward his future.

A few weeks of summer can change a child forever. I felt taller, framed by less space. I was never so clean. Between all our swimming and shampooing, my hair seemed wet as often as it was dry. I owned clothes, possessions, shirts, shorts and several pairs of sneakers and rubber beach shoes. Tato refused to wear these.

Even at my age I could detect Zia's wonderful strength. Tangerine seemed like a child in comparison, too silly sometimes, but so entertaining. Zia tried to teach us to clean up after ourselves, to help with the dishes. She cooked, swiftly and joyfully—salads and fish and nuts and juices, cereals, lobster and chicken, parsley soup and cold zucchini with capers and lemon. (We ate the capers only to please her.) Zia let us have our own glass of wine at dinner. She taught us how to open champagne and how to set a table.

Tangerine was the opposite—a clown constantly playing her song. She knew all the words to "Tangerine" by heart. She drank a lot. Sometimes her fire would suddenly go out. Her face puffed up and she seemed lost in herself.

My father apparently had asked his sister to help him meet some of her female friends. Poor Pumpkin. I wondered what had become of her. Tangerine had fallen in love with my father's photograph and eagerly accompanied Zia from Argentina to meet him. He was supposed to meet us in Southampton but hadn't shown up yet. I was not sorry. Neither was Tangerine. She was fascinated by Tato.

"Look, an eagle." Tato pointed to an osprey beating its wings over the water not far from where we were swimming one day. It lifted a fish and flew off, clutching it in its talons. The fish was still flapping high above us.

"Birds don't carry suitcases." Zia laughed.

"They don't wear shoes or underwear." Tato giggled. "Can we stay here for good?" he asked.

"Do you see there, that white cloud like a ball on the water?" Zia asked him.

"Yes."

"That won't allow us to stay here. That's the winter. Tangerine! Madonna! Your back is red as a tomato." Zia stood up in the water.

"His lips are blue." Tato pointed to me.

"Enough, come. Tangerine, you make hot tea and I'll make a bubble bath."

"I am a fish." I splashed Zia.

"You are a swan." She splashed back. We swam to shore under the warm sky. We were swans, testing our white water wings. Our laughter floated up into the great vault of sky.

Tato dunked me and had to accept Zia's scolding. It was wonderful to watch how much of a child Tato allowed himself to be with her.

Tangerine made Tom Collinses in tall blue glasses. Tato and I had ours with orange slices and maraschino cherries but no alcohol. We drank them down in seconds. Tangerine poured fresh mix over our ice and asked us to carry our drinks up to the bath. Tato, pulling up the rear, stopped at the bar and sneaked some gin into his drink.

The tub was so full of foam that the women touched their noses in it reaching down to wash us. Tangerine turned on the radio:

> "Oh, I'm just a fella, a fella with an umbrella,
> looking for a girl to share her love for a rainy day."

Tangerine and Tato giggled throughout the bath, refusing to share their secret.

We ate lunch in our silk kimonos. Zia's was blue, Tangerine's orange, and mine and Tato's black with dragons on the back. We ate cold chicken, cold celery, cold fruit, and we had club soda to drink. Zia was disapproving as Tangerine was pouring crème de menthe into our glasses.

"Tangerine, stop! That's too much for them."

"Fat hen. All you ever want to do is clean up."

"While you paint your nails?"

"Do you like this color?"

Zia smiled at her audacity. The white curtains ballooned over our heads.

"Cello"—Tangerine turned to me—"you are in charge of the Victrola. That means you are to wind it, but not to change the record." Tangerine's favorite song played on and on:

> *"you are all they claim,*
> *with your eyes of night and lips as bright as flame."*

Zia put Noxzema on Tangerine's back while Tangerine put it on Tato and Tato put it on me. Tangerine jumped up to do the boogie-woogie while Zia and Tato turned the pages of the *Animal Atlas of the World*. But Tato was paying very little attention to Zia's reading. His eyes half closed from gin, he watched Tangerine, her breasts occasionally revealing themselves behind the kimono.

"Put something on," Zia whispered to her. Tangerine pulled light blue stockings out of her pocket and rolled them on. I saw genital hairs. Zia's eyes flashed with annoyance. Suddenly Zia closed the book, stood up and started filling the tray.

"We should have a servant do this," Tangerine said.

"I prefer to take care of myself."

"What a big girl you are." Tangerine laughed. Zia went into the kitchen with the tray. Tangerine made curls with Tato's hairs, giggling and touching her nose to his.

"Show us what you had in the bathtub," Tangerine whispered when Zia was out of sight.

Tato's face reddened but he managed a bold smile.

"What did you have?" I asked innocently.

"Show him."

As if I suddenly sensed disaster, I stepped away.

> *"And I've seen toasts to Tangerine,*
> *raised in every bar across the Argentine."*

Tato leaned back, smiling with drunk, half-closed eyes. He undid the silk belt to his kimono and let it fall away to either side of him. His chest and legs were red, but the rest of him was hairless and white as the moon. His penis stood upright, pink, and hard as alabaster.

"Señoritas stare and caballeros sigh."

"Shall we put lipstick on it?"
"Yes." Tato laughed, looking down at it. "Put lipstick on it." He giggled. Tangerine's large hands spread like a net pressing down on Tato's body, letting through his penis. Her head came down over it. His smile dissolved. "No. Oh." Tato grunted. When Tangerine finally threw back her head, Tato's penis glistened with saliva, and father was standing in the doorway.

Tangerine jumped under the billowing curtains behind the couch. Tato wrapped himself back up in his kimono. My father walked to Tato, looked down at him and suddenly lifted him over his head. Tato grabbed a lamp.

"She's got them all on the run,
but her heart belongs to just one."

My father threw Tato, lamp and all. The plug flew out of its socket and followed Tato to the hall. He crashed in a heap against the door frame and fell to the floor like a marionette. Tato's head was bleeding. Tangerine ran out the French doors onto the porch and down the beach. When Zia came into the room, my father's face was white. Zia's eyes scanned the scene. Father threw over the Victrola and wiped his hands.

"Buzzy, you fool," Zia screamed from the doorway.
"Shut up. Pigs! Whores!"
Tato's hand held his eye. Blood ran between his fingers.
"Let me see." Zia gently forced his hand away. The cut crossed his eyebrow. Blood matted the hair. Tato's old expression came back. The child was gone from his face. My father ran down the beach after Tangerine.

Tangerine returned with the marks of my father's hand on her face. Later my father drove us all silently to Southampton Hospital, where Tato received four stitches in his eyebrow, and my father's face received iodine where Tangerine had scratched him. He looked like an Indian in war paint.

The next day Tangerine went musseling alone in a large straw hat, while Zia and my father talked on the porch. It was a hot day. There were no clouds. When we attempted to sit with them, Zia frowned. "Go play."

"We're too sunburned," Tato complained.

"Then read. Sail the boats in the pond in the shade. We want to talk."

"Let me see your eye." My father reached for Tato's arm. Tato grabbed his hand and held it away.

"Your bandage is loose," my father explained.

"Don't worry."

"I'm not worried." My father's face flushed.

"Then let go of my arm!" Tato said with incredible coolness.

Tato and I pretended to walk to the pond, but we cut back and when we reached the corner Tato lifted the latticed flap to the crawl space under the porch and we crawled along the cool sandy bottom until we were directly under Zia's chair. The flooring gave with each squeak of father's rocker. Zia's foot thumped whenever she uncrossed her legs. The sun imprinted our bodies with squares of light coming through the lattice. Tato looked like a leopard.

"Listen, tell me, Fanny, you like my boy, don't you?"

"I like both of them."

"Okay. How would you like a little son?"

"Cello?"

"Yes."

"Are you crazy? How can you be such a child about life?"

"I never volunteered for life, Fanny. I can't take care of that kid. How am I gonna take care of him?"

"The way all fathers care for their children. The way your father took care of you. How ridiculous for you to ask such a question."

"I never asked for him."

"You never asked to be born either, so why don't you shoot

yourself, eh? The way you accept your own life, accept the life of your son. He needs a woman, a mother. You are surrounded by women constantly. Tangerine adores you already."

"That slut. Where did you dig her up? You want her to be Cello's mother?"

"No. That's not what I meant."

"I hate her."

"The woman came six thousand miles to meet you."

"Get rid of her. I can't stand that type. I'm interested in someone else."

"Who knows? Maybe Tangerine would make a good mother."

"Don't be funny."

"I'm serious."

"Fanny, I'm making you a clear, straight offer. Give me ten thousand dollars and the kid is yours. I'm not kidding. I'm desperate. You're never going to have a kid of your own anyway and you know it."

"Are you completely insane? Where are your feelings for that boy?"

"I have *too* much feeling."

"And you want to sell him to me for ten thousand dollars?"

Please *understand*! You never *understand* me," he shouted. "If you can turn good to bad with me, you'll always do it."

"But what good is there in what you're suggesting to me? Tell me?" Zia's voice flew up.

"I'm broke, goddamn you. *Can't you hear me?* How am I gonna give that kid what he needs? You, you're drowning in money. Look at this house—all this for a goddamn little whore like you."

"You pig." She slapped him. "A woman knows when she sleeps in a man's own bed she is not a whore."

"You sleep in Maldonado's bed? And who has the secret apartment in Buenos Aires, his wife and kids?"

"You are a pig."

"I'm a pig because I tell you the truth? Don't pull your airs on me, okay? I'm your brother. I'm asking for money because I'm desperate. I'll take *care* of the kid, okay? Just give me the money so I can take care of him."

"Do you think I'm a millionaire? This house Maldonado won in a card game. He gave it to me with his left hand. I don't even have five thousand in my bank account."

"How am I gonna send him to the right schools?"

"I'll pay for his schooling," Zia snapped. "Send me the bills. I'll see that both boys get schooling."

"Then give me the cash, because I'm taking the kid out of the country. I have to."

"What cash?"

"The kid's school money. Let me have the first installment. Give me an advance, okay?"

"Bastard."

"I swear on Christ on the cross, I'll educate the kid. What are you crying for?"

"That poor child."

"Look at me, Fanny. I'm your brother. I'm gonna do the right thing for him. Trust me. Be good to me, Fanny. Give me the money and it'll be good for his sake and mine and everybody's. I found a good woman this time. You understand? She's rich. I'm gonna marry her. Her name's Lucille Meyer. She's a widow I met in Florida. She's got a place in Europe. She thinks I have money. I don't want to queer things up by letting her see how goddamn poor I am. She's a smart German woman who'd be a good mother, 'cause she never could have any kids of her own."

"You bastard," Zia repeated, drying her sniffles.

"Give me the kid's money now and I swear he'll have the best bringing-up in Europe, plus a number one mother. I swear to Christ! And listen, Fanny, get rid of the redhead. Do me the favor."

"You told her you loved her, you lunatic."

"I got carried away," he said.

"Get yourself out of this one."

"You gonna come through for me about the money?"

"Let me think about it."

"Think. And get rid of the redhead. If you were married—now no offense—but if you were married to some rich South American

74

instead of just hangin' around one, you wouldn't have to be seen with that class woman."

"Get away from me," Zia said.

"I'm goin', but just get rid of her, okay?"

His shoes, with metal taps nailed to heels and toes, slapped the steps as he went down. We could see him through the lattice, walking on the sand toward the blue water. Zia did not make a sound. The wind came up, making a slight whistling noise through the lattice. We had to wait until we heard her go inside.

When we finally crawled out from under the porch, the hot red Southampton sun was about to slip into a silver bay, turning the sky to icy pink. The wind had changed becoming cooler, out of the north.

For several days there were no towels on the buffaloes in the foyer because of the temperature drop. We wore new sweaters that Zia had picked up in Southampton. They smelled sweetly of new wool.

Night came early. Tangerine and Zia spoke often very quietly in some corner. The snowy egrets were white only at noon. Mornings and afternoons they were pink as flamingos, tinged with the rosiness of August, and by night they were invisible.

From our cold beds one night we heard voices coming from downstairs. "Why can't I go to Europe with you?" Tangerine asked. "I love the boy, don't I, Fantasia?"

"You love nothing. You are a simple-minded slut," my father said.

"I cannot stand either one of you," Zia said. "Call a taxi, Tangerine. Do you like being abused by him?"

"I don't deserve his abuse."

"Then go away from it. Do you think he will change?"

Tangerine began to cry. "I love him."

"We are strangers," my father screamed at her. "How dare you say you love me."

"You used me; you just picked the plum off the tree. And you helped him."

"I?" Zia said. "I told you he was a scoundrel."

"She calls herself a plum? I have to tie my ankles to an oak tree when I make love to her." My father laughed.

"Tangerine, come home to Buenos Aires with me tomorrow," Zia pleaded.

"No," she cried, "no, no, no, no, no."

"Goodnight," Zia said finally. Zia's slippers clacked to her room. Zia's door closed, but the voices continued from below, my father saying, "Shut up, shut up," and Tangerine saying, "Please, please."

Tato got out of bed, closed his door, then crossed the hallway under the green light and jumped into bed with me. His feet were cold.

"Where's Europe?" I asked.

"It's out there, out there on the other side of the ocean."

"Why can't you come?"

"He would never let me. Listen, we're gonna hafta say goodbye, you and me, tomorrow."

I pretended I had nothing to say, but if I spoke, I knew I would cry. Tato put his head under the blanket. I went under after him. He was crying. I lay on my back like a corpse with the blanket over my face.

When I awoke, it was late morning. Tato was gone. I dressed and went downstairs, avoiding the kitchen, from which there came voices. I ran out of the house, intending to hide somewhere near the pond. I found a place behind the oaks where it was thick with weeping willows and fern. I was afraid, as I sat there with the strange hope inside me, that Tato had already been taken away without my having to say goodbye. But when I heard his voice calling me in the wind, I walked out gladly to meet him.

"She gave in to him. She gave him the money. You're going to Europe." His face lit up with fear, his eyes wide as a continent. His dark brows, his breath, all of him was becoming quickly fixed and frozen in my mind. My nose was stuffed. I couldn't breathe.

"Zia is looking for you," Tato said.

Through the phragmites we saw Zia walking down the stairs of the porch. A taxi horn beeped for her a half mile away near the cracked asphalt. We ran toward her. A golden scarf wrapped her head tightly, and a green silk dress totally bared her back except for thin orange straps. Her shoes were high wooden platforms of lacquered orange with transparent plastic straps that revealed her feet entirely. Her green eyes shone near the golden scarf, and her silky tanned face was beautiful. But her eyes were troubled.

"I, I have to leave, my loves." She put an arm around each of us. I squirmed against it. Then I started to run from her grasp, but she held me back.

"Hey, do you see that great ball?" she said.

"Where?" Tato asked.

"See it, on the horizon?"

There was the gray-white cloud again. "That is the great ball of winter coming. We have to get out of its way. But it will pass and get warm again and we will come back here again. I promise."

"Take me with you," I begged.

"I can't do that."

"Pay my father what he wants. Buy me from him."

Her eyes filled, startled. "I don't need to buy you, because you are my nephews, my father's grandchildren, both of you. I love you. Look at the presents I have for you." She took out the bottle of perfume with its white bird of frosted glass on top and put it into my hand. "When you want to remember me, lift the bird and let the smell escape. And Tato"—she pulled the *Animal Atlas of the World* from behind her—"this is for Tato. I have the dingle shells the two of you collected for me. I will take them out and look at them when I want to remember you."

I didn't believe her. "Where are they?"

"In my bag on the chair." She pointed, and I ran and got her bag for her. It was a bag like a clothespin bag, hung on two bamboo circles, and it was green silk like her dress. It jingled when I lifted it. She had told the truth. There they were, every shell as I remembered it.

We walked her toward her taxi, but she would not let us go the full way. She kissed us on the sand and hugged us several times. "Goodbye, goodbye." I kissed her, but I would not say goodbye. We continually waved as we walked backwards toward the house. We saw the driver put her bags in the trunk. Then we watched her step into the taxi. She looked back, not only at us but at the whole peninsula, the house—as though she knew she might never see any of it again, or us, as though she were waving goodbye to the past which was drifting like a huge ferry away from her shore.

The sun was brilliant, though it was September first and cold in the living room. My father and Tangerine slept upstairs almost all day and night. Tato and I sailed a model boat in the pond. There was not a cloud in the sky, nor a plane, nor any boats on the still bay.

"I'm going to take a walk," Tato said. He walked the beach, almost a mile north. I followed. I couldn't let him out of my sight. I climbed the rocks below the cliffs after him, up the sandy cliff, grabbing baby cedars for support, then back homeward with water on both sides of us. He knew I was behind him. There was a burning feeling inside my chest which I can only describe as my need to be near him. It continued through that evening. When Tato went to the bathroom after supper, I felt lost in the middle of the living room. I lay awake that night watching him.

The next day Tangerine's face was puffy and sad. No one spoke. I watched everything that Tato did. If he ate, I ate. If he read, I read. When he went out, I went out. During dinner he didn't take his eyes off my father and Tangerine.

"We're going to the point," Tato said, getting up.

"Who? What for?" my father asked.

Tato slid down from the dining-room chair and casually answered, "We hafta say goodbye." He motioned for me to come.

"Goodbye to who?" my father asked. "Hey," he called as Tato ignored him and I turned. Tangerine's eyes, glassy and afraid, darted between my father and Tato.

"You could die," Tato said to my father.

"Who the hell are you? Cello, get back in your chair."

"No," Tato ordered. Tato's face was dark gray, a face tired from grief, a man's face, a man's pain.

My father stood up and pointed his finger. "Back in your chair, Cello."

"I could go crazy if you try to slap us around, and when your back is turned, I could knife you. If you could be crazy, I could be crazy." Tato's eyes were glazed. My father's mouth was open as he stared at Tato.

"Sit down, Buzzy," Tangerine whispered. "Let them go."

My father sat down with uncertainty as Tato and I walked toward the great red couch and through the silent curtains. We walked out to the porch, downstairs, and around the back of the house to the pantry, where Snow's carrying case was stored. I followed him to Snow's pen, wondering what he intended.

Tato grabbed the case. "I'll take Snow with me," he said, opening the latch on the pen door. Snow walked out.

"Where will you take Snow?" I asked.

"You're going away," he said.

"Me? Where?" I asked.

Snow walked in a circle away from Tato's hands. Suddenly Snow's wings brushed past my face and he was up in the air over our heads, crazily, dizzily flying the way he did the first time on the old man's roof. Tato ran around the house. By the time we were able to see the horizon on the other side of the house, Snow was over the water, flying farther and farther west. We stood numbly watching until he became a tiny black dot. I kept my eyes on the spot where the dot disappeared, trying to imagine that it was rematerializing.

I turned to Tato. "When am I going away?" I asked as the wind rubbed its back on the water. Tiny waves tickled the shore.

Tato's face was unforgettable. "There's a taxi coming for me tonight," he said blankly.

"How do you know?"

"I overheard them. A taxi's comin' for me and there's a limo comin' for you. I go home to Brooklyn. You and Tangerine go with him to the airport. You're gonna fly in a plane to London tonight. Tangerine flies back to Argentina."

I didn't understand it all perfectly, but I knew the news was bad and that Tato was going to be separated from me.

"The house gets boarded up and the pipes get drained tomorrow. Tonight they're putting us to sleep early. Your old man said, 'We'll hafta sneak the Puerto Rican out or else the little one'll go crazy.' So Tangerine asks him, 'What'll you tell Cello when he sees Tato gone?' And do you know what that stupid fuck tells her? He says, 'We'll tell the kid Tato asked to go home and we just had to get him a taxi.'"

Tato's eyes went back to the sky. Snow was still nowhere in sight, but I don't think he was looking for Snow. Then he said, "Goodbye, Cello," and held out his hand. He was acting as if it would be as easy for me to say goodbye as picking a flower.

I pulled my hand back. "I don't want to say goodbye," I said.

He didn't look at me. "It's not bad," he said, looking down.

"It is bad," I insisted.

He stood there like stone, his face turned so that he wouldn't have to look at me. I felt almost too weak to stand. How small we were in comparison to the sky and water. I had no idea where Europe was or how large the world was. I was in shock over how easily we could lose each other. Tato's once-wise dark eyes seemed frozen.

"You gotta say goodbye," he said. What was he talking about? He seemed hurt. I worried suddenly that I was hurting him. I didn't understand enough of what was going on. I was missing the importance.

"Goodbye," I said to cheer him up, but my voice didn't alter his expression.

He turned, looking straight at me. What did his eyes want from my face? Were we waiting for Snow to return? Why were we standing silently on the beach, the mosquitoes biting our legs? We had said goodbye, but we hadn't disappeared. If the word goodbye had done something to us, I didn't notice. It must have been done in a split second. I didn't see blood; I felt no pain.

When we got back to our rooms Tato crossed the hallway under the green light. He left two packs of Tangerine's cigarettes on my dresser, went back to his room and closed the door. I dropped the cigarettes into my little laundry sack. I wrapped Zia's bird perfume in a pair of undershorts and put it into the sack. By the time I crawled into my bed, I was all packed and ready for whatever was going to happen.

There was no moon. My room was very dark. I heard a car far away stopping at the cracked asphalt. Then I heard footsteps coming up the stairs, whispers and footsteps under the green light, the sound of footsteps going down the stairs. I heard the front door close, thumping feet on the wooden porch under the window. I imagined Tato and the cab driver walking on the sand toward the cracked asphalt. I heard the taxi engine start up. I imagined Tato sitting alone in the back of the cab in the dark, looking out the window at the house. And as the engine sounds began to rise, I sat up and listened painfully for every last note of the car. I was able to track the cab until a rustling noise was all I could pick up, just the land breeze making lace of the tiny waves at the shoreline.

I pretended to be asleep when the door of my room opened. My father carried me downstairs and all the way to the waiting limousine. I kept my eyes closed, kept my mind in the air above the house, for a long time pretending sleep, until I sensed the sharp strobing lights of the airport highway. I didn't sit up until we stopped to drop off Tangerine.

She refused to get out. My father had to push her out. She yelled back at him, shouting over the noise of the landing planes. She held onto the door as the car rolled away, crying, screaming angrily, her scarf flying, her mascara running. As the limo picked up speed, she whirled around. I looked out the back window and waved to her as my father pulled the door closed. I felt foolish waving at the angry woman in the middle of the road, but in spite of her anger, she found it in herself to wave back to me.

We flew up over the ocean until the United States of America became a little island in my mind. Tiny people below were going to sleep in tiny houses. Tato was tiny, in a tiny taxi riding to his tiny house in Brooklyn. I thought of mother in a tiny box buried in a tiny cemetery and of the great shack on Jessup Neck with its globe of the world, its great red couch, our water wings and the point of sand where we watched the snowy egrets flying over the bay. I thought of Snow flying somewhere below us, the tiniest white bird in the world, getting tinier in my mind until he became a tiny black dot.

CHAPTER IV

OUR plane landed in London. Lucille Meyer was a thin older woman. She was wearing a blue suit and a gold bracelet. My father dragged Lucille and me along for hours, from place to place. Finally waking from a sleep in my father's lap, I looked out a bus window at rain and a school. A bell was ringing and boys were running. They enrolled me in St. Stephen's boarding school and stooped to kiss me goodbye. My father held a finger before my face. "You'll love this place. It's an expensive place, you hear?" He kissed me with cigarette breath.

Lucille left me a postcard of her house in Geneva, a structure of multicolored brick combined in unusual patterns. A tiny leafless tree stood before the house, sticking up from a frozen lawn.

My father had explained that Lucille's former husband left her the house in Switzerland, which they were going there to sell before moving permanently to England. That would make it possible for me to continue at St. Stephen's and to come home every night to a cozy life with the two of them. I didn't believe him, but it didn't matter to me anyway whether he intended to keep his promise or not. I was relieved to have his finger removed from my face when he left, although my legs were a bit shaky as I walked off with my laundry bag in one hand and the fat hand of Father Ivan, the rector, in my other. He was so huge I couldn't see his head. Walking the hallway to my room, I was afraid he would fall on top of me.

The chapel was always open at St. Stephen's and I spent a lot of time there. I tried to keep Tato alive in my mind. For some reason I kept expecting to see him among the students at St. Stephen's. Whenever I saw the thick dark head of hair of the master of ceremonies on the altar, I imagined if he turned around it would be Tato. But after a while I gave up expecting it. Gradually I began having trouble remembering what Tato looked like.

I took ill at Christmas. Brother Gerard, the infirmarian, told me it was raining in my lungs. Pneumonia. I was in the infirmary from Christmas Day until after the New Year. Father married Lucille in Switzerland that Christmas. They never came to St. Stephen's. Years passed. I spent every Christmas in the infirmary with bronchitis.

In the summer I was among the very few who didn't return home. We had conversations on the phone. Lucille's voice was helpless. She tried to find materials with which to build a conversation, but she never had much luck.

"How are you, dear?"

"Fine, thank you."

"Do you feel well?"

"Yes."

"School is all right?"

"Yes."

My father had little more to say. I learned to stop asking when he was coming to see me. He hated the question.

The teaching brothers of St. Stephen's were like fairy-tale men with shiny red faces. I quickly learned the secret that we were all in one great pot. The great organ roaring in chapel was the huge fire that cooked us into stew. My favorite pastime was sitting in chapel alone, watching the candles burn. It would have made a great pigeon coop, with round stained-glass windows that flipped to allow the birds to escape.

I had my own world, a true territory. No one challenged it. They interpreted my isolation as a virtue. My loneliness was endearing to them. The farther away from me they stayed, the better I liked it. Still, when everyone went home at the beginning of every recess, I wound up in the infirmary with a cold and a fever. My body had learned somehow to give father his excuse for not taking me home.

Each year I repeated the same conversation with Lucille. Each year I accepted father's excuses.

One Christmas I received a transparent plastic box of white almonds from the Perugina Candy Company. They looked like pigeon eggs. They were from Zia Fantasia.

Brother Catolicus—we called him Brother Cat. Once he urged me to talk to Jesus in chapel. He promised emphatically that Jesus would answer me.

"What should I say?"

Brother Cat smiled. "Ask him to be your friend."

The next afternoon in chapel I waited until everyone was gone. I sat on the aisle side, then out loud I asked, "Jesus, will you be my friend?" I heard the echo, the ringing of my ears, but no answer from Jesus. When Jesus didn't answer after a couple of months, I gave him up. I didn't exactly disbelieve in him. At best, Jesus was like Tato, far away, like my father, like Zia, like Mother. When anything was that far away, I didn't care whether it existed or not.

One night when the brothers were away chanting Compline, I took out Zia's white-bird bottle, which I had kept along with Tato's still unopened packs of cigarettes. I opened a handkerchief on the windowsill and placed a white almond on it in the moonlight. Then I lifted the white bird from the bottle. I smelled Zia's presence. Jessup Neck came to mind, Zia's warmth, her whispers. I saw Snow flying like a soft silver spirit over the bay, diving and playing among the egrets and herons. Suddenly Brother Cat was standing in my room, although Compline was not yet over. He grabbed the two packs of Tato's cigarettes and stuffed them into his cassock. By the time the brothers began streaming up the stairs from Compline, Brother Cat was pulling me by the hands, downward to the rector's office. We bumped into the rector in the hallway near his door.

"We must talk to you, Father Ivan."

"Is he sick?" the fat priest asked with a little annoyance.

"Saying mass," Brother Cat hissed.

"What? Speak up."

Brother Cat's smallness automatically enlarged Father Ivan. "He was saying *mass*," Brother Cat repeated with a good throat clearing.

"Who?"

"The boy."

"You were saying *mass*?" Father Ivan asked politely.

"No," I answered.

"He had little hosts," Brother Cat puffed.

"Did you have little hosts?" Father Ivan asked.

"I had candy eggs."

Father Ivan took his keys and opened the door to his office. He went inside onto his red Oriental rug. Brother Cat stretched up and whispered something into Father Ivan's ear. Father Ivan's eyes were on me.

"Do you like perfume?" he asked me.

"Huh?"

"Who is the white bird? Do you know?" Brother Cat asked.

"No."

"The Holy Spirit? Do you know about him?" Father Ivan asked.

"Yes."

"Who is he?"

"A white bird."

"Is that who your white bird is?"

"No."

"Who is your white bird?"

"Do you mean the white bird on the bottle of my aunt's perfume?"

"All right. Who is that bird?"

"It's just a glass bird on the bottle."

"What were you saying to the bird?"

"Why would I talk to a glass bird?" I asked.

"Brother Catolicus says you were talking. Who were you talking to?"

"To the moon."

Brother Cat smiled with satisfaction.

Father Ivan was taken back. "Really? You talk to the moon? What do you say?"

"I tell the moon I miss my aunt."

Father Ivan's eyes widened for a moment. Then his huge body bent toward me. I didn't like the odor of his cassock, but I liked his fat red face. He touched his banana finger to my cheek. Then he went to his large desk, opened the drawer and brought out a hard green candy wrapped in cellophane. It reminded me of the stone in Zia's ring. I picked it up from his fingers as if it were the fruit from a large tree.

"You know the way back to your room?" he asked sweetly.

"Yes."

"Then go and get ready for bed."

From that time on, Brother Cat avoided me. Of course, he never returned my cigarettes.

At St. Stephen's I observed the blooming cycle and followed the course of everything green that broke ground in the woodlands that stretched infinitely beyond the campus. Not too far from the school there was a large bowllike depression about one hundred yards in diameter where ferns grew, giant ferns, light green ferns that trembled in the slightest wind. I often went to the center of the bowl and lay back upon the cool dark peat under the ferns. I floated in the iridescent pale greenness. I tried to catch the slow uncurling of fiddle heads. Sometimes I was surprised by the sudden flip of one. I would often slip down my trousers there and examine my penis.

One day a letter came from Lucille and Father saying that they were going to move to Rome, Italy. I was to meet them there at my new school, Collegio Nazzareno.

Father Ivan accompanied me to Rome. We flew from London directly to Rome. I expected to see Lucille and father at Nazzareno, but they weren't there. Father Ivan said mass for the students the next morning, then kissed me goodbye and left me with the prefect, Father Casaluce. My father and Lucille were nowhere in sight.

After a while, I wasn't sorry to be in Italy. I didn't have to talk to anyone, because I didn't know Italian. Italy was warmer. I had fewer colds. At Nazzareno, friendships were frowned upon. It was a rule that particular friendships were uncharitable to the rest of the student body. That had been the Jesuit rule at the seminary where many of our teachers were trained, and they passed on the regulation to the students.

One person at Nazzareno came close to filling the void Tato had left on the night of the mosquitoes. His name was Father Roberto Ciascuno, the young priest assigned to say mass for us in summer school. There were only five students in the school during the summer. I was assigned to him as altar boy. I had to be in the sacristy every morning at six. The first morning I was early. I filled the wine and water cruets and laid out vestments in the manner in which I was instructed by Prefect Casaluce. I waited in my cassock and surplice on a carved gothic bench. The amber-stained windows of the sacristy filled the place with a wonderful yellowness, except where the windows opened inwardly, revealing the blueness of morning and the pale lacy green of early summer.

"*Buon giorno*," the young priest growled as he entered the sacristy.

I would have believed him to be a soccer player or a young businessman, or even an actor. I never saw a priest with his mannerisms. His movements were totally unsanctimonious, but when he kissed the alb and lifted all that whiteness over his head and tied the cincture at his waist, something more wonderful than priestliness began to shine through. Fully vested at five minutes of six, he sat in the great thronelike seat under the electric clock, and I could see that he hadn't washed his face. His eyes were crusted, his hair wet-combed. It still stuck up in back where it had rested on the pillow. His bad breath cut the minty purity of the room, and his breathing was loud. Though gray and velvety, his sharp eyes recalled my father in the days he paced the wooden floors of our apartment over the Hudson River. His eyebrows were blond, though his hair was thick and dark brown. His nose was large and his chin fine. He wore half a smile, the smile of a thief, contagious.

Sitting fully vested, staring ahead, he neither meditated nor recited his breviary as other priests did. He jumped out of the great chair to check the clock now and then. He peeked at the altar to see if I had filled the cruets and lighted the candles, then sat down again. His eyes came to me. They remained upon me for an inordinate amount of time. I straightened my surplice and looked up at the clock. When I brought my eyes back to him, he smiled and said something in Italian.

"*Mi scusi, Padre,*" I asked, not understanding what he had said.

"*Sei americano?*"

"*Si, Padre.*"

"You do not like being stared at, eh?"

"Do you?" I was surprised at my rudeness.

"Sometimes I am insulted if I am *not* stared at," he said, looking away. He stood up, picked up the chalice and headed for the sanctuary.

"It's not six o'clock," I objected. "We have two more minutes."

"You wait the two minutes." He pushed past me into the sanctuary. I rang the bell for the attention of the congregation and fumbled toward the altar. He had begun the prayers without me. I had never seen such arrogance in a priest.

Lucille finally wrote admitting that they were not coming to Rome. They decided not to sell the house in Geneva, but I was to think of it as my home. So I wrote immediately and asked for the fare to come home for the rest of the summer. They didn't answer.

One day all the students had to sit for individual photographs. When they were ready, the photographs were passed out in sealed brown envelopes. I went straight to my room and opened mine as I sat on my bed. The photograph in my envelope was a much older boy with big white teeth and dark hair neatly parted on the side. His eyes were sharp and he had looked directly into the camera.

I ran into the hall. The other students were in groups examining their photographs. I held up mine. "Excuse me," I said. "Does anyone know who this photo belongs to?"

They peered at my photograph and laughed. "*Stupido*, it's you."

I went back to my room and looked at the photograph again. It couldn't be me, I thought. I seem so grown up.

That evening at dinner the summer student body, overseen by Prefect Casaluce, huddled around one table, shipwrecked adolescents in an ocean of fluorescent light. Prefect Casaluce from the dais never took his eyes off us while we ate. Our only view was the cobblestones of the rear court through the basement window. A silver Lamborghini pulled in silently, a faint trail of smoke coming from its exhaust. I could make out Father Ciascuno, dressed in his black cassock, jumping out. He signaled the driver to move over, jumped back into the incredible automobile and roared off. Prefect Casaluce caught us watching.

The next morning Prefect Casaluce knocked on the sacristy door. "I would like a word with you." Ciascuno, fully vested for mass, stepped forward out of the lemon light into the dark foyer, leaving me alone in the large room. I had become proficient in Italian and could understand every word.

"Are you crazy? Whose car is that out there?"

"It was a gift from my sister. It's still in her name."

"It's scandalous. The boys saw you in it."

"So what?"

"You're supposed to observe poverty."

"I never took a poverty vow."

"Kids don't understand that. Who do you think you are? A movie star? Showing up in a car like that? The Rome Diocese is the last place in the world you should be. You deserve to be sent to the African missions."

"But they send only good priests like you to the missions," Ciascuno answered. "The ones they can't trust they keep in Rome where they can keep an eye on us."

"You young fool. One word from me and Monsignor Vicario will dump you. You realize who you're talking to? Your ass is in enough hot water."

"Casaluce, you see this fist?"

"I see it."

"If Monsignor Vicario dumps me, this lands in your face." Coming back into the sacristy, Ciascuno's teeth shone in a big smile. Before entering the sanctuary, he chuckled. "How was I?"

Of course I didn't answer. Prefect Casaluce was watching. But I laughed hysterically into my pillow that night picturing Prefect Casaluce's eyes crossed and looking down at Ciascuno's fist.

I looked forward to the morning. I loved to watch Ciascuno blustering about irreverently. I decided he was stronger than the white marble spires of the main altar, stronger than the dark mahogany walls, the tall Romanesque arches. They merely suggested power; he *was* power. In his light and careless way, he was stronger than the whole Roman Catholic Church. The Church was a toy wagon he pulled behind him.

When the school barber came on his rounds, I insisted upon only a trim so that my hair would grow fuller like Ciascuno's. The barber had to take more time for such a haircut and was furious. In the end he took twice the time as usual, leaving twice the amount of hair on my head, cutting it painstakingly around my ears. When done, my hair did look like Ciascuno's.

That afternoon there was a knock at my door. It was Ciascuno. He closed the door behind him. He sat on the bed saying nothing. His eyes scanned the walls.

"Where is your crucifix?" he finally asked.

I told him the truth: "In my drawer."

"Why?"

"I don't want cruelty always before my eyes," I said.

He could not control his smile. "It is supposed to make you aware of your own cruelty, and the generosity of God," he said.

"I don't believe in God."

He bolted in shock at my words. His smile returned slowly.

"Then what do you pray to?"

"I don't pray," I answered.

"You little fox. You are telling the truth. You don't believe in Him?"

"Do you?"

"Of course."

"Then why were you so uncharitable to the prefect?"

"Casaluce? Do you know who it was in the Lamborghini waiting for me?"

"Who?"

"Monsignor Vicario. Don't you believe I said the right thing to an old troublemaker? You are such fascists, you atheists. Well, what do you say? You want to play tennis, *americano?* Do you know how?"

"No."

"I am going to teach you."

"What did the prefect mean when he said you're in hot water?"

His eyes rolled up in his head. He sighed. "I have been seen in Rome playing tennis too often. My sister is my tennis partner. My *older* sister. When a priest goes near a woman in tennis shorts, it electrifies the imagination of the Holy Office. Now, what do you say, little atheist? Will you let me teach you tennis, or will you sit in this prison all summer and look out the window?"

"Maybe . . ."

He looked at me with disgust and got up to leave. "Tomorrow after breakfast meet me in the cobblestone court."

Speeding home from my first tennis lesson in the silver Lamborghini was like riding inside a bullet. It was August and the day was magnificent.

"Call me Roberto, you hear?" Ciascuno said suddenly.

"You're kidding me."

"No," he shouted. "My name is Roberto. Call me Roberto. It sounds ugly when you call me Father, especially when we play tennis."

"But if Prefect Casaluce—"

"*Dio!* Don't do it in front of Casaluce; but when we are alone, why not?"

"I thought only other priests are allowed to call you by name."

"But do you know how many kids in Italy would give their right arm to call a priest by his first name? Just don't call me Father on the tennis court, you little monster, you hear?" With that he held out a pack of Camels. I hadn't seen a pack of Camels since the days of Zia and Tangerine.

"Take one," he offered with a sly smile. I pulled one out of the pack. That surprised him. Ciascuno held his lighter in my direction. I leaned toward the flame and sucked in the smoke, inhaling it with perfection and blowing out, filling the Lamborghini with smoke. I amazed myself that I could still do it.

"You little addict." He smiled in wonder. "You'd rather be addicted to my cigarette than to tennis. What would Casaluce say to this?"

I didn't answer. I smoked the cigarette dizzily as I watched the Italian countryside speed by. I opened the window a crack to let out the smoke. I loved the cigarette. I felt older as I sat there. My legs were becoming almost too long for the car. A strong cool odor entered the car. It was not the sweet citrus odor of Italy; it was the sharp salty odor of the wind coming off the bay in Jessup Neck.

One evening during dinner, Prefect Casaluce's eyes were on me for an unusually long time. After the prayer which concluded our meal, Casaluce stood, pointed to me and waved a letter. This was not his normal way of giving out mail. I knew the letter had a formidable message.

The letter had been opened, according to the rule of the school.

Dear Cello,

Lucille and I may have to put up the house for rent. This also means I don't have the money to pay your tuition. If I had the money, you'd be the first to benefit from it, believe me. I want you to write after you figure out what you want to do about this.

With love and affection,
Your father

P.S. Talk to them at Nazzareno. Maybe there's a fund.

The next morning was beautiful—blue sky, soft breeze—but I detested the brightness. I had a headache. I was worse than ever at tennis. People were watching. Ciascuno tried to make my game look better, but my headache was distracting me. It seemed crazy to be playing tennis when my life was going over the waterfall.

"Enough," Ciascuno said, pretending he was tired. I was a little embarrassed before the onlookers.

He was taking off his clothes in the locker room. I was putting mine on. He threw a bar of soap at me.

"You never wash. You stink. Take a shower. *Andiamo!*"

"I take my showers at the school."

"After you soil your clean clothes with sweat? *Stupido!*"

I looked down at the soap and decided I would go into the showers wearing my tennis shorts. They had to be washed anyway. He appeared nude at my stall as I turned on the water.

"Get your head under. C'mon. Wash." He poured his shampoo on my head. I thought of Christ being anointed with oil. Then he stepped into my stall and manipulated my head with his hands. I stood stiffly with my hands out of the way while he kneaded my head as if it were a ball of dough. I kept my eyes closed tightly to avoid soap, but also to avoid seeing his penis. He opened the top of my shorts and pulled them downward.

"No."

"Don't be silly," he commanded. He pulled them down, squatted in the torrent and lifted each foot out of the shorts. He turned me around and soaped up my body, my back, my legs. Then he pushed me under the shower and rinsed my hair. He tried to turn me around again, but I resisted.

"Hey!"

The foam melted off my head. I could feel it trickling down my body. He tried to turn me back to him, but I stood my ground.

"Hey. *Che cosa?*" He peeked smiling into the corner where I had turned my head. "Hey, c'mon."

"No."

"But why? Hey?"

"No."

"Are you crying?"

"No."

"Then what?"

"Nothing."

He put the soap in the rack and took his shampoo and left. I didn't want him to see that I had an erection.

On the way back to Nazzareno the silver Lamborghini flew under the cypresses. Ciascuno was driving fast. He offered a cigarette. I refused. I allowed the road feeding into us to hypnotize me.

His voice startled me. "I would like to see the letter your father sent you." I gave him a nod, then pretended to fall asleep. When the Lamborghini inched slowly into the Nazzareno courtyard, I opened the door.

"The letter," he said. Without a word I went to my room for the letter and brought it out to the car.

"Get in," he said. I sat next to him uncomfortably as he read it. "*Bastardo,*" he mumbled. It didn't make me feel better that he called my father a bastard. I was beginning to regret having agreed to learn tennis.

A few nights later he knocked on my door. "Comb your hair and put on a shirt and tie. C'mon."

"Why?"

"I'm going to take you to the most beautiful ship in Italy. Move."

We had dinner early in Piazza Santa Maria, Trastevere, then we drove the silver car into the pink evening light, forty-five minutes outside of Rome to Ostia.

I saw the big ship from a distance, pure white and very long.

It had no figurehead, but at its bow, carved of wood and gilded in gold, were giant tied ribbons. The ribbons trailed as silk would if it were tied to the bow in the wind. They trailed along the port and starboard sides of the sleek yacht.

We parked beneath the stern, where I could read the yacht's name in gold script—*Rosa Senza Spina*. The Rose Without Thorn. We climbed the gangplank into its shiny interior. Inside, like the outside, everything was pure white. The crew was dressed in white. The silk curtains over the portholes, the louvred doors, the awnings—all white. White shining rows of roulette chips recalled holy communion wafers in rolls inside the golden ciborium on the altar, Jesus Christ, the bridegroom of children, girls in white dresses and veils, brides before their time. Boys in white jackets, white shorts, white shoes and long white stockings, wearing white carnations and white ribbon on their arms. Brides too, in long white lines, waiting to have their tongues touched with more whiteness, the kiss of the Lamb of God, the bridegroom Son of God who comes to take away the sins of the world. The ship was too holy, too clean, too liturgical for me, but the moment Father Ciascuno told me the ship belonged to his sister, and the moment we walked into her presence, the ship began to seem different.

"My sister Gabriella," he said. "This is Cello Manfredi."

"I have seen you before." she said to me, holding out her hand. We were on the upper deck of the stern. The hills of Rome were behind her. "Who does he look like, Roberto?"

He shrugged. She was older than him by only two or three years. She sat almost nude in a bikini on a frail folding-type wooden beach chair, her rump filling out its canvas sling, though she was surrounded by a horseshoe of white puffy couches which lined the stern. Overhead, the ceiling was a white cloth awning strung on poles. It cast a pale glow upon us. Gabriella wore white high heels, which she had hooked onto the cross bar of the chair, bringing her knees under her chin. She embraced her legs, seeming to float over the deck, obviously unaware that some stray genital hair was showing. She was one of those ageless women, with the voice of an old contessa and the skin of a young peasant girl. Her eyes were extremely beautiful, gray like his, but brighter because, unlike his, her lashes and eyebrows were black and sharp. Her teeth were perfect. Her lips were painted icy pink, which then was a fashion in Rome. Her perfect teeth gave her smile added power. Still, when she spoke, she seemed a touch conspiratorial. That was the illusion her deep, careless voice gave as she lit her cigarette.

"How old is the kid? Is he your new toy?" Gabriella asked in Spanish.

"He's only fourteen," Ciascuno responded, also in Spanish.

She could tell that I understood. It didn't embarrass her. On the contrary, it seemed to amuse her. "Does he understand Russian too?" she asked, laughing.

Her brother didn't hide his annoyance. She stood up and grabbed what seemed to be a gigantic white towel, but which was her bathrobe, floor length, of extraordinary fullness, which she tied at the waist. Suddenly Gabriella Ciascuno's authority was visible. She was taller than I expected, and in her white robe she suddenly became an extension of her great white ship. She pressed a button for a servant. "Do you realize you look very much like someone in our family?" she said to me. I shrugged my shoulders.

A steward appeared, fully dressed in white suit, cap and tie. She told him in French to go to her bedroom and get a photograph on the dressing table. Roberto seemed displeased with his sister, and asked me to take a walk to inspect the ship. I turned to go and was presented with a crystal glass filled with *limonata* on a silver tray. I took it and walked along the starboard railing, seeing the hills of Rome disappearing in the pink lavender light of evening. In each stateroom there was a small basket of fresh white roses. I walked into one of the rooms and pulled up one of the flowers to examine its stem. All its thorns had been clipped off. I walked in a full circle around the ship from its gold-beribboned bow back to the horseshoe area under the white awning.

A tiny red lamp glowed now under the white canvas ceiling, and the steward was returning with a glass-framed photograph. When she held it out to me, I laughed. I thought it was a joke Ciascuno was playing on me, because it appeared to be my class photograph, the one I couldn't believe was me. But upon inspection, I could see it was Ciascuno when he was younger. She was right; I resembled him.

"You are an American with the name Manfredi?" she asked in English. "I have friends by that name. Roberto . . ." She rattled off in fast Italian to her brother. Then she laughed and said in Italian, "It's not possible he's related to Fantasia?"

"No. *Dio!*" Ciascuno laughed.

"She's my aunt," I said, sipping my *limonata.*

Ciascuno's eyes popped in my direction. "Fantasia's your aunt? She lives in Argentina."

"That's right."

"With a polo player—what's his name?" Gabriella turned to her brother. She clapped her hands with delight and peered with fascination into my face. "*Dio!* Your aunt and I are very good friends. Did you know that? I met her right on this ship where you stand. She came aboard for a party in Rome and didn't leave till Greece. Fantasia is my favorite Neapolitan."

On the way back to Nazzareno that night in the Lamborghini, Ciascuno drove fast. He switched off the radio and then turned to me. I could tell by the sweat on his temples and the serious look of his face that he was excited and in some way vulnerable.

"Hey, listen to me, Cello. I . . . I like you, as my friend. Understand?" He made me uncomfortable when he didn't smile.

"That's good," I said.

When he spoke to me without smiling, I sensed some mysterious emotion working in him. He seemed to want to invade my solitude those times, as if he wanted something from me that he saw there, something he needed. It unsettled me to be in possession of anything so valuable to a man like him.

"You must accept it from me if I arrange to have your tuition paid."

I was suddenly very embarrassed. I felt betrayed, realizing that he had presented me to his sister as a needy orphan, and that while I walked around her ship he was pleading my case to her. She was going to pay my way through Nazzareno, and he didn't want me to know.

"I will accept your charity if—"

"Not charity."

"Well, I will accept, if you realize the benefactor must be paid back."

"The benefactor? There's no need to pay anyone back."

"Only if I pay *back*," I insisted.

"All right. All right." His hand came gently to my head. I jerked out of its way. "What is the matter?"

"What're you doing?" I asked.

"Nothing, nothing," he whispered. His palm pressed my forehead and forced my head to rest back. He wiped my hair back upon my head. I let my neck relax, but tightened my legs even more. He wanted to believe he was relaxing me. I let him believe it.

Summer ended. The rest of the student body returned with suntans. Ciascuno made our goodbye easy. He said, *"Ciao, americano,"* and drove off without a handshake in a small Fiat to his new desk job at the Rota. He wasn't happy to say goodbye to me, but not distraught about it either.

I dreaded the end of my schooling. Ciascuno's letters had become short notes, and then I heard nothing at all from him. One night someone had put on my bed a copy of the Vatican newspaper, *L'Osservatore Romano,* opened to a page on which I could immediately see Ciascuno's photograph. Prefect Casaluce must have left it. The caption in Italian indicated that Roberto Ciascuno had been made a monsignor. The article said that he was assigned to a post of high responsibility in the Vatican. It emphasized that he was the youngest prelate ever to receive the honor of this post. It mentioned Ciascuno's sister Gabriella and let it be known that the Ciascunos were *Romani di Roma,* an old Roman family dating back to antiquity. No wonder Prefect Casaluce couldn't intimidate him. No wonder there was once a Monsignor Vicario waiting in his Lamborghini. During the next four years, I rarely saw Father Ciascuno, although one letter and postcard at Christmas came reminding me of our relationship and urging me to play tennis as often as possible. And then there was a letter from my father:

Lucille has been writing on your behalf to schools where you may continue your education with scholarship funds. But I emphasize that you should not rely on us for anything beyond this. Be industrious about your future. Ask around. Let them know we are not rich.

Your father

Shortly after that I started receiving catalogues and letters of thanks. One letter stood out because it was so very brief and typed perfectly on the finest stock:

You have been accepted for the pursuit of Theological studies at the North American College in Rome.

How could this be? Ciascuno was my first suspect. I immediately called his office. I heard his secretary catch him in passing. "Who?" He sounded annoyed. "Ask him what it is about."

It was the way he said "Who?" that made me hang up. I felt at that moment that Ciascuno not only had nothing to do with it but he had forgotten who I was, or pretended to have forgotten. I reasoned that my father had used his cunning and his selfishness on my behalf. His cheapness paid off. With Lucille's assistance he had obtained for me a free education, at the same time getting me off his back.

For the first time in my life, I was in control of the distance between my father and me. I was old enough to take a train to Geneva. If he was afraid of me, I was not afraid of him. In fact—I hoped—I might even *make* him like me this time.

I boarded a train for Geneva. I was going to appear before him. I was going to talk to him. We were going to deal with one another. I was his son.

On the train I prepared myself for a white-headed man, ruddy-faced by now. I dared to imagine his putting an arm around my shoulder. I felt the power I had: to startle him with my tallness. I wasn't even shaving when he last saw me. The small leafless tree in Lucille's postcard would be much larger. The multicolored cold brick house would be much warmer inside than it appeared in the old postcard. I imagine my father leading me through French doors covered in tight white curtains to a sunny room of blue French tiles and white geraniums. Lucille would still be thin, not as pretty as she was that day so long ago in London, but gentle and perhaps wise enough to criticize my father's insensitivity, making me more than comfortable among their lace curtains and paintings, asking me to bring my chair near their fire.

But when I stood before it, the multicolored brick house in Geneva was much more elaborate than the postcard implied. The little tree must have died, because there was no tree at all on the lawn. They were living in the best of style.

My father answered the door. He looked up at me, openmouthed. He had grown old. His eyes were tired. His hair seemed dyed and showed gray only at the sideburns.

"I'm Cello," I said.

"My God, you got tall," he said.

Lucille, still quite beautiful and delicate, seemed embarrassed the whole time I was there. She wore a drab wool skirt and sweater. Her thin fingers shook. Both she and my father tried to smile, but I felt like an insurance salesman who had forced his way into their living room. Their cook had dinner ready almost as I arrived. I ate my first bite with exhaustion. They hadn't mentioned my staying overnight, nor had I. Did they imagine I would go back on the next train?

After dinner Lucille put out coffee and excused herself. She turned on a light in the library and disappeared. I wondered what she saw in him, tending to his needs like a faithful nun. Did she call him Buzzy? No. Dear, she called him. *Dee-ahr*, with a trap door in it, through which her voice fell each time. I wondered what she needed from him that he gave her.

I placed the letter before him. He looked at it, put it down and said nothing. Finally I spoke up. "I have no desire to become a priest. I'm not even sure I believe in God," I said with a smile.

He was picking his teeth with a toothpick. Lucille had left a box of them near him. His old eyes turned to mine. "So what do you want *me* to do about this?" he asked.

"Well, when you arranged this, what was your intention?" I asked.

"I didn't arrange this. Why should I want you to be a priest? I don't wish things like that on anybody."

"But I thought—"

"Cello, listen to me. I don't have the strength to live my own goddamn life and I'm going to live yours? I'm getting old, makin' room for the next wave, you hear? Do what you want with your life. You want a gift from me? I give it to you. You're free. You don't have to consult me about anything anymore, okay? The sky and the dirt are paid for; your oxygen is free. Go breathe. You're a man." He held out a hand for me to shake. His skin sagged around his jaws, and puffs under his eyes dimmed their old sharpness; they were tired, colorless eyes. "If you want an education, take my advice and write a nice letter of acceptance." He held up the letter. "This is worth money, you understand? I'm broke."

I looked up at the huge chandelier over the dinner table.

"Don't look up there," he shouted. "This place is hers." He threw a broken toothpick into an ashtray. "Lucille pays. You're a poor man's son. Worse, you're a poor man yourself now." He smiled. "This letter is the only thing you own. It's more than I had to start out with."

I decided to take the night train, even though Lucille finally asked me to stay. I became very formal, thanked them, and excused myself.

"C'mon, for chrissake," my father said, slapping my shoulder. "What you got to be so stiff about?"

I had a lump in my throat as I took his hand. I'd rather have grabbed his throat.

The night train could have been a train to anywhere in the world. I wouldn't have cared. Perhaps it was a premonition of my father's death, or a function of the huge changes we both had undergone. But I felt that I would never see him or Lucille again.

When I closed my eyes to sleep on the train, I became dizzy. I wished for someone to talk to but feared that if anyone got close to me, I would frighten them by my lack of equilibrium. I managed a trip to the lavatory, where I threw up. Later, in the dining car, I fell asleep at the table.

I dreamed I was shipwrecked. When I woke up I discovered I

had knocked over the little vase and its fresh red rose. This rose had thorns. The water soaked the cuff of my shirt.

A few days later I mailed my acceptance to the North American College. Some time later I found out that it was Monsignor Roberto Ciascuno who had arranged it after all. He with his power had provided for my adult education. Gabriella with her money took care of Nazzareno. It hurt and embarrassed me, but I was scared enough of what seemed an insane world to swallow my pride and hide inside their charity.

The North American College was the envy of all seminaries in Italy because we were allowed to smoke. We looked quite slick as we walked about in the recreation hall in long black medieval cassocks, lighting cigarettes with our silver lighters and turning our heads to blow our smoke into the dark corners. Sometimes the smoke lay high under the rafters like ribbons of fog. From the highest point of the recreation hall, a statue of the crucified Christ looked down at the waving smoke ribbons.

The seminary was another planet. We were men who did not work in the true sense. We *pursued studies.* We were not trained to generate money; there was no need. I looked with disdain upon money. It was not intentional snobbery. Although I felt that persons who worked hard at boring tasks were fools, I began to believe that seminarians' work was more the function of omega man. We were future men, dealing with life as it would be when the industrial revolution took its last gasp, when everything for which man had to sell his body and his time would come automatically, leaving him free for contemplation and leisure, which were the basis of culture. We were living ahead of the rest of the world, in a capsule where existence was a higher responsibility than survival. We floated about in black capes in the rare cool atmosphere of a special world that was under complete control. It was like living in a terrarium, except it was the outside world which was the teeming, steaming place of noise and work.

Sex had no place in the seminary. It was presumed we would brush aside sex as easily as giving up sweets. The strange thing was that we succeeded. We were above our bodies. The whole time, I was never sure of the existence of God, but I respected the rhythms and ideals of the ascetical life. Perhaps that was all I had.

I needed to be exceptional and I was willing to pay the price. Our intelligence was constantly challenged by the intellectual gymnastics of philosophy and theology. The gears of life could not snag us in their fads and errors. We grew sharp and articulate and we were safe from every danger imaginable, except the danger of being too safe. I had made a choice, confirmed my identity, and with that identity came my home and the satisfaction of closure, closure of all the possibilities that stretch out before an unlived life. My possibilities melted into one neat fact: I was going to be a priest.

Chastity was painless. Sexually, my body was a refrigerator, in a long cool dormancy. I relished it. I was an eagle soaring effortlessly above the chicken farms where thousands of common vulgar birds reproduced and were killed every day.

I worked at the Rota each summer for Ciascuno. He was becoming powerful in Rome. He had acquired a quasi-messianic reputation along with a famous temper. He physically threw a bishop out of his office and was admired throughout the Vatican for having done so. I was a special person in the minds of other clerics simply because he was my confessor. Officially he was my spiritual director; he was to be my sponsor at my ordination.

I gave up my dreams of Jessup Neck long before that. Right up until 1967 white almonds from Perugina arrived every Christmas with the name *Zia Fantasia* signed by the staff calligrapher.

I often tried to imagine the kind of man Tato had grown into. I received a letter from him forwarded by Lucille. It was written in a clumsy hand:

Dear Cello,
Do they still call you that name? I heard the weirdest wildest thing, that you're going to be a priest and I don't want you to forget that I'm your cousin Tato still. It seems like yesterday. It's a funny thing sending these words over across the ocean. I don't know what else to say. I hope you still remember me. I think of you a lot.
We're all okay over here. Brooklyn hasn't forgotten you,

especially my mother who is still very fat. I put in a couple of years in law, but I may take the police test this summer because the books get to me. You think I'll make a good cop?

I'm a pretty bad Catholic, but I think it's a groove, what you're doing. If you ever come to Greenwich Village, look me up. If not, you have my best wishes for a holy life.

Your cousin Tato

He enclosed a card with his address and telephone number.

The letter depressed me—the mistakes, crossed-out words. I resented the line "best wishes for a holy life." The letter scared me because it meant we were both men now. I was twenty-four. I had nurtured a precious idea of Tato, he never stopped being my protector. He was like one of the saints to me, a fiction. I realized that I had been carrying on an interior dialogue with something other than Tato. I had imagined a soft man of wisdom, of contemplative beauty and intelligence, not the man who wrote that letter. I went to bed anxious and fearful.

I answered Tato with a short note the next day. It was a perfunctory thank you. He never wrote to me again.

Before the ordination ceremony and the taking of the final vows of the priesthood, we were given a meditation period of two weeks, during which I became deeply depressed. It had to do with my gnawing guilt of disbelief in God. I had expected my theological studies to reveal God—theology's logic was so concise and intellectual—but there I was at the end of my studies, no more sure of the existence of God than I was when I started.

As I moved about my room packing things one morning, I suddenly felt totally drained. I *was* tired but would not give up my constant reasoning, wrestling with my doubts. I wisely forced myself to put on my cassock and walk out of the seminary and into the sunlight, crossing St. Peter's Square to Ciascuno's office.

When I walked in, he could tell by my face that something was wrong, because he grabbed his cape without a word and ushered me out the door. After he felt my forehead with his hand and assured me I had no temperature, we walked along the Tiber.

The breeze filled our cassocks, turning them into bells. In keeping with Ciascuno's rebellion against protocol, we ate a *gelati* in the streets. The old Roman women approved. They bowed in the wind as we passed, smiling at the monsignor. His hair flowed back like silver silk, neatly over his ears. He was so handsome, dark-skinned from tennis. He was smiling, feeling well. "Cello, you will be the first American pope. When I am one hundred years old, I will retire and appoint you."

I didn't laugh. "I'm still plagued with the fear that I don't believe in God." I was glad I got it out.

"This is a very logical time for such a plague. Have you heard from Zia Fantasia?" he asked.

"What has she to do with it?"

"Nothing. I wondered who was coming to your ordination. Gabriella tells me she is ill in New York."

My stomach tightened. "Ill? Zia?"

He looked as if he may have regretted telling me. "I don't know, a cold perhaps. Perhaps she is making excuses for not being with you at your ordination. Have you heard from your father?"

"He has nothing whatever to do with my problems."

"Your father is not coming for your ordination with his Coquille, is he?"

"Lucille."

"Pardon me. Lucille." He tried to hold his laughter.

"How do you know he isn't coming?"

"Should I expect your father to change suddenly? Cello, look at me. Your classmates are gone. You are motherless, fatherless. You dare not feel that God has abandoned you, so you blame yourself that you have abandoned God."

I stared at him. He always turned my doubts into virtues. It was not good for me. Nor did it help my feeling of isolation. He pulled me down to a bench. He took out his checkbook and began writing *one thousand dollars* in my name.

"Go home," he said with prophetic finality, "and come back to be ordained in two weeks. I'll take care of the Pope."

"What? Home? Where?"

"You are an American, aren't you?"

"I have no place to go there."

"What about Fantasia's house?"

"It's a summer place."

"So, it's warm now."

The scene flashed in my mind—the gulls, the bay, the herons. "What about your cousin. What's his name?"

"Tato?"

"Call Tato."

"Telephone Tato?"

"Of course, telephone him. That's what phones are for. Have him meet you."

He was a sorcerer. My heart beat faster. In my wallet there was Tato's card; I hoped its mutilation hadn't erased his telephone number.

"Why not?" Ciascuno laughed as he grabbed my shoulder. "Do you know how to reach Fantasia?"

"No."

"Gabriella has her number." He swept me along with him away from the bench. When he left me, as I walked slowly alone in the gentle May afternoon wind, I pictured myself in Jessup Neck, as an adult walking freely, anonymously. Dare I expect to see Tato and Zia? To laugh and speak English all day? I felt childish for accepting Ciascuno's solution. I felt ashamed that I hadn't offered more intelligent resistance. But I was happy for the first time in years.

At four in the afternoon in Rome, it was ten in the morning in New York. I poured lire into the phone in the booth at the Michelangelo Hotel.

"I have a long distance call for anybody from Cello Manfredi."

"Cello? Holy Jesus! Put him on. Hello?" It was too simple to believe. Tato's voice couldn't have been so close all those years. He couldn't have always been this accessible.

"Tato?"

"Yeah. Is this really Cello?"

"Yes."

I hardly remember the words we spoke, just the feelings that pushed them out. It was so strange to speak in adult voices. How are you? Fine. Wonderful. Words tumbled inside balloons of laughter.

"When are you coming home?" When Tato said the word home, I choked up.

"Tomorrow. I have two weeks."

"Damnit, we should go to Jessup."

"That's exactly what I thought."

"I'm due to take a law exam the fifteenth," Tato said.

"I have to be back in Rome on the twelfth."

"That gives us two weeks."

The wind of Rome blowing through my sleeves reminded me of curtains in the main room at Jessup Neck, sheer fields of white riding high over the great couch, curtains lifting toward a flat blue bay. Curtains swelling, beckoning me back to that wonderful room—its books, the old sailboats, the wind-up Victrola, the globe of the world on wheels. Had sand buried the porch? Had hurricanes blown the place apart? Did a giant full moon still sneak out of nowhere sending a hot south wind rushing noisily around the cliffs?

The night before I left Rome I fell asleep with my hand resting on a suitcase.

My plane landed at Kennedy Airport at 3:25 A.M. Tato and I did not recognize each other. But after milling through the crowd, we were among few possibilities left. A short man with a dark beard and soft brown eyes like Rembrandt's Christ—that was Tato. The black hair of his chest curled over the neckband of his tee shirt. I was afraid of him at first. It was the first time that someone I loved reappeared in my life. It was like coming up from the cellar after a long tornado. Tato *hadn't* died as my mother had.

"Hello, Tato." It felt strange to pronounce his name, as if doing so would turn him into an illusion. But his eyes saved me. His eyes hadn't changed.

"Welcome home, Cello." He grabbed my bag, hooked his arm into mine and pulled me away.

"Where are you taking me?" I laughed when we reached the parking lot.

Tato threw my bag into a faded red convertible Volkswagen. "Straight out there to Jessup."

"Is the place open?"

"I have no idea. So we climb in a window if not."

"Did you find out if the house still belongs to Zia?" He looked blankly at me. Had a jet drowned me out? "Zia—is it still hers?" I shouted.

"Don't know." He shrugged.

"She's in New York," I screamed.

"Well, let's call her up."

I dialed Zia's number from an expressway telephone booth as cars shot past and jets boomed overhead. I let it ring a dozen times. No answer.

We headed for Jessup. Tato was not at all the clumsy, inarticulate stranger who wrote that letter. He asked about my life, the Catholic Church, the priesthood. I answered with formality and self-consciousness while the wind whistled through the speeding little car. Suddenly my adrenaline had run out. Tato noticed. He smiled understandingly, so craftily. "Sleep," he said.

It was close to dawn when we arrived at the place of the cracked asphalt near the phragmites and the bay. In the light of predawn the house emerged dirty and gray. We locked the car, took our suitcases under our arms and made the long trek through sand toward the house.

Red police warnings were posted everywhere on the house. Large drifts had washed up on the porch. The paint was almost entirely gone. Steel braces were screwed into the front doors and fastened with a padlock. We walked around the porch and found one of the dining-room windows broken and nailed over with boards. The boards pulled out easily. Tato reached in and unlocked the window. It lifted, the weights rumbling down into their chambers. We walked past the dining chairs, around the big table and into the foyer. The sky barely lit up the colored glass around the front doors, casting an eerie illumination on the two bison still standing there. They seemed much smaller. In the living room the frail colors of morning began to spread behind the red couch. Blue glasses were on the coffee table. Checkers from an unfinished game were still on the chess board. I picked up one of the glasses and blew out the dust. With my finger I felt crystals of dried anisette.

"My God," Tato gasped, "do you realize somethin'? This place hasn't been touched since we left it."

"That couldn't be."

"Look!" He lifted the top of the RCA Victrola. Inside the green felt shone. The needle was still down on the 78 record. He lifted the needle and we squinted in the dim light to read the label. "Tangerine."

"I don't believe it. Zia never came back here. No one has been back here."

We went our separate ways, up and into the house, two men walking in the same dream. Thrown into a corner near the bolted French doors was a black tarlike flattened pile on top of which were the two pairs of blackened rubber beach shoes that Zia had bought us in Southampton. I lifted the blackened folds. They were swan water wings. In the kitchen there were unwashed coffee cups, and in the pantry I recognized Mr. Possilippo's crate in which we had carried Snow. As I walked upstairs, the wind in the attic wailed like a senile ghost, welcoming us home. Beds had not been made since we slept in them. I looked down at the sheets and the cream-colored blanket. Little drifts of sand had gathered in the folds where I had slept. I lifted the covers. There was a little shell.

I met Tato in the hallway. He turned the switch of the green-tulip light.

"Never used to be able to reach this," he said. The light did not come on. Tato's bottom teeth showed in a grimace of hurt. "Call me crazy. I can't explain it"—his voice choked—"there's just something sad about this place, being like a mausoleum like this, I mean the ashtrays are still goddamn full. Rugs faded on one end where the window is and mildewed on the other end where it was dark. That couch used to be dark red. Now it's like pink from the sun. Sand instead of dust. What a waste. I mean . . .

"I deserve nothin', right? I'm a half Puerto Rican nobody from

Brooklyn that came from her bum brother, but one day she takes me here to taste everything. She comes on like a fuckin' fairy godmother, she takes us here to taste it, then she splits, like who needs a couple of poor relatives? She leaves, and she leaves all this to rot because . . . because she doesn't *need* it. This green light; this is a Tiffany. *Tiffany.* Probably the whole goddamn ceiling downstairs is Tiffany. All the fixtures. I mean, she coulda sold something and helped somebody out with it. People suffered because she didn't sell a fuckin' piece of glass or a rug. She used it all for confetti. Happy New Year!"

For a moment he seemed to be on the verge of tears, but then he was laughing. "Happy New Year, Cello. Happy New Year." He opened the window on the landing and pushed out the shutters. "Happy New Year," he yelled to the gulls, then jumped down the stairs. "Where's the brooms?"

The sun broke over the horizon as we opened every door and window in the house and dusted everything. We shoveled the drifts of sand off the porch and set up the chairs. We opened the French doors of the big room and let down the awnings. They were rusted and caked with salt, but the canvas within the roll was as richly colored as ever. We pounded the red velvet couch and turned the cushions on their dark red side. We hung the salvageable sheets and towels in the sun out of every window. By noon we were starved, but beds were freshly made and driftwood was piled on the porch for the fireplace. We went to Southampton to eat and buy groceries. We tried to reach Zia again by phone several times; there was no answer. We bought kerosene lamps and candles at the paint store. The proprietor upon hearing our story advised us to stop at Long Island Lighting Company nearby.

"Look at this." Tato called me over to a pyramid of paint cans that were on sale. "White mold-resistant outdoor latex, half price. Should we do her a favor and paint the house? We could chip in for the paint."

"I don't know. I never did that kind of thing," I said.

"Well, what are we gonna do with ourselves out here for two weeks? I mean the season out here hasn't even started. Water's still cold for swimming."

"Fine with me," I said.

We stopped at the Long Island Lighting Company office and discovered the house was still in Zia's name. They gave us no trouble arranging to have the utilities turned on. That evening we ate a celebration dinner of Chinese take-out food on the porch in the light of hurricane lamps. The peepers in the pond screamed a million tiny screams.

Our tired bodies were flopped into our chairs. Tato looked like an escaped convict taking his first rest. The sun had gone down, but the water reflected the daylight left in the sky. A heron walked in the pond grass. Tato's eyes were pinned to it.

"What are you thinking about?" I asked. He dropped his feet from the railing.

"My wife," he said, honestly but reluctantly.

"You're married?"

"Divorced."

"I didn't know you were married. What kind of woman was she?"

"Oh," he breathed, "very pretty. You know, California. You've got to see California. If anything new happens, it probably started out there. There's like a spirit there, and I was all caught up in it that summer I met her. One of those classy-looking real neurotic ladies who really have a lot of balls and talent. A great dancer. She'll be famous. She deserves it. But it was crazy for a type like me to tangle with that kind of chick."

"You sound like she still means something to you."

"Well, she does in a way. Certain people are hung up on the truth, the truth about everything, and I think I'm one of them. It's my gift and my curse—the truth. Understand what I'm tryin' to bring out? Maybe she just wasn't the right person; not her fault. I mean pairing up is a wild thing. For me she was just not the one; not her fault. Was that the truth? See? I'm dedicated to the truth, but it's not dedicated to me." He laughed. "I'm crazy."

"I'm sorry to hear about your divorce."

"There's no sorry."

"Then nothing was lost?"

"Just the hopes that keep ya goin' day after day."

"There are new hopes." I felt foolish trying to support him. I was acting like a clergyman and I didn't want to.

"True, but the old hopes—they're dead, and they were nice and original." He smiled. "I don't believe in God like you. That makes dead hopes worse, doesn't it?"

"Don't you even wish there was a God?" I asked.

"I would hate it," Tato said, standing up. He frightened the heron. The bird spread its huge wings, its neck pointing east, frightening the sandpipers, which flew into a constellation that curled sharply west then southward. Tato yawned and walked into the blackness of the house. Our hurricane lamp was the only light for miles.

After three days of scraping, our muscles ached and our hands swelled. But when the first shock of white hit the thirsty gray shingles, we shared a powerful feeling of achievement. We painted alongside each other and talked. We talked about the schools we had gone to. Tato told me Aunt Silva had married again and that Tabs had died of a heart attack. Ruth inherited Mr. Possilippo's house. She went to live in the old man's apartment on the top floor and made a tomato garden on the roof. I told Tato about Lucille and my father, about Prefect Casaluce, my tennis lessons, Gabriella Ciascuno and her brother Roberto.

"Does it bother you that I'm not into believing in all that religion stuff?" Tato asked.

"It fascinates me, actually. I didn't always believe in God," I said as the paint brush slipped from my hand.

"But now you do, right?"

"I need a rag. What's the question? Do I believe in God? I should say yes."

"You *should* say it?"

"Well, it's always been a thorny question for me."

"Wipe your hands on my jeans. Where do you come out?"

"What do you mean, come out?"

"What's your final opinion on God, you know?"

My hesitation became a long silence. He let me off the hook and continued painting.

112

The porch roof was pitched, a visible part of the facade of the house, and we were unconsciously letting paint fall upon it. "Shit! I'm gonna get a drop cloth," Tato said, jumping like a chimp from the roof. He made his way down the beach toward the cracked asphalt and his Volkswagen. Like him, I jumped onto the sand from the roof, but the jump was not easy for me, though I was glad I tried it. I was trembling a little. The bay water looked delicious. I decided to swim until Tato returned. I undressed and ran toward the water, knowing it would be quite cold. It meant something suddenly. I gave the act importance—plunging in. The cold took my breath away.

As I came up out of the water gasping, I saw Tato pulling what looked like a red, white and blue parachute from a canvas bag. It puffed before the porch in drifts. The parachute was going to be our drop cloth.

"What were you looking for when you decided to become a priest?" Tato asked when we were back up on the roof painting.

"I had no choice. My father ran out of money. I had no place to go. Monsignor Ciascuno arranged it with his rich sister to pay my tuition at Nazzareno; and later with his influence I got into the North American College in Rome. It seemed the only thing to do. I had no choice." I was revealing it to myself as well.

"Do you mind if I ask you something personal? When you become a priest—how can I put this?—you're going to have to give up sex."

"Oh, I already have."

"Well, how do you manage to get through your day?"

"Huh? The way I'm doing now."

He poised his brush and looked at me quizzically. "Just the way you're doing now? You mean you don't engage in it?"

"Of course not."

"How long have you been . . . that way?"

"All my life," I said.

"Except you masturbate."

"No. It would be a sin."

"And the sin, what would that do to you? I don't understand."

"A sin is an offense against God, or mankind," I said.

"What difference does it make to you if you sin or not? You're not even so sure that God is there."

"Well . . ."

"And sex doesn't hurt mankind. It keeps him going, right?" Tato pressed.

"Well, I don't want to talk about it. It's much more complex—"

"Don't cop out on me, buddy."

"What do you want me to *say*? I don't need sex. I don't think about it."

"See, *that's* hard for me to understand."

"I'm not lying."

"I'm not saying you're lying," he said, "just that something's fishy. Now this comes out of my own ignorance maybe, but I don't see how anybody can really give up sex when they never let themselves be turned on to it in the first place. It's like havin' a baby stillborn and not slapping him." Tato's questions seemed to be casual, but he was relentless.

As he spoke, I was feeling dizzy. I even worried for a moment about falling off the roof, but I didn't want to let him know that. I painted on. My heart was beating faster, my stomach was queasy, a feeling of pressure came over my shoulders. I took a deep breath and suddenly felt like I could black out, and he caught on. "I feel sick."

"Okay." He quickly dropped his brush.

"How am I going to get down the ladder?"

"Let's wait up here till you feel steady."

"But the sun, maybe it's the sun."

Tato guided me down the ladder to a chair in the shade of the porch. He put a fat pillow behind my head, lifted my feet and went inside to make lunch. I let myself sink into the comfort of the cool pillow. The wind was cool. My face was cold. I wanted to cry with no idea why.

Tato came out with a tray of spinach salad, bread and beer. He placed the tray next to me, grabbed his bowl and fork and started eating. "I put a lot of salt on your salad. Eat up."

"In a minute."

"Feel any better?"

"I think so." I reached for my salad. "It must seem crazy to you that I say I don't believe in God but I practice chastity."

You don't hafta talk about it. Nothin' seems crazy to me. Maybe you just don't wanna *feel* anything. That's your privilege. People are all different. Take her."

"Who?"

He pointed toward the shore, where a woman and a yellow dog were walking. The light behind her was blinding, but as she moved south, she and the dog became more discernible. "She's been trying to get us to notice her for three days. What do you think she wants, Cello?"

"I haven't the vaguest."

"She's been hovering around. She was sittin' around the Volks yesterday."

"Do you think she wanted to *steal* something?" I asked.

He laughed. "She's at that age she wants something else."

"What age? What does she want?"

He grinned at me, then looked back to her. "She's just a kid," he said, avoiding the question. "Tell me something"—he turned his chair to me facing me head-on—"what would happen if you didn't go back to Italy?"

I looked away, shocked by his question. Ciascuno came instantly to mind. "Ciascuno," I said, "would be hurt—more than hurt."

"I'm askin' how *you* would feel."

"I don't know."

"Why do you care what this guy Ciascuno feels?"

"I owe it to him to discuss it. He has the knack of turning my doubts into proofs. He's more than my spiritual director."

"What's a spiritual director?"

"He advises me."

"Does he push you around?"

"No."

"It's up to you to stand up for your rights, to defend yourself," he said.

"Maybe that was the problem."

"What?"

"Maybe I have no identity to defend. Maybe I have to be steered or I'll just rot."

"Listen to me, cousin." He pulled his chair closer. "I'm worried about you. Do you understand what I'm sayin'?"

"Fox." The girl called her dog. "Fox."

I turned to look at her. I must have stared longer than I realized, because when I turned back to Tato, he stood up smiling and walked inside with the lunch plates and beer bottles. Two egrets were perched on a dead branch near the pond to which the girl and her dog seemed headed. The sun peeked under a cloud, trimming the willows with yellow. Poppies bled inside the tall grass. She was barefoot; her hair matched the color of the dog—yellow.

I leaned back in my chair, mesmerized by the breeze humming through the rose trellis, the waters flashing, the gulls riding invisible mountains of wind and Fox, the yellow dog, running after the yellow-haired girl with the dress fluttering between her legs. When Tato reappeared, the girl and her dog were headed for the rushes and the cracked asphalt.

"I'm going for a ride," Tato said flatly.

He left me there, making his way toward the blinding bay, then he started walking briskly toward the cracked asphalt. She lingered there, leaning against his Volkswagen. The dog ran to Tato. I slipped my foot from the chair and stood up. Tato played with the dog as they spoke, then he got into the car and drove off away from them.

After a dinner of hamburgers that night, Tato trimmed his beard and put on a clean shirt. He said once again that he was going for a ride, but I suspected he was meeting her. He came home after midnight.

By noon the next day my body was sunburned. My face glowed like an electric bulb. I would stand out before the Holy Pontiff at my ordination in white vestments and a tomato face. We planned a ride to the village to rest from painting and the sun.

Copper-colored people in summer cottons floated in and out of the tiny shops of Southampton Village. Sparrows fed near the

116

sidewalks in complete trust of pedestrians. Tato helped me buy two pairs of jeans. He treated me to a giant sundae with chocolate fudge.

She passed the frame of the ice cream parlor window, dressed this time in a white silk dress. Her hair was long and wavy, like Botticelli's Venus. She wore those floppy rubber thongs on her otherwise bare feet. Her dress was antique. It fit badly, but that only served to exaggerate her good looks. This white dress had once been quite formal. She wore it as if she knew it might fall off her at any minute. The V-shaped collar was so wide that one of her shoulders actually came out of the dress. She passed swiftly, Fox following like a scarf along the ground. They disappeared, out of frame, as abruptly as they appeared.

Tato held out a spoonful of banana split, chocolate dripping off the cherry. It was too big for my mouth.

"No thanks," I said.

We stopped at the liquor store. Tato bought an expensive bottle of French wine.

The car top was down as we drove back. I leaned my head back to watch the elms going by. I thought of Italy. Italy was like Gabriella, centuries of instinct in her and luxurious, but the girl with the yellow hair and the yellow dog was America. She walked like the wind, as if there were thousands of miles before her. She was like the snowy egrets Zia told me about who fly from place to place with no possessions, like angels.

Tato pressed the brake. I looked up, surprised to see her up ahead with the yellow dog, hitchhiking.

"Should we pick them up?" he asked.

"No," I said instantly. We flew past her. I caught hurt in her face.

"You afraid of dogs?" Tato asked.

"No."

"Then you must be afraid of girls. She's pretty far out, isn't she?" He mussed my hair. It surprised me that he would do that. I ran my fingers through it to restore it. My hair was beginning to grow over my ears. I parted it with my fingers. Then Tato reached out and messed it again.

"I don't like that," I said flatly.

"I'm sorry."

I leaned back again to watch the trees, but they were gone. Tato reached out again and gently brushed back my hair, the way Ciascuno once did in the Lamborghini. Only this time I didn't tighten up. I let the touch pass into me like a ray of light.

Next morning I woke up to wind whistling through the screens. The temperature had dropped during the night. The bedding felt crisp and cool as I slid out. Gulls shrieked overhead. Tato leaned into my doorway. "Today we drink the wine," he said. I yawned. The odor of sea was coming through the screens. "We'll paint this morning, then take a swim and eat lunch near the pond."

"When did you plan all this?" I asked, half awake.

"Yesterday, when I bought the wine." He grinned.

"I'm too sunburned."

"We'll be under the trees."

I worked on the shady side of the house. At noon I put away my things and followed Tato into the bay. Afterward we showered. Tato came downstairs dripping wet and totally nude.

"Let's go," he said matter-of-factly.

"Aren't you going to wear something?" I asked.

"Too hot," he answered.

I kept my bathing suit on. I was suspicious of Tato's nudity, yet I willingly followed him to the oaks, to the ferny mound of dappled sunlight where we threw down our sheet and our lunch. We drank our wine and ate our cheese.

I had never noticed the overgrown garden behind the tall rhododendrons. That garden was what the girl probably had come to see every day. Peonies bloomed and wisteria hung off the oaks in blue clusters. Clematis vines grew wild, blooming white and blue into the green of maples and dogwoods. Willows danced like crazy ladies, and the phragmites waved toward the bay. The oaks let out new leaves, wrinkled as bats' wings, and above the oaks clouds flew on the wind. Blue jays, drunk on berries, screamed as they zoomed through the forest of trees.

Tato seemed comfortable in his nudeness, lying upon the clean white sheet. I felt no need to remove my still wet suit. It would dry in the sun, which fell like flower petals through the trees, spotting our backs. We lit cigarettes. The smoke rose in lavender ribbons from our hands into the branches. We lay on our stomachs, smoking and drinking wine. I blew smoke on a young fern.

"They move by themselves, these things," Tato said dreamily, "especially when they've just uncurled. That's when they're nervous."

"There's that girl," I interrupted. "She ducked behind the marsh reeds. I *saw* her."

"Where?" Tato sprang up. "I don't see her."

"You will. She's got to come back around, or else she has to go into the water."

"The dog with her?"

"Yes."

"She definitely wants to get fucked," he mumbled. The word paralyzed me.

She came up over a dune past the phragmites. She was barefoot, wearing an old blue nylon dress, and over it a short-sleeved dark blue sweater. He hair seemed even longer and so yellow, like the dog's, except hers was flying up behind the sun. "Here, Fox." I couldn't believe my ears. It was Tato who called. Tato shouted it again. "Here, Fox." She stopped in her tracks.

"Shut up," I commanded.

"Here, Fox," he called again, then ducked. I pressed down flat upon the sheet, knowing that there was very little I could do to stop him.

"You are going to embarrass me," I said.

"She's coming." He ducked down again.

"Put on your suit. Cover yourself."

"Shut up. She's just a girl." The dog appeared before she did, wagging his tail. When she appeared through the reeds, she was smiling at us. She came directly to the sheet. Up close, I could see the blue dress was printed with violets.

"Hi." She squatted inside the dress on the brink of the white sheet as if she didn't even notice that Tato was naked.

"This is my cousin," Tato said.

"Hello."

"His name is Cello."

She stared at me a moment, then turned back to Tato. "Why are you always teasing him?"

"My cousin?" Tato asked.

"No. Fox."

"I'll tease you too, if you feel neglected." He laughed.

"I'll bet."

Tato gently wrapped his hand around her ankle, and immediately I realized they had been together before. His penis began to change shape.

"Put on your bathing suit," I reprimanded.

"Don't worry." She smiled at me. Her teeth were perfect. "My name's May."

"Say hi," Tato ordered me.

"Hello," I muttered, "how do you do." She laughted at that.

I knew this was an occasion of sin, something I would have to confess if I didn't act to remove myself. In a few seconds I had passed the point of no return. No one said a word. Tato's hand had moved up her dress. The sun dappled her face. She lifted to her knees and pulled the sweater and the dress over her head. In one motion, she was naked. She reached out to my face. Her thumb touched my mouth. She leaned over Tato's body to kiss me. Something broke inside me at the touch of her lips, spilling warmth. Tato was pulling down my bathing suit. I brushed his hand away, but he kept at it. Kissing, our heads fell lost in the cool earth, crushing the fern. Tato was yanking my suit from my ankles. My whole body shook. My hands lost control. I didn't know where my hands were. My heart was a huge bell inside my chest. There was agony in her kisses. Out of the corner of my eye I saw Tato lying with his face between her legs. What is happening? I asked myself. For a moment I felt the power to reverse it, but I let the moment go. I willed to be there, nude with them.

Unbelievably, I had a vision of myself upon my knees in my cassock confessing it to Ciascuno. Ironically, that impelled me forward. Next thing I knew, Tato was inside her. I was face to face with him as he was having intercourse with her. He smiled. He bit his lip, then said softly, "Cello . . . Cello, it's wonderful. Oh . . . Oh . . ." He was coming. I watched his face grow tight and pale, his skin radiant, like St. Francis of Assisi. Sweat beaded his brow.

"You . . . now you, Cello." He took my hand. "C'mon." He breathed heavily. His smile said that it was all too simple. "C'mon, Cello."

Her eyes were still closed. I knelt in Tato's place. Her knees came up. Fox tilted his head curiously. She opened her eyes. Sweat poured into them. Her eyelashes thick and yellow brushed like fans in the sunlight. Her breasts were hard and pink. I leaned toward her. The screaming blue jays hurled themselves. Tato's hand brushed the hair from my forehead and held it back from my eyes. The sun fell through the trees like flower petals upon my back. Tato's hand slipped between my buttocks, leading my penis into place. His hand came down from my head, pressing on my back, pushing me forward, forward.

"Oh," I said, "oh."

May said nothing, rocking her head.

Tato's mouth was on my ear. "You're in," he whispered. "Now pull out. Yeah, push back in. Out again. In. Out. Yeah. Push. Don't be afraid. Good. Push. Push. Again. Yeah. Again. Again. Again."

"Oh . . ."

"Don't worry."

"Oh!"

"C'mon."

"I'm going to . . ."

"Let it go."

"I'm going to . . ."

Her thighs rubbed my hips. I yelped. I couldn't keep down the groans rising up from my lungs as my rod melted, as I came, all tingling from my heels up to my buttocks.

That night the moon appeared, a sharp crescent; the remainder of it glowed like black jelly. We sat without conversation on the porch by the light of a gooseneck lamp. Tato read a law book, while my eyes drifted over my breviary to the bay. I felt no guilt. On the contrary, my thoughts traveled up into the glowing night. I felt fully apt to be a man. More than that, I felt not alone for the first time, like a star in a constellation among other stars, part of a shape of a whole, upheld magnetically by others.

Tato's hair was curled from the dampness, but his face was peaceful in the orange light. He was easy in my presence. What a day it had been! A thousand times more different than any other day of my life. I was a new man on a new planet. The cool night stretched out, empty, clean. I didn't care if I disinherited the past. I longed for the future. I wanted to run loose into it like a wild beast.

"Do you think I could get a job in this country?"

Tato looked up from his book with amazement. "Sure," he answered.

"I'll have to go back to Rome, just for a couple of days." He watched me intently. "Do you think Zia would let us live here?" I continued.

"It's only a summer place. But for the summer, why not?"

"Does it shock you to hear me talk like this?"

"No, man. Will it be easy to do what you got to do in Rome?"

"No."

Tato offered no words of comfort. In a way, he dreaded Ciascuno too.

Tato drove me to the airport. Swallows leapt and dove like roller-coasters across the Long Island Expressway. We said practically nothing to each other the whole drive. At Exit 60 small-craft airplanes, like toys overhead, were gliding and tilting in the sky. Other convertibles passed us, tops down, one full of young people snapping fingers and singing to the rock and roll on their radio. America was so blessed. I swore to myself to become part of it. I swore it over and over, and just to make it definite, when we took the last exit to the airport, I swore it out loud, upon my own soul, that I would be back in a few days. We didn't say goodbye; we smiled instead. He let me out in front of the Alitalia building.

The flight was delayed for hours. It was after midnight by the time I left.

I reached Rome the next afternoon in the rain. From the airport I called Ciascuno's office.

"He's here," his secretary offered.

"Don't bother him. Just book me for a confession tomorrow."

"Just a confession?"

"Yes."

Short and sweet. I would take care of the whole thing in confession. At first I had planned to confess the sin of fornication; that would force him to recommend postponement of my ordination. I could then say that I wanted to spend time in the United States. Then I'd write after a few months requesting dispensations for sub-deaconate and deaconate on the excuse that I had changed my mind. But Ciascuno deserved my honesty. So I made a firm decision to tell him outright that I didn't want to continue with the priesthood. I would say it all in the dark of confession where my every word would be under the seal of the Sacrament of Penance. He would never again be able to pursue the issue after he gave me absolution. Besides, in the dark I didn't have to look into those gray eyes.

The sun shone through the Roman rain. As my cab sped in the warm downpour, rumbling on cobblestone streets toward the North American College, I tried to see the expressions of the Italians on the streets. The fountains blew whiteness into the rain, and flowers were everywhere. I tried to ignore the majestic colors shooting from the side streets, where the sun was throwing gold from the west. I tried to concentrate on my mission, to leave the priesthood and the Church forever, but it didn't work. I wrung my chilly hands and closed my eyes to the beautiful city, radiant in the aftershower.

The shrill cries of a knife sharpener on the street outside pierced the shutters of Ciascuno's office. The rain had long since stopped. It was eleven A.M., and the day was going to be hot. His secretary had closed the shutters against the sun. For confessions there was no greeting. His secretary let me into the dark room. I knew from habit that Ciascuno was hidden in the confessional compartment behind the prie-dieu. I knelt there and whispered into the black silk screen, "Bless me, Father, for I have sinned. My last confession was two and one half weeks ago. Since that time . . . I have neglected to read the Divine Office . . . several times."

"Deliberately, Cello?"

"Yes."

"You failed to read the Divine Office how many times?"

"Five. . . . Monsignor, I—"

"Willfully?"

"Yes."

"Go on."

I took a deep breath. "Monsignor . . . I have something to say . . . that is very difficult for me."

"Have you finished reciting your sins?"

"I—No . . . I—"

"Shall we get through that first?"

"All right. I also committed a sin against the sixth commandment." I could see his profile now through the screen.

"What was the species of sin?"

"Monsignor, I had intercourse—"

"Intercourse? With a woman?"

"A girl," I answered.

"A child?"

"No. Not a child. A woman."

"In America?"

"Yes."

"Was she married?"

"No, I don't think so."

"Fornication?"

"Yes, Monsignor."

"The number of times?"

"Once."

"*Dio, Dio* . . . Cello, *perchè?*"

"Please, let's not use personal names, Monsignor, or else I don't know how I'll get through this." There was a long silence after I said that. He had taken out a handkerchief and wiped his brow. His breathing was getting loud, the way it used to be mornings when we sat waiting to say mass in the sacristy at Nazzareno, with his crusty eyes and bad breath. Now he sat in a black caped robe with purple silk piping, soft shoes of silk, his hair flowing back like silver, and his breath sweetened by mouthwash.

The odor of Italy came through the shutters, the odor of his Persian rug, the dry-cleaned odor of his robes.

"Do you remember the recommendation that you must be pure at least six months before ordination?" he asked.

"Yes."

"Then *why?*" he demanded.

I couldn't imagine an answer. I heard the sound of a motorbike on the cobblestones.

"What am I to do now? You tell me," he said.

"I have made a decision, Monsignor."

"How could you have fallen into such a trap?" He shifted impatiently in his chair.

"There was no trap."

"What?" The confessional compartment creaked from his squirming. He wasn't hearing me. "Do you know this girl—this woman?"

"No, but can I say something? I've thought about it and I have decided not to be ordained tomorrow."

"This is incredible! You want to postpone your ordination?"

"I want to give up the priesthood altogether." The knife sharpener's cry . . .

"Let me give the penance," Ciascuno said assertively.

"Monsignor, there is a defect in my faith. There always was."

"There's a defect in everyone's faith. Before ordination, everything happens, crazy things. Don't worry, you will take ordination tomorrow. I don't subscribe to the opinion about six months of sexual abstinence. You have proved yourself to me long ago. I don't need their medieval rules to guide me in my decisions. I am your spiritual director. Do you hear, Cello? I have the authority to direct you. I'll take responsibility for this decision." His breath ran out.

"Monsignor, please listen carefully. I don't *want* to be ordained.

I don't *want* to. It has nothing to do with this sin I am confessing. My volition is no good."

"You expect everything to be perfect?"

"I don't believe in God. I know I don't."

"That again?"

"Well, of course."

"Cello, you are no different than the rest of us. If anything, you are better. Do you know that? You are more fit to be ordained than any of us."

"I don't question my *fittingness*. It's the fittingness of the priesthood I question. I don't want it. I have no desire." My whisper turned to full voice.

"What do you desire?"

"Nothing."

"Don't be afraid. Speak."

"I am not afraid."

"Have you discussed this with anyone?"

"No."

"Did this girl know you were about to become a priest?"

"No. I did discuss something—"

"With whom?"

"My cousin, Tato."

"Does he know you were together with her?"

"Yes. He—"

"He what?"

"He was present."

"He *witnessed* it?"

"Yes."

Ciascuno shifted again. "He took *part*?"

"*Yes.*"

"He *touched* you?"

"Well . . ." It was hot. I sighed. I wanted to be out in the wind.

"Did he *touch* you?"

"He touched me briefly . . . yes, briefly."

"Why didn't you tell me this?" he hissed.

"Does it matter?"

"It changes the species of the sin. You know that."

"Only if I *willed* it, but I didn't. I didn't foresee that he would touch me. I didn't *will* it. Therefore, its species is irrelevant."

"Let me decide what is irrelevant. There could be a triangular affair here, homosexuality, fornication and possibly adultery. . . . Is *he* married?"

"He was. He's divorced, I think. Separated."

"Married validly?"

"I don't know, Monsignor."

It was difficult to hold my anger with his preposterous bluffing. My heart pumped. I found it hard to breathe, to get enough air. I hated being on my knees. I wanted to stand. My shoes scraped against the floor as I fidgeted. He could hear my struggle.

"Do you want to stop—to continue this confession another time?" he asked.

"No."

"I would like you to release me from the seal of confession so I may discuss this," he said quietly.

"I'd rather finish it here, Monsignor. Please."

"Clumsily? This way? With all the emotions that are present?"

"I don't care how. I want to end it here."

"You have tied my hands. How am I going to help you? Cello?" I smelled his perspiration. He switched on the tiny electric fan near his head. Its rubber blades whirled. "I should let you destroy yourself," he whispered. A half minute passed in which the only sound was the whirring rubber blades. When he spoke, his voice was the old Ciascuno's. "Cello?"

"Yes?" I answered softly.

"Don't run away, please. I understand you."

"It's just that, back in America, I felt the whole world had moved ahead all those years without me. I've got to get out from under this life that has been designed for me against my own will."

"Against your will?"

"I dread solitude. I want the love of another person."

"And no one here loves you?"

"Here? That's different love. I need more. Don't you think it would be a terrible mistake to become a priest with these needs?" I said.

"It would not be a mistake. You are human. Nor would it be a mistake to wait, to think, to pause, to postpone. You are destroying everything in a minute here, in this darkness. Let me talk to you later."

"No. I want to destroy it. I want to. Clearly, selfishly."

I expected him to give in to me, to sympathize, but his voice grew tighter, colder. "I might have predicted this ending," he said. "I was the naïve one, to think that your honesty would save you." His anger was swelling. The heat of it was radiating through the black silk screen. I imagined being caught in the explosion of his pain, the confession compartment splintering, our blood, our flesh and our bones steaming in the debris. But he only coughed. I waited until he cleared his throat. "This woman may have had a disease. Be on the lookout for symptoms."

"Look out for *what?*" I asked.

"Pus or sores on your penis." He had no air. He spoke with his larynx.

"Are you all right? Monsignor?"

"Do you have anything else to confess?"

"No."

"Then you are through." In Latin he began the absolution. I recited the act of contrition. Our words mingled with the sound of the rubber blades of the fan. When he finished there was no sound but the whir. I stood and leaned toward the screen of the compartment. "*Addio*, Roberto," I whispered into the screen.

"*Bastardo.*" He was crying.

Outside the confessional, I paused, looking at the compartment as though he were a trapped, wounded tiger inside. I knew perfectly well what I had done to him. Run, I told myself. And I dared actually to run, out his door, down the white marble stairs, and into the sun, across the piazza. The wind like a drowning man, was grabbing at my cassock. I mumbled as I ran: "*Addio. Addio, Italia. Addio, Roberto Ciascuno. Addio Mater Ecclesia.*"

CHAPTER V

HOME. I remember during the last week of spring semester at Nazzareno and North American, the use of the word "home" increased. One heard it whispered in classrooms and shouted in locker rooms. Home. The word always made my spirits sink. Now the world lifted me.

"Would you like a return ticket, sir?"

"No. I'm going home. Home. New York. One way." I wore my white shirt open showing a yellow tee shirt. I carried a raincoat.

My flight was delayed, and they predicted a two-hour wait. I eyed a seat under the clock and prepared to camp there when the loudspeaker sounded: "Lufthansa Flight 202 for Geneva now boarding at gate twelve. Passengers please have tickets ready at the gate." Many years had passed since my train ride. How easy it would be to switch my ticket and to appear in Geneva with a raincoat on my arm and a cab waiting, to force my father, at his front door, to look into the eyes of a man instead of a child, to show him how I survived by my own cleverness and owed him nothing.

I went to the Lufthansa counter, telling myself that I was only investigating. But in a few minutes my Alitalia flight was canceled and I had a ticket for Geneva, gate twelve, with a Swissair reservation to New York for later that night. As my flight lifted off the runway, I felt a little trapped by my own impulsiveness.

At my father's house an old man shuffled toward the door, wearing house slippers. He held a newspaper and glasses in his hand. A cuckoo clock on the wall was ten minutes slow.

"Manfredi residence?" I asked.

"What do you want?"

"Mr. Manfredi."

"Who are you?"

"Cello Manfredi."

He stared motionless. His glasses slipped. He caught them. "What do you want? You shoulda called. *Lucille*. Come in. *Lucille*," he called toward the stairs.

The living room smelled of furniture wax and freshly vacuumed rugs.

"How are your studies? *Lucille*." He nearly screamed her name this time.

"I didn't come to see Lucille." He glared at my audacity, taking me in, then turning away.

"Why didn't you call? We coulda been in China."

"I'm sorry, but you needn't worry, because there's no chance I'll ever come here again." I could feel the anger mounting in me. He sensed it.

"So what's gonna happen? I'll never *see* you again?" He smiled.

"You never saw me in the past. What chance is there for the future? I've come to say goodbye while we're both alive."

"Wise guy. Where you going?"

130

"Home. The United States."

"Are you a priest?"

"Do I look like one?"

"*Lucille!*" he screamed again.

"I want to ask you a question before your Lucille comes. Why did you keep the money Zia provided for me?"

"What do you think she gave me—a fortune?"

"Enough for me to finish school."

He turned away. "This house is the end of everything for Lucille," he said, shaking. "She has nothing after this. We needed the money. We needed it to eat. I didn't gamble it away in Monte Carlo." My eyes automatically went to the splendid chandelier. He followed them up. "Why should I give you an accounting?" he said angrily.

"Why not? It was my money."

"Your money?" He laughed. "You come here to say goodbye— 'I am a man, tut, tut.' Okay, you pay me for your delivery, pipsqueak, pay me for the hospital. Okay? Pay me for the baby food, the apartment. Do you think I'd have married your mother if it wasn't for you? Pay me for that, for the years I wasted. Do you know where I found her?"

My stomach felt like it would cramp. I turned toward the front door.

"Oh, he doesn't want to hear this part. I *found* her on the *streets.* That's how I met your mother. Okay? Do you get the picture? I felt sorry for your mother. She was a baby, fourteen when I found her. I was like her father and her mother. Fourteen. Straight out of an orphanage, a runaway from a little Southern shithole. Pay me for that. Big man comes here to ask questions." He was trembling. "You look down on me because I'm not like those bourgeois jerks whose sons spit on them because they make their kids their slaves. I get blamed 'cause I *didn't* hang on to you. I never needed you; you should get down on your knees and thank God for that, you little bastard." He was as white as the white bristles on his unshaven face. His fingers were tobacco stained.

"Did you . . . ever love my mother?"

"In the beginning, sure I did."

"Are you my father?" He was surprised by the question.

"You look like me." A smile crept over his face. He lit a cigarette, shuffling in his slippers toward the table. He looked so small. But he had always been small, I realized. How little he mattered. I reached for the front doorknob.

"Wait. Lucille won't believe that you came and left without even seeing her." He tried to inject familiarity into his voice. "C'mon, say goodbye to her."

"Goodbye," I said, ignoring his plea. I shook his hand. It was damp.

"Jesus, you're tall." Those were the last words he said to me.

As I closed the door behind me, I caught a glimpse of Lucille coming into the room. She wore a white sweater clasped around her shoulders. She carried a book. I left them both to their reading, clicking the storm door shut. The Swiss air was cold around my head. I was glad to see my cab waiting.

I looked down as we came in above New York City. It was sunless. The idea of people existing like Lilliputians in apartments piled almost into the clouds made me feel queasy. I recalled Ciascuno saying once, in all seriousness, that the United States and Australia were work camps.

As we disembarked, the American men looked like rich farmers in their poor-fitting suits. The women seemed decorated rather than dressed, like objects at a fair. Why did it all seem so different than a few weeks ago?

Tato's dark beard and eyes jumped out as I walked into the terminal. He grabbed me to him strongly, pulling me out of the crowd. "We're going to my mother's for dinner. That okay?"

"I guess so."

"I have to take an exam this afternoon. You can sleep at my apartment. We'll go out to Jessup later."

There was a welcoming committee at Fay's. Albert the hairdresser whipped open the door of our car the moment it stopped. Silver-gray curls swept tightly over his ears. He wore a cowboy

132

shirt and golden chains around his neck. A Gemini medallion spun in my face as he shook my hand. Aunt Silva had grown huge. Her breasts no longer pointed briskly upward but hung like jelly inside the tent of her dress. Her face was a balloon; her eyelashes long and fake. She was a fat circus lady.

Other faces gradually came into focus: Ruth's hair had turned completely gray, the liquor-store man had no teeth in his smile.

Dinner was *arroz con pollo*. Albert and Aunt Silva were disappointed when we excused ourselves to go to Manhattan.

We climbed the el, up two sets of iron stairs that trembled in the wind, up to the train station that was a mere narrow platform swaying high above billboards and the setting sun. I was afraid to look down. A train rumbled in, covered with graffiti. Inside too, the graffiti violated every inch of the car, even the ads for cigarettes, headaches, and hemorrhoids. The passengers ignored Tato as if they had seen him before, but they stared continuously at me. When we descended into the dark tunnel of the subway, the noise was intolerable.

I closed my eyes, envisioning Rome's wide piazzas, people sitting near ancient trees sipping wine. I thought of Ciascuno the first day I had met him, sitting in the big chair under the sacristy clock at Nazzareno. "Forgiveness is the rarest virtue of Italians," he once said. "We forgive with our lips, we pretend forgiveness, but nothing is ever the same in our hearts again."

Tato's room in Greenwich Village was a serene place. Bare Victorian windows looked out to back yards of ailanthus trees growing out of slate. I could hear Neapolitan dialect floating up from the yard. An opera singer, somewhere above us, practiced her scales. Gently, trying to appear unrushed, Tato let me into his apartment and left. The front sitting room of his apartment looked down the street to the Hudson River. And there loomed the bow of a massive white passenger ship, resplendent in the purple dusk. Its presence was a comfort, a promise that escape was possible.

The simplicity of the room, the smells blowing in from the river and the noises of the restaurant below were comforting, but I felt I was soon going to have diarrhea. I opened the refrigerator, poured milk into a glass and walked to the bathroom. I looked at myself in the mirror. I needed a shave. My hair was disheveled. My eyes were tired. I didn't recognize myself. A wave of nausea came over me as I saw the features of my father. I knew I was his son.

After a while I fell upon Tato's divan. My face touched a chenille bedspread. Was it blue? I pulled back to see. Yes. Blue. Could it possibly have been the one from—how long ago?—when Mr. Possilippo flew pigeons and grew tomatoes? When my mother was fresh in her grave. That grave was nearer now than it had been in years, though by now she was bones. Ugly as it was, the thought of her bones nearby comforted me, as did the silent white ship and the blue chenille spread and the cool milk inside.

When I awoke, I dug out the paper Ciascuno had given me weeks ago and dialed Zia's number.

"Hello?" It was a man's voice.

"Hello, this Cello Manfredi. May I speak with my aunt?"

"I'm sorry, Signor Manfredi. We are no longer employed with Signora Manfredi."

"Is she ill?"

"She *was* ill." He paused. "But she is well again, and she did not leave word."

"Is she in the United States?"

"I think so, yes."

"Do you know of anyone who would know where?"

"No, sir."

We stuffed the Volkswagen with our things, tied Tato's bike to the rear-bumper rack and took off into the night with the top down. Mozart was playing on the radio. Tato was eager and laughing. His hair whipped about his face. "We made it," he kept saying as I watched him tapping out Mozart on the steering wheel, as if it were rock. I think he thought I would enjoy the Mozart; I might have if he hadn't insisted on talking above it.

"When you were in Italy, I got us a job for the summer."

"A job?"

"As parkies, starting July."

"Parkies?"

"We're going to park cars for a disco in Southampton. That okay?"

"I don't care."

"I hope you don't mind if I tell you you look shitty." I didn't answer. "I'll shut up if you want, too. Should I lower the radio?"

"If you like."

"You sure you're okay?"

"I'm tired." It took effort to answer him.

"Maybe you're gettin' a bug, a cold."

"Maybe." He looked at me as if he expected me to say more. I closed my eyes.

I felt better wearing sunglasses, even though Jessup Neck had been clouded over for several days. We put finishing touches on the house, using up the last drop of paint. I forced every stroke and was relieved when we threw all the empty cans in the town dump.

There was no sign of May and Fox. I wondered what happened to her and I wondered when Tato would announce that he was off to town to find her. I wished he would go. I needed to be alone. On my fourth morning I awoke at dawn. I took the bike and pedaled along North Sea Road toward town. In the village I wheeled the bike on foot to the Buttery and had coffee and a roll. When I was pulling the bike away from the wall, I looked up to see a woman smiling at me. She wore pigtails wrapped around her head, white shoes and a black waitress dress with a zipper that ran the whole way down the front. She carried a very large leather bag with a hairbrush sticking out of it. It was May.

"Don't you remember me?" she asked.

"Oh, I'm sorry."

"Where's your cousin?"

"He's at the house."

"You're peeling." She pulled a piece of skin from my nose.

"Oh, am I?"

"My tan is going down the drain too, now that I'm working inside."

"That's wonderful."

"Somethin's gonna hafta pay for this," she said, holding out her hand. I removed my sunglasses and looked down at a large ring with a pretty light blue stone. "It's sixty-five dollars, and they gave me one with a scratch on the stone. It's such a gyp."

"Is this a college ring?"

"High school." She laughed. "God, *college*. Well, I guess I won't be seeing you and your cousin—if he's really your cousin—so tell him I'm not working with my dad anymore. That's how I was hanging around Jessup, in case you didn't know. So we're through with that job. My dad cleans pools."

"Oh. How's Fox?"

"Wasn't he a cute dog? He's the dog from the house we were working at, but I *loved* him. He'd follow me anywhere. That dog was so lonely. Tell your cousin I work at Mickey's Diner now, in Westhampton Beach."

I smiled, said goodbye and stepped around her, putting my sunglasses back on. I smiled as I wheeled my bike to the road, smiled as I jumped on. My legs were trembling, so were my arms. My feet couldn't find the pedals. I kept smiling all the way to North Sea Road, past the elms, until my smile cracked somewhere near the open bay.

On Jessup, all the cherry blossoms had died. The tuberous foliage had flattened with exhaustion. We underwent a spell of cloudiness. The days were at their longest, full of interminable gray light with only a thin shock of color at sundown. It was a mere fifty-five degrees. It seemed impossible that we had been swimming a few weeks earlier and burning in the sun.

We bought Marine surplus woolen trousers. I felt uncomfortable wearing them, but they helped me keep warm. My hands were like ice all the time. I wanted to talk very little, which forced Tato into a self-conscious silence. I sensed his annoyance, but I could do little to change it. We made fires at night, and though they heated my clothing, I still had chills. I couldn't imagine May anymore the way she was in the fern grove now that I had met the girl with the short black waitress dress and the high school ring. I avoided the fern grove.

The evening of the second week of cloudiness, the sky brightened to green and the sun turned the cliffs golden. An electric outline of lavender vibrated around the dark pines, and the water was jade, touched with reflections of sky that were the color of my father's eyes. I was as depressed as the morning Ciascuno took me for a walk to talk to me about the existence of God.

I lay awake all night in fear, and fell asleep at dawn. It was still very early morning when Tato bounced into my bedroom. "There's not a cloud in that sky." I rolled over and looked out. He was right, but I had no enthusiasm. "Hear those airplanes? What d'ya say we take the drop cloth to the edge of the cliff and spread it out for them to see? And we can get our tans back laying on top of it."

"I don't know. I'm cold. You mean the parachute?"

"Yeah. C'mon, man. Warm up. The sun is back."

Tato carried the parachute in the duffel bag on his shoulder, sweating under its weight. I must have lost weight; my bathing suit was loose at my waist.

"C'mon. Get happy," he puffed. I tried to smile just to get him off my back. The sun was blinding after its long absence, and its warmth did not affect the breeze, which was cooler as we neared the point.

"Here," Tato finally said, dropping the bag onto the sand. We weren't close enough to the edge to see the rocks about ninety feet below, but I could hear sounds of water hitting them. I could see Shelter Island five miles away, sitting on top of the wind-rippled bay.

Tato was right. It was a beautiful idea to lie upon silken clouds of red, white and blue, overlooking the bay. As I helped him pull the chute from the canvas bag, the material came out, gathering at our feet like clouds of whipped cream. He was right. It would look spectacular to the planes above. It's true I was cold and tired, but maybe it was time to step out, to do light, mindless things.

The wind gently lifted the blue section against our bodies, turning us into art nouveau statues. Then the blue section slipped away and fluttered overhead. We were inside a blue cloud. We laughed like children. I thought of the time, so many years ago, when we were thrashing with our swan wings in the bay. We pulled and pulled and watched the cloud turn red. Tato's laughter echoed inside the cloud. When the white section filled, it was blinding. Tato

137

laughed, stretching toward me. "Hold on or we'll lose it." I tried to grab a fistful of the white fabric, but it lifted too high into a shape that dwarfed us. The red panel then filled up with a bursting sound and flashed orange in the sun.

"Get out," Tato yelled, and he wasn't joking.

"But we'll lose it," I yelled back, trying to grab hold.

"Let the fucking thing go," he repeated. But I had let go. The problem was that I was standing on it. The chute was lifting. I quickly rolled out, free on the sand. I caught a glimpse of Tato rolling free too. Still I was moving, tangled in something—string. Then I couldn't see Tato. I called out for him. Suddenly with a crack the chute filled entirely into a monstrous red, white and blue umbrella. I came to my feet only to find myself being pulled backwards. Now I could see Tato running behind me, reaching, grabbing at me. Then he leaped, tackling me. He held me around the legs, but the chute dragged us both through the sand. He tried to help me out of the lines as we sped along, but the strings were tangled around my leg. I saw blood coming out of my hands, legs and feet. Tato's back was bleeding. Stones and shells in the sand were cutting us.

"Lift your leg," he cried. I tried to. He was working madly in spite of the sand spraying in his face, when I slipped out of his hands. Suddenly, I don't know how it happened, I was on my feet and the chute was still pulling me faster than ever. I slipped string after string over my head, and still I wasn't free. My feet were cut badly. I couldn't stop running.

I tried to understand the system of my entanglement as I ran with the chute, but there was none. Then I realized the chute had passed the edge of the cliff. I was going to go with it. I watched in terror as it pulled me over the edge. I recall only a few seconds of looking down, legs dangling, the terrible vision of the rocks, and Tato reaching for me, leaning farther, then going off the cliff with me, voluntarily. Tato's eyes full of fear and courage, the bursting muscles, the craziness in his hands, fingers trembling, failing him as they struggled for mine.

Strong updrafts caught the chute, lifting me up from the cliff and Tato. I flew like a pendulum, over the rocks below, and felt myself slipping free of the strings. Suddenly I plunged into the cold water, going under immediately. My feet touched sand. I pushed up. Just as my head split the surface of the sea, the meteor-like shadow fell on me; behind it came the chute, softly landing, touching like a collapsing tent, covering me. Tato was in the water screaming my name over and over somewhere under the chute. Tato's head appeared, strangely shrouded in blue. We made eye contact, then he swam under water to check my legs for strings, then he shot up before me gasping.

"You tangled still?"

"Don't think so."

"Are you hurt?"

"I don't know." I wasn't getting enough oxygen. He led me out from under the chute. I paddled behind him toward the beach. It wasn't far. The chute was drifting out to sea like a giant jellyfish, and we were on a small beach under the cliff.

Tato's chest was scraped and bleeding. When he turned to go back to the house, his back was a sheet of blood. He walked quickly ahead of me. I could see he was in pain. I felt no pain, just weakness, the trembling of my legs and chills. I was shaking so violently I had to place each foot carefully. Looking down, I saw that my feet were blue. So were my hands. So blue I didn't want to see them.

We entered the large house like two men who were strangers to each other, each of us not even pretending concern for the other. Tato went straight upstairs. I heard him turn on the shower. As I crawled into my bed, I listened to his groans. I tried to dry my hair with a towel and spread another blanket over my head, then I took off my bathing suit and threw it.

I was not just cold; something was wrong. It was not going to be simple, my life in America. I had no money, no profession. I had nothing planned. Even the summer no longer seemed a refuge. It tilted us now toward autumn. Zia herself warned us when we were children that the house had no heat and we must get out before the great ball of winter rolled over us and crushed us.

Once in Rome, a seminarian returned after vacation with a canary in a cage. The bird disliked where he had been taken and beat

139

against the wires in attempts to escape. He did it so often that we voted, all the second-floor students, to let him loose. It was spring-time in Rome. A pet canary might survive the summer at least. If not, he would die in the freedom he wished. We opened the window, placed the cage in it, then opened the door of the cage. The canary sat for days looking at the opening. Finally, when he flew into the courtyard, everyone cheered. The next day we found him dead under the window. Someone had taken the cage away, and the bird, trying to return, crashed into the closed glass window and was killed. I felt like that bird.

I tried to imagine, shivering and pulling the covers over my head, that I was sleeping in my bed at the seminary, that Ciascuno was five minutes away. I pretended that Tato didn't exist as I knew him. He was part of a bad dream. I pretended I recognized the semi-nary smell in my pillow and that I would wake up much happier, ready to be ordained. To pretend was my only hope.

I fell asleep, but I woke myself making noises. I was grinding my teeth and grunting as I was shivering.

"Cello." Tato was in the room, his hand on my forehead. "You're warm," he said. "What are you scared of?"

"Scared?"

" 'Don't leave me.' You sayin' that to *me*?"

"In my sleep?" I asked.

"Yeah. 'Don't leave me,' you yelled."

"Tato I'm very cold. I think something's very wrong."

"I think I know what's wrong."

"I'm *very* cold."

"But you feel warm. You hit your head when you fell into the water?"

"I don't think so."

He gently felt my skull with his fingers. "No bumps." He sat on the bed. "Wanna go to a hospital?"

"No. What do you think is wrong?" My teeth were chattering.

He propped the pillow under the back of my neck. The air movement gave me more chills. He went across the hall and took a blanket from his bed. He threw it over me, tucking it to my sides and then he lay down next to me. He slid his arm under my pillow and with his other arm over my chest, he wrapped his foot over my feet and gathered me close to him.

"I'll take care of you. You hear me?"

"Yes."

"I love you, man. I'm your cousin and your friend. You hear? I'll take care of you. You're not alone anymore. You hear that? You'll never be alone again as long as you live in this goddamn world. Are you listenin'?"

"Yes."

"We're both loose and flyin' free. Our lives are both in the same place again, man—me divorced, you free now too. Like when we were on the roof with the old man, right? Hey, look there through the doorway."

"Where?"

"At the green wall light there. I remember the night your old man came up here and took me away. We walked under that light and this door was closed. Well, we're big boys now and nobody can screw around with us. The door's open and here I am, Cello. I'm gonna promise you somethin', man."

"What?"

"I promise you I'll go over the cliff with you any time, you hear? I'll take care of you no matter what. You'll never be alone unless you wanna be. Remember that. I love you, man."

"Thank you." My shivers were really sobs. They had been all along. I realized that as the tears came.

We had a routine. We woke at seven-thirty and made coffee. Then we fished. If we caught anything, we planned our suppers around that. We took turns going into town for fruit and vegetables and milk. We spent hours of silence, and the days were full of work and pleasure and contemplation. We gathered wood along the beach for fires, breaking it and piling it evenly behind the house. We read to each other at night. His eyes often stared wild and far. He seemed in pain sometimes, as though a generator were inside him, overworking his faculties. He chewed his fingernails, eyes burning, like a man looking out of his cave.

He seemed more a boy than ever, primitive in his wisdom and

physically very strong. He moved with power to spare, with grace and continuity. I loved being with him.

I leaned into Tato's promise. I allowed it to sink in that I was no longer alone. That was a new feeling. Sometimes it even pained.

CHAPTER VI

BEFORE the disco opened at eleven, the Gorilla restaurant was a quiet place. Soft jungle sounds reverberated throughout the restaurant coming from a self-reversing tape recorder played through the elaborate speaker system. Live parrots and cockatoos sat in cages over the bar. The bamboo furniture was upholstered in black fabric printed with pink hibiscus and green palms.

I was in terror my first night on the job at how the disco room shook the building. An oil-well rig was under the floor, it seemed, pumping to the accompaniment of flutes and tambourines. I wasn't very good in the parking lot. Tato had to make up for my slowness. He moved the cars as if they were rockets, braking and jumping out while they bounced in their places. He worked fast, with glazed eyes. He had a fake smile for every customer and he held out his hand without a wince. Intimidated customers paid out big tips. We had been guaranteed a hundred dollars a day for weekends, plus tips.

The disco was not busy during the week, so we could leave around two A.M. We'd buy take-out food in the Patio Royale Diner and drive to Jessup to eat it on the porch. But on Fridays, Saturdays and Sundays we got home exhausted after dawn. It was really breakfast we were eating on the porch. July had grabbed hold. Nights were warm and peaceful, and the days were filled with day lilies, Queen Anne's lace and sunshine.

When we parked the Volks on the cracked asphalt one night, I noted how darkly tanned Tato was. The whites of his eyes and his teeth jumped out of the dark. In spite of the breezy ride home, we were sweating. It was humid, but it felt good to be dressed in thin cotton, wearing no socks, and pouring out sweat. We sat in a semi-stupor, listening to crickets in the windlessness. The house looked massive from where we sat. One of us must have left lights on inside and it seemed like a party was going on. Orange incandescent lights from the living-room doors illuminated the porch.

Tato was peeling a banana as we walked in the sand to the house with our take-home food. From afar, my eyes fixed on the globe-shaped crystal vase that sat on the wicker table next to one of the porch columns. The globe was illuminated, catching rays of color from the stained glass around the front door. The foyer light was on. The closer we came to the house, the more resplendent the globe appeared, full of water and pert daisies, so perfect and transparent. By the time we stepped onto the porch, I could see oxygen bubbles on the daisy stems. With the repercussion of our feet on the porch, some were lifting away, floating to the top.

"You *are* a romantic," I murmured to Tato. "When did you put these flowers here?"

"I didn't put no flowers anywhere," Tato said indignantly. We looked blankly at each other.

Tato jumped into the house, only to find the bison completely nude of our towels and sneakers. The floors were swept. A scent hovered, of anise cakes and coffee. Two corner lamps, which Tato and I never used, were lit in the living room. Every object had been picked up, dusted and carefully replaced. The dining-room table was set with placemats and stemware. A large globular ruby vase, carved with large beetles, was filled with tall melon-colored day lilies. The dark mahogany bar in the living room was stocked with fresh bottles of liquor, ginger ale and mineral waters. The house was the way it was when we were children, neat and ready to be lived in. Once again it was 1950. Zia and Tangerine would be upstairs. I felt their presence so vividly I got goose bumps.

Feet thumped on the landing and a woman's voice called out, "Are these my men come home?"

Tato whipped around. "Zia!" He recognized her immediately. She was descending the staircase wearing black high-heeled shoes with white ankle socks. A white negligee showed beneath a blue satin robe, which she tied at her waist with ribbon. She had aged, but she was still beautiful. Her hair was quite different, thinner and darker and tightly permanented. She was bulkier, and when she reached the bottom step, she was much shorter than I expected. She had shrunk with the bison. Her cheeks were rosy with rouge. She wore lipstick, and her eyes were the same fantastic color. But her hands were not the color of her face. They were swollen and very white. Zia kissed us, and I caught the odor of perfume (not the perfume I remembered). She held us away from her by the hair of our necks, looking up into our faces.

"What beauties. You . . . are Tato?"

"Right." Tato smiled.

"And this must be my baby, Cello." The sound of my name on her lips made me dizzy. I felt silly standing in the foyer with brown bags of food in my arms. She led us back out to the porch. She sat with effort in an old orange wicker chair.

"I worked harder today than I have in years. I fixed you dinner, but you never got here." She was puffing. She sat staring, waiting for her breathing to return to normal.

Tato rolled up his banana skin and tucked it into his bag as Zia opened a little maple box and took a cigarette and a match from it. He lit the match for her. Her cigarette smoke drifted toward the roses.

"Where's Tangerine?" Tato asked.

"Who?"

"Tangerine, with all the red hair."

"Oh, Elena." Zia laughed. "I haven't seen her in years. She lives in Miami, married to a Brazilian airline pilot. They have three daughters, I understand. Which one of you telephoned my apartment?"

"I did," I said, taking out my tunafish sandwich.

"It *was* you. Well, I called Tato's mother, Silva." Tato seemed embarrassed at the mention of his mother. "She told me you were here."

"We . . . hope . . . you . . . are not put out by our being here," I felt obliged to say.

"Nothing so wonderful has happened to me in years."

"We painted the house," Tato said with a mouthful of meatball hero.

"No wonder it is so white. In South America you don't leave a house like this and expect to find it the same." She was becoming more radiant, her eyes darting about. "Look at you two. You are the most beautiful men in the world. We are lovers, finally, life and me." I thought she was kidding, but she meant it. Her hand trembled when she lifted her cigarette. She seemed about to cry. Still, she took a long drag on the cigarette as though her emotions had a hole in them through which ordinary actions could still pass. Her sudden age and sadness silenced everything.

"We have a job here for the summer," Tato spoke up. "You sure you don't want us to find another place?"

"No, no, no, no, *no.*" She crushed her cigarette, though she had hardly finished it. "This is your house. You stay."

Tato smiled at her as he sucked down his orange soda.

"How long are you here for?" I asked her.

"Does it matter? There is room here." She laughed.

"What will you do when the great ball of winter comes?" I said.

"I will . . . make some plans." She slowly got up. "I am too tired to talk now. Kiss me. Ahhhh." She hugged our heads to hers.

146

"Tomorrow I'll be fresh. I'll cook. We'll eat a civilized dinner and talk till we drop."

I watched her climb into the green glow of the tulip light. The stairwell hadn't changed, not even its red rug, but she had, very much.

The next afternoon I trimmed Tato's beard before the large bathroom mirror. He had tried to talk me into growing a beard but I swore I never would. The bright sky invaded the room as we ransacked the laundry bag for unwrinkled clothes. I put on my seminary trousers and black dress shoes for the first time since Italy. Tato loaned me a white shirt. He wore new jeans and a new tee shirt.

Downstairs the deep orange bands of late sunlight had entered the room. Our legs broke through them walking to Zia, who was sitting on the red velvet couch in a black lace dress. The breeze played with the curtains.

"There's coffee here for you. May I have a Campari and *acqua minerale?*" she asked. Tato went for the drinks. "And in the kitchen there is a wagon with cheese on it. Please wheel it in and serve us," she called out to Tato. He was obeying with pleasure. She held a tiny brass safety pin before me. "Pick me a rose to wear on my dress?" she asked. The late sunlight was filtering through the trellis on the porch. I chose a bud from it. "Not so young a rose," she called. So I picked the largest open rose on the trellis. Its center was yellow with dozens of stamens. I helped her pin it near her white powdered skin between her breasts. She smelled of talcum and lily of the valley toilet water.

"You have decided not to be a priest?" she asked suddenly. "Gabriella Ciascuno wrote to me. It is a good thing. These are Gabriella's words, 'because he is *too* handsome.'" She patted my hand and looked into my eyes with a deliberate purpose. "I'd rather you were Cello picking my rose in the evening sun than a monk hanging upside down in some drafty church like a bat." I sipped a Campari surprised that Gabriella and Zia were still close friends.

Dinner was striped bass. In spite of the peaceful atmosphere, we ate self-consciously. A thread of impatience seemed to run in Zia's demeanor. She carried on gracefully with smiles and polite words, but something about her worried me. It wasn't melancholy. It possessed energy. At first I thought her eyes were failing. A few times she involuntarily fixed her eyes on space. On the other hand, when she needed her lighter, her hand and eye worked together precisely. She smoked several times during dinner, but she ate very little.

After salad Zia lit what appeared to be a hand-rolled cigarette. It had the pungent odor of marijuana. Tato smiled and blushed, but she proceeded to smoke it with seriousness and without apology. She wanted to have coffee on the porch, so we wiped our mouths and stepped out while she got the coffee in the kitchen. She carried it out to us on a tray, and we drank without conversation while the sky turned indigo and blue-black. A pair of great blue herons fanned the shoreline on their way to the pond. They disappeared into the night, like ghostly prehistoric birds. Tato went inside and returned with brandy and three ruby glasses. Zia remained a mystery. She leaned forward at the railing and looked out to the very last smears of daylight and up to the stars.

"With such a wonderful sun at the perfect distance and such a comic moon, this could have been any kind of world we wanted. What do you guess a world like this could have become?"

Tato and I glanced at each other. He poured her a brandy and quietly left it on the railing near her hand. She flipped her joint into the rhododendrons. Then she lit a Camel and watched the curls of smoke rise like chiffon scarves.

"Our planet is a big engine floating in space," she said as she exhaled. "I should shut up or you will surely think I am crazy."

"Don't shut up." Tato laughed.

"He can put up with me." She smiled slyly. Then her face went blank. She closed her eyes as though she were at a seance. "I am in my *agonia*," she whispered. She opened her eyes to the stars and addressed them. Long streams of words came from her mouth and tears from her eyes. She spoke of her young days in Rome, of picnics with her friend Claretta Petacci and Mussolini, how she learned to smoke when she was sixteen, on the Via Veneto. We listened for an hour in the cricket din while she described every dress she owned, the 1930s in Paris, polo and card games in Argentina, winters in Viña del Mar and springtimes in Florence. She smoked Camels and marijuana and whispered to the stars impassioned, maudlin regrets.

"What do you mean by your *agonia?*" Tato asked, sliding down in his chair and propping his hands before his face.

"*Agonia* is the pain you feel when you no longer have the privilege of blindness, when dreams of possibilities are over. It is when you reach the top of the mountain and there is nowhere left to go, when you look down and back at where you've been."

Though I was surprised by her words, I was not fascinated. It sounded like theology, and it bored me. "Do you see God from the top of that mountain?" I asked sarcastically.

She looked at me, drained by her self-indulgence. "I never saw God," she said. "I only wished I were young again."

"What would you do?" Tato asked, smiling.

"I would become pregnant."

"But why pregnant?"

"It's part of love, to give birth. It's part of life. I feel cheated."

"Why didn't you? Couldn't you?" Tato asked.

"He wouldn't allow it. He warned me it would be over the minute I became pregnant."

"Who?"

"My lover. Did you know who he was? Juan José Ishmael Maldonado? I met him in Paris after they killed Mussolini. He was a poet. He brought me to live with three other writers in a small apartment. He told people he was Spanish. He never told me he had a wife, a mother and children in Argentina. One moment, out of the blue he gave me a choice: to come live as his mistress in Buenos Aires or to say goodbye in Paris. But I loved him. Who dreamed that my scruffy Spaniard who read his poetry in Paris from worn pages that he carried around like scrolls, tied with leather strings . . . who dreamed he was Juan José Ishmael, the Polo Prince of Argentina?"

She breathed deeply and said angrily, "He set me up in an apartment in Buenos Aires. Everyone knew about us. He was rich, a famous card player. He won this house in a card game. He never even saw it. He probably won these emeralds too." She started taking off her earrings, cupping them in her hand, then seemed suddenly impelled to remove the ring also. It didn't slide off easily. Three emeralds shone in her hand—the large green stone in the ring and the two lesser stones of her earrings. The three emeralds had no decorative gold around them. They shone in her palm, deep green and quite large.

She looked down at them bitterly, her eyes filling. "I loved him. He loved me. He would not rest a day without assuring me he loved me above everyone else and everything. I would have rather had a husband, and a child."

Her fist tightened over the jewels. I expected her to throw them into the rhododendrons any moment, but instead she knocked her fist gently on the table. "When he gave these emeralds to me, he said, 'There is a gift of love that one gives only once, to only one other, once in a lifetime, and I give that to you. Emeralds are plentiful as sea shells in comparison to that gift of my heart.' " She grimaced, opening her hand with difficulty. "Still, I would rather have died young than to never have heard those words."

"You're lucky," I spoke up, offended by the grandiosity of her melancholy, "lucky to have been so spoiled. You never knew loneliness, really, until now."

"What?" She was surprised. More bitterness had slipped into my voice than I intended. It was too late to take back my words, so I charged ahead.

"I was a child, alone in Italy, with no one, nothing but a box of Perugina almonds and your promise to talk to the moon. And you say you longed for a child to care for?"

She looked at me as though I were going mad. "What promise? What moon?"

"Don't you remember? You carried me along that beach and you promised me whenever the moon was full you would talk to me."

"I? People invent things for children. Perhaps I didn't mean it so seriously."

I felt foolish for remembering. I felt the blood flooding my cheeks.

"You are angry with me?" Zia asked.

"Yes." I began to cough.

"Shall we try again?" she asked.

"What do you mean?" I cleared my throat.

"Whenever there is a full moon, I will talk to you."

Tato walked away embarrassed, into the house. Zia waited for my answer.

"I hope I am never that lonely again. But I'm glad for the little boy I was"—I had to speak between coughs—"that he never knew you weren't listening." I saw the pain in her face.

"I'm glad the little boy learned how to be such a strong man," she said.

Tato came back with a glass of water for me and more brandy for Zia, which she refused. She stood, facing the water. The moon was not visible, but its light was everywhere. The beach stretched under the moonglow. The sea shimmered like silver and the sand seemed touched with frost. Some petals from Zia's rose had fallen. They appeared icy black, purplish on the moonlit floor, while the bright yellow fruit from which they had fallen hung upside down from her little brass safety pin. She leaned out over the railing, touching her face to the moonlight, shuddering a little.

"In the coming days, I want the joy of *rest*," she whispered to the sky. She turned and held out her arms. "Come. Kiss me good night." I stood. Tato moved close to her. I followed. "Don't be mad at me. I'll make it up to you. Forgive me."

A strangely muffled voice came up from Tato. "How can we forgive you, when you really didn't do anything?" Tato took her right hand and opened it, revealing the three jewels. He picked a small emerald and fastened it to her ear. He did the same with the other, then took the ring and forced it back on her finger. He wore the sly smile of a magician. The three of us were so close, I smelled his beard, his breath mingling with hers.

"Forgive me? Cello?" Zia whispered. Tato's eyes were on mine, waiting for me to speak. I caressed Zia's back with my hand. I simply couldn't give any other answer. She stepped away toward the candy colors of the stained glass surrounding the front door, entered the vestibule and went slowly upstairs.

Tato opened her maple box. He pinched out a joint and lit it with her lighter. I looked at the bay, longing to swim in it. I slipped off my shoes stepped down onto the sand and walked to the water.

Looking back at that night, through all the years, I see that my mind had all the pieces it needed to figure out who and what I was, and yet I didn't want to see. Somewhere in the front of our brains, I suppose we design ourselves—foolishly, stubbornly, inartistically—and we refuse to recognize who we are. We are orphaned to ourselves.

Why was I so blind? Was I too young to see? I wouldn't recognize anything about myself that didn't fit in with my presumption. Our egos pay much more heed to our imaginings than to facts. And yet I believed I was trying to understand. I believed I was willing to admit the truth. I loved them both so much. I needed them both so desperately, and all I could think of as I approached the point was that I was angry.

The water was cool to my feet. I removed all my clothes and threw them up on the sand. I entered the bay slowly. My eyes had adjusted to the dark. I swam under tiny clouds of fog until I was in deep water. I could see the lights of the house a mile away, to the right.

The moon was glowing inside the fog like an orange candle when I got back on shore. Haul seiners were loading a catch. They had worked in such silence I hadn't noticed them. They were dressed in sweaters and rubber waders. Their silhouettes resembled baboons, thick legs spread apart, lifting the last of the nets onto the trucks. One of the trucks flashed its headlights, catching me nude in the beams. When they spotted me, they quickly turned off the headlights and used their yellow parking lights. The haul seiners passed close by in their pickup trucks. In the back of the last truck sat six or seven of them, rocking in unison as the wide beach tires plowed and spun in the sand. Each of them stared back at me from out of his hard skin. They all had startling yellow hair, cut roughly, and faces hard as lobster shells, but their eyes were young. They stared, not judging, but watching, like children. For the moment, I would have exchanged lives with any one of them. From afar I could see Tato's light upstairs.

The porch was desolate when I got there. I walked into the kitchen, turned out the light. The darkness amplified the music of crickets.

I switched out the living-room lamps. The fog had invaded the house and was actually hovering over the Oriental rugs. The odor of stale books filled the living room. On my way up the stairs, toward the green hall light, I could hear Tato snoring. As I passed his doorway, I looked in. The bare overhead light glared down on him. Moths and beetles thumped his screens trying to get in. A damp sheet was twisted around his leg. The rest of him was bare. The dark hair of his body, his beard and head jumped out of the whiteness of his bed. His snoring was loud.

I felt guilty for being so close to his body, looking upon it without his knowing. A book was open at his side. Sweat beaded his forehead. My father's scent was in the room. Maybe it was a common human smell—perspiration, flesh, or breath.

Tato stopped snoring. I jerked the string of the overhead light, throwing the room into darkness. His snoring returned. A heron flapped away outside, as though the light going out were a warning. When my eyes adjusted to the dark, I could see Tato again, partially illuminated by the hallway light. He had uncovered himself even more when he stirred. I thought I saw his penis flinch in its black nest. It had. It was growing. But his snoring was genuine. He was asleep. I watched his penis more than double its size, although it remained limp upon its side. Beetles continued to hit the screen, making Oriental music. As I lifted the sheet to gently cover him, he took my wrist.

"Cello?" His voice was loud.

"I'm covering you," I said. "I turned out the light for you."

"C'mere," he mumbled, pulling me down toward him.

"What do you want?" I asked, looking into his face. He didn't answer. I withdrew my wrist from his hand, turned and left the room.

I slipped into my own bed, watching him for a long time. He didn't move. He might not even remember the incident, I thought. He had acted unconsciously in his sleep. But suppose he wasn't asleep?

In bed, I touched my own body, feeling it with my fingers with new curiosity. Eventually, I masturbated, slowly, without anxiety, looking at Tato through the open door, his body in the green light, his leg hanging off his bed. Tato's body hair was thick and curly, not like my father's, but the odor coming from him was the odor in my own bed. It was also of my father. An aura, a power, hovered between our two rooms, enriching my imagination, making the years disappear, time dissolving into odors that pass through the years like a drawstring pulling the fabric tight. I was a Manfredi. Tato's blood was in me and mine in his. If I had allowed him to pull me down closer to him, I could not be closer than I was now in my own room several yards away. We were branches of the same tree. At some point the sap ran together. That thought helped me breathe in the foggy Jessup night. I breathed safe, connected. It was almost like love, the thing that helped me breathe.

I came. I turned my mouth into my pillow. I sounded like an animal. I wiped my hand on the sheet. As I fell asleep, the strong odor of come hovered in the room.

Weeks went by. Zia became less self-indulgent, more mobile. She was becoming more and more her old self, keeping house for us and surprising us with dinners at two A.M.

One Saturday morning after a busy night at Gorilla, we had breakfast in Southampton at Dillon's off Main Street. It must have been well after eight A.M. when Tato and I dragged our tired bodies from the Volkswagen on the cracked asphalt and started making our way, with shoes in hand, through the warm sand toward the house. The sun shone, but there was also fog which made the air doubly brilliant, as each particle of moisture mirrored the sun. The house was transfigured, shining like a ghost; though to the north there was blue sky and no fog. The air was still.

154

As we drew closer to the house, I made out two people sitting on the porch—women. One was Zia. The other, in a large-brimmed hat, was hidden behind dark glasses. Dressed in tan, she sat with a hidden face, legs crossed.

"Hello," Zia called out as we stepped up to the porch. Still sitting, Zia pulled Tato to herself by his hand. "This is my nephew Guglielmo. Tato, we call him. And the other—come, Cello—I believe you two know each other?"

"Who am I?" the voice spoke playfully from behind dark glasses. Her teeth were white and perfect. The voice was familiar. She wasn't American. "Gabriella Ciascuno," she said.

"Oh"—I took her hand immediately—"I'm sorry." A wind blew the brim of her straw hat away from her face. It *was* Gabriella. Roberto flashed into my mind for the first time in months.

Gabriella was dressed quite well in a flesh-colored skirt and blouse that almost matched her straw hat and shoes. In my soiled undershirt and damp jeans, I felt embarrassed.

"And how have you been?" she asked politely.

"Very well, thank you." I spoke to my double image in her sun glasses.

"Now I really must go," she said, suddenly turning to Zia. "*Arrivederci*, my darling." She kissed Zia from a sitting position, then pulled Zia to her feet. They exchanged tender Italian whispers, kissed and kissed again. Gabriella had to clear her throat once; Zia's eyes filled. Tato looked at me quizzically, then followed Zia inside. I remained on the porch, surprised that there should be so much emotion over a simple parting, and I surmised that something dark had overshadowed their meeting. The smell of sorrow, almost sweet, like the odor of wet sand, was in the air.

Gabriella walked carefully down the steps. We hadn't seen a car when we parked the Volkswagen, so I wondered. Where was she going? She walked a few yards in the sand, then turned back and looked at me. I didn't want her to speak first.

"How is your brother?" I blurted, coming down the steps toward her.

She didn't answer until I was quite close. She took off

155

her glasses, revealing her beautiful gray eyes. In that instant I recalled Roberto so well, and the day on the *Rosa Senza Spina*. Her eyes were tired and she shaded them with her hand. I couldn't stand still.

"I'm sorry I have to say that my brother is not too well. Will you walk with me?" She turned, and we continued toward the shoreline, which glowed with fog. I felt it was possible for Roberto to jump out of his sister's eyes and grab my throat.

"What is wrong with Roberto?" I asked.

"He is working too hard. Why don't you drop him a note, an invitation?"

"An invitation? To here?" I asked. Was she being sarcastic?

"Why not? He's always wanted to see this country, although I must say, I can't imagine why. Don't you miss Italy?"

"Not one bit. No."

"Italians weren't meant for this climate. It is too strict." She held my arm for balance.

"Too strict?"

"Yes. The sun seems confused here. It acts like it is afraid of something. I fly to Spain in two days."

"Tell your brother . . . Give him my best wishes."

"*Write* to him." She tugged my arm. "*Invite* him. He has a place to stay nearby until September."

"What place nearby?" I asked.

"There." She pointed to the water. At the shore there were two men and a small boat, but beyond them, about a quarter of a mile offshore, there was a long white ship waiting almost invisibly in the fog. I had never seen so large a ship in those waters. "The *Rosa Senza Spina* is here for repairs," she said.

"Where do you keep it?"

"In Sag Harbor. Roberto will be no trouble to you. He can live on her. But I'm sure he will not come if you do not ask him to."

"What makes you say that?" I asked. The oarsmen sprang to attention. One jumped to the helm of the dingy to help her into it; the other went to the bow and pulled up the small anchor. He dragged the boat to the lip of the water. I awaited her response while they helped her into the helm seat.

"*Aspetta un momento,*" Gabriella ordered.

"*Siamo pronti quando volete.*" I could tell by their accents that the oarsmen were Romans.

"I should talk to you privately, Cello," Gabriella said.

"All right."

"I do not want to make you uncomfortable." She was uncomfortable.

"Not at all."

"You may think it is none of my business." I felt a blush coming on. She put on her glasses. "But it *is* my business after all. I have only one more day in the United States . . ."

"Where would you like to meet?" I asked, cutting her short.

"On the *Rosa* in Sag Harbor. The yacht club. Do you know where?"

"I'll find it."

"Tomorrow at this time then?"

"Fine," I said.

She reached to kiss me. I gave her only my cheek and reached around her to pat her back. I watched the three of them in the small boat, disappearing toward the great white ship. They seemed to me people from as far away as the stars.

When I went back into the house, the place was silent. Upstairs, both Tato's and Zia's doors were closed. I was glad to be left alone. I wanted to see the ship going away. I ran downstairs and took the pair of binoculars out of the bookcase. They were impossible to adjust because corrosion had kept them at a particular focus, but fortunately, it didn't matter, because by the time I reached the roof of the house, the *Rosa Senza Spina* had moved into the glasses' range. The sun hit the ship squarely, and in the clearing air she appeared sleek, aloof and powerful, her golden ribbons trailing in the wind. I longed to walk on board again, to step on its rugs, to see its marble, its white thornless roses in the staterooms, to sit in its odor of Italian cooking, to hear Italian spoken all around. I could make out the figures of the crew. I wished the binoculars could focus in their eyes. I wanted to smell Italy again.

* * *

157

I napped lightly all day, through dark dreams of Italy. When I woke I expected to be in my seminary bed in Rome.

Zia had dinner for us at seven. Tato came down crusty-eyed. He globbed butter on his bread and gulped coffee. Zia dished out her tuna salad with black olives and pimentos, and poured blue-white sparkling water over ice and lemon in tall glasses for us.

"How the hell'd she *get* here?" Tato asked.

"Gabriella?" Zia said.

"Yeah. There was no car parked."

"She came by water." Zia laughed and looked at me.

"What's so funny?" Tato asked.

"There was a boat anchored out there," I said.

"Oh." Tato was satisfied. I didn't know how to describe the *Rosa Senza Spina,* or even if it were necessary to do so.

"A beautiful boat," Zia said.

"Big?" Tato asked.

"Yes," said Zia.

"It figures," Tato said, standing up. He stretched and picked up his coffee and ambled down to the sand.

I called after him, "Can I borrow the car after work?"

"Yeah," he yelled without turning back.

"He didn't touch any food," Zia said with worry, watching him walk down to the water. "Where must you go with the car after work?"

"Oh . . . for a ride," I answered. She didn't pursue it.

I had saved over five hundred dollars from working at Gorilla. I stuffed it all into my pocket. I decided to have every penny of it with me when I went on board the *Rosa Senza Spina.* If Gabriella referred to my ingratitude at her paying my tuition at Nazzareno, I would insist she accept partial recompense. What right did she have to summon me? Why *had* I to go? So that she could burden me with guilt for her brother's unhappiness? Had I sold my soul to Gabriella Ciascuno? Yes, I said to myself realistically, checking my hair in the mirror. The money in my pocket was good defensive ammunition.

It was a Saturday night, so Tato and I worked until sunrise. We'd had breakfast. It was after eight when I dropped him off at the cracked asphalt. I had brought a clean white shirt and my black trousers with me and was dressed to board the yacht, wearing white sneakers in respect for its teakwood decks.

Sag Harbor Village was having its annual Whaling Festival. Cars were backed up along Ferry Road. It took me twenty minutes to get to the peak of the bridge. I could see the *Rosa Senza Spina* instantly. She was more than conspicuous. The ship dwarfed the other yachts at the club dock. As I sat in the chugging Volkswagen waiting for traffic to clear, I thought of what Gabriella could say to me: "You have hurt my brother. All Rome is gossiping about your cruelty. Roberto is very ill. He misses you. He won't eat."

Gabriella greeted me from the deck. I walked the hemp carpet of the gangplank, up to the starboard passageway of the middle deck, then made my way to the stern, where Roberto had introduced me to Gabriella a long time ago. She was on the phone. The whiteness was gone, everything redone in neutral tan shades, which made the space seem larger. Even the overhead awnings were tan. Gabriella was wearing a navy blue robe this time. She waved her cigarette at me as she spoke on the phone and gestured for me to sit. A steward brought me a Coke, then disappeared. My heart beat faster. I had to go to the bathroom. I was about to search for the head when Gabriella hung up and came to me. She kissed me, took me by the hand to the soft semicircle of couch that rimmed the stern. We sat high above the harbor, overlooking Shelter Island, surrounded by light but shaded by the awning. Her eyes were startling.

"How old are you now, Cello, dear? Tell me."

"I'm twenty-four."

"You're quite old enough to take some responsibility." Her expression hardened as she crushed her cigarette.

"I have never been irresponsible."

"I don't imply that." She looked at me in slight alarm.

"Then what do you mean?" I asked, fixing my eyes upon hers. She didn't expect that much assertiveness.

"What do I mean?" She shrugged. "Not to insult you certainly, Cello, as you seem to imply."

"I never asked you for the favor," I said.

159

"You didn't *ask* me?"

"I didn't ask your brother either."

"Ask my brother what?" Her brow wrinkled now. She reached for another cigarette, then realizing she just crushed one, she threw the pack down.

"I never asked him for a penny, and when he brought me to you, I had no idea of what was going on. I told him I'd repay every cent, and I have been working—"

"Wait." She clapped her hands. "I'm confused. What are you talking about?"

"I'm . . . I'm talking about the money you supplied for my education at Nazzareno."

"I supplied no money. I don't know what you're talking about."

"Didn't your brother bring me aboard this ship to meet you once?"

"Yes"—she winced—"and so?"

"Why?" I asked, confused. "Then why did he want me to meet you?"

"He *loved* you." This time her eyes nailed mine. She couldn't keep the resentment out of them. "He loved you *and* me," she said. "He wanted us to *meet*." She grabbed her cigarettes and lit one after all. "Roberto never needed me to help him with money. He has more than I. He always did," she said, blowing out a cloud of smoke, annoyance winning over her voice. "He certainly did not bring you to meet me so that I could pay for your schooling. He no doubt paid for it. What does it matter? If you have a personal quarrel with my brother, that is not my business."

"I have nothing personal with your brother," I said, matching her tone.

"What has he *done* to offend you?" she asked.

"Nothing," I answered. I wanted to go, but she held me with a sudden smile.

"You are just like him. He is the king of stubbornness and you are the prince."

"What do you mean?"

"I would never dare to try to explain it to either of you. Cello,

160

you are a little late arriving here, and I am so busy. I must be brief. May I speak of what I invited you here for?

"Yes. What is it?"

"It's about your aunt."

"Zia?"

"Yes. How much do you know about her illness?"

I stared speechless. "My aunt?" I repeated.

"Yes. Fantasia."

"Is this what you want to discuss?"

"Yes. You are aware she is quite ill?" Her eyes pinned me, though the lids fluttered rapidly.

"I . . . I knew she was hospitalized."

"Cello, she has cancer." She blinked, watching me intently.

"What do you mean?" I asked. "She *did* have it?"

"She has it *now*. She was undergoing chemotherapy at Columbia Presbyterian Hospital. She discontinued treatment against their advice."

I could feel my throat throb. "Why? Doesn't she want help? She must go back."

"That's what one says at first, but your aunt knows she is beyond help. That's why I wanted to talk to you. She needs you more than you realize."

"I don't believe this. *Why* is she beyond help?" I couldn't hold down the anger in my voice.

"They would have to cut both her lungs out. One cannot live without lungs."

"What can the treatments do?"

"Postpone her death."

"Isn't that good?"

"She would rather pretend nothing is wrong. She says she has a plan. She assures me all is fine, but I know I shall never see her again." Gabriella turned away to hide her tears.

"When did she tell you this?"

"I heard in Italy that she was ill, but I didn't realize it was serious. I was just visiting her yesterday when she told me, just before you appeared with your cousin. Poor thing. Maldonado in

161

Argentina is dying with the same disease. It is bizarre. His family cannot stand her. They pretend your aunt doesn't exist."

When I got back to the house, no one was about. I ran straight up to my room. I closed my door behind me and leaned against it with my hands behind my back clutching the knob. I let out a long groan, and almost immediately there was a soft knock. I felt a hand grab the knob. I knew it was Tato. I stepped aside. He opened the door slowly and came in.

"Hey, you all right?"

"I don't want to go to work tonight. I feel sick," I said.

"Okay." Tato paced in an arc around me with a look of wonderment. I could see the spotless sky of a perfect day behind him through the window.

"She's gonna die," I said, unable to control myself.

"Who?"

"Zia."

"Shut up," he whispered. Tato's eyes darted to the hallway. I turned. Zia was there. She had heard what I said.

"Who told you that?" she asked. Her face had fear in it. The fear gave me hope. It never occurred to me that Gabriella could be mistaken, at least in part. I spilled her name out with some relief.

"Gabriella?" Zia blinked at me, then made a face of disappointment and sadness. "That Gabriella," she said, "that silly woman."

"Is it true?" I asked. She turned without answering. She walked into the hallway as if going to her room. But her own hand, grabbing the molding, seemed to stop her. She turned and looked back at our faces. She said no words, but she nodded her answer: yes.

She went to her room and closed the door behind her.

The next morning she sat on the porch with me. There had been no more mention of her sickness. Tato was a half mile down the beach. I didn't like being alone with her now.

"Are you in pain?" I asked as calmly as I could.

"No. They tell me it is arrested for the moment."

"I'm sure it's true then." I sounded like Ciascuno.

"The past few days have been heaven for me. For a year and a half I have been in hell." She breathed a deep sigh of relief and looked out over the water. "Doctors, hospitals, talk, talk, talk. It is the most boring thing in life—illness."

"I wish there was something I could do."

"It's something everyone has to do for oneself. I've slain all my dragons. There is nothing to do now but—" she stopped short.

"Wait?" I asked.

"Wait for death? I never heard of anything so sterile. Fantasia Manfredi never waited for anything in her life," she said. Her face turned as far away from my gaze as possible. I said nothing.

I watched Tato throwing stones into the bay as he walked toward us, stopping to exercise, to flap his arms to the sun like a bird on the beach. I felt infirm sitting with my old aunt on an old porch while Tato spun and jumped like a marvelous baboon, totally happy to be with himself. When finally he began to come toward us, I was relieved. His black bathing suit made his dark skin seem deep red. He had a peasant's body, apelike indeed, but wonderful, powerful. I wondered how anyone with the body of an ape could possess the eyes of Rembrandt's Christ. I tried to hide my desire for his presence. It was more than a desire. It had become a need.

He lit a cigarette and looked at the water. His eyes became lost and I was able to watch him long and intently. I watched his smoke rise through the trellis and up into the mimosa tree, like ghosts escaping from his chest. Then Zia lit one. Her smoke rose like a column, dipping under the ceiling toward the sky. It mushroomed over the rhododendrons and disappeared into the birches.

"I'm glad we are together." Zia spoke abruptly. "I want to invite you to a party. You will need tuxedos."

"A party? For whom?" I asked.

"In honor of you both."

"In honor of us? Who's comin'?" Tato asked, his cigarette hanging from his mouth.

"Well," Zia said, "it will be a very private dinner party, for a very private purpose."

"What purpose?" I asked.

"That is the surprise." She smiled. "There will be just the three of us."

"And we need tuxedos for that?" I interrupted.

"That's right," she said without looking at me. "Others will join us later, others of no importance, part of the surprise. Don't force me to say too much. But I can assure you that nowhere in this world will there be a more glorious dinner that night. We will eat here, on the porch with the French doors open to the living room. Palms everywhere, and music."

"For just the three of us? Why?" I asked.

"Don't be too suspicious." She patted my face.

"Sounds good," Tato said, flipping his cigarette over the railing.

"We don't have tuxedos," I said.

"We'll get 'em." Tato's face recalled the boy on Mr. Possilippo's tar roof. His teeth glowed in the largest grin I ever saw on his face.

"Cello," she said, "go upstairs to my room. On the dresser there are two leather envelopes. Bring them down."

She had turned her room into an office with telephone numbers from Paris, Montevideo, Rome, the whole world, tacked on her walls. Her bed was neatly made. On her bureau was a bottle with a white-bird top, the same as the one she had given me, except this bird was made of plastic. A book, *Wildflowers of North America*, was on the bed near her eyeglasses. I would have known I was in her room if I were blindfolded. The room had the faint odor of anise, stale marijuana and that particular fragrance of her body, an odor I recalled from that evening long ago when we fished at the point in front of the giant moon. In the hall the old green-tulip light was lit, even though the sun was shining. I sat on her bed in unexpected calm, staring out her window at the flat sea, almost forgetting what I had come for.

The instant I touched the leather envelopes on the dresser, I knew there was money in them for Tato and me. Coming down the stairs with them, I felt a child, a taker, but I also felt cared for. When I walked onto the porch, Tato and Zia were laughing wildly. Zia reached toward me, impatiently taking the envelopes.

"There is in each envelope," she said matter of factly, "ten thousand dollars—one thousand in cash and a certified check for the rest. The reason for the cash"—she smiled—"is so you can buy your tuxedos."

That night we drove to New York City. The next morning we were fitted for our tuxedos. I cashed my certified check, preferring the nine thousand in cash. Tato put his money in his checking account and urged me to do the same but greedily, suspiciously, I did not want to let go of the real money, which was too bulky to fit into my wallet.

We saw the city for three days, then picked up our tuxedos on Thursday. We celebrated with champagne at a place called Gregorio's. We were both very tired by the time we reached Tato's apartment. We opened the convertible couch and fell upon it. The apartment was very still. We both fell asleep instantly. In New York City the nights were much warmer than on Long Island.

About three in the morning I awoke to find Tato's knees curled up behind my own. We had slept that way on the roof in Brooklyn under the old man's grapevine. But now we were men, and at the base of my spine I could feel Tato's hard penis, but his breath was the heavy breath of sleep. I rolled away and fell asleep again.

I woke up later, abruptly, from a nightmare, calling out for help. I had dreamed Uncle Marco was in bed with me, chanting Latin in my ear. I sat up and lit a cigarette. Tato's snoring was very loud. Suddenly I felt mischievous and snapped the elastic of his underpants. It stopped the snoring. Suddenly he lifted himself on his elbow and looked at me, laughing. He pulled me to him.

"Wait! What are you doing?"

"I want to whisper something."

"No one can hear us."

"I don't want to take the chance," he said with sincerity. I leaned my ear toward his lips—and then I felt the tickling of his tongue. I jerked away as he laughed. He pulled down his shorts and threw them on the chair. "Take 'em off." He tugged at the elastic band of mine.

"No." I brushed his hand away.

165

"Whatsamatta?"

"Forget it," I said. "Keep your hands off."

"Oh, is that so?" he said, smiling with embarrassment. He jumped out of bed and went to the bathroom. I turned on my side in a position of sleep. When he came back, I heard him putting on his underwear. I realized something terrible had just happened, something we were going to have to deal with.

Tato was furious. "I feel like a fuckin' jerk," he said, jumping back into bed.

"I'm sorry if you feel that way," I said without turning. "I'm not that way," I said simply.

"You're a fuckin' liar. I heard you jerkin' yourself off in your room the other night. I know you were watchin' me."

"I only wanted to turn out the light—to cover you."

"You were standin' there five minutes."

"No, I wasn't."

"What do you think I want? Hey, turn around and talk to me, shithead."

I turned on my back.

"You think I want your dick? I got my own, man. Animals have dicks. Everything has a dick," he said.

"What do you want?" I asked. He hesitated.

"Don't make a fool of me by pretending with me, Cello."

"Who's pretending? I'm not."

"Just don't treat me false, is what I'm warning you. Okay? Christ almighty, you really think I don't know the truth?"

"What truth?"

"That you dig me, for chrissake."

"That's not true," I exploded.

"Take it easy."

"That is not true."

"Okay."

"And you have no reason to say it." Every part of me trembled.

"Forget it." He turned around. "Go to sleep," he said.

A minute of cold silence passed in which neither of us moved. Then he spoke. "You stood there in my room, lookin' down at me." He punched his pillow, then buried his head in it. Once again, no words, no movement, not even our breath. Suddenly: "Goddamn fuckin' son of a bitch." He jumped up. "I wanna drive back. I'm not gonna be able to sleep now, so why waste time lying around here in this fuckin' couch together."

As soon as I got out of bed, he tore the sheets off, flung the blanket, lifted the foot of the bed and folded it back into a couch. I started to put on my pants.

"I'm a jerk, a goddamn jerk," he muttered, throwing the pillows.

"You didn't do anything wrong," I said.

"Goddamn right, I didn't."

We were out in the hall in a flash. He was locking the door. I was only half dressed. I had to say something strong, something greater than his anger. "You're my only friend . . . in this world."

He didn't answer me. He turned and started down the stairs. I followed him.

"Shove it up your ass," he said finally when we reached the street.

Back at Jessup Neck, after passing two silent hours in the car, we marched through the sand toward the house, our tuxedos in long white boxes under our arms. We stepped up to the porch to find it covered with crumpled green florist paper, palms and ferns, countless orchid plants, clivias and wispy oleander trees. On the wicker table were burgundy flannel sacks with *LaCross Party Corporation* printed on them, containing silver and dishes. The smells of oleander and waxed paper made me want to be happy. But when we entered the living room, we found Zia all but unconscious on the couch, glasses and cups surrounding her, tiny joint butts, clips and ashes in the ashtrays, discarded tissues everywhere—as though she had used the couch as a bed while we were away.

"Help me to my room," she begged.

"Why do you smoke that stuff?" I demanded as we escorted her toward the stairs.

"My doctor prescribed it to counteract the effects of my chemotherapy." She looked terrible. She wanted no fuss, so we left her alone in her room.

When Zia closed her door, Tato murmured good night to me, went to his room and closed his door too. Tato closed his bedroom door every night thereafter.

We had phones installed in the living room the next day and we stuffed linens and blankets into the downstairs closet in case Zia would need them again. She let us wait on her upstairs for a few days, and to our surprise, she was making a comeback. One night she sat up and drank tomato juice and insisted we go to work. The next day she worked on herself in the mirror and spoke French on the telephone.

A lot of people came around making deliveries and discussing the party with Zia. A helicopter brought the chef for a preliminary visit. He spoke with Zia in her room while his assistants set up the kitchen. Zia rang the extension to ask me to meet him in the foyer. His name was Alain Charles. When he arrived, he was smiling, but soon he was in a sweat, annoyed that no one had any ideas or preferences for the menu he was to plan. I assured him that any of his suggestions would be acceptable. This only annoyed him more.

"Do you like fish?"

"Yes."

"Meat?"

"Yes."

"What is your favorite food?"

"Risotto," I answered.

"Risotto?" he repeated in half shock. "Rice?" His assistant rolled his eyes.

Alain Charles forbade us to use the kitchen until the night of the dinner. A woman came from a shop in Southampton with several selections of dresses and shoes for Zia and various garments for her to try on. She refused to get out of bed, telling me to tell the callers to leave everything they brought and to go away. The only people she allowed in her room were the hairdresser and the manicurist.

The phone rang constantly. Musicians, private police, helicopters. Tato was always away. I didn't enjoy sitting on the porch alone with Zia, knowing she was dying, watching her ignore her food, smoking marijuana, especially while Tato was gone off on his own, free and moody somewhere.

That night when I went to sleep, the upstairs reeked with marijuana. Zia called me in and with glassy eyes asked where Tato was. I told her I didn't know. Zia told me my face looked worried, and I answered by saying that I thought the constant odor of marijuana was affecting me. She apologized, reminding me that her doctor had prescribed it. She wanted to be strong for the dinner, she said, and she believed that she was methodically building up a reserve that would carry her through it.

It was cool for July, about fifty-five degrees that night. Tato came home about midnight. I heard him thump up the stairs. He put on the overhead light in his room. His eyes glanced blindly in the direction of my door as he started closing his.

"Tato," I called.

"Yeah?"

"They need us back at work. They called—"

"I'm quittin' the Gorilla," he murmured.

"Why?" I asked.

"Tired." I smelled beer and stale cigarette smoke on him.

"Tomorrow's the dinner. Zia's dinner."

"Right," he said.

"I though you forgot," I said.

"What made you think that?" He smiled. I had never seen that smile on Tato.

The clothes I wore the night of the dinner were the lightest and most comfortable I had ever worn. As I looked in the mirror, I would agree with anyone who said I looked handsome. The black clothes reminded me of those days in the seminary, but I was never quite so tan before.

"This is only play," Zia said excitedly as I accompanied her downstairs. "We are taking a little trip to far away. We will all return to where we belong soon enough." Zia wore a frock of a rather colorless hue, beige-gray. Two panels fell like capes from her shoulders, trimmed with ostrich feathers of the same shade. It reminded me of the fox-trimmed dress she had worn to my mother's wake.

To me, Tato looked like a clown in his tuxedo. He was all teeth, laughing constantly at himself as he walked about accepting hors d'oeuvres and drinks from the nervous waiters. If it hadn't been for the perfect-fitting black suit, he surely would have seemed out of place. I don't think he even combed his hair for the occasion.

Three waiters simultaneously pulled our chairs away from the table. We sat and began to eat quietly, with far more enjoyment than I anticipated. The table was bright with a yellow tablecloth, yellow napkins, candles in clear glass holders and a bouquet of fully opened summer roses. We sat between the rose trellis and the French doors to the living room. The dark red tea roses and the fragrance of oleander, aromas of food and wine, and Zia's Lily-of-the-Valley perfume—it was almost too much.

Charles and his assistants had prepared fresh foie gras and truffles wrapped in a pastry called *feuillet*. The first wine was a Château D'Yquem 1937. We ate quail in Madeira sauce. An array of vegetables in tiny silver dishes spread in a great arc around each main plate: peas, potatoes, artichoke hearts, shredded zucchini, braised celery, string beans, kohlrabi purée, sautéed plum tomatoes, chanterelles and morels. The wine was Romanée-Conti 1959. Tato ate the quail with finesse and used the spoon for his vegetables. He kept asking for bread. We ate without much talk. I thought we were finished when they brought out a side table of special French cheeses that Charles had brought with him from France, which they served with more red wine. For dessert they placed before us raspberry sherbet, strawberries, caramelized cream puffs and more champagne.

The music stopped just as we finished our coffee. A sudden breeze from the water, slightly cooler than the air, came as a blessing, cleaning away the odors of food and candles. The sky was perfect, clear and open. The soundless power of night surrounded us.

Zia became truly alive. Even her laughter had authority again.

The quartet returned to their chairs, smiling from their champagne, and began to play what turned out to be a medley of Puccini arias. The waiters entered to replace the yellow tablecloth with a maroon felt cover and to replace the large bouquet with a tiny one of dark roses and fresh spearmint.

Zia was absorbed by the music, her face a little radiant, yet pensive. "I was always ashamed to admit how much I loved 'Musetta's Waltz,' " she said. "Everyone who made me ashamed is dead now. 'Musetta's Waltz' outlived them. How foolish of me to have believed something better would come along. To Puccini!" She raised her glass.

"I want to dance. Up, both of you." We stood. The musicians nodded their approval, then lowered their eyes, giving us privacy. Zia touched both our cheeks. "I wish I had always known I would live to dance with my father's grandsons, his handsome cavaliers, giants with my father's smile, strong enough to carry me to bed as if I were their child." Tears were in her eyes. "You look afraid of me." She poked my ribs. I didn't answer. "Well, I'm not afraid of you," she said, "not afraid in the least."

We waltzed, the three of us, in a manner of speaking, until we decided it would be easier to take turns, Tato with Zia, then I. As I danced I thought of Tangerine. She and Zia were so young when they had taken us away in the Packard only eighteen years ago, such little time when you think of it, only enough for me to finish school, and here Zia was, close to her end. Living life took as little time as preparing for it. Her eyes fastened on mine as we waltzed. Now the childhood romance was all but lost, the simplicities shattered by experience, still I couldn't rise above the deep love I felt for her. I almost screamed out: *Don't go away. Don't leave again.*

A helicopter, not visible but close enough to hear, sputtered noisily. Large red blinking lights appeared on the beach before the porch, and potted palms bent as if in a hurricane. The musicians continued in a shower of rose petals from the trellis that blew past them all the way into the living room. Zia pulled us each by a hand inside, under the stained-glass archway of the front door, between the two bison, and she slammed the front door.

"The surprise." She hesitated, as if incapable of pronouncing something. "Tonight." She groped for words. "Tonight I shall be a guest in your house."

"What d'ya mean?" Tato said.

She encouraged us with her smile. "This house, all the property. The beaches, the cliffs . . . A small country all your own." She spun us around. "These." She knocked the bison with her knuckles. "Everything is yours. You painted your own house. I'm giving it all to you both while I'm alive." We stood dumbfounded, as she smiled.

Tato looked as though he had been hit in the back of the neck with a log. He put both his hands to his temples. "Holy Jesus!"

"My attorneys have come in the helicopter to draw up the papers. Come. Straighten up." She opened the door.

Two men, one older, marched toward us through the sand, dressed in business suits and ties, carrying attaché cases. She introduced us: "Cello Manfredi, Tato Manfredi."

Tato shook their hands. I held back, still in shock.

"I am Henry Boisvert," the older man said; then turning toward the other, "My son, Carter. We represent the firm of Bartholomew, Hennessey and Boisvert." The old man was crisp. He wore a smile that seemed part of his outfit. His son had one of those faces that could have been designed with a ruler.

In the dining room, under the stained-glass ceiling, they talked to us for an hour and a half, explaining how Zia's death would automatically give us title to everything only if we co-owned it with her beforehand. This would avoid the tremendous inheritance taxes when she died. So there under the stained-glass ceiling we signed into the deed, which represented several millions of dollars of property—the house, its contents and almost all of Jessup Neck. Tato asked why the Boisverts had to sign too, and Zia answered with a smile and a finger to her lips for silence.

After handshakes and goodbyes, father and son walked down the porch steps toward the copter. The copter blades blew their suits against their bones, their ties out of their jackets and gave their hair parts in the wrong places. Then the copter lifted, taking its blinking red lights with it and heaving itself into the blackness out of sight.

My ears were ringing of the silence. Tato and I looked to each other several times to reassure ourselves we weren't dreaming. The quartet reassembled. The musicians poised their bows, and with the promise of no further noise, other than crickets, they began to play.

Zia removed her emerald earrings. "Some woman will be happy to have these." She handed them to Tato. She unscrewed the ring from her finger and slipped it into my hand. Tato objected, smiling, trying to fasten the earrings tenderly on her ears. "No. Give them to the woman you love. Give them with your heart, the one time, the once, the way they were given to me."

I held the ring in my fist. She was so proud, a free creature now, like the snowy egrets preparing for flight in the fall, no bags to pack, nothing to carry. And though she looked relieved and beautiful, her eyes smiling as she lit a joint, I had a premonition she was going to say something painful.

"Now I have only one wish left:" she took a deep drag, held it, then blew out the smoke with relief. "I want to die tonight in the woods, like a doe, with you two near me. To die suddenly in the fresh air, surrounded by all of nature. Will you help me do it?" she asked, tears rolling down her face as, at the same time, she puffed to keep her joint alive.

"To get *rid* of yourself?" Tato's head popped up. He was still holding the emerald earrings in the palm of his hand.

"Yes. I need help, advice how to . . . I want to go to the woods before the pain gets too uncomfortable. Tonight. Do you see those pines there?" She pointed to the bluffs. "I'll bring enough pills. I have all I need. When the musicians leave, I want you to carry me there. There is where I want to die. Tonight." She was calm enough as she spoke.

"Don't do it," I said, looking into her eyes. "I'll hate you. I'll hate you for the rest of my life."

"We don't hafta talk about it now," Tato interrupted me.

"You can keep the house," I went on. "I don't want the house. Just promise me you won't kill yourself."

173

"Shhh." Zia put her hand to my mouth. I kissed it, fighting back tears.

Tato walked away, out the French doors. I heard him dismissing the musicians.

"Do you promise me?" I pressed her hands.

"Cello, why must you make a problem over a simple thing?"

"Simple!" I said. "Zia, you started something in me about your death that is very frightening."

"What did I start?"

"It's my mother." Zia was facing death, yet this seemed so important to me. "You are right there with her in my mind, and it's going to happen to me all over again."

"Shhh."

"It will kill me. I can't . . ." She pressed my hand. Her warmth felt so precious. It brought the blood back to my face. It calmed my stomach. I was a child again. I loved her. How could she have thought she meant so little? I caught Tato watching us with the face of a frightened boy, peering from behind the palms of the porch.

"All right, Cello," she said.

She promised me there, holding my hands, that she would not kill herself, that she would die in a natural way. Tato had come inside while she spoke. He shocked me by offering to walk her to the pines that very moment, but she refused. Her face lost its glow. She kissed me good night, hardly able to bend over. Her face had taken on the pallor of defeat. She stood up clumsily, letting go her old insistence upon dignity and grace. The waiters were packing in the kitchen.

"I want to get out of these clothes," Zia said on her way to the stairs. I felt better as I watched her climb. I had done the right thing, the Christian thing. The woman had been smoking marijuana; she might even be mad. She was halfway upstairs when she called Tato for assistance. She was stuck, standing on the ostrich trim of her cape. Her foot had stepped right into it. Tato knelt, pulling it out roughly but swiftly.

"I'm finding it difficult to breathe," she said suddenly. Tato jumped up.

174

"Bring her down. Get her off the stairs," I said, running toward them.

"No," she said as I came near. She pulled in air. "Just wait here with me." She breathed deep, forcing air into her lungs. Her face had grown pale, then flushed. Her breathing began to normalize. She simply grabbed the banister with a trembling hand and climbed the rest of the way. Tato accompanied her to her room and helped her undress.

It cooled off after midnight, but I couldn't sleep. I took my money out of my drawer and went back downstairs. I lifted the cover of a Chinese ginger jar that sat conspicuously on the mantel. I placed my emerald ring and my ten thousand dollars inside. (I hadn't spent any of my money yet. Tato had paid for the tuxedos with a check.)

For the next few weeks Tato nursed Zia while I looked on from a distance with unexpected guilt and confusion. I tried to cling to the idea that I was right, that suicide under any circumstances was masochistic and defeatist. I believed that from my days at Nazzareno. I had put Christ and his cross into my desk drawer when I was thirteen years old. I refused to have him hanging over my bed. I refused to believe in the virtues of victimhood. To die like Christ was crazy.

How perfectly romantic it was of Christianity to view man as so precious that his own authority was not enough to govern his dying. On the other hand, to be forced to live against one's will seemed crazy, when with a few sleeping pills one could just leave all the foolish ugliness behind. I had felt the fascination of suicide. Why did I stand in Zia's way? Who was I?

Zia's condition worsened with surprising speed over the next two weeks. It was as though she had given up her own support systems, put her mind on the other side of her life, where it waited for her body. Tato stayed close to her. He was finding it difficult to get her to ingest even soup. It was my turn to walk the beach. I visited her room on days that she sat up. If I saw her speaking on the telephone, I took that as a sign that she would not refuse to talk to me. She tried to be friendly whenever I came into her room, smiling often, but there was a lot unspoken between us. She stopped smoking marijuana and began giving herself injections of morphine.

It was August 1968. The days were becoming shorter. The day lilies were all spent, their stems knobby with seed pods. The Queen Anne's lace had dried. Nothing new bloomed anywhere. The landscape was cruelly stark with no surprise of flowers. Tato and I made fires downstairs at night while Zia slept. He was speaking to me now in a friendly enough way, but only of Zia, her condition, her needs. He would not elaborate on any other topic, as though he were telling me that Zia was the only thing left that linked us, as though all other ties had been severed by my foolishness. Though annoyed, I tried everything that might rekindle the old spirit between us. He knew I was trying, but he was too committed to his new attitude to give in to me.

We were having exquisite days, the kind the summer people wish for—clear blue skies, cool breezes, hot sun. Sailboats were racing north of the house about a mile off the tip of Jessup, right about where Gabriella's ship had come out of the fog on its way to Sag Harbor. The weather was like Italy in August, although I couldn't imagine what sad and isolated place in Italy Jessup could be like. In spite of the sun and blue skies, we were in colder waters than Italy. We were in a more sprawling place, too, a lonelier place than Italy, of sandy islands and flat seas, a place of wind and emptiness.

It was hard to believe that Zia could be ill in such pure weather. I felt sorry for Tato, confined to the house with her. I hoped he understood that in my state of mind, I couldn't perform for her and that I was out walking toward the point every day because of my fear of the situation. I cooked dinner now and then, but Tato didn't seem happy with what I prepared, so he volunteered to cook if I would clean up afterwards.

One of those windy afternoons at about one o'clock, I was surprised to see Tato running toward me on the beach. His tan had faded somewhat, and it seemed odd that he was wearing shoes as he ran in the wet sand at the water's edge.

"You better come say goodbye to her," Tato said, out of breath.

"Is she dying?"

"No. She's leaving."

I didn't understand. "Where? How?"

"A helicopter is coming from Columbia Presbyterian."

We both started back. He walked ahead of me at a fast clip. I had to run to keep up.

"She's in pain," he said. "Really crazy pain. She needs a hospital. The morphine isn't enough. They're sending an ambulance copter. I never seen her like this."

As we approached the house, I could hear her. She wasn't screaming or calling a name. Her voice was full of surprise, as though many different demons were attacking her in rapid succession. Tato ran up the stairs, but I couldn't. Inside the house the guilt had immobilized me, the guilt for the confusion, for her pain, as if all the complications were my fault. The helicopter, Tato's nervousness—the whole mess caused by my unwillingness to let her die the way she wanted, up in the pines on the bluffs, in her lovely frock with its ostrich feathers, with both of us near her. I had forced these hard days upon her, upon Tato and myself, those bland, flowerless days of August, each day like the preceding one, sunny, cool at night, all the green dying for rain.

Moments after the medical people got to her, her cries stopped. I steeled myself to look at her as the stretcher came down the stairs. We all go off alone that way, borne away by strangers. But when I saw her face, I was crying, sucking in air like a vacuum. She tried to smile. Everything was happening too fast. I knelt, surrounding her with my arms. "Goodbye," I said.

"*Addio*, Cello, *figlio bello*. Goodbye, Cello, my beautiful child."

Squeezed between the two bison and the stretcher, I watched them carry her out, then down the porch steps into the sunlight. As the stretcher approached the copter, I turned and ran up the stairs. The copter noise was forcing itself through the whole house. When I closed the door to my room, it only grew louder. I leaned against my door, my eyes battered by the pressure of noise. The noise changed in tone, and suddenly out my window I could see the helicopter rising. The flat sea and the sky stretched behind it. I saw Zia's face; they had lifted her head so she could see out the

177

window. Just as Snow did when he flew away from Tato and me, the copter tilted and drifted deep into the horizon, becoming smaller and smaller, until it was the size of a mosquito, then a dot. Only the wind stayed behind breaking the silence. It whirred through the bedroom screen; it died down after an hour, when the sounds of birds replaced it.

I must have stayed against my door for several hours. My mind drifted back to the seminary. There used to be a small sign over the main portal: LEAVE THE WORLD HERE BEFORE YOU PASS INSIDE. I imagined myself passing under that sign as I had done so many times, reaching deacons' corridor where only deacons may pass. Another sign on another archway read: SUMMUM SILENTIUM. I passed it into deacons' corridor to my room with its dark stone walls. That is where I wanted to be—in Rome, in my seminary room on deacons' corridor, in my old room carved out of the center of the great rock where the world has no right, no power to penetrate.

When I finally opened my bedroom door, I smelled coffee in the hallway. I walked downstairs. Things had become so quiet that the sounds of the waves were in the house.

Tato handed me a cup of coffee on the porch. I accepted it, welcoming its heat on my lips. We sat there looking at the water, drinking our coffee as the sun died.

"I was thinking," he said without looking up at me, "where would I like to be more than anywhere right now, and you know what I came up with?"

"What?" I asked.

"The Beverly Hills Hotel."

"Where is it?"

"California."

"Why there?"

"I don't know. The Beverly Hills Hotel is freedom from shit, freedom from this world and bill collectors and scraping your bread and butter together. When you go to the Beverly Hills Hotel, it's because you're not scraping anymore. It means you're flyin'. You're Flash the Flying Man. You don't drag your ass into the Beverly Hills Hotel; someone drags it in for you. You walk in on air like a fuckin' fairy godmother, and you fly out in a white car, a white somethin' on wheels to some cliff overlooking the goddamn Pacific Ocean." He stood up with tears in his eyes. He lifted on his toes and stretched. He yawned, and the yawn turned into a scream. He took a pack of cigarettes out and bit into it with his teeth. He roared and ripped and tore at the pack, spitting out tobacco, cellophane, paper. "Goddamn fuckin' coffin nails. Goddamn fuckin' coffin nails. Murderers."

That night we cleaned her room. Tato put her marijuana into his pocket, but he threw her cigarettes into the toilet bowl and flushed it. We took all the upstairs ashtrays downstairs to the kitchen and ran hot water in them. We changed her bed, throwing her sheets in the garbage, and threw a pale blue bedspread over it. We put fresh ivy in a vase and took down all her telephone numbers. From the hall her room looked serene again, so pretty. I felt that the house would disappear before anyone ever slept in Zia's bed again.

We hadn't smoked all day. We ate no supper. It was nine-thirty when we finished. We drank brandy and mineral water, in bare feet before the fire that night.

He turned to me with a smile. "Did you throw all your cigarettes away?"

"Yes, I answered, "but I have some stale packs in my suitcase, from Italy."

"Get them," he ordered, "before I have a heart attack here."

I ran upstairs and took two packs out of my valise. I threw a pack to him and joined him at the fire. We ripped them open and lit up. We breathed in deep rivers of smoke. I inhaled with such gratitude, such a need, that I mockingly blessed my cigarette.

"How are we ever gonna give up these motherfuckers?" Tato asked.

"Don't know," I said. My temples throbbed peacefully. My cigarette was my peace.

"Let's make a pact. September first we give them up," he said.

"Okay." I was happy to agree, happy to have more time with him, happy to have any agreement with him. I was happy that the house was in order, happy that upstairs her room was quiet and clean. The image of the pale blue bedspread, neatly tucked under and around a pillow at the headboard, comforted me. The house was clean and empty of confusion, a neat place once again, dark on the inside and white on the outside. In its middle there was a fire warming our bare feet, and we were together again. Tato was talking freely to me again. We were together again, safely.

The next day Tato told me that each day Zia had made him promise that we would not try to follow her. It was hard to know if she just wanted to spare us the visions of her deterioration or if she simply wanted the privacy to die without embarrassment. She even had made arrangements for her own cremation with a funeral director named Crosby. The lawyers were well paid in advance to execute the details. She was probably going to be under morphine for the rest of her days. Our goodbye was real. It was final. Even her disappearance would be swift and smooth.

Carter Boisvert, the younger lawyer with the geometric smile, gave us a follow-up call. He reminded us that expenses on the house were being taken care of by reason of the ample value of Zia's house, its contents, and the surrounding properties. Since the law firm was included on the deed, there was no need for us to worry about the expenses or details of her death and burial. He told Tato that, at most, a few hundred yards of beachfront south of the large peninsula of Jessup Neck was all they would take as collateral, and of course, we had the option to buy it back whenever we could. In the meantime, all Zia's expenses were taken care of by the Boisverts in advance. Zia wanted it that way.

Given the situation, it wasn't hard to say yes to Tato when he asked if I would go to California with him. My first chance alone, I went to the ginger jar and counted out five thousand dollars for traveler's checks. The other five thousand and Zia's ring went back into the jar. I wanted to leave them hidden safely, something to come home to.

We woke up in the Beverly Hills Hotel in Los Angeles on September first. We had flown the night before, first class, smoking to our hearts' content, since it was the last day before our agreed cut-off date, drinking champagne, eating lobster thermidor. It had been two A.M. when we collapsed on the large bed in our cottage apartment at the hotel.

I jumped out of bed and pulled the long drapes. Rain puddles on the cement patio reflected the sky; clouds moved fast inside them.

"I wanna see the Pacific Ocean," Tato said, half asleep. He felt the night table for his cigarettes.

"We don't smoke." I laughed. "It's September first."

"Oh, my God, Cello." He sank to the floor in mock death. Suddenly he snapped to his feet. "Brush teeth, take shower, healthy, no shittin' around here. Get them fuckers on the phone and have them bring in the most far-out breakfast. Everything, one of everything." He sang it in a high tenor voice. He danced, shuffling to the bathroom.

Three wagons came to our room loaded with strawberries, blackberries, Cream of Wheat, dry cereal, steak, eggs—scrambled, sunnyside, poached—orange juice, whole carved-out pineapples, two mangos, a silver pot of coffee, a silver pot of tea, a silver pot of cocoa, seeded rolls, honey buns with walnuts, pancakes with blueberries and cream, honey syrup, real maple syrup, confectioners' sugar and pink roses in stem vases. We ate slowly and we ate a lot and watched the clouds go by in the puddles.

"We should take a picture of breakfast," I said.

"No more stills. It's movies from now on, baby. *Real* movies."

After breakfast, I would have liked a cigarette. Instead, I put a berry in my mouth, then a roll with some butter, then a forkful of eggs, and then a pancake with syrup. We ate a second time.

"Let's go," Tato said, holding his stomach. "Let's see that gorgeous Pacific."

We drove in a rented white convertible Mustang, down the winding hotel road into Beverly Hills. The houses we passed were formidable, like mausoleums. The sun came out; still I felt like we were in a giant indoor stadium.

"I've had enough," I said after a while.

"Yeah," Tato said. "I want to see Bobby Brown's Surf City Shop." He zoomed onto Sunset Boulevard and turned on the radio.

The weather man announced record cool weather and predicted rain. The Beach Boys sang,

> *"East Coast girls are hip.*
> *I really dig the styles they wear. . . .*
>
> *I wish they all could be California,*
> *wish they all could be California . . . girls."*

At Malibu it appeared we were the only people on the beach. "Where the hell are all the surfers?" Tato asked. He was acting silly, slightly hysterical; his quest for fun was too urgent.

"Isn't that a surfer coming out of the water?" I replied, pointing.

Tato called, "Hey." The surfer turned, and we hurried toward him. He was a boy, no more than twelve. "Ever hear of Bobby Brown's Surf Shop?" Tato asked.

"Nope." The boy's skin was goose-bumped and blue.

"It's a popular place in California," Tato pressed. The boy shrugged. "How come you have such a small surfboard?"

"It's not small."

"Surfboards are supposed to be twice that long, aren't they?"

"Those are the old-time boards. My father has one like that." The boy was shivering. "My pop used to surf down here with a big Hobie."

"Yeah, Hobie, that's the name." Tato smiled.

"Gotta go."

"Wait. The beach this empty every day?"

"Pretty much," the boy said, hardly able to hold onto the board under his shaking arm. Water still dripped down his face.

"Where does your father surf now?"

"He works for the telephone company now."

I couldn't tell what Tato was feeling. Embarrassment, disappointment perhaps. He held out a five-dollar bill to the boy.

"No thanks." The boy blushed in shock.

"Take it." Tato blushed back in anger.

The boy took it, out of fear, and walked away from us.

It began to rain as we drove north up the Pacific Coast Highway.

Tato acted unconscious of me; I kept silent. He chewed his nails and drove with one hand, looking ahead steadily. I knew he was a man of moods, but I had never seen him this nervous. Big water drops began to hit us. Up ahead it was pouring. Two hitchhikers were huddling under a newspaper. Tato pulled over for them, a girl and bearded fellow carrying a guitar. Tato put up the convertible top.

"Hi." They laughed and jumped in the car.

Tato's spirits picked up. "Hi." His voice flew like an adolescent's. "We were sent from above to rescue you."

"Lifesavers." They giggled.

The fragrance of rain and the sweet smell of wet hair filled the car.

"My name's Murph and this is Caroline." He licked the rain from his lips.

"This is Cello and I'm Tato."

"You guys New York?"

"How could you tell?" Tato's smile was big.

"Oh, we can tell." They laughed a little. "We have to pick up our daughter at the baby-sitter's," Murph said. I was surprised they had a child; they were so much younger than I. Caroline had skin and face like the pregnant woman in Vermeer's painting—blond, almost invisible eyelashes and eyebrows—and he had a thin handsome face and friendly brown eyes.

"What's up with the guitar?" Tato asked.

"Oh, we sing," Murph said.

"We went for an audition this morning. Don't ask how we did," Caroline said.

"Yeah." Murph looked out the window and smiled weakly. He changed the subject. "What are you two up to?"

"We're sort of on a vacation," Tato answered. "We came out here looking for some action. Any suggestions?"

"Depends on what you like," Murph said.

"The California scene," Tato said.

"What are your hopes?" said Caroline.

"What's she talkin' about?" Tato smiled at me.

"Tell us your fantasy, what you hope to find here."

"Oh, blondes, you know, very blond-headed people, all sun-tanned. Surfers swarmin' on the sand, movie stars, fancy old cars, Bobby Brown's Surf Shop, the Beachboys singin' at a beach party." He laughed. Murph and Caroline watched him with fascination. "Your types"—Tato turned with a smile for Caroline—"except raggier maybe, carrying flowers."

"C'mon, that's a whole other crowd."

"How about those mountain people who live in Topanga Canyon with nanny goats and Porsches?"

"Don't go there," Caroline said with real sadness. "The original people are gone, really."

"Where'd they go?" Tato was serious.

"San Francisco to drink and do coke. Some went to New York to tap-dance class. The ones who remained who they were, they're in Oregon and Colorado. The ones who changed, well, they just aren't who they were, so you won't find them on this planet." Her words confused Tato. He kept his eyes on the road, his smile frozen. There were beads of sweat on his forehead. There was a long silence. Murph and Caroline whispered semi-private ordinary things to each other. Then Murph spoke up, directing us to a ranch house near an orchid farm.

"Good luck, and thanks loads," Murph said, hopping out.

"Yeah, good luck," Caroline said. She caught my eyes as she left the car. Her skin was tight and freckled; her eyes blue and brilliant. Another couple waited at the aluminum screen door of the ranch house. The man had a moon face and a long brown beard. Three fingers of his left hand strained to keep open the aluminum door. The woman was short, standing under his straining arm. If she were not so pregnant, I'd have taken her for a much older woman. She wore old rainbow boots, stitched every which way, of many colors of leather, and a dress of unpressed cotton. She smiled at Caroline and held out one hand as she came up the steps. The other hand rested self-consciously on her large belly. The moon-faced man stared at our car as though it were a rhinoceros. He ushered Murph and Caroline inside under his arm. He let the aluminum door close, but he didn't move away. He watched suspiciously through the screen until we left.

Tato spun the wheel sharp left with one hand, crossing a double line, heading south back toward Malibu. "I'm gonna buy a pack of smokes. Fuck it!"

"We've only been off them a half day," I said.

"I don't give a good fuck."

We drove a long time without the radio, just the squeaking of the windshield wipers and the squishing of our tires on the wet asphalt. The air conditioner was on low, blowing cold dampness into the car. Tato seemed to be heading back toward the hotel along Sunset Boulevard.

We spent a lot of time in the hotel. Tato didn't start smoking but he never got over his moodiness. He spent an hour each morning with his coffee, sitting beneath the hanging bougainvillea that puffed out from the patio wall, watching its magenta petals dropping onto the cement. He didn't read or watch television. I watched his features changing, recalling the dark-bearded man who sat with me on the porch at Jessup Neck.

At midnight one night Tato grabbed three tambourines he had bought and was about to leave.

"Can I come?" I asked.

"To a *bar*?" he asked. "*You*?" He raised his eyebrows. Finally he muttered his approval and we left.

We inched our way inside a jam-packed bar on Santa Monica Boulevard. The jukebox vibrations pounded on my face like wind and drummed through the floor into my legs. It smelled as though they had mopped the floor with a mixture of urine and beer. And not a woman in sight! The customers were all men, reminding me of monks in choir, each in his own solitude.

Other tambourine players jangled perfectly to the thumping, but I couldn't see them in the crowd. Tato gathered stares as he pushed through the crowd of men only, men standing in the orange light and smoke, men dressed as cowboys and construction workers, men with mustaches and beards, men with shaved heads, wearing earrings, men dressed in ties and white collars. They stared at us with cold hunters' eyes.

Tato and I didn't talk to each other while we were there. I

185

gripped my bottle of beer. It was still full as we walked out. Tato rolled his tambourines into the street one at a time under an oncoming bus.

I called Columbia Presbyterian from the hotel lobby to get a report on Zia.

"Fair," the hospital operator said.

I wondered if she was in pain. A list of questions was growing in my mind: Who would be at her funeral? Should I let Gabriella know? My father?

At four in the morning Tato woke me. "I feel like going to Colorado," he said.

We flew out of California that same morning. Our bill at the Beverly Hills Hotel totaled $2889.65, not counting the car. He had made reservations at a place called the Star Vue Motel in Boulder, in spite of my suggestion that we both fly back to New York. I thought I'd call Zia's lawyers at the airport for more details about her condition.

"Where are you?" the senior Boisvert asked urgently.

"At the Los Angeles airport," I said.

"Where are you going? Don't hang up." He obviously had put his hand over the phone.

"Colorado," I answered.

Someone picked up an extension. The old man's voice grew thinner: "Where in Colorado?"

"Star Vue in Boulder." I hesitated, feeling for some reason that I shouldn't have let him know.

"I'm sending my son Carter there tonight," he said.

"Is my aunt all right?"

"Carter knows everything," he answered. "Look for him tonight or tomorrow."

"How is my aunt?"

"Carter's got all the information for you. Everything's fine. Just stay there in Boulder."

"Is she dead?" I asked. He hung up without answering.

I said nothing to Tato about the call.

* * *

The Star Vue was a large mountain motel—a main building, with separate cabins around it, with overhanging decks for star gazing. Posters in the lobby read, "Welcome to the land of the stars." There was a photograph of an Indian guru named Jai Dheviada Namada; notices of yoga courses and lectures on transcendental meditation were posted. There was a large framed photograph of a geodesic redwood temple with nothing but a bare wooden floor and an octagonal eye at the top, open to the weather.

At breakfast the next morning, I saw Carter Boisvert sitting at a corner table. He acknowledged me with a small salute. Tato's back was to him.

"Who is it?" Tato asked.

"Carter Boisvert."

"What the hell does he want?"

"Tato, I called them in New York."

"What? Why?"

"To check on Zia."

"Why is he here?"

"I don't know."

"Is Zia okay?"

"I don't know."

"Why didn't you tell me? Goddamnit!"

"I didn't want you to worry."

Tato threw down his napkin and stood up. I followed him to Carter's table, where Carter smiled and shook our hands. "Let's go to your room or somewhere where we can talk," Carter said. He gulped his coffee and stood up.

"Talk here," Tato insisted.

"I'd rather not." Carter warned him with his eyes.

"How's my aunt?" Tato asked.

"We should go somewhere," Carter said.

"Is she close?"

Carter smiled his biggest smile. "Look, you guys, the poor woman, your aunt, she had no right to give you that house or even all this money you've been blowing."

Tato looked at Carter without moving an eyelash. "I don't know what you're pullin'."

"Mr. Manfredi, do you want to know what is happening to you?" Carter smiled.

"Just talk."

"Can't we talk in your room?"

Tato held still for a moment, then he walked stiffly into the lobby toward the elevators. Up to the third floor. When we reached our room, Carter immediately poured himself a glass of water.

"We'll fight this thing. I'm a tiger," Tato warned, throwing the room key against the wall.

"You won't win," Carter said, drinking calmly. Carter took out eyeglasses and wiped them with a handkerchief. "The Maldonado estate has money to burn. They take tax losses in the millions." He put his glasses on. "On top of it all, they're in the right. I don't know if Maldonado ever knew it, but the documents your aunt was given by his lawyers—those weren't real documents of title; they were *assigned* with what is called future interest. In plain English, what she owns, she only sort of owns. It is not transferable to anyone when she dies. In case of her death, everything reverts back to the estate of her benefactor. That means my firm gets screwed along with you guys. We're into this thing with a hefty advance. Her hospital bills read like science fiction, not to mention the money of ours you gorgeous guys are spending this very minute. Maldonado died last week in Argentina. His law firm is Madero, O'Shea and Obregón. They're tops and hot in Argentina. If you've got a couple million bucks to lose, we'll fight for you. But we won't win. Guaranteed. Maldonado's wife and kids hate your aunt for obvious reasons. Her lawyers have been hound-dogging your aunt most of her life. You don't think they're going to let a mistress take off with the family jewels. Not that they need any more than they've got, but with those strict Catholics down there, it's the principle of the thing."

Tato stared at Carter. "Is this some kind of joke, you mother-fucker?" Carter laughed. Tato jumped up, grabbed Carter, hesitated, then pushed him free.

Carter blinked. He lifted his knee to support his attaché case and snapped it open. His fingers shook. "Would I follow you across the country to pull a joke?" Carter said. He pulled some papers out of the case, held them in his teeth and shut the case. "These are the papers you both signed at her house in Jessup Neck."

"Wipe our ass with them, right?" Tato said.

Carter turned, red-faced, forcing a smile that did not mask his discomfort. He walked toward the hall door, opened it and turned. "Your aunt owes us money. The money she gave you was advanced to her by us. We want you to know that we're going to attach that money. Are those airline tickets for New York?" he asked, glancing at the dresser and talking to me.

"Get him outta my sight," Tato said to me.

"You'd better fly home before you make things worse for yourselves." Carter closed the door behind him with those words.

Tato picked up a chair and threw it at the closing door. Then he walked out to the deck.

I ran into the hall and caught Carter at the elevator. "I'd like to talk some more."

"I'm sorry for you and the old woman."

"Can you help us?" I asked.

"Help? What is help at this point?"

"You came here to help, I presumed. Your father made it sound that way."

The elevator came. He stepped inside and held the door from closing. "Your aunt's still alive. I'll give you some free advice: Go back, get your personal stuff out of that house before she dies or it won't be yours anymore."

Tato was on the deck where I left him. I came close to him, waiting for him to say something. I was angry—not at him—and the words came out wrong. "You must be crazy. You acted like a crazy man," I said.

He whipped around. His eyes were glassy. His finger lifted and pointed in my face. "I'm tired of your pussy mouth. Get out of my sight." But it was Tato who left.

There was no sky. Just a colorless claylike mass overhead that made being outdoors seem like being in a gray room. Below, two waiters raced their bicycle carts. The rattling noise had nowhere to go. It fell around like a heap of junk. Wind hummed in the pines, reminding me of Rome—pungent smells, smells of new leaves.

Tato came back onto the deck smoking a cigarette.

"Where'd you get it?" I asked.

"I bought a pack downstairs." I decided to be silent.

"I'm sorry," Tato said as he looked out to the horizon. His eyes squinted as if he were trying to see something. I scanned the sky. Nothing was there. "The one time I thought I had the upper hand on the system, I get fucked out of it. That poor crazy old lady."

Leaves cartwheeled along the sidewalk below. Tato took a deep drag and looked down. The pines stirred. I thought of the Lamborghini days and Ciascuno zooming up the back roads beneath the old Italian pines. Then I wondered who occupied my old room at the seminary now. My classmates would all be priests, assigned to posts or parishes, hearing confessions, blessing the dying, and there I was, bottomed-out in the Star Vue Motel in Colorado.

"I smell it coming—the big ball of winter," Tato whispered. "Summer's all wrapped up. All wrapped up in big crates, on trucks headed south. I'm scared."

"What of?" I asked.

"Of being poor? Maybe not that. I don't know. Of not bein' somethin'."

"Zia's house and money didn't make you special," I said.

"Money doesn't save you from doom"—he smiled—"or from the big final axe, but it can save you from a lotta little deaths." He turned to me, his eyes filled with tears: "Jesus Christ, this morning at breakfast, that was forty thousand years ago, Cello. It's gonna be goodbye time again. Do you feel it comin'?"

"Yes," I said.

"It doesn't have to be, if we make some kind of effort. Cello, c'mon and stay at my apartment in New York." He was pleading, and it unnerved me coming from him.

"Maybe." I turned away.

"I have this premonition that I'm not going to see you anymore." He followed me.

"We got through something like this once before, when we were kids," I said.

"When we were kids, there were sixty million days of life ahead of us, but now I can already see the end of the road."

"I'm the one who should worry. You have a place in the world, your law books."

"I flunked out. The report was in the mailbox when we went back to my apartment for the tuxedos. What are you gonna do?" He was pleading again. I hated that strangulated voice. I'd rather have heard him crying.

"I'm not worried," I said. "I've never had a home, really. I need air right now."

I left him quickly, taking a sweater. I ignored the elevator, slipped into the stairwell and walked down to the front entrance with no idea whatever where I was going.

I saw the Star Vue bus—a "daily service for guests." It waited at the lobby entrance with a sign in its window that read, ROCKY MOUNTAIN TOURS. The driver stood in a gray and green uniform at the open door of the bus, a white-haired man of about sixty. "How about some sightseeing, mister?"

The only passenger in the dark, upholstered sightseeing bus, I thought of my pigeon. Poor Snow. Did he find a female to nest with, a flock that would accept him? Did he get lost over the ocean and die, drowned, his heart given out? Did a shark eat him? Or did he find his way back to Brooklyn and the black tar roof, only to find no one there? Did he return to the house and die under a bush on the beach, wondering where we went? How cruel I had been keeping him in that tight, tiny prison, then give him too much freedom when he was powerless to understand it.

Kids, leaving school for lunch, carrying books and skateboards. Boys talking loudly and laughing while the girls huddled and whispered. We passed a neighborhood of houses; the cloud-filtered white light shed equal accent on each one, making them appear like a primitive painting. Small houses in rows seemed quaint and lovely to me, each one representing a commitment of people to live together. Each house was a tiny estate, a small country with its special citizens. But the houses went on for miles for fifteen minutes, changing very little. They were too alike, a huge bag of jelly beans spilled on the grass.

When I arrived back at the room in the Star Vue, all our clothes were out of the drawers and folded into our bags. Plane tickets, keys and wallets were all laid out in a line on the bed.

"Our plane leaves after midnight, so there's time to get some sleep," Tato said without looking at me. He moved with assertiveness and intention, pulling his stuff out of the medicine cabinet and lining it in his bag. He took a bottle of tequila from the dresser and handed me a glass. "I picked up some celebration liquid." He poured the tequila and clinked my glass. "Good luck to both of us." He looked at me, not with anger this time, but with caution.

"*Salute.*" I sipped the tequila and went to the bathroom.

Tato went down to the coffee shop for some food. I undressed and took a hot shower, then I wrapped a sheet around me and went into the sauna. After a few minutes Tato entered the sauna, wearing a sheet and carrying the tequila with two plastic glasses filled with ice. We drank and leaned back into the heat and silence. I felt good, very safe in the redwood dark. After ten minutes we left the sauna, drenched in sweat. Tato lit a stick of marijuana and we smoked it without conversation on the deck.

The sky's milkiness was changing to pink. The sun, moving westward, had begun to peek beneath the blanket of sky. The pines below murmured. Tato passed me the stick. It was the first inhaling I had done since I had given up cigarettes. I felt a powerful rush to my temples and a gentle throbbing. I had gained weight. My body felt strong. I didn't remember leaving the sauna. I wondered how I got outdoors. Tato poured two more glasses of tequila.

"Your friends have power to kill you," he said, slightly thick-tongued. I ignored the statement.

I inhaled, imitating his sucking. He smiled. I smiled back. They were our first smiles since Carter Boisvert came from New York.

"Do me a favor," Tato said. "Curse. I'm dyin' to hear you curse."

"Shit," I said. "Okay?"

He laughed. "Say . . . son of a bitch."

"Son of a bitch," I said.

"That's good, for you. Now say cunt."

"Cunt?"

"Say motherfucker."

"Motherfucker."

"Now in French—mouthair feuckair."

"Mouthair . . ."

The dirty whipped-cream sky was blowing away like smoke. The pink in the west had changed into glowing red-hot coals which reflected in the sliding glass doors, turning them into molten sheets of red. I was feeling very, very good. I had pretended not to hear his remark about friends killing you, but I had. He was getting high, bolting down tequila as though he were taking aspirins.

"Are you referring to me when you say your friends have power to kill you?" I asked finally.

". . . No."

"You don't sound too sure. Do you mean Zia?"

"Nope. I trust her. I dig Zia. It's friends that fuck you. Only friends have the key to your heart. They know your mind 'cause you invite them in there over and over. Sometimes they even make themselves at home when you aren't there. They walk into your ear with their flashlights. They fall asleep in your head. They help you commit murders."

I had to control an urge to laugh.

"Like you," he said. "You walked with your little flashlight into my ear a long time ago. You made a home for yourself there. You know you did, buddy."

"Excuse me for smiling if it doesn't fit in with what you're saying," I said.

"You pierced my hands and my feet," he said mysteriously. I let go the laugh deliberately, hoping to douse his mood. He ignored me. "I ate your holy communion," he went on.

"I'm not impressed with your theology," I said.

He smiled. Suddenly he leaned his head on my shoulder and curled his body into mine like a snail into a shell. "Admit you're scared shit of me," he said.

"Okay, I'm afraid," I said. Why did I then put my hand to his head, pressing it to my shoulder? I pressed his ribs with my other hand. I meant it to be a brief tenderness. I felt sorry for him. His arms came around me. I felt his heart beating.

I don't remember how we came to be lying down on the pads on the deck. I don't remember the bed sheets being out there, but he covered us with sheets and lay close to me. Stars were vaguely showing in the deepening blueness. Tato's eyes were closed. I lay there a long time feeling his breath in the coolness blowing warm on my face.

It was very cool when I opened my eyes. The night was in full black bloom. The sky was blasted with a million stars.

I was shivering, but I felt a perverse love for the cold that caused it. I lay there a long while, feeling lighter and loving my shivering. I was extremely happy. That is the only way I can describe it . . . so glad I possessed my body. I could hear my blood rushing, wrapping flesh around me. The sound of it in my ears was the same sound of the sea of the planets outside me. I was a fine clock, wrapped in veins and dreams, who had come across a sea of time. I stood up, feeling taller. I imagined I was Jesus Christ, passing through the roof into the sky. The blue night sky was an ocean above me. Its coolness tightened my face. Its stars talked. The sky-ocean did not hold still. The ocean moved above me in one piece. But I hadn't passed through a roof. I was outside standing on the pads of the deck.

"Friend." A whisper. It spoke into the shell of my ear. A word on my neck from behind me. The voice was a breath. "My friend." Father carrying me into the elevator, his lips clucking into my ear? Or was it Tato? Tato stood close to me, behind me. His hands slid under my arms. I felt their heat. My feet were cool, my face cool, my body cool, and his arms were rays of sun around me. His hands pressed lightly into my chest. He pulled me backwards.

"I love you." On the wind, past the shell of my ears, a voice. Tato's voice. Then his hands rose beneath me, sliding slippery between my buttocks like some warm-blooded creature, running up my back to my head, through my hair. I smelled suntan oil; its perfume rose, filling the caverns of my head, touching me behind my eyes. Then something slid between my buttocks. Tato knocked

194

out my knees. His hand pushed my head down. I felt my body open; something had entered me.

"Who? What do I feel?"

"Your friend." His arms, like iron, were trembling, holding me.

"No," I cried, but he was too deep inside.

"Yes," he screamed, his voice shattering me like his arms. His strength was incredible. He had me face down on the deck. He was on top of me, inside me perfectly. I kicked out from under him and scrambled to my feet. But it was too late; his semen was running out of me. He was laughing. I felt the cliffs giving way under my feet. I moved farther and farther back, but they disintegrated faster than I could run, till I fell, sliding all the way down to the irreversible truth. He had raped me.

"Don't tell me that in the back of your mind you weren't hoping for that fuck. It's very hard to get up a man's ass. Try it some time." He was folding the sheets like a housewife.

"Do you love me?" I asked sarcastically.

"You're a cockteaser."

"Do you *love me?*" I shouted.

Tato laughed guiltily, putting on his socks.

"Don't call me your friend, ever again," I said.

"You want a fairy-tale life. You're afraid of the real stuff that goes on between people." He was scared, acting flip.

"Don't ever call me a friend."

"You've decreed that, Caesar?"

"*You have,*" I shouted.

"Cello, you commit the worst sin of all, ya know that? You lie to yourself." He leaned over, dressed already, grabbing his suitcase, still looking at me. His trousers were wrinkled. He was wearing worn leather dress shoes. He put his hand on my shoulder, then up around the back of my neck. I tried to slip free. He held me harder and dropped his suitcase. "Kiss me, you goddamn heterosexual. Let's find out what you feel."

I hit him in the face. He grabbed my throat with both hands. I tried to relax, keeping my hands off him. He tried to squeeze back tears as he squeezed my neck.

195

"Let go," I said calmly. But he didn't let go.

"You poor little man of honor. Your heart is in a fuckin' coffin, buried somewhere." I avoided his eyes, which let go their rivers, and slowly he began to relax his hands. "Get out of here before I kill you," he sobbed.

He walked into the bathroom and slammed the door. I quickly got dressed, grabbed my bags and left. As I closed the door, I could hear him crying.

CHAPTER VII

JUST as my plane began stacking procedures coming into New York, there was a sudden roaring drag, after which the captain announced a half-hour delay. "We are now over eastern Long Island. Connecticut is on our right and the Atlantic Ocean on the left."

I looked down. The earth was misty, but the ocean sparkled, catching the first rays of dawn. We circled New York City, and the captain pointed out the tallest building in the world, the Empire State building, as well as the Hudson River and the Statue of Liberty. From up there, looking down, it all seemed for once containable. The apartment where I was born on the West Side. Jessup Neck stretching out to the east somewhere. My mother buried down there somewhere; Zia in Columbia Presbyterian. As the plane hit the runway, I thought of the mantel in Jessup and the Chinese ginger jar with the dragon on it in which I had left the money and the ring.

After we landed, I picked up my baggage and dragged it toward the sliding doors of the terminal in the same direction as everyone else. Taxis moved past, picking up passengers. I wanted to drop into one, but where would I go? I looked at the line of telephones where everyone was calling. I moved toward them. Who would I call?

I called Columbia Presbyterian. "I'd like to inquire as to the condition of Fantasia Manfredi, please."

"Just a minute." I waited. The operator clicked back. "Sir, Miss Manfredi is no longer at this hospital."

"What do you mean? Where did she go?"

"I'm sorry, sir. Would you like to talk with one of the nurses?"

"Yes, yes."

"Let me see. Just a minute." Another click.

"Nurse Hennesy."

"My name is Manfredi."

"Oh, yes. How is your mother?"

"Where is she?"

"You don't know? She was discharged a few days ago. Where were you then?"

"Pardon me?"

"She needed help. I don't know how she got out of the taxicab."

"Taxicab? Where did she go?"

"Don't *you* know? *I* don't know."

"Why did you let her go?"

"She refused an ambulance which would have taken her to a public hospital."

"Why did she have to go to a public hospital?"

"She signed an AMA."

"What are you talking about?"

"She signed a slip against medical advice."

Taxis came and left as we talked. I was frantic.

"Why did she have to go to another hospital?" I roared. There was a pause. I wondered if we were still connected. "Nurse?"

"Sir. If you shout, I will hang up. Now. Your mother had no hospitalization. Listen, let me see if I can find out where she is right now."

"She's not my mother."

"Who are you?"

"Her nephew."

"Well, your aunt then. God! Hold on," she said with disgust. Then: "Hello?"

"Where is she?"

"At the moment, nobody here seems to know where your aunt is."

"Thank you, thank you."

"But this is not the fault of the hospital, sir. You should have been here." I hung up.

Where was Zia? Who would know? I looked up the name of Carter Boisvert in the Manhattan directory. It was seven-fifteen in the morning, too early to call the firm. I dialed a number. A woman answered: "Your call is being answered by an electronic answering system because it cannot be answered personally at this time." I hung up. Seven-fifteen. Where did Zia go? Since Zia was still alive, the house was still hers. Of course! With no money, Zia would have gone back there, the only home left to her.

I ran through the electric-eye door and hailed a cab.

"Where to, sir?"

"Southampton, Long Island."

"That's a special rate, sir." I dropped into the back seat of the cab, folding my arms around myself while the driver put my bags in the trunk.

When we reached Exit 62 at Manorville on the Long Island Expressway, the driver pulled over. "Could you hitchhike from here?" he asked.

"What do you mean? Why?"

"This trip is gonna bust me. We've been driving almost two hours. I don't have no ride goin' back, and I'm gonna be way overtime."

I paid him fifty dollars plus a ten-dollar tip. I was picked up by the first vehicle that came on the by-pass, a pickup driven by a plumber from Shelter Island. He dropped me off near a fish store at the edge of Southampton Village. I had to hitch again from there.

The North Sea Bakery truck gave me a lift to the Texaco station. I walked the half mile from there to the singing phragmites and the cracked asphalt, hoping I'd find a car parked there, some indication of Zia.

But there was no car; just the cold and clear day stretching wide over the bay. The water shone like ice in the sun. Gulls glided motionless on the wind. A jet burst like a cannon shot in the air, and left a trail of silence.

I tried from the distance to make out any possible signs that Zia was in the house. The porch was empty; all windows appeared closed. Up close I found fresh footprints in the sand at the porch steps. Drifts had gathered on the porch. I could make out fresh footprints there, too, going into the foyer. The front door was ajar.

When I stepped into the foyer, I sensed the house had not been entered since Tato and I left it. Odors of stale marijuana and tobacco reached me from the rugs and drapes. The house was warm and still. I left my bags in the foyer on top of one of the buffaloes and I entered the living room. I went straight to the Chinese ginger jar and held my breath as I lifted the cover. Money and the ring were there. I counted the money and it was all there—five thousand dollars. I stuffed it into my right pocket, the ring into my left. The emerald was, no doubt, worth a great deal. I heard a creak above me.

I walked cautiously to the stairs and started up. I smelled the dust of a closed house, but there was something fresh mixing with it, like the odor of damp earth. Someone was in the house. I felt the presence now. Whoever it was had entered recently, trailing fresh air into the dusty house.

I stopped in the yellow and lavender light of the stained oval window at the landing. Suddenly from Tato's room came a sound of floors creaking, the soft thud of footsteps on the rug, then on the wooden floor.

A woman—tall, thin, wearing a black coat—stood opposite me, unaware of me. She stopped at the window of the hallway looking south to the sky and water, the sun hitting her straight on and pushing past her onto the floor.

"Excuse me?" I said. She whipped around, startled, and faced me. Her eyes, though surprised, held strong to themselves, light brown, the whites blue and healthy. Her chin was small; so was her mouth. Her lips were thin but perfectly shaped. Her neck was long. She was frail. Her hair, very long chestnut, fell silken over her black coat. The coat was a little worn at the cuffs, an antique coat from the 1930s, yet it seemed very chic on her. Her light skin accentuated the blue-green veins on her forehead. She seemed the frail kind of woman a man could simply lift and carry off.

"Who are you?" she asked sharply.

"My name is Cello Manfredi."

"Oh." She seemed to recognize the name. "I'm sorry, I thought the house was empty."

"It was. I just arrived. Who are you?"

"Amelia Murphy. I'm not even sure I am in the right house."

"Are you from the lawyer's office?"

"I'm just trespassing. I'm not from a lawyer's office or anything like that." She smiled a little. She had not totally recovered from her embarrassment. Her face began to color. She may have felt trapped at the landing, having to pass me to leave.

"You're not trespassing, I assure you." I felt responsible for her embarrassment.

"I was just leaving anyway," she said, boldly coming toward me. I immediately stepped aside, letting her pass me on her way downstairs. She walked straight through the vestibule, out the front door, onto the porch. I followed. She turned and put a hand on her hip inside her coat. "Goodbye," she said, holding out her other hand to me.

"Won't you stay for some tea? I was just going to make some." In the light she was beautiful. She was so thin; her clothes seemed alien to her body.

She hesitated. "If you *really* are having tea, I would love some."

"I really am."

I put on the water to boil and found some of Zia's Chinese green tea in the kitchen. The woman drifted back into the house, examining the bookcases of the living room. I watched her from the kitchen, using the time to pull myself together.

"Sugar?" I asked, coming toward her.

"No, thank you." She didn't remove her coat. But she took the tea with both hands and continued walking, clasping the cup tightly as though she needed the warmth. She seemed shy, even more than I.

"You live nearby?" I asked.

"New York City." She looked at her watch. "I'll be going back there in a little while. This house—it's quite wonderful. You live here?"

"Yes."

"All alone?"

"No . . . I didn't get—What is your name?"

"Amelia," she answered. "Who else lives here?"

"My aunt. She's sick in New York."

"Oh, I'm sorry. Was it just the two of you?"

"What do you mean? Oh, no. My cousin Tato was living here too."

"My goodness, I thought the place was empty. It seemed so . . ."

"It *was* empty."

"Well, where is everybody now?"

"I told you. I have to find my aunt yet."

"You said you had a cousin?"

"Oh, he's in Colorado, I think. I don't know."

"So are you going to *stay* here?"

"No. I have to go back to New York, I guess."

"Would you like a ride back? I'm riding back with friends in a few hours."

"Would they mind?"

"Not at all. They keep a place in Noyack and are closing it up."

"Closing it up?"

"After Labor Day it's all over."

"I don't understand."

"The season. You homeowners have such bleak realities to contend with before the frost comes bursting your pipes."

"Oh," I said.

She waited, drinking her tea, while I went to my room and packed a few things.

Soon we were walking toward the cracked asphalt. We waited there only a minute, when a red BMW pulled in from Noyack Road. Amelia introduced me to Wendy and Pete McGibeney. Wendy slid toward the windshield to let us in back. She didn't realize she was crushing her straw bag. The car interior was black. The engine purred quietly as we sped away.

I was embarrassed to inconvenience them, but when I eyed the red telephone booth under the big Texaco sign on North Sea Road, I asked them to stop. It would be late by the time we reached New York, and I wanted to call Carter Boisvert before the office closed. I jumped out of the BMW.

Carter's secretary asked first who I was, then said he was in a meeting. She pressed me for what I wanted. I had only to mention Zia's name when she put me on hold.

Carter picked up. "Your aunt's in Bellevue."

"Bellevue?"

"Bellevue Hospital. She's holding her own. Still alive."

"Thanks. Fine. Thanks." I hung up.

Lavender streetlight lit the brownstone steps where Amelia lived in the West Village. Pete pulled our bags out of the trunk. It was an exhausting ride with Wendy chattering nonstop the whole way.

"Thank you," Amelia said, "and good night, all."

"Would you like some help?" I said.

Wendy's face popped out from the car window beneath us. "Don't let him carry that bag, Amelia. We could be setting up a rape here." Amelia smiled, politely amused. "You want us to drag him away?" Amelia pretended not to have heard. "Hey, cutie"— Wendy pulled my trouser leg—"come home with us and carry *my* bags up."

The BMW started to roll, separating her fingers from my trousers. The car nearly went through the red light at the corner. Pete and Wendy were silhouetted in its glow. Suddenly he hit her —once, twice, three times to her head. She put her head down. The light turned green and the car sped away.

"God, that poor woman," Amelia said, watching the car go off.

"They friends of yours?"

"Yes." She answered embarrassed. She was like a deer, ready to leap, her hair shining, lavender in the streetlight. I carried her bags up two flights of maroon carpeting. The staircase was a drum under our feet.

At her door she turned. "Where are you staying?"

"I don't know."

"You're kidding."

"No."

She spoke with difficulty: "I . . . this apartment was painted over the weekend, and the floors were shellacked. That's why I left. There's not a stick of furniture in the whole place, but you're welcome to sleep on a blanket. That's what I'll have to do."

"I intend to go straight to the hospital." I held out my hand. "Nice to have met you."

"Oh, nice to have met you." Her hand was freezing. "If you change your mind, I'm listed. Amelia Murphy. Good night."

My cab dropped me off near Con Edison's smokestacks, which were ejaculating their creamy white poisons into the night sky. I took off my jacket. It was a humid, hot night in Manhattan. I walked down a steaming First Avenue and through blocks of corridors before reaching the right Bellevue building.

I was facing a beautiful black woman who sat in an air-conditioned compartment behind a large wheel of cards. Her arms were folded, a gray sweater draped over her shoulders. She unfolded herself to peer into her wheel of cards.

"Man . . . Freddy?" she said. "She's in Ward Eleven. That's on the third floor. Take the elevator."

I stepped into the large square metal-lined room she called the elevator. Going up, I realized Zia was really going to die, right in this strange place. Where were all the people who had touched her life? Would they be there to say goodbye? Friends from Argentina? Friends of hers from Maldonado's ranch? Tangerine? Gabriella Ciascuno? People from Italy and Argentina? Father? I felt a twinge of guilt for not having written to him about Zia. But on second thought, I was glad I hadn't. I didn't want to hear his excuses.

I walked through a hot corridor of shiny pale green, past healthy-faced nurses dressed in their white immunity, past the sighs of spirits in the dark wards on either side of me. I found Ward Thirteen and backtracked to Eleven. I stepped through the portal.

It was a dark ward of several beds. Clattering noises rang outside its windows. I could see reddish light outside. A small bulb burned on my left near the room's only empty bed. To my right, deep in the corner, there sat a figure, a visitor—a man, dark and thin, motionless, sleeping. His head was a black lump in a landscape of white peaks the feet of patients made under their sheets. He looked up when I approached.

"Cello." A whisper blew from his mouth. It was Tato, more tired than I'd ever seen him. He looked so much like my father in spite of his beard. I walked toward him. I didn't think to glance at Zia in her bed. When I did, I was shocked. A halo lined Zia's skull where her dyed hair had grown in white. She was unconscious, breathing fast. Her eyes were closed, no movements. Her arms were out of her sheet, neatly, helplessly at her sides.

A woman in the bed next to hers had followed me with her sallow eyes, her gray hair flying in every direction. "My name is Margaret," she said to me.

"Hello," I said and turned away to look at Tato, who stood up. Zia's bed was near a window on an airshaft. Garbage cans rattled below. Music came down the opposite windows. I was glad Zia was unconscious. I dreaded to think of what she had been through while we were roaming about spending her last money. I couldn't breathe.

"Too noisy," Margaret whispered.

I left them and walked into the open corridor. I went a long way until I saw a nurse. She was eating an egg salad sandwich at her desk. Her tag read *Lincoln, R. N.* Her eyes were made up with mascara and blue eye shadow. Her lipstick imprinted her cigarette with a brighter red than was on her lips. Her hair was sculptured, like stiff silk, into one large black wave. The white uniform was a cruel shock to her soft, deep blackness and her make-up.

"Do they have to collect garbarge at this hour?" I asked. "My aunt is very ill in Ward Eleven."

"That's not garbage." She caught a square of egg white with her long bright fingernails. "It's the kitchen getting a delivery. Is your aunt Manfredi?"

"Yes."

"Well, she can't hear anyway." She dialed a number as I stood there. "Eddie? Could you get those clowns to stop banging that stuff down there? Thanks honey." She took a drag at her cigarette. "That happens," she said, picking a speck of celery off her chest.

"Hey! Shut up!" Eddie's voice echoed up the shaft as I entered Ward Eleven. Immediately the ward became quiet. I heard the whirring of a fan, or some large machine, far away. It didn't drown out the sounds of Zia's breathing.

"Was she conscious when you got here?" I asked Tato.

"No," he answered. He pulled a chair to the bed for me. We sat there silently next to Zia for several hours, not saying a word to each other. I had diarrhea and had to leave the room a couple of times. Tato left too, to smoke.

Daylight began to creep into the ward, pink and misty. Though it was September, it promised to be another hot day. Whenever I was alone with Zia, Margaret stared at me.

A short stocky woman, a visitor, bumped me, squeezing next to Margaret. It was Margaret's daughter, a woman with puffy eyes and long brown hair. She was wearing a tight bra under a tight red blouse. The welting of her skin showed through, and wetness was creeping up from under her armpits. She carried a straw handbag which had the word Bermuda sewn on it. And under her arm was the *New York Times*.

"How are ya?" she asked and smiled. Margaret began to weep. "C'mon, Ma. C'mon, c'mon." The woman in the red blouse pulled tissues from a box on the bed table and placed them on Margaret's chest.

"Eleanor."

"What, Ma? Go ahead and blow ya' nose."

"Ya promised."

"I'm keepin' my promise. Who said I ain't keepin' my promise?"

"Don't lemme die here."

"Ma, you ain't *dyin'*."

"Don't lie, Eleanor." Eleanor looked at me as if to say, Bad girl, isn't she? "Talk to me, honey," the old lady demanded.

"What? I'm talkin'. What d'ya want?"

"Take me home. Please, Eleanor, baby."

"How are you gonna get better home, Mama?"

"I'll get better. I swear to God."

"Tomorrow I'll talk to the doctor. Okay?"

"Today."

"I'll be late for work today."

"Today. Please, Eleanor."

"Okay, okay. I'll call him up from work. *Okay?*" Her daughter turned her face and rolled her eyes at me. Margaret turned to me too.

"She's gonna let me die in this shithole. I'm gonna die in this shithole."

"Ma, the people don't wanna hear you." Margaret blew her nose into a tissue.

I turned my eyes away, only to have them caught by Zia's white face, her open mouth, breathing hard. She looked awful. I felt like I was invading her tomb. I wished I had power to be something, to give her the sacraments, Extreme Unction—wishing there, watching her, that Christ were really the Son of God, wishing that God really did exist and that there was a place like heaven to gather up Zia and Margaret and the rest of them on that floor.

Once Ciascuno had told me, "We are still in the Garden of Eden. That is the secret no one has uncovered yet. Everything we need is right at our fingertips. Someone keeps cheating us out of it."

Why was Zia dying this way? That's all I wanted to understand. She wanted to be alone in her death, somewhere among pine trees, and here we were peering into her privacy. She believed we, Tato and I, were so wonderful, her family to trust, her cavaliers. She would never know how much ugliness had crowbarred its way between us while we spent her money out west. When Tato appeared in the doorway of the ward, he had no importance to me. He was common, lost in my memory, like my father, my mother and Ciascuno. I had that facility.

The three of us were anything but together in that hospital. I touched Zia's hand. It was cold. Amelia Murphy came into my mind in such a full and rich way, like a hope that transcended everything. She was present; my mind kept her present. I postponed being afraid.

Tato was waving me out from the doorway. When I reached the corridor, he was talking to Zia's doctor, a young man with a beard and very thick glasses that enlarged his brown eyes. His nose was sharp. He looked Italian, but he was a Jew— Dr. Levine. He spoke very, very quietly. "In these terminal cases, we try to keep the patient as comfortable as possible. We try to help the pain, so we do this with morphine injections every four hours. She's really in a comatose drug state right now at this point. You understand me?"

"Couldn't you hold off on these shots so she could catch a glimpse of us?" Tato asked.

Levine drawled out a long no.

I turned to Tato in shock. "You want her to suffer?"

Levine nodded his head in approval of what I was saying.

"I just want a chance to reach her," Tato said, "to tell her she's not alone."

"But she is alone," Levine said, "and you'll never change that." Levine looked to me for approval. He shook my hand, then Tato's, and walked off.

Tato took out his keys. "Go to the apartment and rest up. I'll call you when I'm ready for relief." I resented his speaking to me as though nothing had happened between us in Colorado.

"You go. You've been here longer," I said.

He pushed the keys on me, trying to speak softly. "I *feel fine.* Go wash up. I'll call you." He was still presuming I was a weak and helpless seminarian, a newcomer to the world.

"I'll go, but I don't need your keys."

"You can't hang around the streets."

"I'll take care of myself," I said, passing around him and touching the elevator button. He stood glaring at me, the keys still in his hand. The elevator came and I stepped into it. He kept his eyes on me until the doors closed between us.

* * *

There was no answer though I rang Amelia's doorbell twice. I put down my bag and waited. It was only eight in the morning. Then the vestibule door opened and Amelia stood before me, completely dressed and looking beautiful.

"Cello!" She was surprised to see me. I hadn't slept or shaved and must have looked awful.

"How's your aunt?"

"It's any time now. We're taking turns."

"Taking turns? Who are you taking turns with?" Her eyes had a kind of nervous pressure behind them, as though she were a spy asking a dangerous question.

I shrugged off that idea, still I didn't answer her.

"There's still nothing but the wooden floor and two windowsills in my apartment, but you're welcome to try to sleep there if you can. The bed's still on its way." She held up her keys.

"Where are you going?" I asked.

"To ballet class."

"I'll go with you. May I?"

"Aren't you exhausted? Shouldn't you rest?"

"I would rather be with someone."

"Okay. Put your bag upstairs and we'll go."

Her ballet teacher was a middle-aged woman with gray hair tied up in a bun. She smiled at me. She wore lavender tights under a violet costume, and she walked about watching everyone's feet and snapping her fingers to the piano music. There were eight dancers; only two were men.

Amelia moved perfectly, her body and mind as one. Her perfect movements were betrayed only slightly by her feet; I watched their power and their struggle. She was far better than I expected. I felt happy knowing and watching her, glad to be there. At last I was in the life-stream.

I loved the smells, the dusty old iron staircase leading to the third floor of the dance studio, smells of old wood, of disinfectant in the hallway, totally new smells, smells of New York surrounding me as I looked around the large white room stinking of new white paint, with its long mirrored wall from which Amelia and the other dancers reflected like black swans in their black tights, dancing to

Mozart's music, which bounced out of the grand piano in the corner. There were the goat smells of perspiration mingling with vague smells of underarm deodorant and perfume, animal smells, the salty odors of sweating men and women and the musty odor of the cracked leather couch in the waiting room. I waited an hour and a half before the dancers ran past me to their dressing rooms.

Amelia bought mung bean sprouts in a plastic bag and ate them as we walked through a small park on our way back to her apartment. She was acting as if she had known me for years. At some moments I felt I couldn't be the person she thought I was, or she would have talked with more caution, kept more distance.

"Walking after class is like floating on clouds," she said.

"Really?"

"Your muscles are in top form. Imagine walking fifty times more effortlessly. How are you holding up?"

"Fine," I said.

"You look tired."

"I am. But I'm feeling good." I smiled.

"You are? Why?"

I wasn't able to say much. I didn't understand my feeling good. I felt as though I had been injected with a powerful drug that simplified everything and made me twenty pounds lighter. How can one explain that?

The hot day didn't bother Amelia. She stuffed sprouts in her mouth and smiled at me and looked at everything as though it were wonderful. "Do you mind if I stare at you sometimes?" she asked.

"No," I said. "Tell me what you see."

"I think you're beautiful."

"Beautiful?" The word threw me off. I wondered for a moment if she was setting some kind of trap for me, and I looked brazenly into her eyes.

"I'm not insulting you, am I?" she said with surprise. "Beautiful is the word I use for a man when handsome is too shallow. It means *smart*. It means his eyes are from heaven. I'm a slave to a man with beautiful eyes. Do you believe me?"

210

I was happy to be with her; still she was making me anxious. I wanted us to talk about something else.

"What does the word beautiful connote to you?" she asked, pressing on.

"I'm not insulted, Amelia."

"Is it feminine to you? Well, answer me."

"No."

"I think you're a very attractive man. Let's get that straight. Okay? I mean I detect nothing that should embarrass you. God! What am I trying to say? You're a good-looking *guy*. You got that straight?"

"Well, I won't object."

"Well, *smile*." I smiled for her "Jesus"—she stuffed more sprouts into her mouth with slight annoyance—"you're sensitive."

"Well, don't be too sure." I smiled very wide this time to indicate I was lighthearted too. "I mean about my being too smart."

"Why?"

"You don't know me. I could be pretty dumb." I let my shyness show, hoping she would approve.

"I would like to know you," she said.

"Yeah? Why?" I was imitating Tato's voice.

"Because . . . you're beautiful." She laughed.

"Are you really interested?" I asked.

"I don't know what you're saying. What do you mean?"

"In me. Are you *interested?*"

"Sure," she said, blushing a little. "Listen," she said, stopping in her tracks, "let me be perfectly clear and honest to the hilt. Okay? I—how do I say this?—I . . . am not what you think. Okay? Let's get that straight right now."

"I don't understand."

"No, let me get it out. I—you have an idea who I am. Right?"

"Are you famous?" I grinned.

The fine, thin blue-veined skin under her left eye trembled. She couldn't stop its twitching. "I'm *not* famous." She didn't smile. "I was married to your cousin Tato."

"You were—"

"I'm Tato's wife—former wife."

I didn't question how Tato's name could spring out of her mouth. It seemed plausible enough at first, but after a moment I did feel trapped. Something was entirely wrong with what had been going on.

"I know who you are, too," she went on.

"Where do you know me from?"

"I heard of you from Tato. When you were coming from the seminary, he told me about you two out there at the house."

"He told you? You are the girl he was married to? The girl from California?"

"Right."

"Then why—"

"Well, I was visiting friends in Noyack to begin with, but I knew Tato was supposed to be there. I thought he was."

"He still talks to you?"

"Uh, minimally."

"Why didn't you tell me all this right away?" I said. I was very frightened and I couldn't hide it. "I don't like surprises."

"It was very manipulative of me." She blushed. "I didn't want you to see me as his wife right away."

"Why not?" I persisted.

"You were terrific up in that hallway. Suddenly there was this incredible face of a man before me. I knew I would like you, and I felt you might run away, and I wouldn't get a chance to know you some. I'm not sorry I didn't tell you." She threw the plastic bag into a garbage basket. "I started out wanting to see Tato. I've been missing him. When you asked me to have some tea, and you were so nice, I forgot Tato. I suddenly didn't want you to see me as his wife. You're angry."

"No."

"I should have told you who I was right away." She shrugged. "My goof-up."

"It would have been better." I couldn't look at her.

"I'm *sorry*. Look at me, Cello." She tilted her head like the dog on Tangerine's Victrola. "I never should have gone to that house. The way things were between Tato and me, I was demeaning

212

myself. If you only knew. But I couldn't goddamn help it. He left me so coldly, the bastard. Don't ever, ever tell him I came there looking for him that day."

"Sure."

"When there was no sign of anyone there, I said, 'Thank God.' I just wanted to get the hell out."

"Then why did you stay?"

"You asked me to. Remember?" Her knuckles brushed mine. She caught my hand and squeezed it. There was permission in her eyes, gladness to be near me, and the need to be forgiven. "I'm so glad Tato wasn't there," she said with a tear in her eyes.

"Why?"

"You're a nice guy. I like you so much. One doesn't often see men like you around. You're not in touch with what you are, but that's what makes you exciting. Forgive me."

Holding Amelia's hand, I was aware for the first time of the sheer power of having life and of having enough intelligence to make life even more marvelous. I could sense there were choices open to me, lots of choices. I had never had such power. I was, myself, a great sun shining on everything in the park. Amelia smiled as though she knew what was going on in my mind.

The park seemed vacated; the sycamores leafless. The light had changed, filtering down. All the benches empty. We seemed alone. Walking through the sycamore leaves seemed mildly sacrilegious. Where were the people who usually came to that park? So many men and women had lived before Amelia and me, their bodies disappearing, leaving behind their music, their poems and their trees, the sycamores.

Amelia sniffed the air like a doe. "You going back to the hospital tonight?" she said.

"Yes."

"Then have dinner with me first? We'll eat early. You can sleep and bathe while I cook."

"That would be nice."

The odor of autumn arrived on a wind that was cartwheeling leaves along the grass.

We stopped at a delicatessen near her apartment. I waited outside, feeling no remorse that she was once Tato's wife. On the contrary, I was feeling lucky somehow that someone needed me in some way and wanted me. I knew by the way she looked at me that I had unmistakable power over her.

We were silent all the way home and thumping up the stairs to her door. Inside, we shuffled around. We both knew we were creating silence as we moved about. We both understood why she dropped her keys on the countertop and why she kept banging the kitchen cabinets. But we didn't deny our nervousness to each other's eyes. I slept while she cooked—my back to her, my knees touching the wall. I couldn't have slept otherwise.

We ate sitting on the wooden floor, with candles burning, even though it still daylight. I was still tired and I must have been poor company for Amelia. She put my things away and threw my bag in her closet. Then she walked me to the avenue and helped me get a cab. She kissed me goodbye when I got in and blew a kiss as the cab pulled away.

The evening sun struck the hospital entrance with flat red light. A dozen Hispanics were hanging around the gates. They turned from the sun's cruelty and lit cigarettes as my cab pulled up. My driver double-parked next to a limousine. The limo's chauffeur sat stiffly waiting, though the limousine doors were open to the sidewalk as though a wedding party was expected to appear. I thought of the Puerto Ricans as rice throwers, well-wishers, waiting for the bride. I paid my driver and looked up. A wheelchair had materialized in the entranceway; some Puerto Ricans had rushed to help lift it. I was shocked when I realized it was Tato who was wheeling the chair. Had he volunteered, like the rest, to help with the wheelchair? But the limousine chauffeur recognized him; he sprang from out of his seat into the back of the limo and helped pull the patient inside. Then the chauffeur ran around to the sidewalk side and slammed the doors. Tato was inside. The patient was so wrapped in sheets I couldn't make out its form until a head pressed against the glass as though unconscious, a woman's head, dark hair with white roots. Zia. It was Zia! The limousine started to move out slowly.

I commanded my driver to follow. He was a gray-haired man of

214

about fifty. He looked at me through the plastic divider as though he had just woke up. Yellow matter, like dried pus, was inside the corners of his eyes. He needed a shave. Gray stubble fanned out on his chin as he smiled. "What are you—a detective, mister?"

I could hardly hear him through the dirty plastic. "Follow that limousine," I shouted into the change bucket.

"I double the meter for this kind of work," he yelled back.

"Jesus Christ, I'll pay," I screamed. We zoomed out immediately but were stopped by a red light. The limo was gone from sight. The light turned green. At Fifty-fifth Street we spotted the limo ahead turning left into Fifty-seventh. When we caught up, the limo was out of sight again.

"They took the bridge to Queens," the driver shouted. "You want me to go on the bridge?"

"Yes, yes," I shouted into the change bucket.

He turned onto the ramp. The cab curled up and onto the bridge. We merged with several cars at the top. Finally, when we were able to see clearly down the bridge roadway, there was no black limousine. Our cab scrambled along the grilled road, and I fell back in my seat. I was sick to my stomach. I wondered if Zia was alive. Tato must have gone crazy. Hospitals don't release dead patients. They have no right to release people near death either. Something bizarre was happening.

"There they are! They took the bridge," the driver shouted. I sat up. At the beginning of a wide boulevard, the limo was waiting for a red light. We stopped at the preceding red light.

"They could be going to China, mister. You got enough money with you? It's double on top of the double if we cross the Nassau border."

"I'll pay, whatever it is." I had only thirty-eight dollars in my pocket. My money was in my bag at Amelia's.

We followed them, unable to catch up for a half hour, past La-Guardia Airport, onto the Northern State Parkway, then we curled south onto another wider parkway of rolling hills of grass lined with huge evergreens. My driver refused to exceed the speed limit but promised we'd keep them in sight. Flocks of crows flushed into the air as the limo suddenly bumped up onto a field of grass that sloped upward toward a forest of pines. The limousine drove slowly up the grass hill to the edge of the woods.

"Slow down," I shouted into the bucket. "Don't pass them."

"I can't go up there," the driver shouted back. "We'll get nailed. Those crazy son of a bitches. This parkway's loaded with cops." We went past the limo.

I looked out the back window. The chauffeur was opening the door. "Stop the cab. Let me out, please," I shouted.

"No dice," my driver answered. "I can't let you out here." I looked back. The chauffeur was counting money. By the time we reached the exit, the big black limo zoomed past us, empty. The exit turned out to be a major cloverleaf.

"Let me out here," I begged.

"I can't. There are cars behind us."

I pulled the money out of my pocket and stuffed all of it into the change cup. I opened the cab door. He jammed on the brakes. I fell off the seat.

He turned, screaming, "You want us to get killed, you jerk-off?"

I jumped onto the pavement and ran as fast as I could down the grass in the direction of the circling crows. The sun was going down behind me, no clouds anywhere, just clear space and green earth beneath my feet. It seemed I could make out the earth's curvature. Was the planet so small?

Fear and a sense of futility made my legs soften. I felt I was getting nowhere, like a man running on a spinning ball. I had to look down, to ignore the sea of sunlight, forget that I was running on a sphere. I had to force Zia and Tato back into mind.

"Where'd they go?" I whispered to myself. "Where are they?" I was running better. When I came into view of the pines, where the limousine had stopped, there was no sign of them. They couldn't have been far. Zia couldn't walk. Tato would surely have had to carry her. They could only have gone into the woods. I ran left into the pines, hoping to come up behind them. After running at least a quarter of a mile through the pines, I decided I had passed them. I looked up for the circling crows. They were exactly over my head. I could hear cars far off, whizzing along, my own panting. And another panting: Tato was looking straight at me. I was jolted to see him in the shadows, stripped to the waist, kneeling, the skin of his face tight as a drum, his eyes black and burning. Zia's head was on his shirt, his sweater over her breast. She looked terrible, her eyes partly opened, her skin very white. She was the whitest thing alive in this world.

"Help me keep her warm," Tato said.

"Tato, you're totally out of your mind to do this."

"Fuck you. This is what she asked for. I would have taken her to the woods at Jessup, but she'll never make another eighty miles."

"They'll call us murderers."

"You stay out of it and they can't call you nothin'."

There were spots like freckles all over her face. They were on her sheet and on Tato's sweater too, and more on Tato's hand near her chin.

"She's spraying blood with her breath. She's hemorrhaging."

"She ain't spittin' catsup," Tato said.

I was sorry I had followed them. He was mad. She was *dying*.

"Call the police. Bring her back to the hospital." I was shaking. My voice could hardly make the command. "Please bring her *back!*"

"Fuck you. You're nothing, standing there with your finger up your nose. What do I give a shit about what you want? She wanted to die in the woods. Why shouldn't she? Who says no? You wanna try to take her back?"

"But suppose she doesn't die? Suppose the morphine wears off?" I tried to bring him to his senses.

"The worse that could happen is that she sees us for a minute."

"She'll have pain."

"So, she'll have pain. Gimme your jacket." His voice became calmer. I tried to remove my jacket, but my arms were so rigid I couldn't bend them. Tato held her in his arms. He was cold. His shoulders danced with shivers. He looked upon her face and spoke to her as though she could hear. "Zia, we're here with you. We're here in the woods with you."

I thought I must be dreaming. There was Zia, spraying blood on her own face, all over the sheets, his jacket, his arms. Zia's blood was on her breath coming from her mouth. She *was* going to die on the spot. Her mouth closed. Her breathing stopped for a moment. She swallowed.

"Ohh." The sound came out of her in a full voice. Her sound rose up into the pines. Her eyes did not open. Her expression did not change. She was unconscious, to all appearances, but an intelligent sound or just a reflex of her vocal cords, it didn't matter. It was her sound, distinct, coming from inside her. Zia's tone, Zia's voice, Zia's sound, as perfectly Zia's as I had heard other times, on the porch, on the beach as a child. "Ohh." A short word, a short note, but I recognized it. It was the voice that came to me at my mother's wake from under her veil. That was Zia and here was Zia.

Her chin doubled. She sank deeper in Tato's arms. She wasn't pulling in any air, no breathing. Her face glowed with a fast rush of beauty. We watched and waited for another breath to come. None came. Tato looked up, then back to her. She didn't move. A minute passed. Her forehead had taken on a waxy shine.

Tato looked at me again. "You look like you're about to shit your pants," he said.

"I am." I turned like a robot and walked a few yards. I didn't want to unbuckle my belt, but I had to. I felt so ashamed pulling down my trousers. I squatted just in time. My face burned with embarrassment. It came out of me as if it were alive.

Oh God in heaven, why isn't there a God in heaven?

I had no paper. I wiped myself with my shorts and threw them out of sight. I pulled on my trousers and buckled my belt. It was cool, dark and still in the woods. The pine needles had cushioned my feet. I looked up and saw a dozen crows sitting in the pines, watching me. They were perched motionless in the twilight, black and blue as coal. We were on their homesite. They were waiting for us to leave, patient as monks, glistening purple and blue-black in the evergreens.

When I got back to Zia and Tato, she was white as alabaster, dead, stretched beautifully on a bed of pine needles in the damp air of a cool wood. She was dead in the darkly tinted air of a fine pine forest where the ground cushioned our feet like straw, where by some acoustical phenomenon the noise of cars speeding nearby sounded over our heads, like rockets in rapid fire.

A red blinking light flashed through the pines in the east.

"The cops," Tato said. "You run. *Run*, goddamnit!" he ordered. "Straight that way." He pointed south. "Go straight to my apartment and don't talk to a soul, you hear?" He threw me his keys.

I caught them in the dark, not knowing how I did it. I turned, but I couldn't run. My legs were too stiff. I could only walk in the direction he pointed to. I walked until I could see the lights of a house. My legs felt like they would break from forcing them to move. My shoulders shook. I couldn't stop their shaking. A man walked his dog. No one else was in sight. I made my way along the service road. Other houses appeared, repeating themselves for miles. People were returning from work. Lights were going on.

Finally I reached the curl where the Northern State crosses another parkway. Cars shot by above me. I stood in the road's curl, against the wall of the overpass where I could see if a police car was approaching. I held out my thumb to westbound traffic. I was in shock. My mind was a movie going too fast, conjuring elaborate possibilities.

A loud black Pontiac pulled over and blinked its rear lights. I ran to it. Its muffler was roaring. Its fenders were rusted. The driver was a black man. He wore a black jacket with a zipper. His hair was slick black. He had a mustache. "Where you goin'?" he asked with impatience.

"New York City. Manhattan."

"How's the Midtown Tunnel?"

"That's good," I answered.

"You pay the toll?"

"I have no money."

"Okay, man, get the fuck in."

Throughout the ride, I smelled engine fumes. He drove to the Queens Midtown Tunnel and through it without a word. He didn't even look at me when I opened my door to leave. I got out and slammed the door, intending to thank him through the open window, but he had closed the window electrically. The car roared across the avenue away from me.

It was after midnight when I reached Tato's apartment in Greenwich Village. I was tempted to call Amelia to let her know I was nearby, but I knew that I would sound completely irrational. Tato, in spite of everything, was the one person in my mind who could make things orderly again. I wished he would walk in the door and tell me that the police took Zia away, that she had been taken care of, her body disposed of in some magical way, that there was nothing left to worry about, the ugliness was over, the matter explained to the police, that there was nothing left to do but to take a shower and leave.

I was too tired to open his couch into a bed. I curled in its confined space and fell asleep. The refrigerator light woke me. Tato was in the apartment. His head was tilted back. His hand squeezed milk into his mouth from a container. When his arm came down, I realized that he had been gulping milk and crying at the same time. His face was wet with sweat and tears. Milk ran down his chin. When he shut the refrigerator door, we were in the dark. He sat down in the armchair.

"I'm glad to be home," he said.

"What happened?"

"They arrested me."

"Where is she?"

He started to sob. "Oh, my God."

"*Where is she?*" I repeated.

"They're doing an autopsy on her."

I didn't expect that. "Why?" I asked.

"They fingerprinted me. Then they brought me to a judge. Next thing I know, they released me with the charge of criminally negligent homicide. I have to go on trial."

I hated him. She probably would have been dead by now, anyway, or dying in a bed. There would have been no mess. The hospital would have taken care of things. Tomorrow would be the funeral. It would be over swiftly. Instead, we had to be haunted by visions of her body being opened, police ghouls cutting her up, tearing at her.

"You deserve it if you go to jail." I stood up.

He didn't say a word. He opened the refrigerator again and took out the container. "Why don't you take a walk for a while?" he said, tipping the container to his mouth again.

"You and your ego, sticking your fist into people's lives."

"Easy on me, Cello."

"I don't remember her asking for an autopsy. I don't remember her wishing for that. She just had a romantic idea about dying in the pines."

Tato whirled away from the refrigerator, toward the bathroom. I made for the hall.

"I feel like throwing up." His voice was tiny, like a child's.

"Throw up," I yelled at him as I slammed his door. I screamed at his closed door, one word, loud enough for him to hear through the door over his throwing up: "Murderer." I don't remember screaming that loud ever in my life. It echoed down the stairs. It felt so good to accuse him, to throw blame at him, so good to escape the blame, to shut him in with it. As I ran down the stairs toward the light of the street, I knew I'd never be the same again.

All the next day and night I spent in Amelia's apartment. She was very kind to me, bringing tea and things for me to eat, leaving me alone, whispering only the most necessary words. I sat on her floor on a pillow most of the time, not ashamed to stare at the wall, compelled to weep now and then simply because of having her, her scent, her presence, someone who cared about me. At moments, I felt wise like the crows. I was about to be set free from an old cave.

Tato was the unlucky one now, not I. His woman brought me cold chicken and sprouts to eat, apple juice in a stemmed glass. She was through with him and beginning with me. He was the past, I the future. He was in the dark; I was in the light. Tato was burdened, tainted, unlucky. Of course I felt guilty—I felt immoral and cowardly—but I had made it to the lifeboats, and I was not sorry. Only once, once more, would I have to see him—for Zia's funeral. After that I'd be free of him. But I had achieved something in my mind. There I was already free.

The undertaker was Howard Crosby. Two assistants were with him at the cemetery, one in a gray pinstriped suit and the other in a brown plaid suit and vest. Crosby wore blue. His few hairs were quite dark and slicked back over his suntanned dome. His eyes were a healthy blue; he might have been a German general of the Second World War. He had the bearing of prelates I knew in Italy who felt they had to appear paternal and warm to their public. I wanted to show him I could resist his beneficent smile.

"She seemed a lovely woman," he said. "Your cousin said you would be the one to receive." Crosby held out the urn. Tato watched from the Volkswagen.

"Is that all we get?" I asked.

"It's all *here*," Crosby answered, a little surprised.

"It? You mean *she*? My aunt?"

"I'm sorry." His face flushed.

"Was she wearing any jewelry? Any pins? Metal that might have refused to turn to dust? Gold teeth?"

"Mr. Manfredi"—his voice opened easily to a louder tone—"you had your chance to consult me all day yesterday. This is not my time to consult." His assistants moved forward. "There was no gold, nothing." I turned and left them standing there.

I sat in the Volkswagen with the urn upon my lap, party to yet another sin. I had been taught in theology that cremation was a heretical act against the dogma of the resurrection of the body. Bodies must not be burned. The human body must not pass from flesh to ash unnaturally, or it will not be able to reconstruct at the resurrection of the dead. I had read that thousands of times from my missal at mass: ". . . *And I look for the resurrection of the dead. And the life of the world to come.*"

"Where should we dunk the ashes?" Tato asked as we sped on the expressway.

"*Dunk* them?"

"Deposit them. Where?"

"It seems a little ridiculous to be going a hundred miles to do it. She's utterly gone. She doesn't know what's going on," I said.

"So what do we want to *do*?" Tato challenged. I didn't answer. "Spray them all over the Long Island Expressway and make a U-turn?" I still didn't answer. He gave up waiting for me to speak and turned on the radio. The wind whistled through the catchlock of the canvas top. Of course we both knew deep down that there was no other way to deal with the ashes but at Jessup. No matter how cremation reduced the problem of death, the ashes still were the last of her. Her image popped into mind several times during the ride. And then involuntary visions of fire—her muscles and bones collapsing to dust—nauseated me.

My memory hadn't gone into the fire with her. I could still imagine her. I heard her voice suddenly: *"Cello, you are too serious."* Her voice rang so true that I jumped in my seat. It seemed madness suddenly that my memory of her should be so rich as I held her ashes. Her dresses and shoes in the closet at Jessup had more reality than she did now. I could see her shoes, their inner lining pressed and smoothed by wear, the dresses uncleaned, still holding some odor of her body, hanging empty in the closet. I imagined pouring her ashes into her shoes and dresses. I wished she hadn't been cremated. With burial, I could believe her body to be still intact for a while, lying underground. I could imagine her face still shining in some dark hollow place.

"We should bring the ashes to the pines she pointed to that time," Tato said, lowering the radio.

"No," I answered. "We should bring them to the point of the cliff, where we fell, and let them go to the wind and the water."

"All right," Tato said. "How do you feel?"

"Okay," I answered. I put my head back, keeping silent the rest of the way. Sometimes I felt his eyes, as if they were trying to connect with me, as if he were waiting for an opening to talk. I wanted to finish the business of Zia's death with him and slip away from him for the rest of my life. I wanted him to get lost among all the other people of the world. I felt his ugliness too strongly now. I sensed his madness. There was no way to speak to it, no way to deal with it. He wanted my destruction. I knew that, in spite of his worried looks at me in the car. He was another Crosby.

Our emotions in the next few hours would link up in some way over Zia. But then it would have its end. Amelia was the cut-off point. Tato and I would never mix, *could* never mix now. It was destined to be over between Tato and me anyway. We were cousins, and we were men. What can happen that is lasting between men? We were connected by Zia in some illogical, ironic way. Her ashes were all that held us together. We were being swept eastward in a frail and flapping faded red capsule—two hearts beating inside it, two minds working, two memories, and one pot of dust, a black handful, a black spot for the sky, a dot, a period after a long sentence.

I had to make it clear to Tato that staying overnight at Jessup Neck was out of the question. The last train to New York was the 4:47 from Southampton station, so there was no other way of getting back to New York except in his car. I had arranged with Amelia to meet near her place at a Chinese restaurant around midnight. Tato would have to drop me off some distance from the restaurant or he might see Amelia. We would have to leave immediately after spreading the ashes.

I had to gain control of the situation. I anticipated that he would say he wanted to talk at some point, that he would make use of our being together to reinstate himself; I didn't want to listen to a lot of explanation, defense, rationalization.

I was sorry I had suggested the cliffs. We would have to walk to the point with the ashes, so we couldn't spare a minute doing anything else.

The main problem of the night was simply making sure he'd drop me off somewhere in New York where there would be no chance of his seeing Amelia. I had to prepare someday for his disgust, his outrage when he found out about Amelia and me, but I wanted him out of my life, clean and complete anyway. So why did I worry? Simply because I hated anything that would give him an excuse to have words with me again, ever.

It was close to dark as we walked toward the house. He didn't offer to carry the urn, and I didn't push it on him. He looked up at the sky. "Christ, there'll be stars tonight," he said.

The water radiated the last hint of gray light. The dusty rose trail of the sun had just about dissipated. The wind was up. It was cool. A planet burned low in the north. I could have kicked myself for suggesting the cliffs.

When Tato veered toward the house on our way to the point, I had to speak up. "I don't want to stop at the house. I have to be back in Manhattan by midnight." He didn't react. "I think we should go straight out there now," I said.

"But I have to take a piss," he said.

"Take it here."

"But we'll need a couple of flashlights soon. I wanna pick them up."

"We can do it without flashlights," I said.

"You wanna go off the fuckin' cliff again?" He kept on his course for the house.

I followed him up the porch to the dark house. He opened the front door and switched on the foyer light. I turned my back to the terrible green walls and the two monstrous bison. I placed the urn on the porch table and sat down.

"Aren't you coming in?" he asked.

"No," I said. He had closed the front door. Light poured out on me from the stained-glass panels. It was almost dark now. That foyer bulb was too bright. The panels glared like circus colors. I sat in a low wicker chair with my back to the colors. I heard Tato thumping up the stairs.

I examined the urn. It was cheap gray-colored ceramic, an imitation of something Victorian, but really a product of industrial stupidity in which detail was melted down to a disgusting degree of simplicity. It was something brand-new, pretending to be old. Hardly anything Zia would like. I had surprised myself by placing it unconsciously on the table in the place where Zia usually ate. I changed its position and turned my chair to face the rose trellis. Roses were not in bloom any longer, but there on the floor was a champagne glass left by one of the string quartet. I thought of "Musetta's Waltz" and our dancing with Zia.

Tato flushed the toilet upstairs. The water trickling down the pipes was a welcome interruption. When he opened the front door, I jumped onto the sand into the long beam of light.

"Hurry. It's getting very windy," I said. Tato turned out the light and followed without hesitation.

We walked north toward the point on the sand about a quarter mile when Tato stopped short.

"Cello, I have to say something that's gonna shock you."

"I don't want to talk. I know what you're going to say." He blocked my path. "You want to tell me that you're sorry?" I said. "Okay, fine. Let's just say it's too late."

"Oh, c'mon." He smiled.

"I can't forgive people like you, and this is not the time. I knew you'd do this."

"I'm not asking for forgiveness."

"You press in on me."

"Take it easy." Tato smiled.

"I have no reason to know you anymore, and I want to be left alone. I have a lot to do—a lot to do."

"Gimme a chance to say something."

"I *know* what you want to say."

"You're full of shit."

I stopped in my tracks and faced him. "What do you want to *say?*"

"We forgot the ashes."

"We forgot the ashes?" He didn't have the urn. It was back on the table.

"I don't have *time.*" I started to run back. He started running behind me. "Let's get rid of the ashes there, at the water in front of the house," I said.

We ran along the shoreline silently. When we were close to the house, Tato veered off for the urn on the porch. I waited at the water. It seemed as if the whole universe was one clear and windy place, stars everywhere. When Tato arrived at the water's edge, he offered the urn to me.

"You do it," I said. There was a strong sea breeze at the water. It was going to be difficult to keep the ashes from flying back toward the house.

"We'll have to go in." Tato was taking off his shoes and socks. I did the same, rolling up my trousers. I held both flashlights. They clunked together in the blackness like two small suns. The water was very cold. Tato released the lid of the urn and tried to hand it to me. I refused it. He threw the lid into the wind, scaling it. Then he began to spin, to whirl, like a discus thrower, one hand gripping the urn. In the beams of the flashlights I saw chunks of matter spewing out. I turned my face away in case it would go into my eyes. Suddenly, something came flying out of the night, a stone or something. It hit me in the head so hard that deep orange rings of light appeared in the blackness. I heard a terrible ringing inside my head.

"I got you in the head with the fuckin' urn," Tato yelled, grabbing me. I walked toward shore and simply rolled down my trousers. I felt dizzy. I didn't want to pass out. A wave of indigestion hit my stomach. I felt nauseated. "It was an accident," Tato pleaded. His fingers examined my head. He turned the flashlight on me. I pushed it away.

"It's nothing. I'm all right." I wanted him to disappear. "Let's go," I said as briskly as I could.

"What should I do with the urn?" Tato asked after a few seconds.

"Throw it after the ashes." He flung it into the wind. I listened for its splash. It came in a few seconds. "Goodbye, Zia," I whispered.

On the way back to New York I fell asleep to the music of the wind in the catchlock. I didn't wake up until we hit the Queens Midtown Tunnel. The roar of the tunnel and the lights woke me. My mouth was dry. My eyes burned.

"Where do you want to go?" he asked.

"Right here."

"You want me to stop in the tunnel?"

"Outside."

"Okay." He wore his tough-guy smile, his tolerant smile. When we reached the incline and came out of the tunnel, he laughed. "When am I gonna see you, you bastard?"

"Whenever," I answered.

"C'mon, jerk-off." He laughed. "When?"

"I don't want to see you, frankly."

"Cello, c'mon now." His smile made me furious.

"This is *goodbye*," I roared.

He blinked. His eyes begged. "C'mon."

"No. Goodbye. Final, complete."

"C'mon. Talk to me." He stopped the car at Third Avenue. I

opened the door and jumped out, slamming the door behind me. He called out my name so loud that even with the windows closed, I could hear it. I pulled open the door and peered back at him. He said nothing.

"What?" I asked.

His expression had changed in the few seconds. His eyes bore the wild, dolorous expression of his Puerto Rican mother, and his lip curled out of control as he attempted to get the words out: "Please don't be like the rest. You are exactly like the rest, exactly like them. Please."

I slammed the door. He shifted and moved the car forward, but the light had turned red. He waited, looking straight ahead. He pulled the visor down, shadowing his face. The light turned green, and he left.

Amelia and I ate chicken and broccoli in oyster sauce at the Chinese restaurant. It was two A.M. when we finished. I had needed the food. Amelia wanted to walk home, so we did, very slowly. I was safe with her. I was her moon, a satellite following her homeward under the great sycamores of the West Village. I'd decided at some point to trust this stranger who was fast becoming the closest human to my heart. I took deep breaths as I walked and leaned into the early autumn breeze, knowing that the future would reel me in and take care of me. She walked, relaxed too, seemingly content. We were an alliance.

I got into her new bed while she showered, but I didn't attempt to fall asleep. Our walking and holding hands silently had been a bridge to something, not necessarily sexual, and I couldn't turn my back on her this time. I sat up in bed and waited for her to appear in the room. She came out of the bathroom smoking a cigarette and wearing a very light skin-colored satin jacket trimmed with lace. It had been carefully ironed. As she got into bed, her bare feet lifted the scent of Urethane shellac from the floor. She turned out the light. She lay flat on her back smoking. The lavender streetlight bounced off the shining wooden floors. I watched her face in the scant light. Her eyes were fresh and awake, looking at the ceiling. She took a final drag, then fumbled across my chest for the ashtray. I held it for her while she crushed her cigarette, renewing its rank odor.

"Cello."

"Uh-huh."

"Hold me?" she asked. I waited before doing so, as if some automatic desire would come out of the dark to impel me. I put my arm around her. She turned and wrapped her leg over mine and put her hand up my tee shirt. Her perfume mixed with the cigarette smell. She lowered her hand to the elastic band of my undershorts. "Take these off," she said, pulling them downward. I lifted my body and helped her drag them down. She collected them with her foot, lifted them up from under the sheets and threw them at the chair. She put her arm back under the covers and slowly ran her hand down my chest to my genital hair. She took my penis in her hand and gently nestled it. "This is so miraculous. It grows like magic and it shrinks. Do you mind what I am doing? I won't hurt you."

"I don't mind."

"Kiss me?" I turned and kissed her lightly many times in succession until her tongue touched my lips and we opened our mouths. I turned, lifting my leg between her legs. She straddled my thigh. We pressed together for many minutes that way, breathing into each other's ears, pressing and relaxing until she threw herself back on her pillow. "Cello, please come into me. Come."

I lifted myself into place, hovering over her, and then, carefully, pressed forward. I was only partly inside her when I spoke: "Amelia, I want to feel close to you." She answered by pulling my hips toward her, pressing, holding my buttocks, bringing me inside her. I moved inside her as she rocked slowly. My only wish was to make her happy. She began to thrust up to me in rapid movements, panting and moving as if compelled. It went on for a long time. Several times she cried out. Her hands loosened from my back. Still she mumbled and continued to rock with slow thrusts. Had I known she was through, I would have withdrawn. She laughed for a moment, then I heard sobs—she was crying.

"Oh, God," she murmured. I wasn't sure what her tears meant. I thought they were part of her passion. "Cello. What are you doing?" she murmured. "What are you *doing*?" She was irritated. I withdrew. She touched her knees together.

"Are you all right?" I asked.

She leaned for her cigarettes. She lit one, quickly shutting her lighter. The flash caught an angry face. She sucked in smoke, then blew it out with relief and sobbed quietly.

"What's wrong?" I kept asking.

But she ignored my questions. She smoked and cried. Finally she asked, "What were you thinking as you were doing that?"

"Doing what?"

"Fucking me?"

"I don't remember. I wanted to make you happy."

"Didn't you want anything for yourself?"

"I don't know."

She threw herself back on her pillow. "I've been thinking," she said. "I can't *stop* thinking."

"Of what?" I asked.

"God! I'm such a jerk. Such a jerk. You are a homosexual, aren't you? Are you in love with Tato?"

"You're crazy." I bolted up. "What did I do to make you think that?"

"I attract you people."

"I am *not* homosexual, Amelia. Was I so different from other men?"

"Yes, you were different."

"I don't believe that."

"Don't look at me with those mopey eyes. I've been ripped off by your type before. You are the worst, the deniers. And you *need* women. God, you need women *desperately* to keep the information away from your door. You fuck with your mind on the moon, but you succeed in keeping the wolves away from your door for one more day."

"Amelia, I swear to you, you're wrong." I wanted to express myself. I tried.

"Words! Cello, this second, here as you look at me with wide,

wide eyes, you are sincerely ignorant. But, oh, what a time you are going to have when my words hit home; and don't hate me when they do. I'm so worn out from your kind of bullshit, so tired of it. Pass me the ashtray."

I was dumbfounded. She looked at me, her eyes filling with tears. Suddenly she was on her knees. I caught the ashtray before it emptied on the sheet.

She pulled my head to her breasts. "God, forgive me. Cello, forgive me. I'm so paranoid. Rest, just rest. Don't think." We both lay down again, my face between her cool breasts. Both her arms were wrapped around my head. I could hear her heart. "Forget what I said," she kept saying.

My mind was going blank. It was not a peaceful blank. It was the hurricane eye.

"Cello," she said, "I don't care about anything, of who or what you are, or think or do consciously or unconsciously, I accept you here. Believe me. You don't have to *service* me. You don't have to work on my body, but, Christ, try, try to be as transparent with me as I am with you. Don't hide. I don't care who anyone *is*, but I can't love someone who has his mask on. That is *my* hang-up, and thank God for it."

"If I'm wearing a mask, I don't know it," I said.

She let me go and lit another cigarette. "Tell me the truth about Tato."

"Huh? What about him?"

"Do you love him?"

I pulled back. I knew I would say yes, but I was trying to prepare my explanation.

"A difficult question?" she asked.

"No, not difficult. I must say yes, but only in a pitying way. He— I find him not anyone I'd care to know, really."

"Did you ever find him sexually interesting?"

"He's my cousin, for one thing."

"Forget that. You never had sexual feelings for a man? Everyone does, c'mon."

"Once."

"Once what? Tell me." She waited, looking at my face.

I was afraid to deceive her. "I wanted to touch him out of curiosity. He was asleep in his room in Jessup."

"There's nothing *wrong* with that, Cello. Did you?"

"He reminded me of . . . Huh?"

"Who'd he remind you of?"

"My father, I think."

"Where did you want to touch him?"

"Please, Amelia, I—"

"Oh, c'mon. Did you *touch* him?"

"Of course not."

"You should have." She shifted and turned on the lamp. "I want to see your face," she said, bringing my head into the light. "Your eyes are scared. How beautiful they look, like an endangered species caught in a floodlight." Her eyes were puffed and red.

"But I don't think that means I'm homosexual—what I just told you about Tato."

"Touch my breasts." She lifted my hand to her breasts as she tested my eyes. "In a way, you have given me more than anyone else has. Let me feel your teeth on my nipple, gently."

I complied, feeling a bit foolish. I had given her my trust. It was a large investment. She held my head as she pulled away from my mouth. She stood and walked to the window. She simply stood there, waiting for me. I felt ridiculous.

I was embarrassed to get up, but I did. I walked toward her. I chose to kneel, to sink away from her gaze, before realizing that kneeling was ugly, submissive. But I didn't want her eyes again. I kissed her with tiny kisses as I descended, hoping that would seem manly, realizing as I went down that she was so beautiful and even maybe a little crazy, but that she was the gentle Amelia who fed me tea, and privacy—the dancer, the startled doe, no less frail than I.

She leaned over me, covering me with her hair. I touched her ankle the way Tato had touched May's ankle in the fern grove.

I had earned a strange power by kneeling. I felt it in my arms, my fingers. I was the man, after all, between the two of us. Only I had the penis, and with that thought I became hard as marble. My other hand wrapped itself around her other ankle. Her head went back, far back. My lips went right to the outer lips of her vagina. I touched lightly with my tongue, imagining it as my place, the place for my tool, which was standing hard and strong, my sudden wand of power over her womanliness. She bent forward now to kiss me. My head was a planet. Her hair was my tides and my winds. Her lips pressed mine.

Now that I had strength, I relished giving in. I wanted to crumble, as though dying, as though surrendering was my gift to her. Her breathing was very fast. I raised myself to enter her. I did, pressing confidently into her body, filling her totally. She gasped. I looked into her eyes as the window light lit her face.

She stopped me from coming with her voice: "I love you," she whispered. I closed my eyes to her words. "I love you," she repeated.

She postponed my coming again. She took my dizzy head in her hands. "Cello, listen to me."

"I'm listening." I looked to the lavender ceiling; it was glowing.

"Did you ever tell someone you loved them?"

"I think I did."

"When?"

"I . . . don't remember. My mother."

"No one else?"

"I don't remember."

She pressed me closer. She touched her mouth to mine and spoke. "I just want to hear the words. You don't have to mean them. I'm so lonely for the words. Tell me you love me."

"I love you." I said the words blankly. But the next moment tears began to gather behind my eyes.

"Why are you crying?" she whispered.

"I don't know." I didn't understand.

"Say the words again."

"It's very hard for me."

"Please."

"I love you," I said, crying more now.

She picked the words from my lips with her mouth; she touched her tongue to my tears. I was coming. Nothing could stop it this time.

"I love you," I said over and over, louder and louder. With the words, ghosts, prehistoric birds and monsters flew from my lungs. The vibrations of their exodus thrilled me.

"I love you," she called back over and over.

Her voice rang in the bare room till she came.

We became silent. Her nails were pressed into my shoulders. Our juices soaked the nest of my hair. Our odors filled the room.

She led me by the hand to the shower. We both went under the stream. She scrubbed me with the eagerness of a servant. Now, I was amazed at the courage of my nudity. My abdomen tightened when she grabbed my genitals with soapy hands. She slipped her hand between my buttocks. I tried to slip away. She laughed at me, stood up and pushed me under the stream of water. "Just like a virgin." She giggled. She stepped out. She threw me a giant towel.

I felt so comfortable with her on the bed this time. We were both wrapped in large towels, sitting in the lamplight. We had been as close as possible. There was no expectation of anything more, except being together. Her drying her long hair was beautiful to watch. I felt healthy, fresh.

"Tato would die if he walked in right now." She laughed.

I wished she hadn't brought him up. I said nothing.

"I don't have one ounce of guilt, Cello. Not an ounce." She went on drying her hair. "You want to know something? Tato was the one who wanted to get married, not me. Oh, I liked marriage after a while, I'll admit that. And, oh God"—she stopped a second—"it was beautiful living with him in the beginning. It was everything I dreamed of, everything I thought it should be. Never lonely; I mean, I never wanted to be anywhere else, with anyone else. We had music, plants. We grew herbs, tomatoes on the fire escape. We made paella, half Puerto Rican, half Italian with tomatoes. We made pasta, all kinds of coffees. We spread ourselves out every night with our supper. I read magazines; he wrestled with his damn law books. Poor Tato. Books and him just didn't mix. He was flunking.

"One night he got up out of bed and said he wanted to go for a walk. Perfectly fine with me, but after a while he was taking walks almost every night. Once I made the mistake of wanting to go with him; no, he definitely wanted to walk alone. Fine. But then the walks got longer and turned into hours. He was coming home when I was asleep, with the smell of beer and cigarette smoke all over him. Now he was flunking exams left and right. Still fine, if that's what he wanted. But I was dying for someone to talk to. I couldn't get him to talk. I had to make an appointment to see him. I left a note one night asking him to give me a time when we could talk. That's the night he woke me up at four in the morning and said it right out: 'It's not your fault, but I think the marriage is washed up.' Okay, but there was something about him that worried me more than if he were telling me the truth. You know what I mean?" She was talking too fast. "How can I explain it? I didn't *believe* him. Time after time I would think about that morning saying to myself, Amelia, you just refused to hear what he was trying to *say* to you. You blocked it, refused to accept that he was *tired* of you. Cello, Cello, believe me, I tried seeing it that way, but I just couldn't buy it that he didn't love me. I . . . If he seemed happy, I'd say sure, good luck, but he was so mushy, so droopy. I looked at him asleep and I thought, No, no, this is not the man. No. He's lost himself. Solid as a rock all along, and all of a sudden he was gone, lost, he was lost inside himself."

Her words were racing against each other: "I never once had the feeling of anger toward him, I swear it. And believe me, I'm capable of anger. I was too worried for anger. To this day I have the funny feeling that our main trouble was that we had no troubles; goddamnit, we were *too* happy, too happy. No place left to go, nothing to strive after, to worry about. Tato became claustrophobic. See, he forgot how many times he opened up to me. A lot of the pieces of the puzzle came together. I suppose I understand it better now, as well as I ever will, but it's not enough just to understand."

She caught herself. She breathed deeply, looked down, trying to pull a thread from the pillow, but it held, swelling the tip of her finger with blood. She released the thread. "I told him I could never be less than a friend to him. I dreamed of being more, because once I thought there was more I could be to someone."

"Maybe there is," I said. "What were some of the pieces of the puzzle? Another woman?"

"It wasn't another woman. Good God. He just . . ." Throwing the pillow down, she sighed. "He said he thought he might be homosexual. He had to go out and test it. That was like seeing him off for the war, wondering if he'd ever return, except I was seeing him off to those hidden bars where they play tambourines and juke boxes. Tato found it boring. He didn't deny it, but he told me that was where the mystery man was likely to pop up, that they all weren't faggots. He deplored effeminate men. He felt they robbed him of a chance for some dignity. They cluttered the issue. But the good guys were sprinkled among them, he said, so out he went."

"He never found the good guy?"

"No."

"Suppose he had?" I asked.

"He'd go on from there, I guess." Her eyes focused on a distance. "I'm sad."

"Well, is he worth it? You certainly put up with a lot."

"I can't forget him. He has my feelings tied up. Sometimes I think if I could just forget his face. Your face is like his, much more delicate, but definitely his type, less brutal, your chin." Her eyes scanned my face. "He called me when you were coming from Europe. He said, 'My cousin, four years younger, is coming from Rome.' I don't know, I had a premonition. I said to myself, This Cello could turn out to be the mystery man. When I laid eyes on you at the house, I knew it."

"What did you know?"

"I knew he'd fallen in love with you."

"How?"

"Just looking at you, hearing you. He did, didn't he?"

"Did what?"

"Flipped for you?"

"He tried to trap me."

Her expression changed. She seemed hurt. "What do you mean?" she said.

"Oh, I don't know what I'm trying to say. He tried . . ."

236

"Yes?"

". . . to initiate me sexually once at his apartment."

She pretended casual interest. "And you didn't go along?"

"That's right. I told him no."

"Gently, I hope."

"What do you mean?" I said.

"*Gently*. You told him gently."

"At first, yes, of course. I was gentle."

"And then what?"

"Then what? Why, I told him more firmly," I said with a little indignation.

"What form did that take?" Her inquisitiveness was too intense. She wasn't talking like a friend anymore. She had me on the defensive.

"Amelia, do you know what he tried to do to me?"

"He tried to have sex with you?"

"Exactly."

"So?" She shrugged. "This city's full of it."

"What do you mean *so*? It wasn't just a . . . a request. He took it upon himself. Would you want someone to do that to you? That's *rape*."

"Oh, I don't believe it. You're paranoid, Cello. Didn't he try anything else with you? C'mon, I lived with the guy. Was he fun? Did you talk? Didn't he open up to you?"

"And I *responded*." I was beginning to shout. "But he also wanted to *use* me. He did. He wrecked everything. Wrecked it. Cared nothing about how I felt. He offered friendship, fidelity."

"Fidelity?" Her eyes darted. I wanted the conversation to end.

"Oh, I mean a certain agreement that we'd be . . ." I stopped short. I was angry. Who the hell was she to question me so fiercely? I resented her a great deal now.

"Agreement that you'd be what?" she said.

"*Friends*."

"And he broke that agreement simply because he wanted to have sex?"

"What?"

"He broke the *agreement*?" All of a sudden I didn't remember

237

what we were talking about. "You love him," she said, turning away from my stare.

"Are you crazy? It's the opposite."

"You *love* him," she insisted.

"What reason do I have to love Tato? I resent you. Do you hear? I resent *you*. Who are you to defend him? Do you know what he did? You know nothing. I don't love him. I hate him. I never want to see him again. I wish those were his ashes. I couldn't pay him back for what he did to me if I had a crowbar and hit his face a thousand times, over and over." I caught myself. I put my hand over my mouth.

She had turned toward the window, her shoulders dropped. Birds chirped far off down the street.

"Poor Tato," she said. She seemed so stupid at that moment. Hadn't she heard what I was saying? She turned to me tearfully with arms folded. "You really don't give a hoot for me. Tell the truth, Cello."

"I don't know what you're talking about." I didn't know what I was talking about either. But I knew she was going to drive a wedge between us, a huge axe about to fall. It had no justice, her sentence; justice was not one of her objectives.

"You're only using me," she said. "It's him you want, but you're too dumb, too proud."

"Is that going to be your excuse to get rid of me?" My question surprised her, but she didn't answer. Now, my nakedness disturbed me. I threw off the towel and put on my undershorts and pants. I slipped into my undershirt and sweater and made for the door. "I'm going for a walk," I said.

"Make it a long one," she said, lighting her cigarette.

I slammed the door behind me, walked down the carpeted stairs, and wished there was sand, a beach, beyond the front door. I walked under the sycamores almost in a state of shock. I tried to understand what had happened with Amelia, whether what we had done was normal or strange, whether she was sane or mad, whether *I* was sane or mad, or were we both too innocent? That made the most sense. We were just children, both hurt, both with many people to blame for our scars, both too wary of one another.

I was tired by the time I returned to the apartment. Amelia was asleep.

We kept missing each other during the next week or so, it seemed to me. I found myself alone in her place most of the time. She was coming in late, too tired to talk. I attributed it to embarrassment on her part, to remorse, exhaustion. Our bodies didn't touch the whole week. She was always rehearsing, preparing for a project at the dance studio. Friday morning before she left, I told her I would have dinner for her when she came home.

"Thanks," she said without looking at me, slinging her dance bag over her shoulder, thumping downstairs without closing the door, absentmindedly, without a goodbye, without a glance back.

I had been eating in Sandolino's Cafe every day. Ignorant as I was about food, I found it difficult to provide my own meals. Amelia's refrigerator only yielded things like butter, orange juice and salad dressing. So on Friday afternoon I brought home from the delicatessen some dinner candles, rice pudding, smoked fish and two containers of Greek salad.

When Amelia walked in, she was delighted. She ate ravenously, then made our coffee.

"I want to talk to you," I said as she lit her cigarette.

"I want to talk to you, too," she said quickly, blowing out smoke. "You have to leave."

She smoked several cigarettes and went on about how uptight I was making her by staying in her apartment. She said she was worried because Tato was bound to find out about it, and she didn't want him to be hurt, nor did she want to deal with his rage toward me. I offered to talk with Tato, but she wanted no part of it. She begged me to let her off the hook.

When she went to the bathroom, I decided that was as good a time as any to leave. I took my bag from her closet and checked my wallet. The five thousand was still there. I knocked on the bathroom door. "Amelia? I think I'll go now."

"Okay," she answered.

I took a room at a hotel uptown called the Claret and spent the whole weekend ordering sandwiches and looking out the window. Sunday, as the dark came, I showered and shaved, put

Zia's ring in my pocket, and my money, then took a taxi to Amelia's apartment, hoping that some change in her would have taken place, hoping that some new element had altered her attitude. When I walked in the apartment door, I found Amelia surrounded by boxes.

"What's all this?" I asked.

"I have a job in London. Why do you think I've been dancing all my life? For jobs. And I got one, so I go."

"Are you giving up the apartment, going forever?"

"Yes, I'm giving up the apartment, but I'm not going forever."

"When will you be back?"

"Cello, please don't give me a hard time."

"I want to talk some more," I pleaded. A quick sharp pain flashed in my head as I spoke, but I pretended not to notice it. The fact that nothing could stop Amelia's leaving forever was all I could focus on.

"I don't want to hurt anybody," she said, her hand touching my arm. Tears came to her eyes. "Especially Tato. No matter how we tried, we would hurt him, with twice the hurt that either of us ever got from him. We'll forget each other, but this he would never forget, and for what? We have to take care of it now before we feel too much pain, Cello."

I panicked. "I love you," I said desperately. This time the words didn't fly, didn't thrill me.

"You don't know me. What do you know about me?"

"I admire you. I need someone. I'm alone in this country now."

"Do you really believe that it's me you need?"

"It's you."

"It's Tato. His scent is on me. He's tied by a long cord to me, and you know it. You say goodbye to Tato, you slam his door and walk away, then you sneak around to his back door. You come into his house, sleep in his bed."

I was shocked that she put it that way. "I didn't know you were his wife. We made love and I still didn't know."

"Oh, that's wrong." Her eyes flashed. Her finger pointed. "I told you in the park, after my class."

"All right. True."

"When you walked up these stairs to this room, you knew who you were going to *fuck*."

"Why are you saying these crazy things?"

"Because I don't want to waste any more time, and they're not crazy."

"Waste time?"

"I realized you were his cousin Cello right from the start. Don't you ever wonder why I turned on to you? One look at you, and I knew how I would feel about you. One word from you, and I knew I wanted you." She was crying. "Cello"—she turned to me— "Jesus Christ, I *used you*. We're both using each other. Admit it, goddamn you."

"You're wrong; I swear you're wrong."

"Maybe you really believe that. Okay. Still, we're going to have to stop this whole thing," she said.

"No, I won't let you."

"*Yes, you will*," she screamed, "or else someday it will kill him. I'm afraid; somewhere unconsciously you are my way of doing that to him. I'll take all the blame. Okay? I'm a cunt. Okay? There's too much going on. You've got to split, Cello."

The buzzer rang. She walked to the kitchen and pressed the button which unlocked the street door downstairs. She came back blowing her nose in a tissue. Her voice dropped. "My brother's here for the boxes. Goodbye." Both hands clutched the tissue under her nose. Her shoulders began to shake.

I tried to hold her, but she pulled away. She was crying in spite of herself. I turned the knob and pulled, revealing the red carpet and the smooth banister of the stairwell, the white wall, a shadow of a man ascending, a man looking up at me. It wasn't her brother. It was Tato.

He smiled with surprise when he saw me. Then he stopped in his tracks, peering through the spindles. His eyes passed rapidly from Amelia to me. Amelia was frozen in shock, tears still on her face.

"What the hell's going on?" he asked in a friendly tone. There was silence. "I heard you were leaving," he said to Amelia.

"Yes," she answered, turning away. He glanced up at me. We

stood motionless for what seemed a terribly long time, until it dawned upon him to turn and leave. He walked down the stairs and out, quietly pulling the door closed behind him.

I stood there a long time, between the click of the street door and the sound of Amelia's sobs. She sat on a chair in the kitchen crying. I attempted to move back inside. Her face was so pale and her sobbing so intense, she could only hold out her arm with her hand up, like a policeman directing traffic. "Go," she was saying, but her mouth couldn't form the word.

Outside, the rain was full and steady. Few leaves were left on the sycamores; the rain had pummeled them off. Yellow and wet, they gathered at curbsides, splattered themselves over parked cars. The air was not cold. Ahead, on Seventh Avenue, light-streams of fast-moving cars reflected off the blacktop. Not a soul on the streets, but lights were on in houses and apartments. People at home, cozy, planning for Thanksgiving, trading the summer sun for the evening glow of incandescent General Electric light bulbs, laughing people back together after summer, making fires, cooking soups, wondering what to buy each other for Christmas.

All at once, the streetlights came alive. It was six o'clock. I was glad I had Zia's ring and my money on me. I decided to forget about going back for my bag at the Claret Hotel and to catch the 11:20 train for Southampton. From there I could hitch to Jessup. If anyone disturbed me there from Carter Boisvert's office, I would tell them I was collecting my things. I had to be back at the house to focus on my next move. Only from there would I be able to see into the future. And I was longing for the house.

I bought an umbrella for two dollars from a man on Seventh Avenue, although I was already drenched. He took my money without looking at me. I walked slowly, even though it was pouring, the thumping rain working an insistent cadence on my umbrella. I walked uptown on Seventh Avenue toward Penn Station. I tipped the umbrella several times, letting the rain hit my face.

People were smiling under the waterfall inside a restaurant. People chatted, safe from the rain, in a glass-enclosed sidewalk cafe. How did they meet each other? People laughed in the orange light of another bar. A girl waved to me from the window. She was with a man, a black man, singing. I wondered if the windows at Jessup were open to the rain.

The 11:20 arrived in Southampton at 1:41 A.M. Eddie's Taxi, a rusty black Checker, waited for the one passenger on the train. For three dollars Eddie, a quiet old black man, drove me to the cracked asphalt.

Next morning, the sun tried to peek at the earth a few times. From the beach I could see smoky gray rain clouds moving west behind the house, which seemed frail in its new whiteness. Its oaks had shed leaves, allowing light to ravage the house.

I came upon Zia's urn. The tide had washed it ashore. I walked around it, contemplating picking it up and burying it out of sight, but I decided instead to ignore it. I didn't even want to touch it.

The sun came out once or twice the next day. Rain clouds loomed motionless to the north. There was nothing but tea in the house. I hitched into the village for supplies. I bought fish, bread and milk and made it back without getting wet. That night after I ate and fell asleep on the red velvet couch, I had terrible headaches, terrible dreams. It was late in the morning when I woke up. I made coffee and took it with me as I walked along the bay. Smoky gray rain clouds were moving west this time behind the house. Now the house seemed *sad* in spite of its white paint, a dying old dame in a new white dress. Even its interior refused to wake up for me: it was a forgotten place, and my presence alone couldn't wake it.

I never went upstairs. I used the kitchen bathroom and spent as much time outside of the house as I could, even though it was chilly on the porch. A west wind hit it straight on. I sat there motionless for hours, watching the water. I felt stiff. My nose was stuffed. Movement took too much effort.

Night came early, and yet I could hardly keep awake until dark. I slept in my clothes on the red velvet couch each night, stretched out on its huge pillows, pressing out the dusty days that were trapped inside. Winters filled my nostrils as I slept, and long-ago summers. I smelled salt, fresh sunny days and the remnants of damp nights, faint traces of perfume and people's bodies. I dreamed of lions and silver Lamborghinis. One time I slept so long that I awoke in the afternoon of the next day. It alarmed me that I could sleep that long. I didn't remember the details of my dreams, but they were dark and continuous. Once someone was banging on the front door. It wasn't a dream, but the noise didn't have the power to wake me.

In the bathroom mirror I could see I had grown a beard. Headaches had made my eyes red. With no one around to wake me, I had become lost in mazes of light and dark, day and night. I had to hold onto the walls to get from the bathroom to the porch. I stepped carefully down to the sand. It was cold; very bright white clouds had replaced the gray ones. I made note of those very bright white clouds that were speeding eastward like locomotives.

Suddenly the sky was gold, and winds tore at the sheets—or was it a lace tablecloth—I had tied in a large knot around my neck? I was standing before a wall of water, standing next to a roar of white water and wind. The booming wind out of the west had lifted a fan of red clouds. The white moon rising in the east screamed at the fiery west, silver fighting gold, as the bay rushed eastward like a river, whole waves higher than my head, not breaking upon me because of the wind. Or was it the full moon in the east sucking in the bay? How did it get late?

Why the tablecloth? I remembered it under the red bowl in the dining room. How did it get around me? Next to me—what was the bamboo liquor wagon doing at the shoreline? I looked back and saw its tracks in the sand. I had dragged it, not remembering, not remembering . . . And the urn, Zia's urn in my hands. What was in it? Campari? No, God! I threw it. I dared to throw the urn at the screaming wall of water? Yes! Tear off the tablecloth. I thought I was saying mass, my first mass, pretending to, the way I had rehearsed it in Rome.

"Sleeping too much," I shouted to myself. "Wake up." I walked into the wall of water with my clothes on. The chill made me feel better. The bay threw me about, tossed me. I was grateful to it as though it were a mother giving birth to me. "Wake me," I pleaded. "I'm afraid. Take care of me."

When I walked back to the house, I found myself drifting to the right. In spite of it, I gathered kindling on the way, small pieces. I piled them in the living-room fireplace with a mountain of crumpled newspaper. I placed three of the heaviest logs on top and poured oak leaves all around them. I set them on fire. The flames burst out, almost licking the mantel. It was exactly the fire I wanted, the fire I needed. I spoke to it softly. "Help me. Warm me."

"Che paura." I began to speak to the fire in Italian. Gradually my voice became a strengthening rod inside me, pulling me together. My clothes were drying. I felt better.

I sat up on the velvet couch. I didn't want to sleep again. The curtains lifted unexpectedly over my head and waved toward the dying fire. They returned, brushing my forehead. I turned and looked into the bay. I thought I saw ships, but they were swans flying low in the moonlight, swans hovering, inching against the wind. The wind had changed to northwest. The air was very dry and much cooler, as though the huge gears inside the earth had started it turning in a different direction with a jolt. The old and the very sick would die from the shock. Fetuses would bolt out of their wombs. The great ball of winter was coming, rolling out of the north.

I decided to hitch back to New York, to the Claret Hotel for my bag, afraid to think of what I would do after that. I folded the shutters in the dark. I felt so empty-handed as I left, but there was nothing to take. I looked back into the great living room. There was the ginger jar. I felt my trouser pockets; the money and the ring were there. "Goodbye, Zia," I said.

I turned on the terrible light in the foyer to check the bolt on the front door: first the brass stays on the inside on the top, then the bottom. There, near the brass fixture, was a dark yellow envelope that had been slipped under the door. I tore it open. Inside was a cablegram that had been opened and placed back in its envelope. The cablegram inside was dated September 13, 1968, and addressed to Argentina. It read:

TO MANFREDI, FANTASIA, AVENIDA ROSA, BUENOS AIRES.
YOUR BROTHER DIED YESTERDAY. FUNERAL MONDAY 16,
GENEVA. OVERSEAS OPERATOR 8774. LUCILLE MEYER
MANFREDI.

Zia's brother? That was my father. My father had died.

I flicked off the bright overhead light. I was standing between the two bison. The moon lit the porch. There was the chair he sat in with Zia the afternoon he tried to sell me for ten thousand dollars, while Tato and I listened under the porch. I stepped outside and pulled the wicker chairs into the foyer, piling them up.

The house never had a key. Even if it did, what point would there be in locking the door? Who was there to leave a key with? I closed the door simply, as though I would be back in a half hour, and walked down onto the sand recalling the day Tato, Tangerine and I hid, smoking under the porch. My eyes burned as I walked, and I had to compensate for my drift to the right. That disturbed me, but I had awakened quite well, and the moving about had sharpened my senses. I might have had a flu, a high temperature.

I walked slowly to North Sea Road to the telephone at the Texaco station. When I got there, the station was dark. My hands were freezing as I dialed, my fingernails very dirty. The overseas operator connected me, collect. Lucille accepted without hesitation.

"Are you all right, Lucille?" I asked.

"Yes. Who is it? Cello?" Her voice hadn't changed.

"Yes," I said.

"Do you know?"

"Yes. Did he suffer?" I didn't know what else to say.

"A little. He expected it. He didn't want anyone to know."

"Why not?"

"You knew him, Cello. He was proud. It was a lovely funeral. He wanted to be buried in Switzerland. I hope you don't mind."

"It's all right."

She cried a moment, then, half recovering: "There are some

papers you should look at," she said. "I don't know what to do with them."

She had to leave the phone for a minute. My eyes went up over the telephone wires. The sky was flying by in chunks. The wind was cold. The egrets had surely gone. How could they fly south in such wind?

I thought of Mrs. Sadowski's white brocade against my cheek, my father's strong arms lifting me up from it, his black hair slicked down, his lips chuckling in my ear, gentle noises. I could feel sobs stirring inside me.

What was there to mourn? Just the hopes, those old hopes that once kept me alive, that he would take me out of school, home with him, hopes that there was a place somewhere he was making for me in his life, hopes I had on the train to Geneva, as though something miraculous, inexplicable would emanate from him, compensating for my pain, making everything all right retroactively. As though, before his end, he was destined to become a man of final wisdom who would accept me as his son. Those old hopes dashed, not his dying, made me want to cry.

Lucille had come back to the phone. "Letters, documents," she said.

"Yes? What letters?"

"Letters from your mother."

"My mother?"

"Not now. When you come, you can see them."

"Letters to whom? Lucille?"

"There is the letter she left him when she died."

"Read it to me, please."

"Cello, they are *yours*. You may have them, but please, don't ask me to read them now."

"Read them. Read them," I demanded. She left the phone. I thought I could hear the roar of the ocean while she was away.

"Hello?" she said.

"Yes."

"This one is from your mother. I will send it to you if you like."

"Just read it."

" 'My dear husband. I don't hate anybody. Why do you hate

247

me? Goodbye. Take care of your son.' And there is the letter to
you."

"From my father?"

"From your mother."

"Huh? What are you talking about?"

"There is the letter to you from your mother."

"I don't remember any letter. Read it. Please, Lucille."

" 'My baby. Remember you are named after the musical instru-
ment. Don't let him tell you anything else. I love you, my baby,
because you are a very good boy. You have to go to school so you
can learn. I don't want you to be mad at me because I had to go
away. I can't stand it no more. Forgive Mommie and pray for me.
I'll watch over you from where I'm going. Ha, ha—' "

"What was that last word?" I asked.

"Ha, ha."

"Spell it."

"H-a, h-a. 'Hugs and kisses, your mommy.' " Lucille was silent.
I could see my mother's wide eyes, large through the thick glass
of her eyeglasses. I remembered the Flamingo, her voice, her sad
smile of pain, her smile of confusion. I don't remember if I said
goodbye to Lucille before I hung up.

I pulled the folding doors of the booth toward me. The loud
voices of wind hit my face. The dust of leaves hit my nostrils.
Above me trees roared loud as a waterfall. I stepped out into it,
the moonlight. I walked. The Texaco sign creaked over my head.

I tore the cablegram to pieces, letting them fly behind me in the
wind. I saw the flash of headlights up ahead. I crossed the street
and lifted my thumb. I was near Trout Pond. The car shot by
me, leaving me in darkness and dust. I walked away from the pond
on a road I had walked so many times before, but this time it
seemed unfamiliar. I kept my right hand out in case I would hit
a tree, because I was still drifting to my right as I walked.

By the time the next car showed up, I had to make a very
concentrated effort to walk on line. I didn't want to appear drunk.
I turned, facing the oncoming car. High beams burned my eyes.
My head hurt. I raised one hand to shield my eyes and the other
with its thumb out. The headlights belonged to a pale green Ford

LTD with dark green tinted glass. It pulled slowly up to me. The window on the passenger side opened slightly.

A gray-haired woman smiled and put her lips into the narrow opening. "Where are you going?" she asked.

"New York City," I answered. She turned and spoke to her husband. Then her lips came back to the window. "Are you all right? We thought you were hurt."

"I'm all right."

Her husband started speaking to her. Her lips came back to the window. "We're going as far as Center Moriches," she said.

"That's good." She lifted the button unlocking the back door. I opened and entered the dark, quiet car.

The tinted windows closed out the moonlight and the rushing river of noise outside. The car smelled of jasmine perfume or shave lotion, mingling with the industrial odors of new vinyl and upholstery. We drove for a few miles in silence. The husband reached to turn on the radio as we took a curve. The sign said fifteen miles per hour.

I was leaning to my right almost against the door of the back seat, still dizzy. As our headlights scanned the woods on the big curve ahead, a voice came over the radio advertising delivery of the *New York Times*. I heard the antenna behind me rise out of the car. The voice became clearer. I wondered if my father had really died and if I had really talked to Lucille. I knew I had told the man and woman sitting in front of me that I was going to New York. I was glad I had managed to remember that, because I was losing sense of where I had come from and couldn't think where I was headed or why I had to go there. I was finding it very hard to put together all the things that had happened.

"Look out," the woman in front said, trying to sound calm at first. Her husband jerked the wheel with haughty indignation.

"The fool," he cried out. She gripped the dashboard. In spite of the tinted glass, the other car's lights filled our car. I could see her hair was whiter than I thought. Her lips were very thin. Her lipstick was too greasy, too red for an old lady. When she screamed, I could see that her lipstick had strayed into the cracks and wrinkles around her mouth.

He was wearing a seat belt, so I flew past him from the back seat, right between them. I could see her face smashing against the dashboard as I flew past. Suddenly I was on the hood looking in at them. They were screaming. Above the screams I could hear the river of air. I remember thinking the lipstick had run all over their faces. Her hair wasn't white anymore; it was straight and blond and . . .

Then I realized I was facing different people, two of them women. They were young, screaming. I had gone completely through the windshield onto the hood of the other car, and was looking in on them through shattered glass. I tasted blood. Oddly, I felt only a slight pain, burning at my right temple. I wanted to touch the pain, but I couldn't tell where my hands were. I heard the river of air, though, and the cries, and smelled the gasoline. I kept my ear tuned to the river of air and my eyes on the moon.

CHAPTER VIII

I WOKE up in Southampton Hospital, in a dark room. It was daytime though, and the sun glared around the edges of the window shades. There was cleanliness all around me and the odor of alcohol.

"My name is Dearstyne," said a young man, smiling. "Can you see me?"

"Yes," I answered. He was tanned. His eyes were blue, his mustache turned almost white by the sun. His front teeth were large. They held back his smile. His hair was many tight blond curls close to his head.

"Try to breathe through your mouth, because you have a broken nose."

"Huh?"

"We're going to try to rebuild your nose as soon as your face heals a little."

"What's wrong with my face?"

"You received a pretty bad gash, from your forehead down to your chin. It ran through your eyebrow across your eye. If the cut heals without infection, you won't need plastic surgery, but we'll want photographs to use as a guide to rebuild your nose."

"Photographs?"

"Your nose is fractured pretty badly; we can only try. I have to warn you about this because there will be changes in your face— nothing radical, nothing too drastic but . . ." I reached up to touch my face. He caught my hand. "No, you can't do that."

"My eye burns."

"Okay. Your cornea has been grazed minutely. It'll heal itself, but you have a lot of bleeding in the eyes."

"Give me a mirror."

"Now just relax."

"I want a mirror. Take off these bandages."

"No." Dearstyne's hand was firm on my arm. "Now the gash crossed your eyebrow. Your eyebrow will be interrupted." I turned away, but he went on: "We can't replace the hair follicles in your eyebrow or along your chin, but you can eventually grow a beard to hide it."

I was getting nauseated. "Don't tell me any more."

"There's no more to tell. Except that your face may turn out more interesting than before. Wouldn't you like that? Do you feel any pain other than the eye?"

"No."

"None in the head?"

"Who are you?"

"I told you. Dr. Dearstyne. I'm the resident neurosurgeon. Now will you tell me *your* name?"

"My name?"

"Yes. We'd like to get in touch with someone for you."

"Who?"

"We don't know who. Who do you want us to get in touch with?"

I was willing to answer—but I couldn't. The impulse to form a response was there inside me. It rose to my throat, to its threshold, but it had no power to turn into a word. "Give me a minute," I said.

"Take your time." He tried to hide his seriousness behind a wide smile. I wanted to answer his question. The impulse to answer again gathered power, but once again something blocked the words, and the impulse escaped my lips without its cargo, like a bubble floating away.

"I can't."

"Don't try. We can wait." He held a light up to my eyes.

"Can't think of it," I said.

"Well, you can relax."

"Why can't I think of it?" I asked.

"You will."

"Why can't I now?" I demanded. When it dawned on me how blank my mind had become, I screamed; how many times I don't know. Someone had robbed me mercilessly, siphoning off images before they could form. I was desperate.

Dearstyne must have buzzed for help. Two nurses ran into the room. They flung up the cages on the sides of my bed.

"Where will you go?" Dearstyne was asking, straining against me. "Where will you go?" he repeated. His hand pushed me back toward my pillow.

"What the hell are you talking about?" I asked.

"You said, 'Let me go.' You're trying to go somewhere. Where will you go?" Once again I tried to answer, but no pictures, no words could form. I started to cry. They gave me an injection. In an instant I was falling asleep.

I felt them wheeling me around, lifting me from one table to the next. I must have been getting X rays.

That night Dearstyne was back. This time his approach was totally different. He wasn't smiling.

"First, let me say you are all right and there is nothing terribly critical going on here, but the X rays indicate you received a bad blow on your head. It has caused a subdural hematoma, a blood clot on your left side above your ear. Do you feel any numbness or lack of control on your right side?"

I lifted my hand. I felt no numbness.

"There's a big mystery here." Dearstyne sighed. "The hematoma isn't where it should be, behind the swelling. The X rays show your skull's fine there."

"So?" I asked.

"So, it means there was another blow." He waited. "Couple weeks ago maybe, before the car accident. You remember anything?"

"No."

"Headaches? Dizziness?"

"Don't remember."

"Well, it doesn't matter. We"—he took a deep breath—"we should get at the hematoma, because it is unusually large and dense. It's what's making you irritable, and it may be interfering with your ability to recall things or to express certain words."

"How do I get rid of it?" I asked.

"We cut a small hole in your skull," he said simply. "I know it sounds terrible, but it's routine. We cut the hole over the hematoma and suck it out. When the pressure is removed, things should return to normal. In the meantime, you're suffering from a little shock, pure and simple. Now because your nose is interfering with your breathing, we're going to have to rebuild it while you're under anesthesia for the hematoma. You're luckier than the others."

"What happened to the others?" I asked.

He hesitated, as though he wasn't sure he should tell me, then he blurted out, "The older couple—they're both dead. She was DOA. The husband died a few hours ago. The two women in the other car are sisters. They're young and have a good chance. One's on a respirator. If we can prevent pneumonia, she'll make it. Punctured lung. Both legs broken on each of them. The older couple are probably related to you. Have you thought of that?"

254

I couldn't answer. I could feel no concern for either of them.

The next morning after breakfast Dearstyne appeared with some people. He asked them to wait and came into my room. His front teeth were in the way of his smile again. He asked me how I was.

"Okay," I answered impatiently.

"I have some people here who may be related to you."

"Okay."

"You don't have to talk to them," he said.

"What do you mean?"

"Okay. I mean I don't want you to react until I talk to you first. Do you understand? Just let me know later if you recognize any of them." He gave a signal and four people entered the room.

I wanted to leap out of bed, knock them over and run out of the hospital. I didn't want to be related to any of them. I was afraid they would lie, say they knew me and take me away. The older woman was dressed all in black. She took out her handkerchief. "No." She gulped.

Dearstyne tried to quiet her.

"He's no one. Were you in my father's car?" She flung the words at me. "Who are you?" A nurse pulled her away. "I have a right to know who that man is," she called from the hallway.

The other couple stood scared. She was pregnant. "No." They shook their heads. "Whose fault?" he whispered to me. Dearstyne caught him and gently pushed them out.

The next day they removed my bandages so that a policeman could take photographs of me. Then Dearstyne came in with the resident psychiatrist, who just observed while Dearstyne asked questions.

While they were there, an orderly wheeled in a tray. "Do you want your whole head shaved or just the part they have to, you know, cut?"

"Just the part they have to cut," I answered. Dearstyne and the psychiatrist ignored him as he worked on my head. I said, "I don't remember," to all their questions. I did some color-matching tests. I read aloud. Then Dearstyne left. The psychiatrist gave me more written tests, sitting patiently near the bed as I completed them. Then a nurse gave me an injection. I was feeling good when they wheeled me into the operating room.

I woke up in the intensive care unit. When they wheeled me back to my room, I discovered there was a new nurse assigned to me. Nurse Foster. I had never seen her before the operation; she had been out because her mother had recently died. I was glad to find someone like her when I came down from intensive care. From the start, Nurse Foster took a very serious interest in me.

She kept curiosity seekers away from my door. She kept the room dark and the hallway silent. She rarely talked, but she came often to check on me. I was grateful for her silence and her energy, but it didn't have the power to head off periods of depression that were becoming worse every day.

Not only was it impossible for me to come up with connecting links, but I was beginning to find it difficult to concentrate on things that were taking place. One morning I looked out the window with complete certitude that what I saw was a dream, that everything, even the accident, was a long dream over which I had no control. I had no choice but to wait to wake up. It calmed me to believe it all wasn't happening.

I went through the rest of my tests cooperatively. I didn't try to hide my helplessness inside the dream. I answered their questions. All the while, I hoped to escape the dream, but day dawned after night over and over, and I was becoming very tired of putting faith into small acts like conversation, eating and going to the bathroom. I needed the dream to end so I could go back into the life that was waiting for me. I had no papers, no identification, no passport or connections. I envied the characters around me who did. I envied their sense of purpose, the way they took action as if they had been given a list of orders from somewhere high above. The land of my dream was really their territory, not mine.

Rosie Foster often wore a pale and wounded expression. She had been very close to her mother. I admired the way she forced life into her eyes for me in spite of her own sadness. Her dark hair and her blue and white nurse's uniform always appeared to be in sharper focus than anything else in my field of vision. Her smile came from outside my bad dream. Her smile was truthful and guileless. Her smile was innocent.

"Guess what?" she said one morning. She wouldn't look at me as she puffed my pillows. "My father is Police Chief of Bridgehampton town." She made statements sound like questions.

"Yes. So?"

"He's gonna be working on your case."

"Doing what?"

"Checking all the high school yearbooks around here for someone who looks something like you might have. I think you were a little before my time, but wouldn't it be funny if we went to the same high school? Lift your head please, Jim."

"Lift your head please, Jim."

"You call me Jim?"

"Yep."

"How come?"

"Who knows? Maybe Jim was your name." She laughed. "It was the name of my favorite actor. He died in a car crash. Why let the name go to waste? Don't mind me."

She was a shy and a very simple woman. Attractively shy to me. The name Jim became the North Star of my dream. Since my dream refused to end, I decided to live by its rules. Okay, I *was* Jim.

One morning Rosie came into my room with bags from a shop called the Woodsman. Inside were jeans and underwear and two light blue shirts.

"I had your clothes cleaned," she said. "But when I picked them up I said, 'Uh, uh. They didn't come out of the accident as well as you did.'" She laughed. "So I got you this stuff as a present. Put 'em on. Dearstyne wants you to hit the air."

I got dressed in the shirt and jeans but had to wear my bathrobe on top of them because it was cool. Rosie held my arm. The outdoors was bright and noisy. Blue jays screaming far off pained my ears. The oaks were almost bare, but the maples were still leafy and yellow. Tired geraniums bloomed at the tips of long crooked stems, small blooms, but their redness shocked the fall air. She had spent

her own money on me. I had been wondering how I would pay
for the hospital.

"My roommate got married last September," Rosie said, her
face flushing. "I . . . I don't like living alone. The place is too big.
It's *small* really, but too big for one person, and I don't know.
Temporarily, if you want . . ." It took me a while to realize she
was struggling for the words to invite me to come live with her.
"Why not let's share the place?" she finally said.

"I have no money," I said.

"What about that money you came in with?"

"What money?"

"Your clothing sheet said you were carrying forty-nine hundred
somethin' dollars and a woman's ring with a green stone."

I checked out of the hospital, signing the name James Smith,
and went with Rosie to her apartment on Jobs Lane in Southampton Village. It was a three-room apartment over a bar. Two bed-
rooms faced north; the bath was in the hallway. A large living
room faced south. The ocean was less than a mile away. I could
hear it.

Rosie worked days. She made dinner every night at her father's
in Bridgehampton. She brought him a plate to the police station
and two plates back to the apartment for us. We spent mostly
the dark hours together each day. She seemed a much different
person without her tag that read R. *Foster*.

On her days off I became a little nervous, but gradually I began
to feel she wasn't concentrating on me when we were together.
She gave me privacy and made me feel safe. Dearstyne had
prescribed an anti-convulsion drug. Rosie left my dosage on the
countertop each morning. I sat in the apartment alone all day
watching the sun on her ficus tree. Sometimes I could hear the
ocean.

One night she came home with no dinner, so we ate hamburgers
in the bar beneath the apartment. Her face was tired and she
hadn't changed her uniform.

"My father told me to tell you that the yearbooks didn't pan
out. I don't think they tried too hard." She wiped ketchup from

258

her chin and looked down at the hamburger. "And"—her eyes avoided mine as she pulled a fresh napkin from the container—"he knows you're living with me."

"What does he think about it?" I asked.

"He thinks I'm crazy. Suppose you have a wife and kids somewhere, he says."

"Suppose I do?" I asked.

She shrugged. "Dearstyne says that unconsciously you haven't the slightest intention of becoming the man you were, ever again."

"What? Did he tell you that?"

"I overheard him talking to the psychiatrist. And my father, he still believes a man and woman should be married before they live together."

"How do you feel?" I asked directly. She pulled another napkin. I couldn't get her to look into my eyes. "Do you feel we should be married?" She laughed quietly at the question, still not acknowledging my eyes.

"I love you." She blushed. Tears came into her eyes. She tried to continue to chew in spite of it. She dropped her hamburger in a heap on her dish and she put her face into her hands. "I love you, Jim." She shook. People were watching. It made me a little angry that those feelings were in her, that she saw me in a romantic way and had never indicated it until now. She knew about me medically and emotionally; probably even talked to Dearstyne about me. She nurtured me to this point of privilege, where she could cry and say, "I love you," making a fool of herself and me, while the bartender pretended to be watching television. I was angry with her for the first time since the accident. Though I should have been flattered, I suppose, it only made me feel more alone. Rosie had turned her kindness into love. She had turned all her good intentions into a word, into a tool. Now I was responsible for her feelings. I could make her sad or glad. I could no longer be her friend unless I answered, "I love you, too." If I chose not to, I would become the man who hurt her. I would have to leave.

"Do you want to marry me?" I asked. I couldn't find it in me to say otherwise. She looked up with wet eyes.

"I've been so afraid to become another problem to you," she said. "Do you love me?" She lifted her head to support the daring words.

"I don't love anyone else," I said.

She took my hands quickly, holding back a smile. "We can live together awhile, then get married. I think the law lets you."

I nodded my consent.

"What does that mean?" She smiled.

"Yes," I said. "It means yes, Rosie."

At Christmas Rosie gave me a corduroy jacket and a gift certificate from Arnold's Men's Store. I bought a pair of loafers and plaid trousers to go with the jacket. I got a haircut on Christmas Eve, a very short one that finally matched up with the shaved side of my head. We ate dinner with her father at his house in Bridgehampton. The Chief hardly spoke to me during the whole thing. He didn't have a present for me, and he ignored the tags that read *From Rosie and Jim*. He thanked her as though I had nothing to do with it. But later, when we were leaving, he held onto my hand with a hard angular grip and asked me if I liked boats. His shyness had no defense. His eyes danced wildly away from mine.

"Sure, I like boats," I said confusedly.

"Well, you got a job then. I got you a partnership in a little marina goin' up out east." His hand quickly urged me out the door. "I'll tell Rosie about it tomorrow. You can get the info from Rosie."

"Thanks," I said. "Thanks Chief. Merry Christmas. Good night, Chief."

When we got back to the apartment, I called Rosie to the Christmas tree before she took off her coat. I asked her to close her eyes and hold out her hand. I slipped the emerald ring onto her finger. She opened her eyes and stared down, steadying the loose ring with her thumb so that the stone faced up.

"My God!"

"Jeweler says it's a guaranteed real emerald. You mind an emerald for your engagement ring?"

"Do I mind having a real emerald?" She answered by throwing her arms around me. She cried, taking my head in her hands, pressing it to her face. "Oh, I love you so much, Jim. I love you with all my heart."

"I love you, Rosie. I really do."

PART III

CHAPTER IX

DOWN in the tool room sometimes these recollections were so sharp, so vibrant and sudden, that I had to catch my breath, as though I were a bird suddenly lifted high on a great wind, seeing below my whole life with its different compartments, like patchwork, a small town or a map with its short limits and its clear boundaries. After all, I had colored in all the spaces on the map now. Jim Smith was trying to make peace with Cello Manfredi.

I had built up the marina so that I could buy out the Chief's interest, which I did. The Chief carried both my daughters home from the hospital when they were born. I allowed things like that, hoping he would mellow if he was assured of his inclusion in our lives.

It only had the effect of making me feel excluded. If it weren't for Rosie's peace-keeping efforts, I don't know how I would have gotten through those past ten years with the Chief. Ten years of geese killed for the Christmas table, ten capons for ten Thanksgivings.

For ten years Rosie and I had lived on Garden Street in the Village of Bridgehampton, less than ten miles from the big house on Jessup. It stunned me to realize that ten seasons of snow and ice had hit Zia's house, so close to us all those years.

Had the Maldonados sold her? Or had she languished all those years, boarded up winters, too isolated for rental in the summer? I was tempted to drive along North Sea Road, and over to the phragmites and the cracked asphalt, but I was too afraid of what I might find.

Dearstyne was wrong when he said I'd never let the other man emerge. By Thanksgiving Day, the last piece of the puzzle fell into place. I came up from the tool room that morning and walked about my house in wonder.

We were steeped in that long hot Indian summer when my daughters Karen and Erica set the eleventh Thanksgiving table for the eleventh capon Rosie had ordered killed fresh from Iacono's Poultry Farm. It was the warmest Thanksgiving Day on record in Long Island. We had local tomatoes and bouquets of our own roses for the table; something, they said, that had never happened before.

The bird was fourteen pounds. We had to juggle things in the fridge to make room for it; we couldn't have left it on the pantry shelf like other years, because it would have gone bad in the heat. Rosie stuffed the bird and put it in at ten in the morning. She walked to the living room, wiping her hands, and went to the window.

"Lawn needs cutting," Rosie said without looking at me.

The sound of a low-flying helicopter entered the house. The windows rattled. When it passed, I heard Erica and Karen laughing outside. It was summertime to the ear. We hadn't lifted the screens and put on the storm windows yet. There seemed to be more flies than in summer, flying clumsily, in a stupor of having lived too long.

"Jim, while we're alone, I want to talk to you."

"About what?"

"Your arrest." Her eyes struggled with her shyness to pin me down.

"Rosie, it's Thanksgiving. Not now."

"Not now? When? When you grab the fireplace poker and break the house apart again?"

"Goddamn, Rosie, don't turn into a bitch on me. I know it's hard for you. I'm not sayin' it's not. Just give me some trust. *Trust* me."

"It's like eating and sleeping with a stranger." She turned into a child; I could see Erica in her.

"C'mon." I tried to pull her down on my lap.

"Yes, a stranger." She pried her wrist from my grip. "That's what it does to ya'. How much more can I trust? Why don't *you* trust *me?* Trust me and *talk,* for cryin' out loud. You're the one not trusting," she said. I just looked at her, not speaking. She calmed herself, took a breath. "What am I gonna tell my father this afternoon? He keeps on asking me if you've talked to me." Her face was grim.

"Lie to him," I said, realizing it was a foolish suggestion that wouldn't work. It totally finished her. She started walking away. "What time we eating?" I asked.

"Two o'clock." She drew back, haggard in defeat, and disappeared into the kitchen.

I pulled myself out of my chair and went to the garage. There was half a tank of gasoline in the power mower. I dragged it out and started on the lawn like Rosie wanted, though I had heard it was unwise to cut a lawn after September, because it halts reseeding.

The lawn did look much better when I was through, though. I left the cuttings unraked, hoping seeds would fall from them and germinate. Rosie watched me from the kitchen window as I dragged the mower back to the garage. I entered the house through the kitchen door. There was an iced tea with lemon waiting for me on the countertop. I thanked her, but she didn't look up. She set the timer and began to wash out a colander without a word. I drank the iced tea at the window. Smells from the kitchen were mingling with the odor of the cut grass. The helicopter was returning.

When I carved the capon breast at the table, I could tell it was overdone. "Looks delicious," I kept saying. "Goodness, look at this meat."

For once I welcomed my daughters' chatter and giggling. We were all quite civil to each other with our grunts of thank-you for the gravy and compliments on the brussels sprouts and the stuffing. The Chief corrected the girls' table manners and directed all his talk away from me.

"Helicopters looking for a hunter. His shell turned over at Barcelona Point," he informed Rosie.

"What was he hunting?" I asked.

He closed his eyes and continued looking at his daughter. "Fella was hunting ducks."

"I was wondering about that helicopter." Rosie jumped in with great interest.

"Heart attack, they said."

"Oh, really?"

"Found him in the water," the Chief said warmly to his daughter.

"A shame," Rosie said, chewing.

We all chewed and made a few more grunts. Rosie heaped the Chief's dish with lots of crisp skin and second helpings and urged everyone else to take more. At the table, it was hard to put a finger on the trouble between Rosie and me; she did nothing to indicate it. But she was still in a long, cool anger, the same anger that she had been nurturing since I wrecked our living room a fortnight before. The Chief's presence didn't help.

Over pumpkin pie the Chief mumbled, "Someone better rake that hay on the lawn before it rots. Makes yellow spots."

"I want it to reseed," I said. Rosie told Karen to wipe her mouth.

"Lawn reseeded months ago," the Chief muttered to his dish.

After coffee the Chief left the table and floated behind Rosie like a paralyzed man in flight. He had his second cup of coffee in the kitchen with Rosie, then said he would have to go. After he left, I pulled my jacket out of the closet. "I'll be at the ocean a couple of hours," I called out.

"You were gonna make cocoa," Karen whined. Erica never seemed to care if I came or went, but it always meant something to Karen. I found myself too often disappointing her. But as I backed the truck into Garden Street, it was Erica who was watching from the window.

I drove to Sagaponack ocean beach. The sun was low at four o'clock. A woman walked barefoot with a golden retriever in the surf.

The ocean couldn't hold my interest. I thought of Willie Warren. I whipped the truck into reverse and headed toward Montauk Highway, coming out at Warren's Nursery. There they were unloading a shipment of Christmas trees, all the Warrens in tee shirts. I parked and got out to check the prices of some of the balled trees that lined the highway. Willie was on the job. He waved when he saw me.

"Hi doin', Jimmy?"

"Hi doin', Willie."

He walked over. "Thinkin' on puttin' up a live one this year?"

"Too early to be thinkin' of Christmas trees, ain't it?"

"Got a cool dark place?" he asked.

"High prices is the problem, Willie," I teased.

"Tol' my father that. Don't tell me." He laughed. "With this weather, tol' the ol' man we should be sellin' banana trees."

"What's really happening?" If anyone knew, Willie did.

"Things changin' up there, I guess." He glanced at the sky. I detected the slightest fear in his speech. "All's I can say is, it never used to be like this. I 'member as a kid we used to hitch the horse and sleigh before Thanksgiving, delivering milk by sleigh November till March. 'Course the roads was dirt out here then. You don't remember that. Otter Pond in Sag Harbor was frozen two feet thick the whole winter. You'd skate with your girlfriend

269

and the band'd play on the ice every Saturday night. It's an awful changed world."

"Gotta go, Willie."

"See ya."

I left Willie and the Christmas trees with a wave and drove westward aimlessly, then took the north road that skirts Seven Ponds and comes out at Scuttlehole. The ponds were fields of perfect blue set in the rich green of winter wheat which had grown almost as high as corn with no frost to hold it back. I could smell spring, though I knew it couldn't be spring on Thanksgiving Day. The maple trees in the woods hadn't given up a single leaf to autumn yet. Their yellowing suggested sweetness, like the first shock of forsythia.

I turned into Millstone Road toward Jessup Neck. I had often avoided this road, maybe because I knew it came out near the Texaco station on North Sea Road, not far from where the accident took place. It also is close to the narrow road that leads to the cracked asphalt. It was time to see the old house. I was ready, not calm, but willing to get it over with.

I drove twenty miles an hour, letting the truck take me as though it were a wagon, rolling, on automatic cruise. I watched the unfolding woodlands, the tall maples and willows, still holding every leaf in the rosy light. I stopped at the stop sign. The old Texaco sign was still there and near it the red phone booth, the phone Tato and I used when service was off at the big house. I crossed Noyack Road and rolled down the narrow road toward the bay, so slowly I hardly had to brake when the truck rolled onto the cracked asphalt.

There, on the right, was the old white house, just as gray as it had been before Tato and I painted it eleven years ago. From where I stood, nothing seemed to have changed. Bays are timeless. Seasons cannot change the configuration of sky and water. It was 4:45 and Thanksgiving Day. The light seemed the same as 8:45 in June, eleven years ago.

I walked to the house along the beach, then up to it from the shoreline. No birds anywhere, not even gulls. Sand had drifted up to the windowsills. The chimney on the west side was standing about three inches away from the house. So many shingles were torn from the front that the dark undersides of the house showed through. Six two-by-fours had been crudely nailed across the front door.

I strolled toward the fern grove, feeling quite old for the first time in my life, thinking of May, wondering at the improbability of a girl pulling off her sweater and dress in one motion in order to make love with two cousins. I stood on the spot where it all happened. The place seemed so tired now. I looked around for egrets, but saw none. There was much more light than I remembered. Unlike the maples, the oaks had dropped their leaves. Vines still twisted up the bare trees. The long perverse Indian summer had kept them leafy and yellow. I felt like a trespasser walking in a cemetery with no one to pay respects to. It wasn't until I turned to leave that I realized the blue jays hadn't abandoned the place. They screeched from afar as I walked back to the cracked asphalt.

I drove home in a quiet daze, the pickup tracing an imaginary line between the big house on Jessup and the low ranch house on Garden Street in Bridgehampton. It was like completing a circle as wide as the earth itself. I drove through the Noyack woods toward the Bridgehampton potato farms and the ocean. My truck came out onto the farm roads, high above sea level. I could see the ocean, flat and twinkling, a couple of miles ahead, and church steeples from Water Mill to Sagaponack—all golden in the late sun. Our house was buried in trees somewhere between the Presbyterian steeple and the Methodist steeple. Rosie and the girls would be there, tiny dots in the distance. Rosie'd be cleaning up, tired.

I was glad Thanksgiving was over. I had forced every morsel down. I didn't care so much about the Chief's disrespect; I had grown used to that and his tenseness with me. But Rosie's disrespect worried me. Oddly, there was something hopeful in the Chief's behavior that afternoon that suggested he might never tell his daughter everything he knew about me. If that were true, should I consider not telling Rosie the whole truth of why I was arrested?

It was a precarious situation. If I didn't tell Rosie, the Chief could always hold the information over my head. But suppose, in spite of it all, Rosie found out some other way?

Why was I fooling myself? If Maggie at the Bridgehampton *Seagull* had made a headline out of a sixteen-year-old baby-sitter who stole a damn ring from a dresser jewelry box, then what would she make of me?

About eight o'clock that night I was surprised by a knock on the tool-room door. I jumped up and opened the latch. Erica's little face peeked in. Her blue eyes were startled. I made the effort to smile, but it didn't change her expression.

"Come in, honey," I said.

Her eyes took in the walls as she spoke. "Grandpa's on the phone, Mommie said." She swiftly turned and left. I followed behind her up the wobbly stairs.

"Hello, Chief," I said into the phone. Rosie got up from her chair and started walking into the kitchen. She motioned the girls to follow her. Karen resented the interruption. She had been working on her stamp album.

"Jim, I wanna talk to you." The Chief's voice was almost friendly.

"All right, Chief."

"I don't trust phones. No big deal. Thought we'd do some fishin' tomorrow, if you know what I mean. No big deal. You got the boat?"

"Yeah."

"Thought we'd do some weak fishin'. I only got a couple hours."

"Sure. What time?"

"Say the morning? Say nine?"

"Sure." I hung up and went back down to the cellar to close up the tool room and turn out the cellar light. When I came back up, the girls were going up to bed.

I took a bath Thanksgiving night while Rosie watched TV. By the time Rosie came up, I was in bed. I watched her undress in the dark. When she got into bed, I rolled toward her.

"Hi," I whispered. I waited for her to ask what her father had called about. She didn't; she just lay there, her arms out of the covers like a mummy. I spoke up in the dark. "What does your father want?"

"Huh? You talked to him, not me."

"He says he wants to talk to me tomorrow, out in the boat, and go fishing at the same time."

"I have no idea what he wants, Jim." She turned her back to me and snuggled her pillow to her stomach. I listened for her breathing to take on the long, relaxed rhythm of sleep, but it never did.

"Let's get out there," the Chief said, walking ahead of me along the ramp toward *The Escape*. I wondered if he might not have heard my good morning. I tried to catch his eyes as we made the boat ready, but he seemed totally unconscious of me, though he accepted my hand as he got into the boat, then quickly let go.

He stood exactly where his daughter liked to stand the few times she rode with me—to the left of me, slightly behind. Inside the boat it was more difficult for him to keep his eyes away from me. He stood with a hand on his hip and one foot on the cabin step, a caricature of Washington crossing the Delaware. Over his uniform he wore his hunting mackinaw, red and black plaid with matching cap. The horizon at nine A.M. was brighter than the sky overhead. It was going to be a cloudy day.

We took to open water. He stared steadily ahead, his upper lip resting a little over his eyetooth in a grimace of self-consciousness. His gun bulged from his hip, swelling the mackinaw on his right side. I turned to indicate my willingness to exchange words, but he wouldn't pick me up with his eyes.

He was getting older. In the cruel daylight, his skin was colorless and deeply grooved. His lower eyelids sagged with that doleful look of age, but his posture indicated an iron spine, strong as ever. The farther from shore, the more imposing his figure loomed in the corner of my eye. I felt I was steering deeper and deeper into his trap. This was his game.

I had to remind myself that it was my boat. I had the controls,

273

yet I couldn't shake the feeling that I was chauffeuring him, so I turned the wheel left, away from the course he was setting with his eyes. The boat angled and pointed toward the Cedar Point lighthouse. I was going to choose the site of the conversation.

Some sense of territoriality impelled me to steer toward the Shelter Island Inlet and Jessup, near the beach where Tato said goodbye to me as the mosquitoes ate our legs when we were children, the same beach where Zia took me fishing as a little boy that night of the giant moon. How easily we might have caught that fish that evening, Zia and I. Weaks, Long Island's sea trout, pass by the thousands along that beach at sundown during july and August.

But a good fisherman wouldn't say, "Let's go weak fishing," there in late November. The Chief didn't know the difference. His garage floor was stained with blood from butchering deer he shot year after year. He was a hunter, not a fisherman.

We rounded the rock under the cliff where the peninsula ended. I put her into low, then anchored about fifty yards off the beach. The house appeared. I felt sacrilegious glancing up at it from the water. The Chief followed my glance suspiciously toward shore.

"Isn't this too close?" he asked.

"Weaks feed close."

"I'm not out here to fish." He threw away all pretensions of civility now.

"Well, I am. I have poles. There's squid in the bait box," I said lightly.

He stepped forward and grabbed my jacket collar. "You trash. You know I'm not here to fish. Now I'm an old man. I'll kill you." His anger was out before he could shape it.

"Leggo, please, Chief." I pulled his hand down from my jacket.

His face flushed; his teeth chattered. He raised his other hand as though to rap me, but his hand held itself off.

"Why the fuck haven't you told my daughter what you are?"

"Now gimme a chance here, Chief."

" 'Cause you know goddamn well that girl'd leave you flat in a second. Don'cha, you slime?" Tears were coming into his eyes.

274

"My grandfather was born on Shelter Island, a minister. His father was a whaler. My mother was first teacher of the Middle School. Rosie was born here and you, you son of a bitch, fall outta the sky and shame me and mine."

"I intend to tell Rosie everything in due time." I wanted to stop his train of thought.

"You ain't got no time. Your daughters can't have a decent life here anymore."

"Why is that?"

"Because you"—his voice cracked—"you're gonna be spread all over that goddamn newspaper for all the world."

"Now, maybe not, Chief." I was stalling.

"Maggie's gonna *print* it."

"Not necessarily."

"I talked to her yesterday, goddamn you." His head bobbed, indicating the tremendous pounding of his heart inside his chest. "She's gonna fuckin' print it, sure as I'm standin' in front of you. I'm so ashamed." His emotions reached a bottleneck. He was going to cry. He turned away, looking across the bay and pulling out his handkerchief. He blew his nose and took a few deep breaths. "Christ." A heron landed in the moment of silence. It pecked the water and swallowed a minnow. "I want you to leave my daughter," he said with finality. "I want you to go away, *permanently,* Jim."

He brought his handkerchief to his face, but he went on: "You leave my Rosie. Why should she be the one to leave? It's your shame, not hers." I watched the heron fly off. The Chief's breathing was normalizing. He took off his hat and wiped his sweat. "This is Rosie's home, not yours, anyway. God knows where you originate."

I decided not to say a word. I sat there looking up at Zia's large gray house while he fumbled and sniffled and returned his handkerchief to his back pocket.

"Oh, God." He sighed through a stuffed nose.

"Haven't you told Rosie anything yet?" I was testing him.

"I ain't got the nerve to tell her. Poor girl, she wouldn't know what hit her. She's got the sense to suspect it's awful enough, but she's scared to hear just what it is. She avoids me tellin' her. Scared of me, my own daughter." He avoided my eyes guiltily.

I myself dreaded telling Rosie. I couldn't imagine how she would handle it. I wouldn't know how to start to tell her. I didn't want her out of my life. I couldn't stand the shift. I was already in an earthquake. An avalanche would finish me. If Rosie left that would be an avalanche.

"Why are we out here, Chief?" I asked, interrupting the silence.

"I'm warning you to leave Rosie is what we're here for. If you can't do the decent thing, then get the fuck outta her life."

"What's the decent thing?"

"Goddamn, you figure that out. I'd shoot my brains out if I were you. Either that or tell her what you did. Tell her what you *are* so she can leave you. And she'll leave you. I'm sure of that."

"Do you really think you know what's right for Rosie?"

"You son of a bitch. Don't tell me I don't know my own flesh and blood."

"I didn't say—"

"Prick," he screamed and grabbed me with both hands. "I know what's good for my wife." He unconsciously called Rosie his wife.

"Your *wife?*"

"My daughter, goddamnit."

"Don't touch me again, Chief." I pushed him away gently.

He recognized my seriousness and he backed off, though he still screamed: "Are we supposed to give you a medal for what you did? A Father's Day award? I'll shoot my grandchildren before I see you do any more good to them. I warned you, I'm an old man. I'll walk right into the fire to save my kind, right into the goddamn fuckin' fire. I warn you." He looked away. The water lapped *The Escape*'s bottom. Crows cawed out of sight behind the cliffs. The wind had quieted. "I thought maybe . . ." He hesitated. His voice changed. He swallowed. He was tired now.

"Maybe what?" I asked hopefully.

His voice was throaty now and more open. "Thought maybe Maggie would consider. I talked to her. Goddamn, she owes me a million favors. She'll only compromise. Her compromise ain't worth shit anyway."

"What's her compromise?"

"She's gonna postpone the story a month, give you time to do the right thing."

"A month? That means it'll come out around Christmas."

"Nice present for your kids."

"What if I take Rosie and the kids away?"

He bit his lip and shook his head. "Who gave you the goddamn right to bust up my family?" He slapped his thigh. "Christ in heaven! You do the decent thing: Leave this town and never come back, or I swear by Christ I'll take those two kids and Rosie outta here. They'll be gone. Some night you'd come home and they'd be gone. I swear on Christ almighty."

"Do you think Rosie would let you do that?"

"I'd rather see you use a shotgun on my daughter than to bring such shame on her. Rosie don't have to agree with me. But you can bank on my doin' you justice. You wipe up your shit and leave us, Jim, before we have to do something about you ourselves." He spat defiantly into the water, then snapped his arm back to his back pocket, pulled out a black swollen wallet, fingered through business cards and pulled one out. "This is the lawyer they say is able to keep you outta jail; you're gonna hafta go before a judge in public."

I accepted the card. *Leonard Hirsch, Attorney, Southampton.* "Suppose this guy gets me off."

He choked a sarcastic laugh. "So what if he does? That's not gonna stop Maggie. What you were arrested for is her juicy meat. That's what the vultures want to read. Six months later she'll run a line on page six that says you got off. The paper don't really care if you're guilty or innocent, and I don't care either. I don't want to hear no appeals."

"I don't have to appeal to you," I snapped. He gave me a mean look. I looked down at the card with a feeling of disgust. "What am I gonna do?"

"Well, what *are* you gonna do?" the Chief asked with the slightest satisfaction.

"About what?" I asked.

"Leaving." He closed his eyes, then looked at me with defiance. "I want you permanently gone when that paper comes out. I want the world to know we burned you out before they read about you."

"What would happen, Chief, if I said I intend to stay? Would you shoot me? Shoot me now. You know how to bring the boat back. Or maybe you can just go back and work on Rosie now. You know, put the pressure on her. You could scare the shit out of her. You know the buttons to punch. You know where they are, the cracks in her strength. Go spill the beans to Rosie."

He ducked under my words. "When are you leaving?" he pressed, ignoring everything I had said. I snapped the little card against my thumb and looked toward shore. I tried to envision the little boy I once was, swimming there in water wings, skinny as a bird. I had walked that beach with Tato, picking shells for Zia. I was through leaving places. I didn't want to leave Rosie, Karen and Erica, my marina, the dunes and the ocean, and the fish. I was home. I didn't want to leave, not after all the years it took me to find everything I called home.

I hit the starter, then looked into the Chief's eyes. I revved the engine in neutral and threw the gearshift abruptly into low. The boat jolted forward. He grabbed the rail for support.

"I ain't goin' no place," I shouted as I threw her into high.

He spun around, almost slipping to the deck. "What the fuck you tryin' to do?"

"Rosie and my kids ain't goin' no place either," I yelled. "You hear that, Chief?" Tears were coming into my eyes this time. I felt no younger than he now. I didn't bother checking his reaction. I didn't care. I looked to the horizon and took my boat on its run, north in a large half circle around the rocks. I ignored him completely as we passed under the cliffs of Jessup Neck going toward home.

CHAPTER X

T HE arrest. It was so easy for it never to have happened. It never would have happened if East Hampton Ford had given me a better price on a Custom Ford 250 than Ray Zaykowski in River-head. Goddamn that day.

It was a Tuesday. There were only a few days of summer left. Labor Day had come and gone. It had been a record summer for fishing. Within the week of the full moon, rod and reel fishermen set a record of 87,000 pounds of fish caught under the lighthouse at Montauk. The marine biology lab estimated that several hundred million fish—blues, stripers and weaks—were much more plentiful than normal and meteorologists were predicting the long Indian summer. *The Escape* was booked for charters into the second week of November. I had made my last payment on her, so I traded in my old truck for a brand-new four-wheel-drive Ford 250 pickup.

I went for the new truck in Riverhead a couple of weeks after Labor Day. I drove it home along Route 27. The paint job was totally black, shiny as a hot stallion in moonlight. Had everything on it—marker lights, extra floodlights, C.B., AM-FM radio and a forty-channel sideband that could reach down to Florida. Even had a shotgun cradle installed over the rear window.

I was headed toward the Shinnecock Canal on the wide Montauk Highway, breaking it in at a leisurely fifty miles an hour. The heavy-duty suspension boosted me so high in my seat I thought I was flying. The day was perfectly clear, the sky shuddering where it met the horizon. I had my truck on automatic, sailing it like a boat. All the windows were open and I stretched out my right arm. I smiled involuntarily as the road lifted me high into the cobalt skies of the Shinnecock Hills, pointing me straight at the twinkling Atlantic.

In the rearview and side mirrors I could see nothing. Ahead was nothing. The highway was open wide as a beach. Behind me was New York City, about a hundred miles west.

In the left lane an old pickup showed up. It surprised me. Its body was painted with one of those latex flat paints—a chalky blue, no shine whatever. The color clashed mysteriously with the sky. An older fellow than I expected to see was driving her, a fellow about forty. He seemed almost to be trying to get my attention, riding alongside me like that. His curly black hair was flying up in the wind, and his white teeth showed in a friendly smile. I gave him a nod. Did I know this man? I didn't think so. Why then did he go on smiling, paralleling me, doing a perfect fifty alongside me?

His white cotton shirt was filling with wind. The sleeves, rolled up, revealed hairy dark arms. I liked the stranger. As we rolled along, his audacious, smiling face started some unexpected feelings in me. I felt the lack of a friend, another man my age, someone like the black-haired stranger who let all of the wind into his cab and who rode high on extra-heavy-duty suspension, high above the road with the recklessness of youth.

He inched out ahead of me. I was a little embarrassed to move up to him, but I did. We were both doing fifty-five now. His smile broadened. I smiled back. I accelerated to sixty; he accelerated too. No cops visible; the road was ours. We brought the trucks up to seventy-five. The wind thundered into our cabs, our hair whipped about our faces. We couldn't hear each other's laughter, but we both laughed as those strange purple flowers blooming on the roadside flattened in our wake.

We reached eighty on the empty road, as if the sharp sunlight was pulling us toward the ocean. Recklessly, I wondered if the black-haired fellow could become a friend, someone to spend time with, taking old trucks alongside the ocean under the cliffs of Montauk and carrying fishing poles to the rocks under the lighthouse to fish the next full moon, and drink coffee out of Thermoses. Images came on waves of excitement, and I allowed them, because soon enough my truck would be parked silently in my driveway. Soon enough my friend would disappear.

He was pointing for me to look at something to my right, but there was nothing to see really. When I looked back, the blue truck was in front of me, flashing its right blinker. By the time I realized that he was inviting me to follow, it was too late. We were on different roads. He shot far to the right of me, going up into the Rest Area, and I was still below on the highway, the woods separating us.

It would take me at least twenty minutes to get off at the next exit, to backtrack westward and revisit the road where I first caught sight of him. By the time I could have reached the Rest Area road, the blue truck most likely would be gone. But I decided it was worth the gamble. I switched on my right blinker and went off at the next exit.

I pulled into the Rest Area some fifteen minutes later. A number of cars were hidden there behind a long row of oaks: a small Toyota pickup, a Coca-Cola truck, an electrician's van, a jeep and several others up ahead. There was plenty of parking room beyond the line of cars, but it was ignored, as if the cars preferred to huddle close, hidden from the road. I passed them slowly. What was he going to think of me, going to all that trouble to find him? I decided I would leave the first move up to him, but by the time I got to the end of the line of cars, it didn't matter; the blue pickup was not there.

But something strange was going on there. No drivers were in sight, neither in their cars or near them, though some engines were still running. With nothing but highway on three sides—ahead, behind and to the left—the only place they could have gone to was into the woods. I looked intently into my rearview mirrors to see if some drivers were lying down. From what I could tell, all the cars were empty. Their drivers had to be in the woods. But why *were* they in the woods? Were they all taking a piss at once?

I cut off my own engine and quietly opened the door of the cab. I stepped out. I leaned against my truck fender, noticing there were several well-worn paths leading from the pavement into the woods, disappearing into a ravine. I walked to the edge of one path and looked down into the ravine, onto scrub oaks, pines and wispy lindens. Next to me was a marker for tourists indicating Indian hunting grounds. I walked a few yards into the woodland, downward, hearing footsteps but seeing no one. I turned in all directions to be sure no one was near. The ground was dry. A rabbit or a raccoon was rustling about somewhere, but nothing appeared, so I continued slowly down the steep path. Oak and pine droppings, year after year, had created a highly acid soil. Wildflowers grew in patches wherever they had sunlight. As I went deeper, beer cans appeared and, of all things, men's underwear that had been rained on so many times it had almost become the ground itself. A sanitary napkin and patches of human excrement lay among wild mushrooms. It was like the reverse side of a tapestry, gnarled and stringy, vaguely suggesting the scene on the other side.

Suddenly, although walking slowly, I almost collided with two men. When they saw me, they spun away, making it impossible to catch their faces. One was bald. The other was a black man. Both wore digital watches. I continued past them feeling a bit embarrassed, trying to pretend I hadn't noticed their surprise, hands stuffing a shirttail into a belt, a quick comb to the hair, a handkerchief nervously pulled from a back pocket, the fragrance of flesh, a nose blowing, odors of sweat, clearing of throats, odors of sex.

I moved quickly on. The path hairpinned sharply upward again, deeper into the woods. My heart was racing as I climbed out of their sight.

The path dwindled to no path at all and soon I found myself standing on the lip of a large bowl of ferns about the size of a football field, looking down upon young oaks and the umbrella tops of dogwood. To my right, half buried in fern, was a thick fallen tree trunk, at least four feet in girth, gray and smooth from sun and time. In that part of the woods the air was cooler. Stepping into the fern bowl was like stepping into a lake of cool air. Something moved, halting me.

I focused to the opposite rim, about forty yards away. Two men were there, one of them half nude. They hadn't noticed me standing in the open woods, freckled by the dappling sunlight. My slightest movement would have brought their eyes to me, so I froze, camouflaged in the dancing shadows, watching.

The taller man must have been a mechanic. A monkey suit was unzipped and peeled down to his boots. His body was thick and well built. His skin was white, except for his face and neck, which were darkly tanned. His hands were black with grease and dirt. His buttocks were speckled with pimples. When he turned, I could make out that his eyes were quite blue and wild with nervousness; they scanned the woods and incredibly did not catch me standing there. He was totally bald on top, though handsome. Blond curls grew somewhat comically over his ears.

The other fellow was shorter, his body smaller, though not slight. His face was sharp, his chin small. Clean, shiny brown hair kept its part, though it kept falling like fringes over his eyes. He wore khaki cotton trousers and a black western shirt which was open, baring his chest. Unlike the mechanic, he was calm. He wore a smile that reflected irony and embarrassment.

As the bald man put his hands on the younger man's shoulders, trying to push him downward, the younger man resisted till his knees buckled willingly, and he yielded to the pressure. His face was opposite the bald fellow's genitals. The younger man self-consciously held his head at a distance but curiously cupped the

283

testicles before him in one hand and tenderly ran the other hand up to a nipple, which he pinched gently. The bald man was too impatient for this tenderness. He took his partner's head into his blackened hands like a basketball, urging the face closer until the fellow accepted the fully grown penis into his mouth. The mechanic threw back his head with satisfaction. He looked up at the sky. His buttocks softened and tightened as he began a slow, almost graceful grinding of his midsection, literally fucking the fellow in the mouth, like a nude man riding a horse in slow motion.

I could hear their murmurs. The mechanic was hunched over, enfolding his partner's head. Suddenly he straightened up, as if to forestall orgasm. He lifted his younger partner up from his knees, his joint so totally engorged and shining with saliva that it seemed not a real part of his anatomy. His clumsy grease-blackened fingers tore at the younger man's belt buckle. It was a western belt with a trick latch. He couldn't solve the puzzle of opening it.

The younger fellow didn't offer to help. He stood there while the bald man tugged impatiently, then angrily. His penis was beginning to droop. Then the younger fellow, with the simplest ease, un-latched his buckle, letting it fall to the side. The bald man tore open the top button, fumbled for the zipper, then yanked it down. After he turned the fellow completely around, in one sweep, he tore down his undershorts and trousers and pushed the fellow's shirt up to his shoulders, revealing a well-tanned body except where a bath-ing suit had been. The bald man pushed on the fellow's head, downward, urging him to bend over. He spit nervously into his own hand and moistened his joint, which once again grew hard. He positioned it between the white buttocks, then with both hands grabbed the fellow by the shoulders. The mechanic's legs rippled as he pushed in carefully. The younger fellow grimaced and beckoned for the mechanic to hold up, which he did—for a mo-ment. Then with grim determination the mechanic thrust himself up entirely until the young man cried out and grabbed a tree for support, though he didn't stop the bald man. In spite of the pain which showed on his face, he willingly provided his body. The mechanic began the same slow grinding as before, as if he were riding a horse. But the trot evolved into a gallop. The bald man's movements became more rapid. He thrashed wildly until a cry came up from him so sharply it flushed the birds nearby.

They dressed themselves with remarkable speed and parted, going in different directions. I remained there frozen. As soon as they disappeared completely, I skirted the bowl until I found a path that seemed to go toward the Indian marker. I ran up the path and soon recognized the marker. An injured catbird flushed out of my way, dragging its wing under a laurel. When I came out to the asphalt, two cars were going off. The driver of the Coca-Cola truck was staring at me. He nodded in a friendly manner. I looked down and passed him on my way to the pickup without a smile.

Perfumed steam from Rosie's scented bubble bath had collected on the blue tile of our bathroom. That's how I knew we were going to have sex. It happened always on nights when Rosie treated herself that way. I noticed she had vacuumed and tidied the bedroom and put on her blue flowered nightgown. She sat up in bed with wet hair, surrounded by magazines and papers and scrubbed to the toenails. She reached for the Bridgehampton *Seagull.*

"My God."

"What?"

"Right here on the front page, Angie Bennet had a ring stolen by a baby-sitter."

"Jesus."

"Who are the Banisters?"

"He's a plumber, I think."

"Must be his daughter who did it." Rosie read from the *Seagull:* " 'Mrs. Bennet reported the ring missing from a jewelry box on the dresser in the master bedroom. Sixteen-year-old Susan Banister was baby-sitting for the Bennet children, Mark and Andrew of the Middle School, last Saturday . . . God!" She flipped pages as the bedroom curtains swelled. I could smell the pond. A mallard quacked. I wiped the fog from the mirror to shave.

Rosie laughed. "They're sayin' we're gonna have palm trees growin' out here."

"That'll be somethin'. Watch and see, we'll have the coldest autumn in ten years."

She read: "Edward Johnston 'Oceanographer at Montauk's Oceanographic Laboratory predicts record warmth as Gulf Stream inches toward New England.' Do you believe it?"

"Not if it's in the *Seagull*."

"Because a woman writes it?"

"Too gossipy."

"Maggie's no more gossipy than you fishermen. I hear the gab at the Country Kitchen. Those men are worse than old women. Who buys the *Seagull* anyway? Mostly you men."

"For the tide tables."

"Baloney! I give Maggie credit. Who wants to wash dishes? God." Then Rosie asked, "Are those the mergansers quacking?"

I had bought a pair of mergansers with clipped wings for the pond, and it outraged the mallards. "It's the mallards," I answered, jumping into bed. I reached to turn out the light.

"I'm *reading*," Rosie objected. She threw down the *Seagull* and opened *Better Homes and Gardens*.

This was before the arrest and Rosie was happier those days than I'd ever known her. She was acting younger than ever, taking risks and going after what she wanted. She even wanted to have sex with the light on a few times. I didn't mind it all that much. Each time it happened, though, she took all that reading material to bed, requiring the light of the bedside lamp, and when I reached to switch it out, she stopped my hand. But this was a warm night, and the ducks wouldn't quit their racket until the lights were out. So I did nothing but lie there, curled on my side in the breeze Rosie made by flipping the pages of *Better Homes and Gardens*. She stretched her leg affectionately, touching my knees under the sheet. "You tired?" she asked.

"Not tired. Just hate that light," I said. "Why can't you read in the dark?" I chuckled. She threw down the magazine, slid down and touched her forehead to mine. "Hi."

"Hi." I slid my face to her breasts and spoke into the blue flowered nightgown. "Can't we have the light off?" I asked.

She stretched her hand behind herself under the shade and twisted the lamp switch, flooding the room with moonlight. In the dark, I threw off the sheet and lifted the frail cotton nightgown to her neck. I rested my head on her belly, facing her feet. She breathed deeply and put her fingers into my hair. I loved the smell of her body after a bath. It was a totally artificial smell, totally unnatural, but so heavenly somehow. I guess it announced her willingness, her readiness for me, her desire. Embracing Rosie when she was so clean was like falling on a pure white cloud. I smelled the baby powder, following the scent with my nose down into her bush and farther, needing to take her by surprise, wanting to excite her suddenly with my tongue. She opened her legs and I hopped between them. She lifted her vagina to my lips and murmured as I reached up, finding her breasts, fingering her nipples, pinching them gently.

I closed my eyes—and unbelievably the mechanic's face flashed before me, his white skin. Rosie's body was his. I pulled my head up quickly.

"Come up," Rosie whispered in the dark. "Jim?" Her hands brought my head up to her breasts. Her legs lifted outwardly, generously. "Come in."

I entered Rosie, but my mind was elsewhere. Inside my head it was daylight, the afternoon in the woods. Rosie was matching my movements, but each thrust only brought my mind further away from her—the western belt thrown open, the younger man's shirt pushed up to his shoulders, his back revealed, his smooth buttocks. In the dark suddenly it was his body beneath me. I was in a slow trot, slow grinding . . . I stopped. I didn't want to move another inch that way, but Rosie's need pulled me into it more and more. I couldn't withdraw my mind from the place where it had put me. Rosie was gone. I was inside *him*. As I started my movements again, his murmurs were in my ear. I couldn't back out, so I pushed ahead, thrusting harder, faster until I heard my own voice rising, my cries flushing birds into the sun, my cries flying high into the dogwoods as I came, roaring.

Rosie jerked away from me and switched on the light. "You'll frighten the girls." Ducks quacked. Rosie jumped out of bed.

"Turn off the light?" I asked.

"You all right?" She switched us back into moonlight.

"I'm all right. I'm all right."

"I never heard you do that."

"I'm sorry."

"You sounded like you were in pain."

"No, it's okay." The ducks were quacking without letup. "Sorry, Rosie."

"What are you sorry for?"

"You okay? You come?"

"I did," she said.

"You satisfied?"

"I'm fine." She turned on the air conditioner.

"Why you doin' that?"

"You're sweating."

"Okay, fine, fine. Fall asleep. Let's fall asleep."

She was turning on the bathroom light, partially closing the door. I opened my eyes to the bedroom. After a minute Rosie flushed the john, switched off the bathroom light and came back into the moonlit room. She jumped into bed quickly, making herself comfortable. She curled away from me, took several deep breaths and drifted to sleep. I got up momentarily to flick off the air conditioner.

I lay on my back awake, listening to the wind starting up. Thunder sounded faintly. I was glad Rosie had fallen asleep easily. I wanted to stay awake listening to the wind. The moonlight was gone. I lay flat on our bed in the pitch blackness, listening, until the thunder became so distant I couldn't track it anymore. The mallards were asleep. The crickets started in. My ears inquired beyond the crickets, above them into the air over the pond. I heard the trees, fat with the fullness of summer, rustling lazily, like silk in the uncertain wind. And above them my ears picked up sounds of the highway a half mile away with its sputtering trucks and dragsters.

The blue pickup, sugary blue under fluorescent light, came to mind. Could it be out there, I wondered, still looking for me? With the black-haired man in the white shirt still inside? Who was he? Someone famous I didn't know enough to recognize? Had I met him before?

* * *

On my way home from work each night, I couldn't stop keeping my eye peeled for the blue truck. I wanted to catch him on *my* turf. I wanted him quietly, in some neutral place, to talk easily, to chat about weather and fish. It was becoming a mild obsession. I even imagined I would see the blue truck parked in my driveway some night. I imagined introducing him to Rosie, and I imagined Willie Warren on the dunes asking me who my new sidekick was. But by November, I gave up hope of seeing the blue truck.

One night on my way home, I noticed my pickup odometer read 003087. She was past due for the 3000-mile inspection. Next morning I put in a call to Ray Zaykowski at Riverhead Ford and he gave me my appointment.

I brought the marina accounts with me to Riverhead on the day of the inspection and I worked on them over coffee in the Howard Johnson's while Ray worked on the truck. The truck was ready about three, so it must have been three-thirty when I hit the main highway coming home. I was in no hurry. That night Rosie was taking Karen and Erica to the East Hampton movie and to a Chinese dinner. I thought maybe I'd catch a bite at Patchy's Diner—kielbasa, stuffed cabbage. He always piled it on for me and talked my head off. But I wasn't hungry yet, so I just drifted, doing a cool fifty along the highway. A gray blanket of clouds overhead was low enough to hit with a stone. The blanket went all the way to the ocean and on to Europe. The highway underneath was clear; the ocean a flat gray line up ahead.

REST AREA ¾ MI. AHEAD. The big blue sign with white letters popped up. I surprised myself by clicking on my right directional signal. Why not check it out? Zoom in, zoom out. The blinking directional signal on my control panel, regular and rhythmical, became my commitment to going in.

I pushed on the brake when the service road came up and rolled right into the Rest Area, separating myself from the highway with woods and the long line of oaks.

The place was empty, except for one car, an old Porsche, one of the first Porsches, a speedster over twenty years old. It looked abandoned. The finish had been stripped to the steel. Either that or the paint had oxidized to a flat gray. Its bumper hanging at a cockeyed angle, it was parked in the open, visible to the highway. I leaped out of my truck and ambled to the woods at the Indian marker. I looked down into the ravine. I wondered what the fern bowl would be like after two months, so I slowly went in, taking the same path I had taken before.

After several minutes of dodging laurel and scraping through the leaf-strewn paths, I was looking down into the fern bowl from exactly the same spot from which I had watched the mechanic and his buddy. There was far more light in the bowl now. The oaks had shed, but the fern carpet was still rich, seeming even greener in the cloud-filtered light. I heard the gurgling sounds of a muffler and an engine coming in. I could barely see the top half of a GTO. It had been turned into a hot rod with a boosted rear end. When its engine cut off, I instinctively made for the fallen tree trunk to hide. Yet another car was coming in, engine cut off. A car door slammed. Then another.

I could make out someone coming down the steep ravine toward the bowl. He didn't see me, didn't even look up. He wore a brown mackinaw, open, over a tee shirt, his hands in his pockets. Dark green cotton trousers and work boots. His hair was combed neatly. He was clean shaven, about forty, might have been in construction work. Some thirty yards behind him appeared the hot-rodder, a much younger fellow, slender and white-skinned. His black eyebrows seemed to have been painted on his shiny face, like those statues of saints. He was slightly cross-eyed. Black pupils jumped out of their whites, two black marbles trying to ignore each other.

I crouched down as the younger fellow headed in my direction through the fern. There must have been bramble beneath the fern. He was getting caught and he had to leap like a deer, up the incline toward me. He came out around to the side of the tree trunk where I was lying down. He unzipped his jeans and turned his head to scan the woods for the other fellow. The trickling sound of his urine hitting oak leaves dwindled into a quiet splash, then drops.

I could hear footsteps, the man in the mackinaw was coming through the underbrush behind me. I lay as motionless as I could as the green cotton trousers and the work boots passed me by once. He hadn't seen me. The younger fellow was not putting away his joint, which had become visibly turgid. They were only a yard apart.

"Hi," the older man said.

"Hi," the younger fellow whispered.

"I don't like to do things here," the older fellow said with a smile. "Wanna come to my place?"

The younger fellow shook his head.

"No? What do you mean?" the older man asked, "that you can't go?"

"Can't go," the young man agreed, looking around.

"Well, what you up for?" the fellow in the mackinaw whispered.

"I wanna get blowed."

The mackinaw man moved closer to him, bringing his hand up into the dark hair behind the other fellow's neck. Then he tilted his own head, and tried to make eye contact, but the young man held his head away to avoid it. The mackinaw man touched his cheek with his fingers, lightly, but the young man jerked his head away.

"I wanna get blowed," he repeated.

"I can't do that," the man in the mackinaw said.

"Lemme split then."

"I'm not a cocksucker," said the fellow in the mackinaw, with a grin.

"And I'm no pussy," the hot-rodder said, smiling.

Still, neither of them wanted to leave. The man in the mackinaw reached once again to touch the silky hair. The young fellow allowed it for a half minute, then pulled away, finally putting away his joint and zippering his trousers, but he remained standing there. The man in the mackinaw once again started the curious touching. This time the young man closed his eyes; a little color was coming into his face. He took deep breaths. The man in the mackinaw was touching his face tenderly, straightforwardly brushing the boy's hair back in a fatherly manner. The boy's face was transformed, his hand went up behind the mackinaw, awkwardly, around the man's back, bringing him closer. Their heads came together, their foreheads touching. They stayed that way awhile in the awkward embrace. The man in the mackinaw had his back to me; the young man's face came into view over the other man's shoulder, eyes closed, soft grunts of relief, deep breaths. Suddenly the black eyes opened wide.

"Who's that?" he said, pulling away from the other fellow.

"Who?"

"Watchin' us."

"Huh?" The fellow in the mackinaw turned, looking in every direction. By the time he turned back, the hot-rodder was sprinting away through the laurel, up the path toward the marker and out of sight. The man in the mackinaw chased, but the GTO was on its way before its pursuer got out of the woods. I listened for the muffler sounds to melt away. Once again there was the calm twittering of birds, and finally I heard the engine of the other car starting up. I stood, brushing leaves from my clothes.

An instant later the man from the blue pickup truck appeared only a few yards away from me in the fern bowl. He had had a haircut. His black hair was shorter, curlier. He wore a gabardine jacket with a zipper. He came toward me.

Suddenly I realized the Porsche was his. He had been there before any of us. The car was parked there empty simply because he was in the woods. I was too embarrassed to continue facing him. I turned and started to walk away, even though I wasn't sure I wanted to.

"You lookin' for a blow job?" the soft voice called behind me.

I stopped in my tracks, not turning around. We were entirely alone in the woods. *Yes, I* dared to think. My mouth felt dry; my heartbeat picked up. I thought of him kneeling, his head in my hands, the thick black curls. I turned, facing him, and as I did, I could understand why the fellow from the GTO couldn't look the older man in the eye. I had to cast my eyes up over his head, trembling. I felt a burning in my chest as he came closer, then a free cool sensation, as if armor were lifting from my arms. My whole body felt so vulnerable and tender. I might be willing, but I wanted it over with fast. I could feel his breath on my face as I unzipped my trousers. He looked down smiling. I felt foolish, wished he would do something right away, but he only stood there smiling.

292

"Would *you* blow *me?*" he asked.

"I don't think I could," I answered. I noticed a swelling in his trousers. This whole thing was a mistake. I had to reverse things.

"Too macho to go down?" he asked. I didn't understand him, his stalling; I didn't understand his smile. Either he had to act fast or I was going to leave, because I sensed a strange inequality growing between us as we stood there facing each other: I was becoming the fool. True, he had risked with words, but his words had long disappeared. I was the one standing there with my zipper opened. That's when I realized he was waiting for a sign from me, of compliance. There was something I was to do to make his action less ignoble. There would be something insulting about my total passivity. I had seen that between the hot-rodder and the man in the mackinaw. I was to *do* something too, give a sign, so I nervously lifted my hand and put it on his shoulder; the other I brought close to the swelling in his trousers, closer, until the mysterious swelling touched my hand. There was no kindness in his face at that moment, nothing to trust in his smile. The healthy whiteness of his eyes, the handsome grin, didn't help my distrust. Quickly, I zipped up.

"What's your name?" he whispered.

I could smell cigarettes on his breath. "Jim," I answered, about to turn away.

"Jim?"

"Yes."

"Jim"—he pulled a badge from his back pocket and held it before my face—"Jim, you're under arrest." He pulled out handcuffs.

Another man bounced up from behind some laurel about fifty yards away and came toward us. It was the fellow in the mackinaw. "I saw the contact," he called out.

"Did you nab that kid?"

"He got away."

"You get the plate number?"

"No. Forgot my glasses." The man in the mackinaw smiled and shrugged.

They were both plainclothesmen. They handcuffed my hands behind me and led me up toward the parking area. I was stunned, smiling as if it were a game, a joke. But when I saw the blue truck parked behind the Porsche, I realized both cars were police decoys and they were plainclothesmen.

"You missed a dynamite duo. Christ, they were screamin' their lungs out. Big Polack was fuckin' a New Yorker, and there I was with no help."

"I was in the truck on the west side waiting for you," the fellow in the brown mackinaw answered.

"I told you east, you dummy."

"This one's wearin' a wedding band," the fellow in the mackinaw said.

"So what d'ya want from me?" my captor replied. "Get him in the truck." The mackinaw fellow pulled me while the other one went to check that my pickup was locked. When he came back, he started the engine and we drove out of the Rest Area, crossing over the grass island into westbound traffic.

"Why are you doing this?" I asked. Tears came.

He looked at me. "You did it to yourself, danger freak."

"He's married," the other one repeated.

"Let Boylan worry about it." He turned on a police siren.

I sat between the two with my hands cuffed behind me. It was too much to believe that the dilapidated blue truck even had a police siren. The absurd siren destroyed any chance of conversation. I kept staring at the dark-haired man, still mesmerized by his face, hoping he'd talk, but he refused to acknowledge me. Ironically, he seemed depressed, biting his fingernails and steering with one hand.

The station house was a tomblike art deco building shining under blue fluorescent floodlights in a meadow. Their icy glow cut into the pink sky where the sun was setting. Chief Boylan met us at the front desk with a clipboard and a cup of coffee in his hand. "Another wood nymph?" he asked, looking into my eyes. His skin was yellow, like a dying person's; his pupils shone like black olives dipped in glycerine.

"This one's a tyro. We lost two whoppers and a hot-rodder, though, 'cause our buddy here forgot his glasses."

"What do we book him for?"

"Lewd behavior," my friend answered.

"That all?"

"He's wearin' a wedding band," the mackinaw man said.

"What do I give a fuck about his wedding band?" Boylan snapped. "We're not the Salvation Army here."

"It was only lewd behavior," the dark one repeated. "He didn't touch me." The policeman in the mackinaw turned away from his lie.

"Do you have twenty-five bucks on you?" Boylan asked me.

"Why?" My legs were trembling.

Boylan's eyes were monstrously intense, glassy; the whites were yellow. "To post your bail." Boylan's voice came out of a nut-cracker.

"No. I have fifteen, maybe sixteen."

"We'll call your wife to bring the rest."

"Easy, Boylan." The one who handcuffed me held Boylan's eyes threateningly, then turned to me. "You can call anybody you like and you'd better think of someone you can trust fast, 'cause he'll keep you in the cage till you pay up." As he spoke, he pulled me into a powder blue fluorescent-lit room, exactly the color of the pickup. He asked me to sit, then pulled out a form and started asking questions without looking at me. "Name?"

"Jim Smith."

"Good. You're not Italian. For a minute there"—he stopped writing and leaned back in his chair staring at me with a quizzical smile—"I thought you could be. *Tu me ricordi?*" he asked.

"No." I answered.

"Oh, so you know Italian?"

"I don't know Italian," I answered.

"I just asked if you remembered me, in Italian, and you answered me."

"I . . . I didn't know what I was saying."

"Holy Christ in heaven"—his smile became wider—"now I know who you remind me of. Your beard threw me off, and that space in your eyebrow. When did you grow that beard?"

"*Who* do I remind you of?"

"Were you cruisin' alongside of me about a month ago on the bypass? In that black truck?"

"Right."

"Right. And I said to myself that night, Who did that guy remind me of? Jesus, now I know. Jesus Christ almighty!" He flipped his pencil into the air and put his face in his hands.

"*Who* do I remind you of?"

He didn't answer. His hands fell with a thud from his face into his lap. "I cannot believe this."

"Who do I remind you of?" I repeated.

He swallowed. His eyes softened. "You." He tilted his chair back and viewed me again. "Are you . . . are you *Cello?*" he asked softly.

"My name's Jim Smith." My heart began to palpitate; I could feel blood coming to my face. An internal buzzing started in my head, so loud I jumped a little. "My name's Jim Smith," I repeated. I felt drained suddenly, bloodless, exhausted, my mind about to blank out.

"My name is Tato. You remember me? Tato. I'm your cousin Tato. I *shaved* my beard and became a cop." He laughed.

I was drowning in air. "Tato? My name is Jim Smith." I could hardly breathe.

"Okay, James Smith," he said, writing the name on the form. "Except if you aren't James Smith, I sure wish you'd've lemme know before I got you into this opera," he said.

"Manfredi." Boylan burst in. "Go sign this guy's personal-belongings voucher." Boylan tapped him. "Get up." Manfredi rose with a strange look of embarrassment. Boylan slid into his seat. Manfredi walked, quite stunned, through the two swinging doors, but he didn't go far. He stood there behind the door, watching through the glass. My quick glances away from his eyes didn't deter him. His pity showed on his face, though his face looked terrified as he watched.

"You're married?" Boylan stated the question as he put on his glasses.

"Yes."

Boylan made a cross on the form. "Don't think I'm surprised.

Wife's name?" I didn't answer. "Wife's name?" I wouldn't answer. "Never mind. How old are you?"

I didn't answer. He guessed and wrote. "Make it thirty-five. Just around the age you married queers come visit the Rest Area."

"I don't like that remark."

"What?" His head bounced up.

"Don't like the way you're assuming—"

He whipped off his glasses. "I see ten of you guys a fuckin' week. Okay, Mr. Smith? And they all don't know how the hell they got here." He laughed. "They all went to the Rest Area out of curiosity, for the first time in their life, they say. Right? Then, in a billion to one shot, we come along and handcuff them to being a queer. Oh, they squirm. And you wanna know why? They ain't lyin' to us, these guys. They swear on a stack of Bibles they ain't queer. We get 'em all in here. I had a football star sittin' here once, doctors. I had movie people, lawyers I had. But they're none of them *queer*. Even with the fuckin' handcuffs on, they deny they're queer."

"So you rub their noses in it," I said, dizzy with anger as I spoke.

He laughed. "That's right, queenie." He lifted his hand to my cheek. I was still handcuffed when Boylan's fingers pinched my face, so I went for his hand with my teeth. A growling sound came out of me; that surprised even me. Boylan jumped away. Manfredi ran in. "Did you see what this motherfucker just tried to do to me?" Boylan screamed.

"I'm putting him in the cage," Manfredi said, grabbing my arm.

"That cocksucker. You leave him here, Manfredi."

"C'mon." Manfredi lifted me gently, ignoring Boylan. He grabbed the sheet of paper and pen and pulled me out of the room. Boylan didn't object. I must have frightened him.

Manfredi took me to another policeman who took off my handcuffs and ordered me to undress. Manfredi left and the other fellow fingerprinted me, photographed me, then led me to a tile cell, where I sat in my underwear. The room was all white tile—floor, ceiling, walls—with a sewer, tiled so they can hose down the juices that ooze out of busted people—urine, shit, vomit and blood. I thought of the fish that come in on *The Escape*, sharks tied by their tails, their stomachs hanging out of their mouths.

Manfredi appeared at the bars with my clothes in his hands. The other policeman opened the cage with his keys, then disappeared.

"Here." He handed me my clothes. "Get dressed." He didn't leave as I put on my pants and shirt. "There's twenty-five bucks in your shoe," he said in a hushed voice. "I'm going to tell Boylan you found some mad money."

"What?"

"There's twenty-five bucks in your *shoe,* so you can get the hell outta here. You can make believe you don't remember me, but I can't let you get torn up by that asshole in there. You hear me, Cello? Call the guard and say you found your bail money."

"What did you call me?" I asked.

"Cello." He looked at me quizzically. "Look, I'm minding my business. You want me to forget who you are?" His face seemed hurt.

"Do you really know me?" I asked.

"You're my cousin Cello." He blinked and his face was gravely serious.

"Cello?"

"You really don't remember me?" He was annoyed. "I'm *Tato.* Tato Manfredi."

"You . . . you know who I am?" I asked.

He looked carefully at my eyes, testing me. "I'm *Tato,*" he repeated with emphasis, "for chrissake. Tato? Don't you remember? Zia and the house on Jessup? Colorado? California?" His face reddened; he was angry. He thought I was making a fool out of him.

"What house?" I asked.

"Christ, did you lose your memory?"

"Yes," I answered simply. "I lost my . . ."

He froze. His eyes darted nervously all over my face, as if they were trying to confirm what I had said, like a man double-checking his bank account. "When?" he whispered. "When did you lose your memory?"

"Eleven years ago in an accident, a car accident."

"You're Cello. *Cello.*" He wiped the perspiration from his forehead. "What happened to you? You mean you never . . . Didn't anyone ever tell you who you are?"

The policeman who took my fingerprints was staring at us. Manfredi turned, glaring at him. Springing up, Tato took out his pencil and address book, wrote a number on a page, ripped it from the book and stuck it in my trouser pocket. Then he beckoned the cop. "Tell Boylan this guy's got his bail." Manfredi walked ahead to the desk. I carried the money in hand like a child, still not understanding. There was a strong buzzing in my head again. My back ached as if I had just lifted a concrete slab.

"Did you call his house?" Tato asked Boylan.

Boylan glanced at me ominously. "There was no answer."

"Well, he's got the bail money. It was in his shoe."

Boylan blinked. "You had money in your shoe all this while?" Boylan asked, "and you didn't try to use it to help yourself?"

"Yes," I answered. I felt like vomiting. I must have looked bad.

"Go on, send him home before he has a heart attack. I wanna talk to you, Manfredi." Tato walked off with Boylan and didn't glance back.

I left the station house with a uniformed policeman. He smelled of one of those leathery colognes. He didn't speak, just quietly chewed gum as we rode. It was one of the white two-doors with uncomfortable vinyl seats. We found the Rest Area under moonlight. A cool wind had washed the gray out of the air and the sky was dark blue. Stars were scattering like diamonds on velvet. My truck was parked next to tall pines in the blue light. The cologne-scented policeman handed me my keys, wallet, and belt.

The gray Porsche was barely visible in the ghostly light. The cricket din was ear-piercing. I waited next to my truck until the white police car bumped over the grass island and disappeared westward. I began walking and taking deep breaths. I wanted to throw up but was not able to. I climbed up into the pickup. I sat there several minutes, smelling the new insides of my beautiful truck, so glad to be alone, so glad to be locked inside my beautiful truck so perfectly alone, so perfectly unthought of. I cried. It was a blind emotion.

I drove home as if by radar, so glad Rosie had promised to take the girls for Chinese food and a movie.

* * *

I crawled into bed next to Rosie.

"You okay?" she murmured.

"Yeah."

"Where were you?"

"Ridin'."

Our bedroom was cool. A safe, secret cave under a waterfall—that's what it sounds like when the wind blows through our oaks, a waterfall. I could hear the patter of squirrels' feet on the roof. I never heard squirrels so busy at night. They didn't quiet down until three in the morning. I could see the time on the electric clock that had a light behind the face, the electric clock that had become the North Star of our bedroom. I imagined the squirrels were like me, blinking awake in their oak nests. They hadn't been deceived by the Indian summer. Maybe they knew that a terrible winter was coming. Squirrels are smart like the oaks.

I wanted Rosie, even though she was asleep. I needed her in a sexual way to prove to myself I loved her. I never needed her so badly. I slid my cool hand up her leg under her nightgown.

"Jim," she murmured. I found the stiff hairs of her vaginal lips. She pushed me away, but I persisted until she wrapped her thighs around my hand, urging me to apply more pressure. I pulled my hand out and lifted her gown to her neck. I lay on top of her, my entire body pressing very close to hers, sliding my hands under her back, up to her shoulders and gripping them. I entered her deeply, quickly, keeping myself there, as far as I could go, as if I were pinning her to the bed.

"What?" she whispered.

I joined my mouth to hers, pulling away only very slightly to say something to her now and then. "I need you," I whispered. "Understand, Rosie? Say you love me. Say you love me, Rosie. I wanna hear it." She tried to turn her head away, but my lips followed hers, insisting, "Say it."

"I love you," she whispered.

Then I began to move inside her, slowly, pressing hard all the while, till she gasped, coming. I caught her cries with my mouth. I stayed inside her a long time before I pulled out and let her roll away.

She quickly fell asleep, like a puppy, curled on her side. I stayed awake, on my back, listening to the wind. I couldn't put his voice out of my head: "I'm Tato, for chrissake. Tato Manfredi, your cousin."

The next morning, like a man who wakes from a nightmare not remembering what he dreamed, I groggily sipped my coffee in the Country Kitchen. Even by lunchtime I hadn't made one mental reference to the arrest. I worked in a stupor. I refused any conversation with those dentists from Virginia when they showed up for that mako hunt.

But by that afternoon, the facts threatened increasingly to unveil themselves. I fled, in work, in exhausting activity, finally losing myself by the end of the day, up in the crumbling roads of Northwest Woods, looking for a place to dump the poor mako head in back. That night I wrecked the living room, scared Rosie and the girls nearly to death as my nightmare caught up to me, grabbing my heels in its teeth, forcing me to acknowledge that it was no mere nightmare but something larger, something far worse. . . .

CHAPTER XI

FRIDAY, the day after Thanksgiving, when the Chief and I had our confrontation aboard *The Escape*, I locked up the marina at four-thirty and drove the truck to Sagaponack on the way home, thinking how I would present my case to my wife. The fish were still around; gulls were diving for bait. I didn't feel like eating. I decided to telephone Rosie from the highway to tell her to get a baby-sitter so we could take a drive to Montauk later. She always said she'd like to fish with me. I'd rig up a pole for her and we'd eat at Shagwong Restaurant, then make for the lighthouse and go down to the rocks to try for a striper. She had the gear. I wondered why I never pushed our fishing together. I figured I wouldn't say a word about the arrest until we were coming home, content and maybe laughing. Then I would stop at the overlook, take her hand in mine, and try to tell her, explaining that I had to get her out of the house so we could talk freely without danger of the kids hearing.

I backed the truck away from the ocean and called Rosie from the first booth I came to. As I dialed, I noticed the wind was out of the north, and did not believe that there could be such a warm wind so close to December, as balmy and sweet-smelling as August.

"Rosie, it's Jim. Can you get a baby-sitter?"

"No. Can't talk."

"Huh? Wait till I tell you—"

"Jim." She said my name, then put her hand over the mouth-piece. "Rosie? Rosie." No answer.

Her hand came off the mouthpiece. "Can you call back?" she asked.

"What's going on?"

"I'm talking with my father. I'd like to talk to my father."

"What you talking about? Rosie?"

"Call back."

"Put your father on."

Her mouth strayed from the phone. "*He wants you,*" she was saying to her father. I couldn't hear the Chief's answer, only Rosie coming back stiffly: "He doesn't want to talk."

I hung up and jumped into the truck. I flew north to the highway, then turned into Garden Street.

When I pulled into the driveway, the Chief's car was gone. I ran into the house the back way. Rosie was in the kitchen, sitting under the fluorescent light, staring into space. The table was set in the dining room. I smelled tomato sauce, but I sensed the food on the stove was cold.

"Let's go to Montauk," I said. Rosie's face was puffed, her eyes glazed. She didn't answer. "I want to talk," I said as I tried to gather her hands in mine.

"Please don't hurt me," she said. "Please, don't."

"Did your father tell you about me?"

"Yes. He wants me to pack and go to his house with the girls. He's got men patrolling. You gotta do me a favor, please, Jim." She was terrified, her lips quivering. "Please don't come upstairs tonight. Please. I'm afraid."

"What did he tell you?"

"No."

"Let me explain."

"No." Her head shook. Her eyes closed tight. Tears leaked. "No." Her voice was a small box closing. Nothing more could come out of her. She was turning to wood, metal; she was a thing, a robot, a bomb that couldn't go off. She was nothing but pain. Her brain was smoldering. She knew about me. She knew everything about the arrest. She knew everything.

There were only eleven more shopping days left till Christmas when Hirsch the lawyer was finally able to see me. He laughed when I mentioned the word innocent. Hirsch had thin slicked-back black hair and very mottled teeth from which the enamel had been worn. His teeth came down out of his gums like sticks; he tried to hide them with his lips. His shirt was crisp, and his tie seemed to have been ironed. His office was behind the parking lot in Southampton Village. From his window I could see seagulls standing in a line on top of the Justice Building, only two blocks from the apartment with the ficus tree that Rosie and I used to share after my accident.

"Why do you laugh?" I asked.

"My dear man, I can hardly tell the judge you stopped in the woods to watch the birds or to take a leak. Do you think he's going to believe that? Everyone knows about the Rest Area." He was the wrong lawyer for me, but it was too late to walk out.

"Just tell me what *can* be done?" I asked.

"Nothing," he said and waited. He was almost amused. "My dear man, you *did* something. *They* say you did it. You *know* you did it. What's the point in fighting them? You'll lose. There was a chance, in the old days, to get people off this kind of thing when the police operated alone. But now they go in pairs. They bring witnesses, and the witnesses are *police*, no less. Do *you* have a witness to lie for you that you didn't do what they claim? Produce him, and we'll start to talk about innocence."

I stared at him, hoping to find a reason for disbelief, but he was too arrogant to be lying.

"You are a cooked goose. You should be glad you've got a lawyer. Other lawyers wouldn't touch this with a ten-foot pole, believe me." There was a glimmer of sympathy in his eyes.

"Can anything be done about keeping it out of the local papers?" I asked. "I have children, my wife. You know who my father-in-law is. "

He tapped the point of his pencil on his blotter. "Did you hear what happened in New Jersey? They published their names and pictures, their addresses, their wives' and parents' names and the names of their children, and their places of business, and they got away with it, and why not? This is a free country. People hate that sort of behavior, but they love to read about it. It's news. You don't have to be *guilty*. The paper doesn't say you did it; they say you were arrested for it. Well, in your case, you did it, didn't you?"

I didn't answer. My face was flushing. I felt my neck bursting at the collar.

"Let's be fair. You made yourself the news and now you are going to have to *be* the news. People who don't want to be the news should stay at home, shouldn't they? Don't you think it's a bit unrealistic to expect them to protect you from yourself?"

I wanted to choke him. He was thumping the eraser, switching to the point, back to the eraser, point, eraser, point, eraser.

"Two years from now it will be nearly forgotten. In ten years people won't even be sure it happened. People forget, if you give them time." Point, eraser, point, eraser. "So shall we plead guilty, and not waste our time and your money?"

I stood up to leave just as the gulls flew off the roof of the Justice Building. "What choice do I have?"

"It'll be painless. That's the advantage of pleading guilty. It'll take seconds."

A week later I went with Hirsch to court in Hauppauge. We stepped before a white-haired judge who spoke to Hirsch only. I kept my head down, looking at the oak floors, thinking about the shotgun. We were before the judge no more than thirty seconds before we walked back out into the sunlight.

305

"You have to visit a psychiatrist," Hirsch said. "Here's the name. He's in Cutchogue on the North Fork and you can go to him tonight, I think. He'll make out a report, and everything will be over but the newspaper. You're just gonna have to sweat that one out alone."

I was glad I'd never have to see Hirsch and his teeth again.

Those poor tired roses were still blooming in front of the Howard Johnson's. Kids were skateboarding the traffic circle. I stopped the pickup at a phone booth under an old yellow maple near the circle. Its last fat rubbery leaves had trapped the sun and glowed yellow overhead. I put forty-five cents into the slot and dialed Cutchogue. Smells of grass and pollen filled the booth. The sight of kids on skateboards in tee shirts made me cold. I recalled the same day four years ago. I had taken the girls to test the frozen Trout Pond for ice skating. That same day Rosie had gotten stuck on North Sea Road and nearly froze. She had taken just a raincoat. We sold that wagon, a Chevrolet. It was our first car.

"Hello," a man's voice answered.

"Dr. Alan Elliott?" I asked.

"This is he."

"I'm James Smith, a client of Leonard Hirsch."

"And?"

"And I'd like to see you, regarding an examination. I was arrested."

"What for?"

"I was arrested . . . in the Rest Area. I . . ."

"I see. All right then." His voice became friendly. He said he would be at home and that I could come any time until nine. I said I'd come right away, if he didn't mind. I figured I'd take the ferry back from the North Fork through Shelter Island and Sag.

Elliott lived on the bay. There were two cars in his garage but no sign of his wife. From the photo portrait on his desk I saw that he had three children, all girls. His wife was much like Rosie—similar haircut and a plaid skirt. They were all posed before their mantel, which I noted had a ginger jar on it similar to the one at Jessup, where I had hidden my money and Zia's ring eleven years ago.

306

"Sit. Sit." He had short wiry pepper-and-salt hair and an open smile. Around his eyes was the brownish rubbery hue of exhaustion that represents years of wakefulness and worry, yet his eye whites were clear and healthy, as if lately he had found the key to the peace of sleep. He was tall, but his nose and mouth and puffy eyes gave him a boyish, impish quality. When he lit his pipe and sat down, he became an elf. He didn't look at me as he sucked in the flame of his match. The sweet smell of tobacco filled the office. "What happened at this Rest Area?"

"Do you know what goes on there?" I asked.

"Oh, yes." He puffed. "You pleaded guilty to sodomy?"

"No."

"You know what sodomy is?" He puffed some more.

"Yes, of course."

"Why do you say of course? A lot of people never heard of it." He spun toward me in his chair.

"It wasn't sodomy." I looked straight at him.

"But you exposed yourself."

"No. I did not."

"Tell me. You touched the cop?"

"Right. I did that."

"With your hand."

"That's right."

"And that's all you did."

"That's right."

"That was the first time you ever did such a thing?"

"Yes."

"I mean with another man?"

"That's right."

"Do you expect me to believe that?"

"I don't want to design your conclusions for you. I'm just telling you the truth. I can't control your not believing me."

His eyes focused on me sharply. "Do you have normal sex relations with your wife?"

"Yes."

"Naturally." He put a second match into the clean ashtray. "Absolutely nothing wrong with being curious about another man.

307

The issue here is why did you go where you could get caught? Do you see what I mean? Those woods *are* public, you know." He smiled. I decided to let him say his piece, to listen and get out as quickly as possible. He talked easier and easier. He asked about my work. We talked about the crazy weather and about a book he was writing on wildflowers of the North Fork of Long Island.

I said only a few words the whole time, wishing I could tell him about Tato, wishing I could give him the whole story starting with that winter long ago when my mother cut her wrists, Tato on the roof, Zia, all those years in the seminary without wanting to touch or be touched, not caring. He stood and shook my hand. He said he saw no need for us to talk further unless I wanted to. I wrote him a check for fifty dollars.

As I stood at his front door, I noticed his wife in the kitchen light. She wasn't like Rosie in real life. She was taller, a lean body, very fine blond hair pulled back, shoulders bare in a wraparound dress. She was lighting candles. They had guests somewhere inside.

"Do you fish?" Elliott asked at the door.

"How did you know?"

"I see you have a pickup. You go on the beach with that thing?"

"Sure."

"Four-wheel drive, is it?"

"Right."

"Stop by sometime and give us a lesson."

"Okay."

"Give us a call. You've got my number."

"All right then, I've got the number."

"Sure. We'll go fishing."

"All right then."

"I'd like that." He closed the door.

"Sure thing."

When I pulled into my driveway, it was midnight. Rosie was still awake, sitting in the jalousied porch watching television.

Since the night the Chief had told her about me, Rosie slept downstairs on the couch. Some nights I heard her cleaning house.

I could smell coffee. The television would be on until three in the morning.

When I walked in, she jumped up and turned off the TV. She blocked the television, facing me like a statue. I reached behind her and turned the set back on.

"Hi," I said. "What's on?"

"I went to Maggie at the newspaper office." Her face was squeezed closed like a trap over her feelings.

I turned down the sound. "Why did you do that?" I asked without looking up.

"So she wouldn't print anything about you. I asked her not to, as a personal favor."

"Did she consent?" I asked.

"No. She's printing it. She said you pleaded guilty today in court."

"She's a speed demon."

"I'm *trying* to *save* you," Rosie screamed like a spoiled little girl, "and you plead *guilty?*"

Her eyes reflected double images of the television screen. The two images deteriorated, turning abstract in the watery mirrors. Johnny Carson had stopped talking, and a dog-food commercial came on. She turned off the television and sat back down. "The horror movie was that someone would walk in and say, 'Jim's got a wife somewhere,' or 'He's a murderer.' Or 'Jim's dead,' but never this. I would even have been able to take it if you loved another woman."

"Rosie, this has nothing to do with love. I don't love anybody. Get to the point. What *are* you worried about?"

"I care about how you feel about *me*." She didn't try to hide her shaking anymore.

"No different," I said angrily. "You expect our marriage to go up in smoke because a couple of men played with each other in the woods?"

"You were one of them. Didn't you have some *need* when you went into those woods?" she asked defiantly.

"Rosie, whatever happened there didn't erase the past ten years between you and me. I don't know a better way to say it."

"The *need*," she repeated. "I asked if you had the need."

"Yes, I had the need, obviously."

I traced the quick involuntary movements of her eyes as she listened to my words. She was a lost child. She had used up all her intelligence, all her strength, and still she could not understand what was happening. She seemed to want to say something, but no words would come. Tears were all she had. She stared at me through them as if I were a ship sailing away from her. She was being left on a far island that no one would ever come back to. Her pain stirred a strange joy in me. I could measure her love by peering into the gaping hole its absence was making, and it thrilled me in spite of myself. Impetuously, I pulled her to me and tried to hold her tightly. She didn't know whether to resist me or to lean into me.

"I'm sorry, hon. I'm sorry," I said. "Please . . ."

She pressed my chest with her hands and squirmed out of my arms.

"Go," she said, turning away. "Go upstairs and let me go to sleep."

Swamp maple and oaks were bare, their red and brown leaves all raked up and packed in black plastic bags. Stillness, and the mildness so close to Christmas were eerie. Wild grapes were still growing all over the woods, their leaves still green. Certain flowers were reblooming. The seed droppings under the bird feeders germinated and were blooming into small yellow flowers.

It stayed around fifty degrees. People were getting used to the mildness. They went about with smiles, enjoying themselves, and at sundown Sunday, when the Merchants Association Christmas lights came on down Main Street, it all seemed like a big hoax.

Fishermen told of unusual happenings at the ocean. Dogfish—some call them sand sharks—were lying dead from East Hampton beach to Sagaponack. The dead fish were ten- to twenty-pounders. Fishermen said a large dark shadow appeared in the water at dusk, when the dogfish started flapping up onto the beach, where they died, some with their young still writhing inside of them.

I folded up at the marina and called Rosie to tell her I wasn't going to make it home for supper. She reacted minimally. I bought a ham and cheese sandwich and drove to Sagaponack, right up to the ocean's edge. I saw the dogfish scattered about. I chose a promontory the outgoing tide had cliffed out.

While the shotgun in its cradle behind my head offered its sensual comfort of the last word, I ate my sandwich in peace. In the last red glow of sunset, seagulls appeared. They were streaming in from up north, no end of them. They were definitely working the water. I didn't see the big dark shadow the fishermen talked about, but I knew something was stirring havoc under the surface. The gulls were feasting on the flesh that floated up. My guess was that the monster was made up of many parts, a school of striped bass, probably the whole northern migration.

A moon rose in the southeast. The wind was southerly, carrying the great racing sound of ocean toward my pickup. I watched the stars form and I fell asleep imagining the other worlds up there. It was a rare sleep, with no guard on my dreams.

I drove home so leisurely that cars honked behind me. I waved them to pass. I turned into the farm roads through the moonlit potato fields. The dirt smelled clean, cleaner than spring to me.

When I got to Garden Street, things did not cry out to me with their usual familiarity. Some ungathered leaves whirlpooled before me as I walked across the lawn from my driveway. Trees were making whirring noises. I was startled by the moon, silver and silent in the bare oaks. A single-engine plane buzzed slowly, invisibly somewhere in the sky.

Inside, the house smelled of room deodorizer. Rosie was not visible. Karen and Erica were sitting in the living room with colorless faces, chewing gum simultaneously, dressed alike, as if they were hiding inside each other.

Karen called as I went upstairs, "Dad?"

"What, honey?"

She came to the archway. "Are you gonna get a Christmas tree?"

"Sure, honey. I'm gonna pick one out for us." I continued on up to my room.

Rosie was packing, throwing things into the largest suitcase we owned.

"Where the hell are you going?" I asked.

"To my aunt's in Pennsylvania."

"For Christmas?"

"For as long as it takes."

"Coward." I forced a laugh.

She turned on me in a fury. "Why? Because I refuse to stay for when the paper comes out? I'm a coward because I don't want to be wife of the village Quasimodo? You're not worthy of my courage. What do I owe you? You owe me."

"What do I owe you? Love? Is that what you're not getting?"

"You owe me to end this mess you put us all in. Love—don't use that word."

"How can I end the mess? Tell me. I'll do it."

"You'll have to figure that out alone." She threw her hairbrush into her suitcase. "I'm not going to be in this town when the axe falls, neither are my kids. Just sign the papers and let me live in peace."

"What papers? Sign what?"

"Didn't you go to the post office today?" she said with surprise.

"No," I answered simply.

"Well, you'll get it tomorrow." She grabbed her suitcase by the handle, refusing my help. She let the suitcase drag her down the stairs.

"Rosie, what'll I get tomorrow? Separation papers?"

"You guessed it," she said. "Get in the car," she ordered the girls.

"I can't believe you'd leave. This is your village, your home town."

"I can't believe it either," she said without looking at me. "I don't know what to think anymore."

I grabbed her arm. "*Think* what you *think*. Say what you feel. You look like you'd rather go away than to say what you really feel to my face. Ask me questions."

"I know all I want to." She pulled away.

"*Talk* to me. Discuss it. Ask me."

"I have asked you."

"What did you ask me?"

"The main question."

"What was the main question?"

"I asked you if you went into the woods because you had the need." I grabbed her again. Karen and Erica were outside waiting for her. She pulled, but I held on. "And you said you had the need."

"Yes," I answered. In the new light I saw that all color was gone from her face. She looked everywhere but into my eyes.

"Yes," she said sarcastically. "Just like that. No shame. You had the need."

"Well, it's *true.*"

"Then why don't you let me go? Or *you* go. Get out of my house." She swung at my face with her other arm and grazed my forehead with her knuckles. "Get out of my town. You shit on my life." She pulled back to slap me again. Her teeth showed like a snarling dog's. I held off her arm. A faraway light was in her eyes. I remembered that look from the hospital days after her mother died. It was an alien light, a glimmer that warned of her uniqueness and her pain. There was a complex woman beneath the haircut and plaid skirt, a yet uncivilized monster that never saw the light of day.

"Rosie, listen to me. Talk to me."

"I don't wanna."

"Talk beyond the woods, beyond the arrest."

"I don't *want* to. I don't want you if you're that way."

"What way?"

"Go away," she screamed without answering.

"Suppose you didn't know about it, like so many women who don't have the faintest idea about their husbands?"

"I *do* know. You saw to that."

"Your father saw to it."

"The paper would have told me. It comes out tomorrow. Thank God, I was told in advance."

"Rosie, we have children. We have this house. We used to sit here and talk about lawns and neighbors."

"Now it's their turn to talk about us."

"Rosie." I caught her eyes. She tried to pull her arm out of my hand. I warned her with my eyes and I pleaded at the same time. "I can't allow you to walk out that door." It was as if she were attached to a string that had healed inside my old scars. I didn't care so much about Rosie; it was only her leaving I was scared of, her pulling on that string, ripping those scars. I pinned her to the doorway. I let all my fear show. It was my last look, my last chance. I felt tears coming. I let them come.

She only screamed into my face. "Am I supposed to be the tragic wife and go upstairs now and hang up all my clothes, go Christmas shopping tomorrow with the whole goddamn town watching me?"

"Pride, Rosie."

"Yes, pride. I wasn't cut out to be the wife of Frankenstein. I didn't volunteer for that. You were the one copped out, not me. You smeared egg on my face. Why blame me if I want to hide?"

"Will you come back? Just promise me."

"No, not unless you're gone." She managed to face me with those words and to hold her position until my eyes grew tired of trying to meet her expression. I released her. She took a breath. She won, just as she knew she would. She took after her father. I would never have believed she could be so strong.

She grabbed her raincoat and her bag and, without looking back, she pulled the door toward her with her foot, muttered, "Goodbye," and dragged the bag behind her down the front steps toward the garage.

"Merry Christmas," I yelled after them. Karen turned, crying, but Rosie and Erica acted as if they didn't hear me. I realized for the first time that Karen had Zia's eyes.

CHAPTER XII

THE next morning I faced the empty rooms, talking to myself. What do I do now? What do I do?

Make yourself a cup of coffee, I answered myself.

In the kitchen I found Zia's emerald ring—which I had given to Rosie as our engagement ring—and Rosie's wedding band. The two rings sat conspicuously with no note, nothing to contain them, alone on a sparkling clean countertop. The emerald ring looked different off Rosie's finger. I stuck both rings into my pocket immediately to get them out of my sight; their messages were becoming too large to swallow in one gulp. I changed my mind about coffee.

I wanted air. I went into the living room and sat in the wing chair, though I wasn't tired. I resented the inertia of the room. How motionless the curtains hung! The clock ticked on the mantel slowly. No fireplace tools near the fireplace; Rosie must have hidden them. But there, next to the kindling bucket, was a miniature Christmas tree only seven inches high, the kind made of straw bristles and twisted wire. The little tree stood upon a box with a logo imprinted in gold: *Arnold's Men's Shop*. The box was tied with a cheerful red and green ribbon. There was a white envelope under the ribbon. I ripped open the envelope. Inside was a card depicting a Victorian snow scene: horses and carriages, women in bonnets, men in top hats going toward a church steeple, in the fallen snow. Inside it said, *Merry Christmas to Dad from Karen and Erica. I* opened the box. Within the white tissue paper was a green and black plaid hunting shirt and a lightweight tan cotton turtleneck. Price tags were left on in case they didn't fit. I felt nothing—no hurt, no panic. I still longed for motion and sound to enter the room. I wanted air. I began opening windows—windows in the living room, the dining room. I turned the thermostat down. I turned on the radio with plenty of volume. A man's radio voice boomed inside the house. Rosie's curtains swelled. Suddenly music filled the place. Palestrina. Palestrina would exorcise the house. In the din the phone rang. I ran to the kitchen and grabbed it from the wall.

"Hello."

"Cello?"

"Yes. No. Who is this?"

"This is Tato." Simple, as if it were eleven years ago and we had just spoken an hour before. He seemed surprised that I didn't recognize him immediately. Palestrina almost drowned us out.

"What do you want?" I asked coldly.

"Nothing for you to be uptight about. I'm just nearby at this place called the Country Kitchen."

"Want to check to see if they put the nails in all the right places?"

"Huh? What nails?"

"Of my crucifixion?"

316

"Don't lay a guilt trip on me today. I'm in bad shape. I need a friend."

"A friend? You must be crazy to be calling me, then. I'm no friend."

There was silence. When Tato spoke, it was a different voice, harder, a very familiar voice. "Could you just forget everything for a minute? I've just been socked with too much, a little too much today."

I laughed. "I was about to blow my brains out," I said.

"Cello, I can help you. I got some good ideas. First of all, I found out that lawyer Hirsch is an asshole."

"Too late, Tato. It's all over. I've been to court. I pleaded guilty." I heard the rattling of dishes in the phone.

"I have something here with me that I want to give you. It's gonna cheer you up, I think." His voice infuriated me.

"What do you have?"

"It's . . . *somethin'*. Listen I can't hear too good. I'm cold, and I know you're right nearby. I'm not driving a police car or anything. You're alone, so what's the sweat if I come by?"

"How do you know I'm alone?"

"I just passed your place a few times."

"Have you been cruising around here, spying?"

"Take it easy. I just got out here from Brooklyn. I figured I'd better go back to the highway and call before I showed up. C'mon, Cello, have an open mind."

"Don't call me that."

"Jim. Okay? I'm sorry."

"Just tell me what it is you have to give me."

"Your suitcase."

"My suitcase? What suitcase?"

"Remember the valise you came to Brooklyn with, when you were a kid, and we couldn't find the thing so you had to wear all my clothes? Well, that valise just popped up in Brooklyn."

"Just get rid of it."

"Oh, c'mon. Your mother packed it with her own hands, for chrissake."

"I don't need the suitcase, valise, whatever it is. I mean, don't worry; get rid of it."

"But I wanna *see* you. I wanna talk. And I have this surprise for you."

"I can't talk."

"I'll take two minutes. I swear to God." He waited for an answer. I kept silent. "We need maybe two minutes, and I swear to God you'll never see me again in your life. That's the God's honest truth. I . . . I just wanna express myself and give you something, something besides the valise. The valise don't matter."

"What do you want to give me?"

He blew an exasperated breath. "*Trust* me, for chrissake. My mother just died. I'm just comin' from three days of hell in Brooklyn. I drove out here with no sleep, straight from the funeral. She was buried this morning. It's Christmastime. I'm feeling funny, and I wanna *give* you somethin'. Christ!"

Aunt Silva in her coral-colored elastic blouse with the elastic silver threads woven in, that stretched over her huge breasts, her laughter, sitting at her sewing machine, sweating—the memory slowed me down. "I'm sorry," I sputtered. "Sorry to hear about your mother. You know how to get to my house."

"Yeah."

"Give me ten minutes."

"All right. Ten minutes."

I paced about after I hung up, passing the mirror in the dining room. When my eyes contacted their reflection, I stopped short, surprised that in the past few weeks my beard had grown so much. My eyes looked wild and tired. I was an older man, a stranger walking through my own rooms. I ran up to the bathroom, turned on the light over the sink and ran the hot water to wash. I opened the medicine cabinet, found my beard scissors. As I began to trim, I wondered, why keep the beard at all? To hide a scar? I suddenly wanted my old face back. I yearned to see it. To hell with the scar. I clipped my beard close to the skin, soaped my face and shaved, hoping to see a familiar face when I rinsed.

The old scar was hardly visible. The wet face was a boy's, the skin smooth, the chin beautiful, but the eyes belonged to an older

318

man, though not wild as they had seemed in the mirror downstairs. The light over the bathroom sink was very kind. The space in my eyebrow was more noticeable somehow, with the beard gone, but the blue eyes shone with a kind of innocence. They were Cello's eyes, beginning to fill up as if they recognized an old friend.

I had noticed at the police station that Tato still smoked, that his face had grown tired. We were both so different from the two young men who fell off a cliff after a parachute one summer day long ago. And yet my face in the mirror looked not very different from my face when I left the seminary in Rome eleven years ago, in spite of so many Long Island summers and winters.

Downstairs, the Connecticut radio station was now playing Gregorian chant, their mistaken idea of Christmas music. I recognized the piece. It was a recording that the director of the Schola Cantorum used to play for the seminarians in Rome. The singers were monks of some Benedictine abbey in France—I recognized their French-accented Latin. I felt lightheaded, off balance, before my mirror, mentally jumping time bands of my life, skipping tracks from one pilgrimage to the next. Rosie and the girls had gone. It was another Christmas and Tato was re-emerging. Suddenly I remembered that apartment on the West Side where I had lived as a boy, with Jeanette the Flamingo.

I tried to ignore a pain in the stomach as I went down to the front door. I peeked out the little window. The gray Porsche was in my driveway. Tato stepped out, smiling innocently and blindly toward my house. His hair was longer, to his neck, going back over his ears. He wore an overcoat, brown trousers and black scruffy dress shoes that had seen better days. He rubbed his hands as he came toward the door. He turned back to the car for something—the small blue suitcase. He also pulled out a long goose-necked object wrapped in newspaper and tied with a silver ribbon. As I stood unnoticed behind the window, enjoying my last hidden moment, the antiphon of matins, Christus Natus Est, began to fill the house. The bell chime startled the chickadees feeding in our Franklinia tree.

His eyes were the first thing I saw when I pulled the door open —dark brown, velvety, exhausted. His hair against the blue sky was still black as crow's feathers except for some gray. Tato, smiling before me—my cousin Tato. He didn't seem so slender and energetic as he did the day of the Rest Area. His eyes lacked sleep. His overcoat collar was turned up. He was unshaven, his stubble pure white.

"Hello, Cello." His voice was the old Tato, exactly the same Tato from the days of Zia. His hand reached out.

I pressed it briefly. "You're cold." I couldn't believe Tato was the cop who arrested me. I bolted at the coincidence as if I hadn't realized it till that moment. It was too grotesque, too wide a truth to pass through the channels of my understanding.

"My car heater's screwed up." His eyes drank me in as he wiped his feet on the welcome mat, though they were dry. He smiled at me as if I were a boulder that he could not pass until his eyes melted my anger, as if he were waiting for forgiveness from my voice. "Isn't this the craziest, most unbelievable thing?" he said self-consciously.

I stepped back, letting him in. "We don't have any fancy coffees like Zia used to brew, but I can offer you Maxwell House." I deliberately used the word "we" to include Rosie. My voice was not mine. "Or a drink?" I was really running away inside.

"No drink," he said, stepping into the living room.

"Put your things down," I said. He dropped the small suitcase from under his arm onto the club chair, took off his coat and plopped it on top of the suitcase. He held onto the goose-neck object, which was wrapped in yellow newspaper and long ago tied with hemp. The silver Christmas ribbon had obviously been added that morning.

"Let's have some coffee," he said, rubbing his hands, glancing at the open windows. "You like the cold?" I went to the kitchen without answering. "Jesus! You have a pond back here," Tato yelled over the music. The curtains were rising as the monks continued.

"Make yourself at home," I shouted as I opened the kitchen cabinet. "We get some wonderful birds because of that pond." He didn't hear me. What was I doing, letting him into my house?

Making coffee for him? Did he want me to close my windows? Why should I?

"You know what I got?" he said, coming toward me. "Remember that green light, like an upside-down flower in the hallway of Zia's house?"

"Oh, yes, the green light."

"I got it for three hundred fifty bucks."

"You *bought* the green light?" I hated myself for pretending interest.

"Sure." He walked toward me with the silver-ribboned package. "Couple years back there was this big ad in the *New York Times,* Parke Bernet auctioning the stuff of Zia's place—the O'Loughlin Estate on Jessup Neck, the ad said. And I said to myself, O'Loughlin, that's the guy Maldonado won the house from, in that card game Zia told us about. So I went to the auction. You wouldn't believe what used to be in that house that we didn't even know about—rare books, Tiffany shit, lamps, glasses, bronze, paintings. Christ! Those paintings were worth thousands. Egyptian stuff, man."

He drifted around the kitchen. "Some of the stuff was so small we could've filled a pillowcase with a quarter million dollars' worth any time we wanted. Christ! The two buffaloes, remember them? They split the pair. But I got the green light. Here." He held out the silver-ribboned package. "Merry Christmas."

I took the package and put in on the countertop. I opened the plastic lid of the coffee can and threw six tablespoons of coffee into the pot. He must have expected me to unwrap the lamp, and when I didn't, he seemed unsure of how to react. He put his hand in his pockets, turned and walked awkwardly back into the living room. Out of the corner of my eye I saw him stop at the drum table near the large window. Both hands came out of his pockets to reach for the brass-frame booklet in which were snapshots of Karen and Erica. Both hands bumped the frame, knocking it over. He scooped it up with clumsy reverence.

While I waited for the water to boil I took deep breaths to hold down my anger. Why did he find it necessary to touch my things?

By what authority did he tip books toward himself at my bookcases? Why didn't he just look at the whale's tooth on the mantel? Why did he have to hold it for a moment in his hand, as if everything were once his?

As I walked inside with the coffee, I tried to smile broadly enough to hide my nervousness, but my mind was speaking. It was saying, I could make you coffee, but if you don't leave in a few minutes, I may kill you.

He noticed my flush when I entered the room with the coffee. "You okay? You're red."

"Just warm. Do you still smoke?" I asked, knowing he did.

"Smoke? Smoke what?" he asked with a little surprise.

"Cigarettes."

"Oh, *sure*."

I fell into a chair, pretending I was finally relaxed. He took out a pack of cigarettes uncertainly, as if to please me. He lit up. "You're not far from Jessup here. Ever see the old place?" he asked.

My chair was a trap. I would have to finish my coffee first to get rid of him. "I do everything to avoid the past, as you know." I could not control a slight shaking in my legs. I sat up and poured extra milk into my coffee. "The past doesn't really exist anyway, except in the mind." I couldn't look at him.

"I think the past exists," he said almost sadly, looking out the window.

The monks' bass chant resonated beautifully from the speakers. The sun was aiming its yellow into Rosie's curtains. Dried-up dogwood leaves twirled on threads, almost ready to blow away. Sunlight came through the dogwood, splattering across the waxed wooden floors, making twirling shadows all the way to the porch.

"Crazy fuckin' weather for Christmas," Tato said, still staring out the window. He freed my eyes to examine his face, so much older. The dancing shadows were mesmerizing him. He looked like he would have welcomed sleep.

"What happened to Aunt Silva?" I asked cautiously.

His expression didn't change. "She had diabetes and she stopped treating herself. She was tired, I think. Can you turn down that music? Christ, I can't hear myself."

I went to the radio and clicked it off. A sudden gassy silence filled the room.

"Thanks," he said. "My mother always used to ask about you, always worried about you. Yeah. She had no idea of our . . . our not seeing each other anymore. You know what I mean?" He smiled with a pretense of embarrassment. "She kept asking me, 'Where did that poor kid go? I figured you were a priest back in Italy; that's really where I thought you were all this time. Last week I had to go through her things with Albert. She married Albert, you know."

"The hairdresser?" I gulped coffee to indicate we were near the end of our visit.

"Yep." He laughed. "She was nuts, you know that. Poor thing. Anyway, Albert found your valise. He asked me to bring it to you. He found it in the back of the closet downstairs in the sweatshop." Tato held up the small blue suitcase. I envisioned Jeanette, my mother, clearly, too clearly, just as she was the day she packed the suitcase, her eyes so large behind her glasses. I took the suitcase and tucked it behind my chair as if it were an old book he was returning. He seemed hurt that I dispensed with it.

"And I brought you this. Here." He held out a white envelope. I took it. I tore it open. Inside was an old overexposed photograph of Tato and me. The one Ruth took on the roof. I was holding Snow. Tato, a head taller, was holding Midnight. We wore shorts and athletic shirts, the kind with shoulder straps. Our skinny legs were dirty and scraped. The sneakers I was wearing were too large, probably his.

The photograph made me queasy; it was too real. I remembered every bit of it too well: the roof, Possilippo's garden, Uncle Marco and Aunt Silva, but I couldn't grasp the years between. In the overexposure, Snow glowed so brightly that he was hardly recognizable as a bird, except for his sharp black eyes. I recalled his heartbeat, feathers over bones, his frail whiteness, shining in my hands. And there was Midnight, whom we had eaten, silken, shiny black in Tato's hands. I handed the photograph back to Tato.

Clever Tato. He had brought tools to work on my feelings. It was time to ask him to leave.

"I never stopped loving you," he said. The words fell, like a glass, a clumsy accident out of his mouth. I gripped my chair as if to pull myself up.

"My wife is coming back." It was all I could think of to say. "She's just dropping the kids off."

"Sure." He sipped his coffee sheepishly with hunched shoulders, knowing I was lying. He sipped small fast sips as he watched me. I said nothing. "You know what I was thinking?" he said, glancing out the window. "I was thinking about it all through the funeral."

"What were you thinking?"

"Of you and me goin' away for good, not California this time, but maybe Canada. Canada's wide open. We'll start from scratch. Buy a farm. Nobody'll know who we are." I deliberately said nothing, leaving him in the aftermath of his own words. I closed my eyes. The silence gave him discomfort. "I . . . I'm sorry you got arrested. I did everything to get you off the hook. I almost lost my job."

"You mean you're still arresting people out there?" I laughed. My question hurt him.

His eyes opened wide. Outrage flushed his face. "It's Gestapo days, man. Don't you know that? They got it so everyone thinks they're Jews, man. We're so dumb, we eat our own bodies with a fork and knife and call it veal cutlets. They've got us wacko, because we're really freaks deep down to them."

He stopped and blinked nervously. He turned to stare once again out the window into the world. Drops of sweat were on his forehead. "There's somethin' you're supposed to get from your father. You know what I'm trying to say? But it's somethin' he's gotta wanna give you, like part of himself, and if you don't get it, because he don't want to give it or because he ain't got it to give, then you bleed like a son of a bitch all your life, like a Jew in the Hitler days. And people smell your blood, small people, jerks; they zero in like sharks, so fast, man, you need a cage to protect you. So you join the army, where you're the enemy of the jerks. You join the Gestapo. You hide there, like it's a movie of the Hitler days."

Trucks groaned by on Montauk Highway, birds twittered. I refused to speak, so he went on. "I wouldn't be a cop if it wasn't for

Boylan. I had stuff on my record and he let it go by. So I got to be his fair-haired boy. I didn't want that shit detail of the Rest Area. Boylan gets his rocks off putting me on it. He's a closet-case weirdo. You ought to see him on the phone with wives of these guys, cuttin' their fuckin' hearts out while he picks his teeth." Tato was making me sick to my stomach. "At the bottom line, I love you, man. I still love you, no matter what. Okay? That's what I came to tell you, Cello."

The words fell like hot sparks on my brain, coming through my skull, not my ears. He blamed Boylan. I recalled Boylan's pasty face. I could believe anything about that man, but I also remembered the smile of the man in the powder blue pickup. I recalled his eyes in the woods, promising what he so well knew the men who go there yearn for and need from other men. He was the perfect bait, promising his body, with firsthand knowledge, becoming the hook that jerks them, like the beautiful mako, out of their innocence.

"Look at my fireplace," I said. My voice shook, warning that the words to follow would be louder.

"What about the fireplace?" he muttered.

"See any irons there? My wife hid them after my arrest because I nearly destroyed this goddamn house. There was a mirror there I smashed, wishing it was your face. I smashed windows, broke furniture. That's what your love did for me. That was my response to your love. Go upstairs. See if you find any signs of a wife or children. They squeezed the TV, dolls, books, clothes—their whole lives—into a station wagon. They're gone. They think I'm scum. That's what your love has done for me. You won. Now I'm yours, Tato. You've earned your catch; I'm all yours now. C'mon." I pulled off my shirt, tearing open the buttons. "Wanna fuck me? C'mon, my friend."

"You're crazy." His eyes nearly popped out.

"Tomorrow the paper will tell the whole story. The whole world has a right to my darkest secrets and you or I can't do anything about it. My family is destroyed. My wife despises me. My father-in-law has given half the county tacit permission to shoot me in a hunting accident. So I have to leave it all—everything—or stay and fight every man and woman, even the kids. You still wanna help me? You wanna move in here and defend me?"

"Huh?"

"How come you're not saying sure?" I nearly laughed in his face.

"Sure." he smiled. "Yeah, sure. I'll help ya," he squealed. He put on an impish grin. "So I quit my job, I always wanted to be a security guard. You wanna go to Canada? C'mon, you're still hot for me. I saw that in your face in those woods." He chuckled.

I couldn't control myself any longer. "Out, you motherfucker." I stood up.

"What?"

"Out of my house." I pointed to the front door.

"C'mon. For chrissake, I was only kiddin'."

"Out." I grabbed the doorknob.

"Wait a second," he shouted. He put down his coffee and stood up. His face was reddening. "Don't open that door. I'll go on my own steam."

I pulled the door wide open. The bright gray sky and red leaves on my green lawn were a shock of color. I smelled leaves burning.

He didn't move. He waited deep in the living room for my eyes to return to him.

"It still fucks you up to hear that a man loves you. What goes on between men and women is not always that pretty either, you know," he said, trembling.

"I don't care about men and women, or men and men; that's not the issue. The issue is me and you."

"What did I do?" He was standing there with both hands outstretched. "What did I *do*?" I stood still. "What in the goddamn *fuck* did I *do*?" he shouted.

I tried to distill a quick answer, but my heart pounded too fast and my anger was too captivating.

He came toward me, white with anger. He held up a shaky finger. "Just let me close this here door a second." He pushed it closed. I waited for him to speak, but he didn't. He seemed not to know himself what he was going to do or say. I tried to pull the

326

door back open, but his hand grabbed my arm. He pulled me close to him. He embraced me. I pushed off his arms, but he held onto my shirt. "Gimme a break, for chrissake," he said. His face was too close. I was a horse rudely held by the bit. He pulled me closer. He scraped his beard on my cheek. "I love you, man. Even if it took you all those years to let yourself touch me, you had to go get arrested when you finally got up the guts to fuck around a little bit." He was chuckling, foolishly trying to win me.

I held still for a few seconds to assure myself of his madness. When he pressed me closer, and his lips touched my skin, I said simply and bitterly, "Get your filthy hands off or I'll kill you." He pulled away. "Get out of my house. Take your three-hundred-fifty-dollar lamp."

His fists were white, yet the vestige of his smile was still on his lips. "You are a cunt," he said, "a true faggot. You don't fool anybody with your work shoes and your pickup truck. Somebody says they love you, and you tighten up your ass and kick them out, just like the same old stiff you always were. And you talk about me arresting people."

"How do you get the nerve to say you love me, you son of a bitch?" I screamed at him. "What did you ever do for me that was love? You hate me. You hate all men. You think everyone is your father. We all have to be destroyed for hurting you. We all have to drink your poisoned wine, and the more naïve the man, the easier you murder him, fuck his ass, impale him to a bed of wax like a butterfly, another scalp, another life snuffed out by a vampire. You and Boylan didn't find each other by accident. Look at you, standing in my doorway, trying to put your arms around me—the cop who arrests men for touching men. How you must hate yourself."

At that moment, I think he realized he would never see me again. He looked about to die. Pain flattened his face. "I'm confused by all this. Very confused," he mumbled as he moved toward his coat. He lifted the coat, stiffly, and came toward me, dragging his feet. "I think you're right. I think I better go."

"You *have* to go. I'm throwing you out." I pulled open the door.

The curtains swelled. The stem vase fell from the drum table. He turned at the sound. I made nothing of it. His eyes pierced me as he approached with the coat in his arms. He was forgetting the lamp. He came so close I could feel his breath. "I'm not sure," he said, "but I think you're full of shit."

I didn't respond. I looked out the door to the milky sky. There had been a wind. The red leaves were gone. He grabbed the door and stood on the threshold, frozen, trying to catch my eyes, but I wouldn't look at him. Instead of stepping out, he stepped back into the house. He slammed the door shut with such strength that the window in it cracked. He grabbed me with both hands and pushed me against the door. The back of my head hit the window. I heard the breaking of glass on the brick steps outside.

"You got fuckin' nerve," he snarled. "Did I ever throw you out of anywhere? Huh, you cocksucker?"

I was glad he made the first move. His physicality justified my own overwhelming need to hit him. I pounded his face with both fists. He grabbed my shirt, trying to place me for a blow. I pulled him back into the living room with more strength than I knew I had. I looked for the irons, doubly angered that Rosie had hidden them. I glanced frantically about for a weapon. In the meantime he landed some punches to my cheek, one to my eye, but the last hit me so squarely that my vision darkened for a moment. My cheek was cut on the inside. He tried to step away and he tripped on the rug, landing with a thud near the fireplace. I took advantage of his fall: I began kicking him in the skull with full power. He turned his head away, reaching blindly for my ankle and caught it. I kicked with the other foot, grazing his temple with my heel. He caught my other foot, jerking both my ankles toward him, and I fell. He scrambled on top of me, quickly pinning my arms with his knees. I was helpless, flat on my back. I tried to reach his head with my feet, but I couldn't. My hands were powerless. He slapped my face three or four times with full power. We were both out of breath. He looked down at me. Droplets of blood were oozing from under the shredded skin of his temple where I had caught him with my heel.

"Let me up." I grunted.

He was pressing on my lungs. "No." he said breathlessly. "Let's not fuck around at the last minute now." He turned my face to him. "And this *is* the last minute, because, I swear to Christ, when I walk out that door I never will see you again, Cello. Tell me the truth, man. Tell me you never loved me. Just tell me that. Look at me and tell me, and I'll go."

"I don't know what the word means. Let me up, Tato."

"No way."

"Tell me what it means. I'd love to know." I tried to laugh.

"Tell me you never cared about me. Just let me hear you say you never cared about me." Tears came into his eyes. He didn't wait for my words. He yelled down at me: "*I cared about you.*" He shook me. "Don't try to take that away from me. You bastard, did you forget the good?"

I turned my head to avoid a thread of saliva dripping from his mouth.

His knees were hurting my arms. "Let me up, Tato, please."

"Tell me you never cared for me."

"When we were children . . ." I couldn't finish what I was trying to say to him. The words had turned into something too large for my larynx.

"When we were children, what?" he asked.

My anger was gone. I was a tape recorder dropped to the floor; my feelings of anger had run off my reels, flapping impotently in my ear. Other new vibrations sounded inside me. I was looking at the face I saw when I stepped off the plane from Rome, the young bearded man with the eyes of Rembrandt's Christ, the boy whom I followed about the large rooms of Zia's house like a duckling after his mother—Tato, my cousin, the apelike half Puerto Rican. I would never love anything with such force again, nor with such pain, such a sad, unsatisfied love it was. My anger was breaking, like a bridge, everything about to fall into the river. I remembered Tato keeping me warm on the roof one cold August night; and years later, when I lay on the old iron bed in Zia's house, missing Italy, missing Ciascuno, longing for the seminary, he promised to take care of me. . . . Now, looking down at me, his knees pinning my arms, and his face hanging off its shell, an old man, I re-

membered him, that wet day we thought we killed Uncle Marco—
a child reflected in a black gallon of wine on a tar roof. Tato,
powerful, loving Tato.

I couldn't hold back the tears. He quickly lifted himself off
my arms as though he had hurt me mortally, looking at me in
amazement, not understanding what he had done, but knowing
that my anger was gone, that the bridge had collapsed.

He lay down next to me, leaning on his arm, watching me. The
room grew quiet except for my sobs and the children's laughter
through the open windows. Then he put his arm under my neck.

He spoke without moving. "You did your share of murdering
too, you know. You got me with Amelia. You killed me with her."

"I'm sorry," I said softly. "Amelia was more of a killer than you
or I." I suddenly felt sorry for his ignorance of himself, his long-
lost irretrievable identity, his perdition and mine. We said nothing
more, just lay there in each other's arms listening to the children
outside. I tasted blood in my mouth.

"It's all paranoia," he kept saying. I almost fell asleep.

I was exhausted, as if my circulation had reversed its flow, like
a changing tide. I pulled myself up, stumbled into the kitchen and
rinsed the blood out my mouth. I brought him back a glass of
water. He was sitting in the wing chair, facing the pond. One arm
hung down. His eyes sagged. He wouldn't like it if he knew how
much like his father he looked at that moment.

"Let's go live in Canada. I'll quit my job," he said, half believing
himself.

"Too late, Tato," I said, looking past him out the window.

Now the years were falling away like loose bandages from my
mind. I remembered Tato's face when he met me the very first
time at the limousine and my father said, "Shake hands with your
cousin." I remembered the smell of Mr. Possilippo's sweater and
the wine on his breath.

Rosie's rug smelled sweetly of dust.

"Chicken hearts," Tato said gently. "What did we get for our
chicken hearts?"

"A wife and two children," I whispered almost to myself.

"Big deal. What are your wife and kids? Grades on your report card?" His audacity had no more power. He was pathetic. His own life was the punishment for who he was. Just like mine.

"I did love her. And my kids. I love them. Just like I loved you too, once." I said it to punish him, his final hurt.

"Shhh." His hand grabbed my forearm tenderly. I turned my hand around into his. How lifeless it was. I held it with curiosity. "You figure your ol' lady may come back to you?" He gave me my excuse.

"Yes," I lied. The sun dancing caught my eyes again. We were both sitting motionless. Nothing seemed important. It must have been the wind, because our words had blown away like smoke from our mouths; the room, like my mind, was empty. I was very tired, staring out my windows. How reduced in my mind Tato had become. What a small part of life either of us was.

"Aren't you going to open the valise?" Tato asked. I had forgotten it. I walked to it and placed it on the table. As he watched, I touched the latch, then lifted the top. There were cottons, molded to the shape of the case. I picked them up—tiny pairs of underwear, shorts no bigger than my hand, little sunsuits, with their own straps. There were several pairs of pajamas, two pairs that must have been new, with the pins still in them, and one pair quite used. My mother must have washed them with her own hands.

As I fingered them, I was displacing her arrangement, disturbing her plan, her design. The Flamingo, the child herself, where did she learn to fold? In the satin pocket of the suitcase, there was a lump the size of a golf ball. I reached in and pulled out what looked like a walnut but it had dark orangy, leathery skin.

"It's a dried-up orange," Tato remarked. "She was a Southerner."

"How did you know she was a Southerner?" I asked.

"That's what my mother used to say."

His eyes held no threat now, beauty all gone from them, and I was so tired. Rosie's white curtains filled up like pregnant brides. The wind was quite cold now. The sun made diamonds on the pond.

He put on his coat. I never saw anyone put on a coat more slowly.

"I'm sorry about your mother," I said clumsily.

"Thanks." We walked out the front door, down the brick steps, ignoring the broken glass.

Children across the way were screeching, burying each other in piles of leaves. We walked toward the gray car. Many people were gone from the planet who were here when we were children. The world was ours at last. We could do what we wished, but oddly, it was also too late—we had already done what we wished.

"Merry Christmas," Tato said. He yawned the words.

My life had been too small; the thought turned my stomach.

"Goodbye," I said, at first not giving meaning to the word. But as his dark head with its few gray hairs tucked itself under the roof of his car as he got into the driver's seat, I knew I'd never see him again. He started the engine, looking everywhere but at me. The Porsche rolled backward. He put it into gear, waved, and then drove off. I walked to the center of the road and watched the squatty Porsche with its broken heater going north up the grade of Garden Street. He never knew what life was doing to him, like his father, like my father, like myself; and I thought of the bars in California that he used to visit with his jingling tambourines.

CHAPTER XIII

THE weekly *Seagull* would come off the presses by eleven that night. Maggie would go to the diner for coffee, stay until midnight. Next morning before dawn Arthur Page's kid Walter and his younger brother would pull the paper wagon from shop to shop, dropping a pile of papers off at each shop: White's Pharmacy, then the Deli, then the Country Kitchen, where the farmers and construction men would show up for coffee with the dawn.

I went to bed before twelve, but I couldn't sleep. The house was too silent. I had closed all the windows; the radio said the temperature would drop drastically overnight. I put the thermostat on sixty. Reports warned that the freeze would hit. I wondered if any birds would be trapped in it, or the lingering striped bass. I tossed as I imagined the begonias and the geraniums finally being put to death. I fell asleep at the first blue promise of day.

I dreamed I drove to Jessup and saw him, old and dirty—Snow, my pigeon—hiding under a beach-plum bush. And I remember in the dream making myself a promise to call the National Audubon Society to find out how long a pigeon can live.

Christmas Eve morning I pulled the pins out of the black and green hunting shirt and the turtleneck and put them on, the shirt over the turtleneck. I had to go to the marina. *The Escape* was dry-docked, but padlocks had to be put on the office door and the storage bins. I went down to the tool room, selected two sets of locks and keys, and left the house out the back door.

Havoc was breaking loose up in the oaks. Squirrels were flying from branch to branch, screeching louder than the blue jays. Birds were going crazy. They weren't just busy; they seemed to fly from perch to perch, screaming, like the red-winged blackbirds on that crumbling road near Barcelona Point.

But beyond the noisy oaks, the seagulls sailed upon invisible mountains of air, facing the north resolutely. Swallows zoomed under the wind in long stretches close to the pond making tighter and tighter circles, as if gathering for a migration.

There were flurries flying sharply southward. I kept an ear cocked for the ocean. The land breeze had silenced the ocean, carried its roar out to sea. Instead I heard trucks on Route 27 and the high pitch of pickup engines pressing from first to second. Rosie's begonias were still healthy. The frost line hadn't quite reached us yet.

I was on the pond side of the house, with the wind to my back, when the Chief in his white patrol car leaned out his window, his eyes scanning the front of the house. He didn't see me.

"Can I help you?" I shouted. He tried to pretend he didn't hear me and started pulling away. But I kept coming toward him so that he had to stop the car.

"Where's my daughter?" he asked half politely.

"She's taken the girls to Pennsylvania for the holidays. Didn't you know?"

He glanced suspiciously toward the garage, then toward the front door.

"Would you like to come in and look around?" I asked. He didn't answer.

"Where in Pennsylvania?" he asked.

"Your wife's sister, I think. Why don't you call her?"

"Why didn't she tell me?"

"Maybe she's a grown-up woman, Chief," I said. He was about to answer me, but instead he turned and lifted something off the seat next to him. It was the weekly *Seagull*. The paper slipped apart before he was able to throw it.

"Here's something for your scrapbook," he said. It fell to the ground as he stepped on the gas. The paper flapped like a dying bird in his wake. I picked it up and walked toward the truck.

A thin column of snow had developed on the north side of the tree trunks. I jumped into the cab of my truck and scanned the paper. The story was on the front page: BRIDGEHAMPTON MAN ARRESTED. I tossed the paper to the floor. But I caught the sub-headline: "For lewd homosexual advances. Citizens upset by immoral activities in local parking area." I lifted the shotgun off its cradle, then I turned on the key and revved the engine. I let it run while I checked the gun. She was oily and bright with just a slight sign of rust, which I wiped off with my finger. I pulled back the lever arm; she was clean. The barrel was dusty, but there wasn't a speck of carbon. She was ready to fire. I checked the glove compartment for my shells; they were there.

Now I was outside the truck with the shotgun, old *Seagull* stories about local suicides flashing in my mind. Artie Moses put his shotgun in a clamp in the cellar and rigged a pulley and wire, even a ring, like those merry-go-round rings, which he pulled while looking into the barrel. Larry Brennan just held it up and fired into his ear. Some young fellow, just sixteen, pushed the trigger with his toes and fired into his chest.

A tiny frail voice came over the wind. "Gonna shoot a poor little rabbit?" It was Nettie Babcock, our next-door neighbor, on the other side of her cedar fence. She was wearing garden gloves and holding shears. The snow was wetting her glasses. Her apron showed beneath her overcoat. Nettie was getting old. She wore a man's scarf around her head, tied in a knot under her chin. Her

335

skinny legs were lost in galoshes. She peered myopically at a rose stem, then with the oversized shears she severed a rose from the rest of the plant and held the bloom aloft. "Snow on a rose," she called out affectionately. I smiled and waved to her, then put the shotgun in its cradle and jumped back into the pickup. The engine had warmed up fine.

I wanted coffee. In spite of everything, my body yearned for its morning coffee. Did I have the nerve to pull up to the Country Kitchen diner? Why not? What could they do to me? Kill me? Let them—save me the trouble. Liz, the cashier girl, can't refuse me a takeout coffee.

I pulled the pickup into a space across from the Country Kitchen, right near where I phoned Rosie the day of the mako head. The windows of the place were sweating, but I could see the neighborhood men gathered around Liz at the counter. She was taking their checks and giving them change. One fellow was reading a newspaper, waiting for Liz to take his money. He was laughing and talking to the fellow next to him. Liz was laughing too as she punched the keys on the cash register. I decided I couldn't do it. I waited in the truck, watching and hoping that the place would thin out a bit. It started to; the men came out the front door in groups—haul seiners in high rubber boots and mackinaws and two farmers in overalls. Georgie Mizinski came running out to slap his howling Labrador. Everyone seemed joyful and laughing. Cold weather appeals to those early morning coffee drinkers that patronize the diner. I decided to get my coffee at Patchy's instead. I turned the key and headed the truck west for Patchy's.

There was only one pickup in the parking lot—Patchy's. I pulled in slowly and sat a minute watching Patchy cleaning the venetian blinds under the neon Budweiser sign. I told myself I'd wait till Patchy went back behind the counter. When he left the window, I jumped out of the truck. The air was freezing. I think the frost must have hit that moment. Puddles were crystallizing, and it felt colder than I could stand. I hoped Patchy had some heat on.

He was on the phone. The bell of the door surprised him. His eyes nearly popped out when he saw me. "Hi, Patch," I said. I never knew Patchy to be shy; still, he didn't answer. He turned, sticking his finger in his ear. I couldn't see his face. He hung up and grabbed a dish towel and wiped the counter. It was nice and warm. "Coffee, black, please," I said. Instead of filling a mug, he turned, grabbed a Styrofoam cup to go, filled it and capped it with a white plastic disc. I noticed the *Seagull* on his counter, the headline facing up: BRIDGEHAMPTON MAN.

"What d'ya think of this weather?" I asked. He made a face as if to say, I'm disgusted with the weather, but he didn't speak. Even when I handed him the dollar, and he gave me the change, and I said thanks, he didn't speak. He went back to his towel and disappeared under the counter. I stood there with my change in my hand, wondering just how long he would pretend to be busy under the counter that way. I heard him shifting crates and decided to walk out without saying goodbye. I pulled the door open and waited after the bell ring to see if he'd pop back up. He did. But he was only surprised to see me still there. "Bye, Patchy."

"Yeah," he said, looking down and wiping. Patchy knew.

I jumped into my truck. I felt frail, fearing a sound might come out of me which I wouldn't want to hear, a cry, a roar. I rolled up the windows, started the engine and let the sound out. I hardly remember what it was, just the ring in my ears afterwards. I shifted and hit the highway. At the first ocean road I took a left and headed toward the ocean with the snow, toward the dunes.

I felt the dashboard ducts. The heater was blowing fast and hot. It wasn't one of those borderline frosts now. It was fifteen degrees out there, and snow coming down on top of it.

I didn't have to see what was happening to the wild grapevines. I knew all those overgrown vines that had climbed like fat yellow ribbons up into the cedars were finally killed. It was a winter landscape out my windows. It wasn't a gentle frost that put everything to sleep slowly, but a killer that fell like an axe, breaking the spine of summer right before people's eyes. I twirled the radio dial and picked up a weather station from Connecticut that said it was going to drop down to nine degrees by midnight.

At the end of the road, I flew right off the asphalt onto the sand. I drove the truck between the dunes all the way up to the cusp of the beach overlooking the ocean. Ordinarily I wouldn't risk it so close, but the freeze had firmed the sand and I didn't care what happened to the pickup anyway.

The snow thinned as it flowed over the warmth of the ocean. Flurries blew across my windshield, whirlpooling. With the heat off, the cab began to get cold. I decided to give in to the new air. I slid down in my seat. My legs and bottom, my belly and chest sank into their own warmth. My nostrils felt the gentle bite of cold from the tiny crack I left in the window. I reached behind me and lifted the shotgun from its cradle and let it lie in my arms like a doll. The steel was cold, but the wood parts were comforting. The gun gave off soft vibrations. I realized its power at my fingertips, glad for the choices it gave me. I felt warmth for the gun, a sudden strong love for it, and I clung to it lovingly.

I could breathe. I could breathe deeply. I didn't need to touch Patchy's coffee. I had everything I needed. I let the flurries whirling across the waves have their way with me, to mesmerize me. I gave in to the cold that was creeping into the cab. I slid down farther in my seat. I gave in to the drowsiness, letting myself drift.

There is a family of lions, a pride, lying around on the maroon rug in the funeral parlor on the West Side. It is her wake in the funeral parlor on the West Side. No one is there with her casket except the child and his father. The father's hands are lifting the boy high into the odor of her flowers. The boy looks down at her, stuffed in her casket below in her blue tulle dress, her hands frozen in prayer, light blue crystal rosary beads; Christ is still crucified at the end of the string of crystals. He looks beyond the boy at the ceiling—a solid chrome Jesus pinned to a solid chrome cross floating upon a cloud of blue tulle.

Her face is a birthday cake again. But her eyelash flutters, a finger flinches, her mouth tries to open. Suddenly she opens her eyes, cracking the icing. She blinks sugar out of her eyes.

"What happened?" she asks.

The father puts the boy down quickly. "Jeanette," the father cries, "don't get up."

She grabs hold of the side of the casket weakly and tries to pull herself up. Her crystal rosary beads roll along the sides of the casket; they are tangled in her fingers. "C'mere," she cries. Her hand reaches for her husband. "Don't stand there. Pull me up."

He wouldn't help her. He moves back. "What the hell you tryin' to do?" Reluctantly, he reaches out his hand to her. She lifts herself.

"My God in heaven, where am I? Help me, dear Jesus." She is sitting up in her casket, putting her hand to her forehead, squeezing her eyes together. "I'm dizzy. What's goin' on here? What did they do to me?"

"You died," her husband says.

"I died? God forbid," she says. "I *died?*"

"You died."

"Oh, no. And what are they gonna do now? Huh?"

"Jeanette, we got to bury you. You're not supposed to sit up."

"Oh, no. Let me out." She struggles to lift her legs, but she is too weak. She realizes herself she is too weak. She bursts out weeping, then she sees the boy and stops. "Cello? C'mere, baby."

"No," the boy says.

"Do what your mother tells you," his father orders.

"No."

"Come sit in Mommy's lap," she says, smiling. "C'mon, get in."

The boy turns. But the lions in the vestibule are lying in his path. One stands up alertly. The others lift their heads.

"Don't you dare try to go," the father calls to his son, who steps back toward the lions. He can see his father is afraid of them. The boy walks slowly toward the vestibule. His father is too afraid to follow.

Lions, beautiful young lions, lick their paws, calmly watching the child. He has to walk very, very slowly past them to the doorway. They smell of urine. Their breath smells foully of raw meat. He sees their eyes up close, the bristles on their faces. He walks past the funeral guest book. He reaches the door, turns the knob and slowly pulls, letting in the winter light. Then he runs down the front steps, past the iron gate into the street. Which way? Left. Uptown. Up the bright, wintry afternoon street where the red sun is low and glowing orange against the orange brick apartment houses. Running, under the leafless sycamores. Running, uptown, past store windows where he sees his reflection—a child fleeing lions, a man-child, a boy with wonderful black hair, flying, a beautiful child, a courageous child, a child of no mother or father, a child stealing his life. At the corner he runs west into the cold shadow of a side street. There is a silver car, a low silver car like the one in Italy. He grabs the door handle of the silver car and pulls fiercely. In the driver's seat, waiting, is Ciascuno—suntanned, silver-haired, yellow eyebrows and lashes—just as he appeared that first day in the yellow sacristy light, puffy-eyed, hardly awake. The young priest's blond eyebrows go up. His white teeth show in a smile. His voice in English says, "Jump in and close the door, *stupido*." The boy jumps in and he is sitting inside the Lamborghini—the very same smell of leather, and the very same dashboard.

Ciascuno turns the key. The fine engine sings, high and powerful. His hand reaches toward the boy's face and brushes the hair out of his eyes. "Had enough?" the beautiful man with the gray eyes asks. "Yes," the child answers. The man shifts into gear, releases the brake and they take off with a screech, to the corner, then right onto West End Avenue with another screech.

But the wheels spin above the asphalt. They are on a roadway that rises, above the apartment houses, above all the streets and avenues. Down below they can see the lions turning the corner in pursuit, the boy's father in the orange winter light, frantically turning north, then south. The lions scatter in the streets. There is nothing to pursue.

In the Lamborghini they fly past the Empire State Building, very close to the top, still moving south toward the Twin Towers, then flying right between the two tall buildings, leaving the smoke of Brooklyn and New Jersey behind, upward over the twinkling Atlantic, leaving America behind, higher and higher, veering eastward with the sun directly at their back, flying east into the pure, unmolested dark . . .

Boom Boom Boom Boom Boom. . . . Boom Boom Boom Boom Boom. . . . Someone's fist was banging on the pickup window.

"Pull her out. Get her the hell outta here."

"Huh?" I woke up to see Willie Warren on the other side of

the glass, banging on my pickup window with his fist. The ocean had risen high.

"Pull 'er out. Turn on the engine, goddamnit." I threw the rifle aside and turned the key. The engine sang. "Now throw her into reverse. Did you hear me?" Willy screamed over the wind.

The snow streaked westward now. I threw her into reverse and gave her gas. The wheels spun, but she didn't pull out. I couldn't see damn Willie Warren. What the hell! I was going to have to pretend I wanted to save the goddamn truck. I couldn't ease it forward because the promontory had eroded from the tide and my front wheels had sunk down. The ocean all but drowned out Willie's voice.

"Jim, turn her off a minute." I turned the key. The engine quit. I brought my hands to my face. My face was hot; my hands rough and cold. I was a fool. I could have taken my shotgun and walked up the beach to the privacy of a dune, leaving the truck to the ocean. I still could. No one would hear a gunshot in the dunes, not in a wind, and there was even a chance of a sand drift covering me up. But now for Willy I had to pretend I wanted to save the truck. I turned the key, starting the engine again. I gunned the silly goddamn engine and threw her into reverse. The wheels spun and she lifted back onto the dry sand.

I was out. I cut her around, pointing her north toward the parking lot, and almost hit Willie, who was waving for me to stop. I lowered my window and he stuck his snowy head in and looked inside suspiciously. "Christ, I thought I saw your truck out there," he said.

"Thanks, Willie."

He noticed the gun. "What the hell were you gonna do, Jim, shoot yourself a fish?"

"I fell asleep."

"Christ a'mighty! One more minute 'n' salt water'd've turned your engine to shit."

"I appreciate it, Willie. I'll run her through those fresh-water puddles on the way home."

" 'Em puddles are solid ice by now. But with luck salt water never got to yer engine. Jeez, Jimmy, you ever see gulls workin' in

341

the snow? Christ, must be a zillion fish goin' south. C.B. says they're breakin' the nets in Shinnecock."

"Gotta go, Willie."

"Who's stoppin' ya?" Willie smiled broadly backing away.

"Thanks for everything, buddy." I shifted into low. The pickup bucked.

"Hey, Jimmy," he laughed, wiping his nose and moving close. "You wanna hear a joke?"

"No."

I drove past Willie up onto the asphalt road. The truck took solidly to the blacktop. Visibility was better inland. I could see a dozen swans, their heads tucked under their wings, hugging the marsh reeds in the lee of the snow on Sagaponack Lake. I turned on my radio, sending up the long-distance antenna. The red and green lights of the dial glowed hot in the cold air of the cab. The dial was set between several stations picking up everything at once from all up and down the Atlantic seaboard. I loved the sounds of confusion that filled the cab—nervous, static, scratching sounds, undulations of air waves suggesting space, distance, the world outside Bridgehampton.

I left the dial exactly where it was and I headed toward the highway. Where the hell was I going now? Did I want to find another beach? Take my walk into the dunes with my shotgun? No. Then where to? Not east to the dead end of Montauk. West was my only alternative, toward New York City. But it gets busy westward. It's a different world of hungry, rushing commuters in their Christmas shopping anxiety. But it might be a relief to see traffic, to see strangers. I thought of going home for the green-tulip light first, and maybe my bankbook, some underwear. But I quickly rejected the idea of stopping at Garden Street. I touched my back pocket—my wallet was there. I had identification and credit cards. I banged open the glove compartment. Yes. There was the spare checkbook. I knew if I turned into Garden Street, it would bring me back to start, so I turned left at Bridge Lane. Stopping the truck on the tiny bridge, I jumped out, pulling the shotgun with me. In the middle of the bridge, in the pink aura of flashing back lights, I spun, letting the gun fly into the air over the water. It grew invisible in the snowy air before I heard it splash, faint in the wind. I jumped back into the truck, punched off the flasher and shifted.

I warned myself not to dare lift my foot off the gas. I sped, doing sixty, right into Bridgehampton town, jumping the red light on Main Street, turning left and flooring it right through town, through Watermill, onto the Montauk Highway, past the College and onto Route 27, where I gunned her to Exit 62 inside five minutes. I made a right, another right, and a left onto the wide-open Long Island Expressway, pointing myself toward Manhattan.

The radio sounded as though every voice in the world was feeding in at once. I increased the volume, increased the confusion. "Christ Almighty, thank you." My voice lifted loud in the cold air.

Tropical air? What was that whiff that came into my cab? Was it something real or in my imagination? Was it the odor of Zia? Or was it the remembrance of a place that I wished to visit once, long ago?

I called out. My cries echoed off the steel roof, "I'm comin'. I'm *comin'*." I moved into the left lane now. "I'm free." I laughed. "Fuck 'em. Fuck 'em behind me." Dolly Parton rushed in on one of the bands, singing "Two Doors Down." The static and weather from Georgia said the temperature was eighty-two. Maybe that's where the robins were headed. And from Florida, twangy announcements blended with Christmas music, Nat King Cole and the New York Philharmonic, chestnuts roasting on top of Handel's roaring Easter Hallelujahs. I let the dial stay where it was, all the way to the Cross Island, south again to the Narrows.

When I turned onto the lofty Verrazano bridge which flies out over the tide waters rushing to the Atlantic, I thought of the migrating fish hundreds of feet below, the water boiling with blues and bass, going south with me.

There was lightning in the snow, blue-white lightning with an orange burning center. The two fronts, cold and hot, were clashing right over the Narrows. Thunder drummed, vibrating through the bridge into the wheel in my hands. It felt like Long Island was crumbling behind me into the sea—Garden Street, Jessup, Montauk—all sinking, and Manhattan behind me, Brooklyn too—all crumbling, sliding into the ocean, leaving nothing behind but the unruly Atlantic.

As my pickup bumped off the bridge, onto the solid cliffs, I knew I would be somewhere the next morning where I could watch the gulls working, somewhere sunny, somewhere unknown in the South.

I turned around for one last glance. Long Island wasn't to be seen through the falling snow, but I knew it was somewhere behind me, stretching long and narrow, a finger of sand pointing east one hundred miles into the Atlantic.

COMING OF AGE

(0452)

☐ **THE FAMILY OF MAX DESIR, by Robert Ferro.** This is the story of Max Desir, a man whose emotions are painfully divided between his Italian-American family—from which he has been exiled—and his lover Nick, with whom he openly takes up life amid the enchantments of Rome and, later, amid the realities of New York.
(255872—$6.95)

☐ **A SMILE IN HIS LIFETIME, by Joseph Hansen.** Whit Miller was gay and now there was nothing to repress who he was and what he wanted: a man to love, among so many men to love. In an odyssey of desperate need and obsessive desire he journeys to the heights and to the depths of the heart—and of the flesh . . .
(256755—$6.95)

☐ **A BOY'S OWN STORY, by Edmund White.** A bittersweet novel of gay adolescence, it has a universality that evokes memories for everyone, male and female, gay and straight: the perplexing rites of passage, the comic sexual experiments, the first broken heart, the thrill of forbidden longing, and the inevitable coming of age.
(254302—$5.95)

☐ **THE BOYS ON THE ROCK, by John Fox.** Sixteen-year-old Billy Connors feels lost—he's handsome, popular, and a star member of the swim team, but his secret fantasies about men have him confused and worried—until he meets Al, a twenty-year-old aspiring politician who initiates him into a new world of love and passion. Combining uncanny precision and wild humor, this is a rare and powerful first novel.
(257530—$6.95)

Prices slightly higher in Canada.

To order use coupon on next page.

OUTSTANDING MODERN FICTION

☐ **THE BLUE STAR by Robert Ferro.** *Direct sunlight hit his shining blond hair. He was twenty-one. He was perfect.* That was Peter's first sight of Chase Walker in a pensione in Florence. Both were young Americans come to Europe to satisfy hungers of the spirit and even more pressing needs of the flesh. Both were about to embark on an intertwined odyssey that would take them further than they ever imagined. (258197—$7.95)

☐ **FUEL-INJECTED DREAMS by James Robert Baker.** James Robert Baker, a brilliant new voice in American fiction, has written an exuberant, breathtakingly original novel that is at once a love story, an exposé of celebrity, a black comedy, a thriller, and a tribute to young passion—in the wild, surreal world of Los Angeles rock'n'roll. (258154—$5.95)

☐ **ANNIE JOHN by Jamaica Kincaid.** The island of Antigua is a magical place; growing up there should be a sojourn in paradise for young Annie John. But as in the basket of green figs carried on her mother's head, there is a snake hidden somewhere within. "Penetrating, relentless . . . Women especially will learn much about their childhood through this eloquent, profound story."—*San Francisco Chronicle* (258170—$5.95)

☐ **THE PLOUGHSHARES READER edited by Dewitt Henry.** From prize-winning established authors and exciting new writers come some of the best stories in America today. The works of Raymond Carver, Richard Yates, and many others offer a striking mix of subjects, sensibilities, and styles. Winner of the Third Annual Editors' Book Award. "A rich collection . . . recommended."—*Library Journal* (258243—$9.95)

Prices slightly higher in Canada.
To order use coupon on next page.